The Sisterhood

THE NETWORK SERIES
BOOK NINE

KATIE CROSS

Chapter One

Rognvald smelled like leather and sweat.

The sweltering summer heat strove to destroy both of us as we stood in an alley, outside a Potionmaker's shop, in a village bordering the Bicker's Mill Covens. Letum Wood surrounded the sleepy place with vines and lush undergrowth. Giant trees soared, cutting shadows like monsters.

The air broiled, a hot bath. Sweat ringed my neck and arms. My shirt clung to my chest. The Volare, my flying carpet, lay in a round case across my back, causing a sweat stain wherever it touched.

A woman with graying hair entered the Potionmaker's shop with a pram and a huff at the witch who left. Transformation magic soaked her.

"Care to review the plan?" Rognvald inquired, gaze tapered as he studied the exterior wall.

"I'll enter the Potionmaker's shop," I said. "Once inside, I'll find the woman in question and distract her. You'll enter and take the baby."

Rognvald, a shaggy-haired, burly-faced witch with beady eyes, nodded. "Sounds good to me. Simple, straightforward. Approaching her *inside* is the key. If she moves outside, we'll have a problem controlling her. She's a wildcat."

"Simple," I declared, as if the weight of my future, the Sisterhood, and prospects for more opportunities didn't depend on the proper execution. As if the entire Brotherhood of Protectors wasn't secretly waiting to see how I performed.

Rognvald cast me a sidelong glance, but said nothing to my bravado. *Simple* didn't equate to *easy*, and I knew the difference.

Curiosity got the better of me. "Remind me how you know this child abductor?"

He grumbled. "The baby is my cousin . . . or something. My old aunt, a real piece of work, said her youngest daughter, Daniella, stole the baby from the eldest daughter and is on the run."

"The Guardians can't handle this?"

"No. It's . . . a family thing. Besides," he added in a mutter, "no one says no to my aunt. Besides that, Daniella is not . . . right."

"In the head?"

Rognvald shook his head, shaggy hair swinging. "She's *right* in the head. But she's not *right*. She just stole her nephew, and now she's in a Potionmakers shop, probably to buy a tincture to make him sleep at night. She's not *right*."

"That makes no sense."

"It will when you meet her," he clipped as he swiped his forehead with the back of his forearm. "Be warned: She senses magic fast. She's good with a transformation spell, and she wants the baby. I could transform and do this myself, but I think it's wise to have a non-transformed witch distract her. If I barrel in there alone, I'll frighten her and she'll bolt with the baby."

He had the audacity to sound disappointed.

"I'm on it," I said.

"I just brought you back into the Brotherhood magic for the mission. I'll remove you as soon as it's successful."

This, I already knew.

Moments earlier, a light pulse of pressure rippled through my mind like a wave. I'd felt something similar in the past. A year ago, the Brotherhood allowed me into their silent communication magic so I could speak with them while defeating the gods during the Battle for Letum Wood. Matthais, the former Head of Protectors died in that battle. High Priestess Scarlett put Rognvald in his spot. He eventually removed me from the communication magic, which made sense. A Brotherhood member, I was not.

Thanks, I said.

The nuance of speaking a thought to Rognvald's mind wasn't difficult. It resembled turning from one intentional topic to the next, but required a little more attention at first. Eventually, it would become natural.

Rognvald nodded to the Potionmaker's shop as he faded into an invisibility spell. *Careful in there. Daniella is unpredictable.*

I strolled into the street. We stood a hundred or so paces from the shop. As I closed in on the building, the same middle-aged woman with a pram and a wide-brimmed hat moved outside. On top of the pram yapped a curious, small dog I hadn't noticed before.

Fantastic, Rognvald muttered in my head. *She's already negating our plan. Do the best you can.*

Right. Being outside complicated things. For one, Daniella could make a scene and draw more attention. For another, it afforded no opportunity for us to corner her in the shop, the interior layout of which we both knew well.

It's fine, I said breezily. *I'm not afraid of improvising.*

Thank the gods for that.

Cautious of each rustle of movement around me, I casually approached. Fortunately, this tiny town barely moved. Few witches were visible. By design, no doubt. What baby abductor wanted to draw attention?

While I trust you to be wise, I don't trust Daniella. My aunt wouldn't take kindly to anything happening to her grandson, Rognvald said.

I'll restrain my womanly impulse to breastfeed.

I could have sworn I heard him snort.

As I closed in on Daniella, a few things became blatantly obvious. First, magic soaked her *and* the pram. Fair enough. If I abducted a baby and then went on the run, I'd change everything about my appearance as well.

Second, the dog perched on top of the pram, teeth half-bared and growling at any witch that attempted to stroll by. A tiny complication. More annoyance than issue.

Easy enough.

I cleared my throat and paused right next to the pram. The bitty dog almost barked out of its skin, nearly leaping free from the pram. I cleared my throat.

"Excuse me?"

Daniella's head whipped around like a bird of prey. Beaky nose. Sharp eyes. She clutched a coin purse to her chest with thin fingers like talons. Despite being a bland witch with undecidedly gray hair and a padded body, everything about her bespoke simmering aggression. She had clearly changed herself into an older woman.

Wildcat, indeed.

It took all my willpower not to recoil.

"What?" she snapped.

"Do you have the time?"

"No."

She swirled around, hair blanketing her shoulders, to face the pram. A chain wrapped her wrist and strung over to the handle on the pram, jostling with her quick movements as she shoved it forward.

She's attached to the pram, I told Rognvald. *Metal chain, easy to snap, but would cost the element of surprise. Unless it's enchanted. She's thoroughly soaked in magic, so it's impossible to tell.*

No transporting the pram away?

No.

I scooted to the side to force Daniella to look at me. "I'm sorry, but do you know whether this potion shop is open?"

She snarled. "I just walked out of it, didn't I?"

"Did you?"

"Yes!"

"So it's open?"

She jostled the pram over a rock, nearly knocking the small dog off the top. It yelped, sprawled its paws, and held on for dear life. With a little tap of her hand, she shoved the pup into the middle of the retractable pram ceiling. I followed at her heels, wondering why the baby didn't cry.

She likes cats, Rognvald said.

Cats?

Yes, cats.

The woman skidded to a stop, forcing me to wheel to the side to avoid slamming into her spine.

"Stop following me!" she screeched.

"You have something stuck on your back. Oh, it's cat hair! Do you like cats? I love cats."

With a quick spell, I conjured a ball of goat hair I remembered seeing on the ground that morning, mimed pulling it free, and held it up. Any fool would understand *this* was not cat hair, but that didn't matter. A cry issued from the pram.

Daniella growled, teeth half-bared. "Now you've done it!"

Baby crying from the pram, I said.

How old?

Can't see it. It's just crying.

It's a baby that walks.

What does that mean?

It's not a little baby.

I rolled my eyes. Rognvald, one of the most deadly and talented men in the Central Network, didn't know the difference between a baby and a toddler. I shouldn't have been surprised.

Once you get her away from the pram, I only need three seconds, he growled.

By any means?

Any means.

With a sigh, I sent a spell, heard the snap of the chain, and tackled. Daniella buckled under me with surprising ease, like butter collapsing under a hot knife. She did not, however, go silently.

The intent was to separate her from the pram first, deal with consequences later, so I wrapped an arm around her head to soften her fall. Her head slammed into my forearm instead of the dirt packed road as we toppled down together. A ripple of magic appeared on the other side of the pram. Rognvald transporting into place, invisible.

Spastic barking filled the air. The commotion of Daniella's wild shrieks, and attempts to gouge my eyes out with her nails, distracted me from the pram lurching away. The dog leaped free to land on my back, claws digging deep. The pram vanished entirely. I shouted as those nails swiped across my shoulder blades.

"Baby stealer!" she screamed. "She stole my baby!"

"No I didn't! I'm right here."

Her shrieks echoed through the village, drawing eyes. Witches congregated in the street, amassing in a closing circle.

"Help!" she shouted. "Get off me!"

I rolled free.

Hair tousled, she bolted upright. Half of her head had grayish blonde hair, the other a silky blue black, like raven feathers. The glossy side coiled around her shoulders, long enough to drop to her waist. The lighter side stopped at her shoulder blades.

The radiating transformation magic lessened as alterations rippled down the other half of her body. Instead of a nondescript middle-aged woman, a twenty-something witch with a surly glare and smooth skin appeared.

Ah.

This was Daniella.

Seeing my surprise, Daniella glanced at her hands. One wrinkled, one young and strong. She screamed again, renewing the transformation spell, but it was too late. I'd seen her, and so had the gathering crowd.

Her gaze tapered, then widened. "I know you!" she breathed, eyes large as saucers. "Bianca Monroe. You . . ."

She looked at where the pram had been, the dog, and then me. She scrambled backward. The dog danced, nipping near her elbows. The woman gathered it in her arms, breathing hard.

"Oh no you don't!" I cried, lunging. I barely managed to grab her ankle before she began a transportation spell. The allotted power wasn't enough to sweep both of us with her, so the incantation died as swiftly as it surged.

Witches crowded us as we scrabbled on the ground, Daniella attempting to bolt away with the dog in her arms. A male wearing a bright purple overcoat with a gaudy flower in the pocket stood in the midst, head tilted to the side with concern. An orange hat topped his head. Next to him, the owner of the shop shouted at us, throwing cork toppers, as if that would break us apart.

Not the baby! Rognvald shouted in my head. *The baby isn't real.*

What?

It was a deception spell.

Daniella hurled a stone at me, teeth bared. I ducked. The rock skidded across the shell of my ear, drawing blood. I shouted, grabbed her other ankle, and yanked. Though I managed to cast a paralyzing curse, she overpowered it as quickly. The dog wriggled free to strike at both of our heels in a tizzy.

"Dog!" she shouted. "No!"

The little terrier spasmed as it tried to bite, frothing with tiny, shark-like teeth. It flashed in an odd way.

A *very* odd way.

Dogs didn't flash. Fading transformation spells flashed, though, right before they failed to renew. I caught a gasp.

The dog! I said to Rognvald. *The dog is the child!*

A savage fist slammed into my left eye. The force sent stars wheeling through my vision. Daniella escaped my grip. Still spinning, I crawled after her, lightheaded, able to see out of only one eye.

"Volare!" I called. "The dog!"

My loyal flying carpet burst out of the case at my back and zipped away. Daniella screamed as the Volare scooped the dog up and rolled around it, hovering out of reach. From within, the muffled yips continued.

A bushy beard appeared before my eyes. The pram returned with it. "It's the demmed dog!" I shouted. "In the Volare!"

Rognvald dove for the carpet as Daniella began to transport, gasping with panic upon seeing Rognvald. Sensing her building magic was more powerful than her last attempt, I clamped an arm around her waist and cast an immobility spell.

Her transportation spell withered just as Rognvald got a hold of the Volare. Too surprised to counter my spell, Daniella plummeted toward the ground. I snatched her head before it slammed into the hard-packed road. Relieved, eye throbbing, I sank to one knee.

The gods.

She *was* a wildcat.

The Volare carefully unrolled, cradling the small child in the dead center. A wriggling toddler cried, replacing the frantic yips and snarls. Tiny ears replaced the hairy, dog-like triangles with each lusty shout of protest.

The crowd let out a collective gasp. They stared at me, then Rognvald, wide-eyed, murmuring amongst themselves. The words

Bianca Monroe and *Head of Protectors* and *mission* swirled in and out. Rognvald hung his head with relief, the screeching child flailing in his oversized arms. Obeying my silent command, the Volare zipped into a roll and slid into the protective sheath at my back. The attached cap at the end of the case popped back on.

"Thank you, B," Rognvald said. "Leave Daniella and meet me at the Gatehouse to debrief."

Chapter Two

Fifteen minutes later, the door to Rognvald's office burst open, spilling towering bodies. I recognized each of the three Brothers that entered. Todd, Caffrey, and Tysen, the youngest Protector. He reminded me of Merrick from years ago, when I first met him.

Strange to be on this side of time.

They didn't see me as they plunged into the room, almost tripping over each other.

"Well?" Tysen asked.

"Did it work?

Caffrey said, "Did she mess it up?"

Their voices halted as quickly as they had spilled into the room and noticed me standing there, like a bunch of gossiping teenagers reprimanded by an adult. I tilted them a wry smile. They drew up, staring at me like expectant puppies.

"Gentlemen," I drawled.

"No," Rognvald snapped. "Of course she didn't mess it up."

Caffrey had the wherewithal to appear sheepish.

Rognvald lowered into his chair behind a utilitarian desk. Unlike almost every other desk at Chatham Castle, paperwork did not clutter the top. Not for lack of trying, either. Council Members, High Witches, journalists, and others attempted to pester the Head of Protectors, but he ignored summons, burned article requests, or said nothing. He answered directly to Scarlett and Grandfather, or no one at all. The Central Network, and Alkarra by some extension, kept all of them too busy to answer messages.

Lucky mongrels.

"It was a successful mission," Rognvald declared. "As expected, the Sisterhood's execution was well done. The Council should take note."

Despite the Head of the Sisterhood, an all but non-existent entity, being involved in this mission, the Council still wouldn't recognize it as such. They hadn't yet esteemed the Sisterhood as an official . . . organization . . . for lack of better terminology. The blatant way they ignored me didn't prevent Rognvald's formal acknowledgment, but even his opinion didn't mean much in the big scheme of things.

One could battle gods and still not be enough for the Central Network Council.

Three heads swiveled toward me with unfettered curiosity, Tysen in particular. After the Battle for Letum Wood, Tysen had been welcomed into the Protectors in an official capacity. He cut his hair short, had umber eyes, and a quick smile. Like many Protectors, he didn't say much.

Their profound reputation for magical prowess aside, most Protectors were little more than boys trapped in giant bodies capable of more than most witches dreamed.

Caffrey laughed outright. "And a black eye for a souvenir. I'd say you won!"

I'd intentionally ignored the throbbing pain around my eye, but it had increased. It wasn't my first, and wouldn't be my last, but it did cast an annoying pall over the event. It was a small price to pay for the safe return of the child to its mother.

"Not any fun without a bit of sparring, and the baby safe," I said.

"Bianca called it," Rognvald said. "She noticed the dog before I did."

Attention piqued.

"Dog?" Caffrey asked.

I said nothing, leaving Rognvald to recount the events, careful to note the way he spoke and structured the flow. His bare-bones sketch provided enough context to paint a picture that left me appearing capable. The mission had been tiny, but at least it was *something*. After the quiet of the last several months, I'd take whatever foothold the Brotherhood offered.

Rognvald turned his attention onto me. "Thank you. I appreciate your help, and the mother of the child said the same." He tossed an envelope to my side of the desk. "This is from her."

I plucked it from the top. Currency rattled inside, which made my stomach tense. I opened my mouth to protest, but he held up a hand.

"Don't bother. She wanted to offer something."

With a frown, I folded my fingers into a fist around it. Currency? I hadn't done this as a hired mission. I craved more than coins, but it seemed rude to attempt returning it when he'd already circumvented the motivation.

Rognvald cleared his throat, waved his hand. "Be on your way then. You lot, stay. I have something else to speak with you about."

Caffrey and Todd descended into jokes about stealing dogs and babies, while Tysen watched me leave. Their joyful camaraderie rang as I stepped out of the Head of Protectors' office and closed the door.

A larger room awaited, with a hearth, stack of firewood, and stone floor. Across the way, a similar office door stood open. The Head of Guardians' office. The space was bigger, with a gargantuan table that sat all the Captains of the Guard.

These interior Gatehouse offices perched directly over the

giant three-story wooden doors that allowed entrance into Chatham Castle from Chatham City road. The Gatehouse had always been the home of the Head of Guardians and Head of Protectors, the two most important protective groups in terms of Network defense. To the left, I spied a spot ripe for a new office.

Just perfect for a Sisterhood.

Chapter Three

The quiet melody of Goat and Other Goat was a soothing soundtrack that welcomed me home.

Goat, who frolicked in a penned cage set on top of a tree branch wider than my living space, shook her head. A bell rang with each movement. Other Goat set his slotted eyes on me and called with a ferocious bellow. They chattered from their pens, which were carefully corralled by fences, magic, and vines.

Warm water lapped around my shoulders and knees as I leaned against my wooden tub, working through sore knots from grappling with Daniella. Thoughts cluttered my mind. The dog. The Volare. The currency. The Brotherhood. These mental meanderings funneled to one spot. The same, inevitable spot as always.

Merrick.

When I opened my eyes, I stared out of the window and into the upper canopy of Letum Wood. Tree branches swayed in a forest symphony. Leaves rattled. Gigantic branches, like impossibly thick and long arms, stretched into canopy roads. Their mossy trunks swooped to the side and down.

Down, down, *down.*

So far down, I couldn't see the ground from my treehouse in

the upper stories of the forest. If one looked hard, trails and earth existed . . . somewhere.

With great joy, I sighed.

The tepid bath water required another spell to warm it to steamy perfection, but the therapeutic effect had ebbed. I slipped out, wrapped myself in a towel and padded across my treehouse.

As I passed a window carved out of the tree trunk in which I resided, I glanced out of the tree in which I lived. It was one of twelve ancient behemoths called the Circle of Ancients. The root of power for Deasylva, goddess of the forest.

Said goddess was a new, infrequent companion of mine these days.

This tree, named Amanthis, was a quiet, stirring thing. It spoke rarely, but called often. A draw to Amanthis often brought me home, as if Amanthis felt better when I was close. I shared the sentiment.

A few months after my humble cottage disappeared in a flood that launched the Battle for Letum Wood, the forest brought me to this hollowed out space in a tree wide enough to fit several houses abreast, and still have room left over.

Magic or weather or time might have carved the living space out. The half-circle shape allowed for two distinct rooms, a living area, a kitchen area, a flat wooden floor without splinters, and the wide, open holes for windows. I could safely assume it was magic. Deasylva, most likely, though she hadn't bothered to claim it.

Only Grandfather and Papa truly understood my treehouse for the escape that it was. Whisked into the treetops, away from other witches, I could sink into the whispering cacophony that the forest provided at the back of my mind.

Whispering.

Always whispering.

You belong to us.

We belong to you.

You always return.

A childish refrain easily comforted by the presence of an indomitable parent.

A breeze warbled through one window on the far end and twined through to the window on the other end in a playful song. Glass panes sparkled, a necessary addition once winter encroached. I left them flung open the rest of the year. Pots and pans gleamed around my kitchen area, where they hung on the wall. Amanthis didn't fear my fires in the winter. A rock chimney spouted the smoke directly out a hole in the back, and the place warmed beautifully fast.

I hummed as I slipped into a sleeveless summer dress and sandals that strapped to my feet. A favorite product of the Western Network. Tiny, bright manulele birds zinged by, chasing each other as they headed toward their homes in the tree trunk overhead.

A message appeared in front of me.

I'll be over tonight.

The lack of a signature was no problem. Only Ava had such atrocious handwriting, and I hosted her for dinner more often than not on the weekends, when she snuck away from Miss Priscilla's School for Girls.

However, the letter did remind me.

I dug into a drawer, withdrew a leather book. The hard cover was a gentle gold. I tucked it under an arm, reached for a pencil, and slipped outside.

My favorite vine hammock swung easily back and forth, cradling my back and sides like a mother's cocoon as I settled within. The playful, hot breeze dried the wet tips of my hair as I drifted, slinking like the tide. The forest cooed.

You belong to us.

She is ours.

The joy will return.

Letum Wood, so attuned to my heart space that it often announced Merrick before he arrived, anxiously waited for him to return as well. Their usual, triumphant cry of, *the joy has come,* had long become, *the joy will come.*

Each time I heard it, my heart galloped, then calmed. The stalwart testimony reminded me that though he had been gone for six months, he would return.

Soon.

I hoped.

My fingers ran over the smooth leather cover, studded with bumps. A very special book, indeed. No title. Ruffled pages ran along the edge in an uneven cut. Thick, black string pulled along the spine, keeping it together. Beads, made out of some sort of wood, and whittled into faceted designs, dotted the edges. A shimmering, golden color shone across the front and back. In the sunshine, it glimmered like a thousand jewels.

All in all, it looked like something a forester might have dropped after a fairy attacked them.

I adored it.

Wherever in Alkarra he was, Merrick held his copy of the same book. The two enchanted books mimicked each other perfectly on the interior. If I wrote Merrick a note in mine, it appeared in his, and vice versa. When a new note was received, the golden exterior altered into a flushed rose gold. A week ago, mine was a lovely hue of light rose, the soft pink bleeding from the edges and toward the interior. It hadn't reformed since.

Until today.

The rose-toned beauty illuminated again, which set my heart hammering.

Another note!

A crack along the middle opened and I peeled the pages apart, reviewing the paper. Messages scrawled in my handwriting and Merrick's littered the inside. The jagged pages held jewels of indefinable worth.

Words.

From Merrick.

For the sake of nostalgia, and savoring the anticipatory treat of hearing from him again, I perused the first message he sent.

Little troublemaker,

I know only that this assignment will be a long mission. What that means, or where I'll be, I cannot say. I'm sorry. This is us truly embarking on what it means to be together. I am a Protector and a Master. You are the Lady Witch of Letum Wood and the Head of the Sisterhood.

After being away from you without contact for three years, I won't go through that agony again. Not so soon after returning to you. Which is why I'm giving this to you. I wish I could claim the idea, but it was Jacqueline.

She'll be unbearable over it.

I have the match to your notebook. When I write in mine, you'll see it in yours. When you write in yours, I'll have it in mine. If the pages begin to run out, more will appear. It wasn't easy tracking this charm down, but it will be so worth it.

I love you, B. Write soon.

—M

The sentimentality hit hard. What an expensive treasure he gave to me after he departed! The assignment happened so quickly it left me in a whirlwind. He received notice from Rognvald, packed, said merry part, and was gone within twenty minutes. The notebook arrived the next day.

That was six months ago.

My reply to his first message.

My love,

I will write, always. I await your return with eagerness and love and support. We can withstand all.

More soon.

—B

I slid to the end, which our messages had reached twice after six months away. Pages filled with my rambling notes about the day shuffled by.

Regina beat me just shy of a bloody pulp in sword drills today.

Letum Wood revealed a house in a tree for me. I wish you could see it. Already, it's changed so much just from me moving inside.

His replies tended to be far less specific, and far more homesick. *I miss you, little troublemaker* and *tell me everything you can* and *I smelled you in a forest last night.*

A forest likely meant it wasn't *my* forest.

Never did he betray details about his location, his mission. No hints, no signs. He existed in the world without my awareness, which would always feel strange. Dozens of words that I refused to write down seemed to fill the page with ghost ink, visible only through my mind's eye. The sloping, curving letters formed all the things that I would never say.

This is harder than I expected.
Come back to me.
I don't like this.

These words didn't belong here. The notebook was a sacred space. On the difficult days, I didn't part with it. On the easy days, I left it tucked away, waiting until the final, lonely moments at the close of the evening to see if he wrote. My heart skipped a beat as I landed at the end.

A new message.

I frowned at the abruptness of it.

Not much time. Just wanted to say—

My lips pursed together as I fought rising anxiety. Why didn't he finish the note? How long ago had he sent it? The cover color changed immediately when a new message arrived. Rarely, I watched the letters appear, the slips and curls and twirls reveal on the page in real time. We had a couple of immediate, back-and-forth discussions that made me giddy for days after.

This?

Nothing.

No more words appeared. I flowed in the porch swing, breath half held, expectantly hoping for more.

No luck.

Why would he cut off? Did something happen? Swallowing a lump in my throat, I scratched a new entry at the bottom of ten other entries, stacked above each other like books on a shelf.

Are you all right?

Another ten minutes yielded no response. Heart in my throat, I forced myself to finish the message I'd been compiling in my head ever since I sank into the bath, but every normal word felt like a rock in my chest.

I helped Rognvald with a personal mission today. It went well, even though it was short and easy. I have a black eye.

My thoughts stalled, as they did every night while I searched for a way to summarize an entire day into a few sentences. Sometimes, I rambled on in writing, giving as many details as I recalled. Other days, like today, the flow gummed up, too trapped by the words that I longed to say, but didn't dare. The traitorous thoughts soared through my mind, behind my eyes, and out.

Please, come back.
This is too long.
I'm not as good without you.

Instead, I wrote, *I miss you. I love you.*

With one last, long breath, I closed the notebook. I had to set him aside. Couldn't stew on what his hasty note meant, or didn't mean. "Doesn't mean anything bad," I muttered as I wrestled out of the hammock. "He might have gotten called away for dinner, or something."

Otherwise I would spiral on the plaguing fears. They could consume my entire day if I let them, and that would make everything worse. But I left the notebook out, near a collection of letters in the middle of my table. Those obnoxious letters would be from Leda. Instead of asking all her questions in one message, she sent her queries as singular lines whenever they occurred. Her habit left piles.

"Or else I'll forget!" she snapped with deepest irritation that I couldn't read her fast-moving mind. "Just answer them, all right?"

I brushed past the collection. I would definitely answer them. Later.

In the meantime, I had a meeting with Scarlett to prepare for.

Chapter Four

Later that week, I transported outside of Grandfather's apartment and knocked on the door. The comforting sounds of Reeves bustling through the High Priest's apartment was a welcome reprieve from the utter silence at home.

From the lack of Merrick.

Within minutes, I sat on Grandfather's balcony, my back to the wall, cooled by a patch of shade while heat radiated from nearby shingles. Turrets and wall sprawled to either side. Papers I spread across my lap rustled in the wind while I stewed over Sisterhood troubles and waited for Grandfather's soothing presence.

Life maps, Leda would call them. More like *hope on a page.*

Tomorrow, I had a meeting with Scarlett to discuss the next step in our plan to get the Council to approve funding for the Sisterhood. *We are nothing without funds,* she said so many times I couldn't count them. *It's more than salary and resources, but belief. What the Council believes in, they invest in. That is how we legitimize the Sisterhood.*

I couldn't bear the thought of showing up to the meeting with Scarlett empty-handed of proof that the Sisterhood had a place.

The mission with Rognvald was . . . something. A very small something.

Grandfather's raspy voice, lined with care, startled me out of deepening thoughts. "I see your plans for the Sisterhood there."

"Hmm."

"To me," he mused, "it looks like you're trying awfully hard to mimic the Brotherhood."

I tilted my head, studied the papers.

Sighed.

One might say that my vision of the Sisterhood mimicked the Brotherhood with embarrassing exactness.

"Imagination was never my strong suit," I quipped. "Merry meet, Grandfather."

He squeezed my shoulder.

"Is it intentional that it is structured just like the Brotherhood?"

I frowned. "It's an existing structure that works. The Council is familiar with it, which makes funding approval more likely. Apparently," I added as a slightly bitter aside, "we need to worry about currency and approval."

A soft chuckle reassured me that, if nothing else, I wasn't taking myself too seriously.

Yet.

A chair appeared at my side. He settled on it with a breath, hiking his pants up around his ankles. "Hot today." He closed his eyes. "I quite enjoy the heat."

"You're mad."

He chuckled as I shuffled all my papers into a pile and spelled them away.

A tea tray appeared on the table, replete with several cookies, a pot with clinking ice cubes, and tea sachets labeled *chamomile*, *mint*, and *rose*. While he set about making his favorite cuppa, and pouring coffee over ice chips for me from a different pot, I pondered his question.

Why *wouldn't* we mimic the Brotherhood?

What alternate path could possibly exist?

As if he read my thoughts, Grandfather said, "We already have a Brotherhood. Maybe we need something new. Something *better*. You could convince some members of the Council as to your adaptability as much as you can to your predictability."

Unwilling to sink into the idea just yet, I replied, "You sound a little like Scarlett, though she's invested in proving funding first."

"A compliment, at any angle."

A yawn split my mouth wide open, so I sipped the cooling coffee. For several pleasant minutes, we stared over the castle grounds. The clink of his ice tea, and the bitter zing of coffee, soothed the wrinkles in my day.

"The Brotherhood is established and predictable and functional," he continued, "it speaks for its own merits. But as High Priest, I'm not seeking *merit*."

"What are you seeking?"

He made a throaty sound. "Different."

"I don't understand."

"I know." He sipped his tea. "Not yet."

Stymied, I stared out. Setting it aside to consider later, I asked, "Do you know what weak spots exist in the Brotherhood?"

He smiled knowingly. "You tell me."

I scratched the side of my head. "Aside from the fact that they don't allow women to join their ranks, I can think of some issues with tradition, the narrow bottleneck of validating men to join . . ."

My scrutiny dissolved.

"Definitive factors against them," he mused. "The predictability of the Brotherhood to create exceptional Protectors comes from their deep-seated and proven traditions. It's a blessing and a curse. You seek their weakness to avoid it yourself?"

"Yes. The Sisterhood began as a service to Scarlett," I said with a rueful breath. "Sort of. I mean, that was the main idea. Problem is . . . she hasn't needed much help. Small things, of course. All dealt with by me on a volunteer basis. But nothing that proves what a Sisterhood could be capable of."

He made another noncommittal noise. "The Sisterhood will require growth in areas you haven't yet imagined existed. Capability will rise to the occasion."

I said nothing, not entirely sure I understood what he meant.

In some ways, the Brotherhood negated the need for an equally similar Sisterhood, as they already had most of their missions well in hand. The Battle for Letum Wood ensured that the Networks had come together to fight as one entity, securing a better peace treaty and general feeling across borders than we'd experienced in years. It proved the possibility of teamwork and goodwill.

"Which begs the question," Grandfather drawled, "of why a second Brotherhood would be required?"

"I don't know," I breathed.

Wasn't that the crux of my problem?

Perhaps the Sisterhood wasn't needed. Unless I could come up with—and prove myself through—missions that required a woman's presence to be successful. A hard sell. The Brothers had been successful at their missions without women for centuries, which negated what I sought to do.

Rock, meet hard place.

Grandfather stood, patted my shoulder, and said, "I have no doubt you'll come up with something. Might I make a suggestion?"

"Please."

"Start with what you enjoy the most. Build from there. Also, come with me."

We left the heat of late summer behind, entering the cooler air inside the apartment. Reeves gave a stiff bow as we slid past, toward a wall of books that had once been spare weapon parts and maps when Papa lived here. I set my paperwork aside to focus on Grandfather's intent perusal.

His aged fingers strummed the spine of a book as we skimmed by, humming under his breath.

"There's great necessity for swordwork and weaponry in a position such as a Sisterhood." He paused to pull a book from the shelf with a thick edge and peeled back a flappy layer of fur, considered the title, and replaced it. "But of greater import to someone in your position is the acquisition of new magical abilities."

I eyed the books along the wall in his apartment. This apartment, dedicated for the reigning High Priest, was protected by layered spells and enchantments. The space felt entirely too big when Grandfather first moved in. Gradually, he filled it with books, parchment, and the acquisition of things that only a lifetime could collect. Though Mildred was nowhere in the mix except through painted portraits, I felt her whisper amongst the memories.

The sheer number of books and potentially rare titles rivaled only the Great Library of Burke. I selected a book off the shelf titled *Potions from the Mulberry Plant* and perused the interior. Potions didn't capture my attention all that often. They required too many details, follow-through, and time, but Leda or Merrick's sister, Jacqueline, would adore it.

The book *Invisibility Magic and Its Sources* caught my eye. I unshelved it to riffle through.

Grandfather hummed under his breath as he breezed behind me. "A keeper," he said. "That book has been a rare treasure. Given to me by a witch from the Southern Covens years ago, when my contingent helped him out of a sticky situation. At the time, I was considering trying to get into the Brotherhood."

My head lifted. "You did?"

He chuckled. "The notion was a vague plan. Because success in the Brotherhood is as much about magical ability as it is courage, I was attempting to find as many rare spell books as I possibly could." He pointed to it. "This was one of them."

"I would say," I murmured, skimming the pages. I'd heard of none of these invisibility spells before.

Few witches knew more than the standard Muran magic invisibility spell, which was so magically obvious that many witches began to learn the skill of sensing magic by detecting invisibility. It was also one of the easiest spells, requiring repetition only after ten minutes, sometimes more, and a single two-word spell.

"Did you try out for the Brotherhood?"

"No." Wistfulness infused Grandfather's expression. "I didn't follow it through because, in the end, I met a librarian that grabbed my attention in very unexpected ways."

A soft smile stretched my lips.

"Mildred?"

He winked at me, reverently saying, "Mildred. Suddenly, the world seemed a bigger place than the small Brotherhood. Inevitably, it was. The Brotherhood leadership at the time wasn't as stolid as it is now," he added with a wry smile. "There were many factors that led to my reticence to commit."

The silky, solid paper was thicker than regular parchment, and more like vellum. Made to last centuries, I would imagine. The ink bled into a dark cerulean and faded around the edges. The lines were written far apart, and the book wasn't all that big. I closed it.

"Sounds wonderful, Grandfather."

"Take it."

My eyes widened. "What?"

With deep love, he smiled. "Take it. I cannot think of another soul that deserves this book more than you, my dear."

A protest rose to my lips, but he tutted. "I have almost no need for it. Not anymore. Not with witches such as yourself going into the world to protect others. You'll put it to far better use than moldering on my shelf. Which, consequently, you'll inherit eventually."

With gratitude, I slipped under his arm in an embrace, enjoying the pulse of his heart and the hold of his sturdy hand.

He wasn't as physically strong as Papa, but his embrace contained the steel of love. He sighed into my hair with a deep contentment.

"I want it noted," he said, huskily, "that if Scarlett did not hire the Sisterhood, then I would myself."

"Thank you, Grandfather."

He pulled away, blinking rapidly. "Now, onto magical acquisition. That invisibility book will give you ideas for different methods of invisibility. The raw invisibility is convenient, as the Muran magic system is for everything, but not the only thing. You cannot be stealthy if you're detected, so that's a good starting point to have a leg up on the Brotherhood. Many witches think that the Muran system, which we tend to use the most these days, is all that we have. It's not true."

My lips parted. "What about transportation?" I whispered. "I thought—"

He smiled. "There's always more out there, my dear. Always more." He drummed his fingers on top of the book with a sprite roll of fingers. "Knowing you, you'll devour it this evening and be back in the morning, which will buy me the time to find the book I'm looking for. A squat, short little thing about transporting that sometimes gets tucked into odd places . . ."

Smiling, I drifted to a chair.

"Oh, and Bianca?"

He paused, and I sensed something in the hesitation.

"Yes?"

"Should anything ever happen to me, I've already bequeathed my entire book collection to you. Reeves has the paperwork, as does my legal witch. But . . . please . . ."

He hesitated. A queer twist of his lips changed his expression into something that I couldn't quite fathom.

"Please?" I softly repeated.

"Make sure that *you* receive the books? I don't want them bequeathed to the Great Library of Burke or other witches without you personally going through them first. It's a rather important collection to me, and I would . . . that is . . ."

To put him at ease, I said, "Of course, Grandfather."

He smiled.

"Thank you."

I returned to my study of the grimoire, shuffling the odd expression on his face into the back of my mind. Sometimes, a fatigue existed in his eyes that I couldn't understand. A mixture of grief and exhaustion and hope. But he continued in his duties, and gladly. I couldn't imagine Scarlett's nightmare without Grandfather here to help.

While Grandfather putted and tucked around his bookcase, pulling books and parchments here and there, murmuring stories about how the books found him, I flipped through the pages and began to study the incantations.

Far more complicated than the easy invisibility that I enjoyed now, but intriguing in their range of versatility. Enchanting objects, then covering myself with them. Spelling the air. The other person.

With Grandfather humming, organizing, shelving, and shuffling behind me, I curled up on his divan, propped my head in my hand, and fell to practicing.

Scarlett, the Central Network High Priestess, handed me a rolled parchment. "For you to read." A request lived in her tonal nuances. Carefully accepting the scroll, I unfurled it with a stretch of my fingers.

Scarlett retreated to stand at the window, her regal form silhouetted against a lovely sky, her chin high, her hands folded behind her back. A slight gauntness affected her cheeks, and the loose material around her shoulders indicated she'd lost weight. I made a mental note to ask Leda about it later and honed my attention on the missive.

Writing filled the scroll with barely a breath on either edge. The cursive, loopy handwriting would have been a painstaking chore to execute. Almost childlike, with whirls and exaggerated dots over the i's that looked like exploding stars.

I skimmed enough to recognize a story and confirmed a hunch at the very bottom. No signature. Glancing at her, I shook it gently.

"What is it?"

"That's for you to answer . . . Head of the Sisterhood."

The emphasis wasn't unnoticed, but I ignored it for now. Implication loaded such a statement, and neither of us were ready for implication. Blood rushed past my ears for a moment.

Was this an assignment?

We *desperately* needed an assignment. A legitimate, obvious mission that could prove value to our work.

"I need to speak with Hiddleston," she said. "If you'll excuse me, I'll give you time to read it in its entirety." She stopped halfway around her desk. "I'd like to discuss it when I return. I believe there's more than what meets the eye."

With an idle nod, I waved her out.

Such informal behaviors around the leader of our Network were a bit unorthodox, but Scarlett and I had more history than most. Grandfather was the High Priest, anyway, which practically made her family. In the absence of Mama, who died years ago, Scarlett was the closest thing that I had to a mother.

I shuffled closer to the window as I began to read.

The young girl named Ellie Victoriann lived in an orphanage.

You'd observe nothing special about Ellie Victoriann.

Silver-blonde hair, knobby knees, wrinkled socks, lusterless eyes, and a dim disposition.

Except for one thing.

She could fly.

At five years old, she discovered her hovering talent. At six years old, she soared down a set of stairs, or fluttered from the lower branches of a tree. At seven years old, she crossed four times that space, and at eight years old, she thoroughly exploited her abilities.

One might call her naughty, but Ellie Victoriann was too responsible for naughtiness. She helped in the kitchen, orga-nized books in the library, and taught the other orphans.

Still, those around her disliked her abilities. You see, villagers don't like a nobody in the clouds. They spat, "She's not going anywhere. There's no hope for an orphan. Put her to work in the school."

Ellie Victoriann didn't listen.

Until the day they ripped off her wings.

Blinking, I extracted from the story.
Odd.

I read it again, more perplexed as to why Scarlett wanted *me* to read it. On my third read, I still couldn't fathom why she'd desire the Head of the Sisterhood to be involved. My questions didn't percolate for long.

Scarlett returned, Leda in tow. Seeing me, Leda's fine white eyebrows shot up. Disparagement lingered there. I still hadn't responded to her letters.

She gave me a silent, inquisitive look, to which I shrugged and held up the scroll. Her brows knitted together in a thoughtful question, but she didn't have time to say anything before Hiddleston wound in, filling the doorway with his broad shoulders, and closed the door.

Leda and Hiddleston couldn't be more different. He was tall, dark-skinned, broad shouldered, and had locks that swept past his shoulders. Set against Leda's short, petite frame, pale skin, differently colored eyes, and white-blonde hair, Hiddleston resembled a hulking tree.

"Did you finish?" Scarlet asked.

"Yes. Several read throughs."

"Thoughts?"

"It's . . . a story."

Prim lips pursed, Scarlett said, "Well observed. What do you make of it?"

Wordless, I shrugged. "I'm not sure. It's written in the sort of script one might find in a children's book. Who sent it?"

An envelope lifted from her desk and sped toward me. The same writing in the letter filled the front of the envelope, complete with a wax seal the color of deepest emerald.

The High Priestess.

"They sent a scroll in an envelope?" I asked, incredulous. Witches did weird things that surprised me everyday, but this beat many others. Scrolls, by nature, negated the need for an envelope. Particularly one sealed with wax, like this scroll.

Scarlett said nothing.

"And no sender?"

She shook her head. "None."

"When did it arrive?"

Scarlett glanced at the clock. "Half an hour ago."

Which made it sometime after lunch. A variable that might

not matter, but I had no idea what else to ask. Slowly, I flipped it over. Revealing incantations resulted in nothing. No hidden ink, tracking spells. Nothing nefarious that I could think of.

"It's not hiding anything. I can't sense any magic on the parchment or the envelope."

"I checked the ink," Leda said. "No poison or other spells."

Scarlett waited behind her desk. I nearly missed her cues of concern. A slight uptick of her lips. A furrowed brow. To buy myself time, I read the story again, puzzled nothing further, and slid it back into the envelope. I set it on her desk.

"What do *you* make of it, High Priestess?"

"Nothing that makes sense, at the moment."

"Are you concerned?"

"A little."

"Why?"

Scarlett swallowed. "The name."

"Ellie Victoriann?"

"Yes."

When Scarlett struggled to answer, Leda spoke up. "The letter arrived at my desk, like all the others. I opened it first. Normally, I wouldn't have bothered to give something so vague to Scarlett to think about, but the name is why I gave the letter to Scarlett in the first place."

"What's the significance?"

Leda bit her bottom lip before saying, "Because her little sister was named Ellie, and Scarlett was also in an orphanage. It . . ." Leda sighed, her face wrenched into an uncertain grimace. "Maybe I was wrong? I just . . . coincidence?"

Scarlett held up an allaying hand. "You weren't wrong, Leda."

"Your sister was named Ellie Victoriann?" I asked.

"No. My sister was named Ellie." Scarlett shook her head. "But . . . Victoriann was my mother's name."

My stomach clenched. Jikes, but *that* couldn't have been an accident. It didn't make it a threat, either, only rather suspicious.

Lack of signature or responsibility increased my wariness. Regardless, Scarlett appeared very uncomfortable.

"There's something . . . wrong with that letter," Scarlett said breathily. Her face had bleached of color. "The orphanage, the kitchen and teaching duties, I don't believe those details are coincidental. They aren't a perfect fit, either. My sister, Ellie, didn't participate in those tasks. *I* did. Excessively."

With new eyes, I reviewed the snippet of the story. Nothing overt lay within. No thinly-veiled threat, no promise of violence. Certainly, the withholding of a sender, the details of the child, were obliquely a problem.

Sort of.

"This story is a letter," Scarlett pointed out, "but not a mission that I can assign to the Sisterhood. Yet. While I'm grateful for any help you'll provide, we can hardly say that it's going to be wildly beneficial in our case with the Council."

"It will help," Leda asserted, "as long as you stand behind Bianca and are willing to talk about it. Whatever Bianca figures out, or no matter what happens, the fact that you assigned her to it will matter."

Scarlett offered no hesitation. "Of course I stand behind her."

Leda nodded, and the subject was dismissed, despite requiring very little input from my end. Not that I minded. Leda stepping in to have something to say on behalf of the Sisterhood was a welcome relief.

A small voice in my head longed to inquire, *Why can't you just approve the Sisterhood, Scarlett? Why involve the Council at all?*

The reasons irritated me. For one, the Sisterhood could end up being a dark mark on her already tempestuous career. Many Council Members considered me a favorite of hers. To put me into a powerful position might erase her hard-won trust amongst the other leadership.

For another, anything attached to the name Derek Black continued to tilt on a precarious scale. Most witches adored and revered Papa, while others hadn't erased the slaughter that Niko's campaign against Papa had caused. His time as High Priest, though hardly of his own making, created giant waves.

Waves that bashed into my life constantly.

Finally, Scarlett strove for a more involved Council than former Highest Witches, Papa included. She didn't want to make bold moves that required currency without their approval.

Until this moment, I'd never seen such stillness or hesitation in Scarlett before. Her sister had been dead for decades. While I always missed Mama, speaking about her death had grown easier over the years.

Had it not been so for Scarlett?

Did we bury secret pockets of pain that unexpectedly rose from our loamy souls to seize us in their claws?

"Can I keep it?" I asked. "I want to try a few more tests."

Scarlett nodded, seeming pleased with the offer. "Please," she rasped, "take it away."

Her back turned to us. She faced outside, appearing to compose herself. Leda tilted her head to the door in a not-so-subtle command. I ignored her.

"High Priestess?"

"I'm fine, Bianca."

"I—"

"I'm *fine*."

Her sharp retort wasn't as frightening to me now as it might have been years ago. Scarlett had been High Priestess for too long, and we had gone through too much, for me to be afraid of a few snippy words. It seemed a natural trait for our recent slate of High Priestesses.

Stella aside.

This tension in Scarlett pointed to something amiss.

"Let me know if another one arrives," I said instead of offering the emotional support that lurked on the edge of my tongue. "As soon as it arrives, please. I'll be ready when I hear from you."

"Thank you."

"Do you want to discuss the Sisterhood today?"

Scarlett dismissed me with a wave. "Another time. Leda? Please send in a tray of tea. That new tea from the Western Network, if you please. I find the taste agreeable. I'll need a little bolstering to get through the next few hours."

Leda's explanation fell like two boulders.

"She's tired."

She perched behind her humongous Assistant's desk just outside Scarlett's office, standing exactly four paces in front of the door. Despite being thin and petite, Leda's prodigious presence protected Scarlett from any interlopers. Any witch that wanted to enter Scarlett's office had to scoot around Leda, and I doubted any fool would try. She eyed passing witches with all the territory of a starving vulture.

"She looks ill," I said.

Leda tilted her head in deeper thought. "She might be," she concluded, and I hid a grimace. Whatever Leda was or wasn't, she made a terrible liar. Thus, I took everything she spoke as truth.

"If she is ill," Leda continued, "it's not egregiously so, and I have not been informed. It's unlikely more than just general fatigue brought on by summer heat, though I've had to clear her schedule more than once so she could rest in the afternoon." Leda swept her arms over her desk and its obnoxious positioning. "Hence my desk stands here. Too many witches take the liberty of walking in without invitation."

"Put Hiddleston in charge."

A fleeting smile found her lips. "I did, but he's also in charge of the Underassistants and often busy away from here. Besides, I really don't mind."

Frowning, I said, "This isn't like Scarlett. She's always taken care of herself."

"I know."

"Has she seen an Apothecary?"

A quick back-and-forth head shake followed. "I'd tell you if I thought she should. For the most part, I have no reason to believe it's not a normal fatigue from the demands of her job. She needs better boundaries."

"But—"

Her voice rose to speak over me. "Today, I think it's something else. Reading that story about her sister had an effect on her. An unexpected one. Within moments, that peaked expression overcame her and hasn't left."

I dropped my voice, leaning my palms on Leda's desk to close the distance between us. "What happened to her sister?"

"Died." Leda's shoulders' slumped. "I don't know much more than that. She was quite young. Both of them were. I would hazard a guess that Scarlett was eight. Her mother died in childbirth, her father from a work accident."

The truth made this situation more complex, but still not dangerous. Leda briefly touched my elbow to nudge me down the hall, subtly tilting her head toward the Underassistants approaching.

Two of them cluttered the left side of Leda's desk as they sat down, chattering happily, swinging two lunch pails. Without a word to us, they settled into two seats, their legs cramped painfully close to the edge as they reached for envelopes and quills.

"Watch the office, please," Leda said crisply. "Not a soul is to go inside."

Both nodded with vigorous zeal.

In sync, we strode down the hall toward the marble steps that rose and lowered either direction. The High Priest's office and

Council Hall lingered not far away, doors sprawled wide. A general hush indicated it was time for lunch.

"Scarlett is more tired than usual," Leda said under her breath. She didn't even glance at me sidelong, and spoke so quietly I could barely hope to hear. "But I think there is something else adding pressure on her."

"What?"

Leda shook her head. "The Eastern Network is a bit of a mess."

"They're always a mess."

Grim-faced, she shook her head.

"It's worse. Baxter has been reporting directly to Scarlett every week."

My thoughts roved to Baxter, my demigod friend. He had an apartment at each Network castle, and rotated through them as politics and duty demanded. As the official liaison between gods and witches, his duties kept him rather busy. He spent the majority of the time in the Eastern Network. Magnolia Castle, set on the sea, scratched his itch for ocean life in a way that Chatham Castle could not.

That cold, condemning stare finally met mine. "She looks at you as her own personal Protector, you know."

The admission thrilled and terrified me.

"I know."

"By any chance," she ventured, with a sudden curiosity that immediately sparked my concern, "do you happen to know if Merrick would join me in the Great Library of Burke one day?"

"Why?" I drawled.

She smiled, and a daring feline lived inside. "Oh, just an idea I had. If the Brotherhood has their own communication magic, why can't the Sisterhood?"

A full five seconds passed before I processed what she said. Nearly choking over my own tongue, I managed to sputter, "W-what?"

With a trill of her hand, she attempted to dismiss the subject. "Don't worry! I'll ask when he returns."

"You can't just—"

"I can," she replied firmly, with a stubborn coldness in her stare that sent chills down my spine, "and I *will* look into it. Whether or not we can use their communication magic remains in question. Certainly, looking at the grimoire in which the spell originates won't kill us."

My mouth had gone dry at the thought. The Brotherhood had their own room in the Great Library of Burke, where they hoarded specific grimoires, maps, and other treasure troves that enabled them to keep some magic away from the populace, thus enabling them to remain hidden, their magic unpredictable. Only a Protector could open the door.

Whether the ethics of the room were fair was up for debate. For Leda to dare? I couldn't help cheer her on, yet fear for her life and career.

"When he returns," I said, managing an even tone, "I'll put the question to him."

"Thanks. It will, at least, give me a focus for the Sisterhood until we can get something off the ground with the Council," Leda added in a bitter mutter. "I can understand the Council refusing my request for a time slot the past several months as they settled all this business with the gods, and Letum Wood, and amulets, but really." She huffed. "A year is more than enough, and business has settled down."

"I thought Scarlett felt it was her duty to schedule it?"

"Let's not be ridiculous," Leda bit out. "*I* do the scheduling for Scarlett. She's been putting it off, too. Not for lack of belief, but lack of energy to remember." She stopped in the middle of the hall, neck red. "In fact, I'm going to apply to them again today and get you an appointment. Merry part!"

Halfway through her pivot to bestow her personal wrath to the ten Council Members that helped rule this Network, she paused. "Speaking of Merrick, any news? It's been awhile since you heard from him, hasn't it?"

Like always, I marveled at her ability to track the small details, like days, times, and Council Meeting slots. The low-spoken question stirred a breath of disappointment. "Yes, and no. He wrote a message but it was cut off."

"Sorry, Bianca. That must be hard."

Shoving through it, I smiled. "Life with a Protector, eh?"

"True," she sang, appearing relieved. "You did ask for this."

With that sublime reminder of self-inflicted painful life lessons, she spun on her heels and left. I watched her go, cognizant that sometimes, if I didn't love her so much, I'd probably hate her.

Chapter Five

A burly witch with slotted eyes, a thin smile, and exuberant cheeks grinned at me, smacking a club against the shield hooked on my arm. When he hit the shield with a *tap-tap-tap* of his heavy cudgel, the impact reverberated into my forearm.

"Just like the sword, no?"

Indeed. The design on the shield *did* look like Viveet, my ever-faithful sword currently sheathed at my hip. Papa, standing only a few paces away, arms folded tight over his chest, hid a grin.

The shieldmaker was a wily witch, and an expert businessman. He had a rotating arsenal of shields in the back of a wooden wagon, all stacked side by side, organized by height. Though heavy canvas blankets lay on top of his product, effectively hiding all that lay within, I'd caught a peek of the shields before he produced them. All had been blank. He designed the ivy onto the shield *after* he saw Viveet.

Brilliant.

"It's heavier than I'd like." I lifted my arm, testing the impact all the way to my shoulder. "Do you have something lighter?"

"That's not the shield's fault!" he cried. "You need to get stronger."

Papa laughed outright.

I sent him a quelling look, but it didn't silence the hilarity. Grandfather, standing at his side, rolled his lips in a poor attempt to calm his own humor. Together, the pair of them were trouble.

"Even then," I drawled, "it's still heavier than would make sense, if I want to be versatile. It's been several years since my battle with Mabel destroyed my shield, but I certainly haven't lost strength in that time."

Wisely, Papa said nothing, but sent me a cheeky wink. The shieldmaker plucked it off my arm and returned to the wagon. He dove under the canvas, rolling like a slug beneath soil. The thud and shudder of shields shifting around gave him away.

"Take your time finding the perfect one, weakling." Papa chucked me in the shoulder with a grin. "Viveet is obviously the most powerful weapon you have, but the shield is still very important too. Worth shopping around."

I rolled my wrist, stretching the forearm. We'd been here for thirty minutes. Twice, Papa sparred with me to test the quality of the shields. Viveet bit into them, but when I yanked them free, they revealed no sign of damage.

My shield work was, to say it mildly, pathetic. Years ago, Mabel shattered my first shield in a Mactos for my life, and I hadn't replaced it.

"Not even sure I'll use it," I mumbled.

"Still," Papa said sagely, "don't you think the Head of the Sisterhood should have a shield?"

There were a lot of things the Head of the Sisterhood *should* do. The list stacked ever higher, in daunting ways.

Grandfather hummed to himself and said nothing.

The rotund shieldmaker returned with a version the same width, but thinner. The type of wood was less dense, but it also lacked sturdiness. After teasing Papa into another round, during which my shield work was slightly less egregious, I handed it back.

"Sorry." I grimaced. "None of those."

The witch's expression sank. He dropped into a litany of curse words, shook his fist at me, and grabbed the reins of his donkey. Before I could ask if he'd make a custom design, the animal bawled as they hauled down the lane. He shouted obscenities at me for wasting his time.

Papa, gaze tapered, watched him go. "A delightful man, isn't he?" he murmured.

This time, I laughed.

Grandfather set a hand on my shoulder. "Come. Regina said that fresh bread awaits at Derek's house, and I am rather hungry."

Papa's house smelled like fresh pine.

Thanks to forest destruction caused by the Battle for Letum Wood, fresh lumber was rampantly available. Once the messy world calmed in the aftermath, Letum Wood obligingly brought fallen trees to Papa's chosen area so he could start his creation. The house, and figuring out how to build one, had been his sole focus for months.

He needed it.

Life apart from the castle, the Protectors, the busyness that was all he knew, would have taken him by the throat and dragged him to deeper waters without something difficult to challenge him. The creation of his living space anchored him to a task, and kept him from wallowing.

Sort of.

Grandfather worried more about Papa now that the house was almost finalized. What would Papa think about when glass panes and attic beams and trusses didn't bother him? The unanswered question hummed in the air, building tension, particularly on the days when Papa stared into the forest like a lost little boy.

I tapped on a wall that hadn't been there during my last visit. "Looking good, Papa. Nice and sturdy, just the way you wanted."

He blinked, returning from concealed thoughts, and smirked. "Turns out, I *can* build a house."

"But," I sang, "you're better taking them down during a Protector raid that cleans up all the bad guys, then lights the house on fire to burn the evidence and creates a more powerful reputation."

He tapped his nose in affirmation.

Grandfather chuckled.

The gleaming walls, freshly sanded, had farther to go. Working from top to bottom, he'd completed the attic, and the main living area, but not the adjoining rooms. His stone hearth boasted enough space for a warm cooking fire, grate, and swinging, cast-iron arm. A sturdy table large enough for up to six witches occupied an area near the fire, so the cozy, incomplete place was a point of high pride.

It wasn't all that far from my tree house, just an hour's run, but he'd built in a more open section of forest. Less clotted, more visible. A stream trickled beyond his back door, winding into brush and saplings.

"The bread smells delicious," Grandfather said, inhaling deeply. The scents of butter and yeast intertwined, making my stomach growl.

"Merry meet!" trilled a feminine voice, preceding a brilliant smile. Regina bustled out from the pantry, a crock of preserves in one hand, a golden loaf of delicious-smelling bread in her other. She'd tied her voluptuous red curls away from her face, and wore a simple, loose dress instead of her usual pants, shirt, and vest.

As the Head Master for the Northern Network, Regina popped into Papa's house every now and then. Transitioning from their old High Priestess, Geralyn, to their new one, Nadira, had been a lurching change in the highest Alkarran peaks. For months, the strain showed on Regina's expression, edging her closer to the idea of *retirement*. Particularly as she watched Papa control his day.

For good or for ill.

"Staying in?" I couldn't help asking, glancing at her casual dress. With a laugh, she set the bread in the middle of the table. A shy smile curled her lips.

"For the morning, I did, and it was lovely. I've always had somewhere to be, and something to do, on behalf of the Masters. Today? Nothing at all, except this bread and meeting with a friend for coffee. And," she added with a touch of pride, "the bread is pretty good, if you ask me. You'll have to let me know, because I'm leaving soon for the North."

Papa put an arm on her waist and gave her a kiss on the cheek. The affectionate murmur of, "It smells delicious," snagged my heartstrings. Though it had taken a while to get used to their tender touches, I more readily appreciated Papa having a connection with someone other than Mama.

Regina was an entirely different witch. She didn't show as much outward affection as Mama used to, and she appeared stiff in social situations when Papa held her hand. She seemed to have grown more used to his frequent, unabashed touching, because Papa held no such reservations.

Grandfather sat at the table first. Papa, tearing a chunk of bread off the end, tossed the loaf to me next. Regina rolled her eyes and muttered, "Savage!" The exclamation earned her a broad, boyish smile. I caught the buttery, steaming loaf, accepted the knife Regina passed my way, and sawed a large chunk free.

"Don't mind me," Regina said as she nabbed her own piece. She glanced at a ticking clock on the hearth mantel. "I'm on my way out." She sent Papa a starry gaze and a smile. "I'll be back later this evening."

With a smile and a wave, Regina transported away.

"So," Grandfather said as he accepted a slice of bread from my hands, "how are things?"

I shrugged. "Fine." The temptation to tell them about Scarlett's letter sat on the tip of my tongue, but I forewent the idea. Despite a few details that didn't make sense, there was nothing to say. We had to wait for a second letter to arrive, if at all.

"Any word from Merrick?" Grandfather asked.

"Not really."

"How long has it been?" Papa asked.

"Six months."

His brow rose. "So long?"

I nodded.

Grandfather made a thoughtful noise at the back of his throat, glanced at Papa. "I don't suppose you have any information on whereabouts?"

"Aren't you the High Priest?"

Grandfather smiled. "Yes, and you should know better than anyone else that this doesn't mean anything when it comes to Protector intelligence. I didn't know if you kept up with anyone in the Brotherhood. Rognvald hasn't divulged to me the exact reasons for Merrick's departure, and I haven't asked. Only," he added with a wry glance sent my way, "because my granddaughter has some entanglement in Merrick's life. I didn't want to draw suspicion."

With a forced chuckle, Papa said, "I don't keep up with them much." His face tightened ever-so-slightly. "Rognvald pulled me from the Brotherhood communication magic a few months ago."

My breath caught. Papa hadn't mentioned it.

"Really?" Grandfather asked.

Papa nodded and tore off a bite of bread. That explained Papa's surlier-than-ever stares and the multitude of reasons he found to visit my treehouse every day with some insufferable request to be useful. Sometimes, the man drove me dotty.

"I'm sorry, Papa. I didn't know."

He shrugged. "I left the Brotherhood. I'm not the High Priest, nor the Highest Witch. There's no reason for me to be in the Brotherhood magic."

A flash of compassion for Rognvald swept me. What an awkward position. As the new Head of Protectors, he wouldn't want to ostracize Papa, one of the most respected—alternately, disliked—witches in the Central Network. Not only had Papa run the Brotherhood for years, ascended to High Priest, and then Highest Witch, but he'd also managed to navigate a hostile Council, remove himself from the highest leadership position, which was something that most witches could only manage through death or drama, and live the life of freedom he'd always wanted.

No wonder Rognvald delayed the decision for months.

The farther Papa advanced into said freedom, the more blatantly obvious it appeared that it may not be the happy place he expected. In fact, it looked agonizing.

Papa waved a hand, no doubt from exasperation at our gaping astonishment. "Not a big deal." He swallowed hard, each word thinning as he spoke, as if he had to squeeze them through a tight airway. "I'm attempting to make sense of the purpose of life right now, that's all."

Brutal.

"And you shall," Grandfather said gently, with eyes brimming with love for Papa. He turned to me. "Forgive me, my dear. I am not privy to all the details of Merrick's mission, nor have I felt it my place to ask."

I set a hand on top of his and smiled. "Even if you were, I wouldn't expect you to report them to me. I will honor the sanctity of the Brotherhood and their missions, as I would want them to do for the Sisterhood, as well."

Grandfather set his free hand on top of mine and squeezed. His smile had a bolstering effect.

"I'm sure he's fine," he stated with cheer. "Do you know anything about the mission or his assignment?"

I shook my head.

"Not this time."

Not all Protector missions were so closely held. There had been times in the past where Papa let us know where he went, wrote every day, or sent trinkets and stories about the witches he met.

Deductions about where Merrick might have been for the last several months weren't difficult to make. Alkarra only had so many places for a Protector to be called, and only so many missions that required their skill level.

After the Battle for Letum Wood decimated Alkarran Guardian forces, and laid open several exposed weaknesses both in government infrastructure and geographical locations, there were two main guesses about where Rognvald sent Merrick.

The North,

Or the East.

For my part, I wagered the North, where the new High Priestess Nadira attempted to grasp onto the reins after Geralyn's growing dictatorship was brought to its knees. Though what a Central Network Protector might do *there*, I couldn't fathom. And with such secrecy, too.

That, or the wobbly Eastern Network. High Priest Niko Aldana and father to my best friend's son had died during the Battle for Letum Wood. Niko's brother, Cristian, had taken over the Aldana throne.

It wasn't going well.

Rognvald may have sent Merrick on a roving mission, too. Merrick might be traveling all the Networks, gathering what reformation looked like. In the Southern Network, Gelas, god of ice, reputedly lived amongst the glaciers and ice flows. His demigod children used his god magic to help the magicless witches in the Southern Network have independence again. The transition in the South had been simple compared to the East.

"Well," Grandfather said with a spry voice, "I'm sure Merrick will return safely, and I hope that is soon."

Seeing Papa's distant, broiling stare, I decided to turn the topic. A little. Without Regina present, it would be easier to ask the question that had haunted me for days.

"How did you do it, Papa?"

"Do what?"

"Handle being a Protector and a husband?"

Grandfather's eyebrow quirked higher. He gazed over the top of his bread, staring right at Papa, who reached for a cup to swig a drink of water. His throat bobbed as he drank, and drank . . .

. . . and drank.

The way he glanced at me, with an edgy uncertainty, told me I'd hit a nerve. He fiddled with his napkin and set the cup down and searched for butter, which told me I'd hit a *big* nerve. Papa swiped his lips off with the back of his arm, glanced over, and saw me waiting with my usual stubborn persistence for an answer.

He scowled.

I elevated my brow. "Well?"

"Badly," he muttered. "I did it badly and I don't want to talk about it."

"Papa!"

"What? It's the truth!"

Exasperated, I rolled my eyes. "It's not the truth from my view of things, and I need help. Insight, I guess."

"Into what? Your Protector is gone."

"Exactly. I need help knowing how to . . . *do* . . . this."

He frowned. "You mean life? It's been six months. You're doing exactly what you should be doing."

I leaned against my chair, realized I hadn't asked a fair question. Nor could I put into words what I sought. Not exactly. There was an underlying insecurity that plagued me. A question of, *can Merrick and I survive this?* that kept me awake at night. This was one mission. Dozens awaited throughout the course of our lives.

I let out a breath, not wanting to voice the words, *I'm not sure I'm cut out for this,* because I knew that wasn't true. Neither was the phrase, *I don't want this kind of relationship,* true either, because I wanted anything to do with Merrick.

"I mean . . ."

Whether he responded to my earnest gaze, or the pleading in my voice, Papa sighed. With a shake of his head, he said, "I did it badly, Bianca. Marie is the one you need to speak with."

I glowered.

He held up both hands.

"I'm sorry, but she was the one stuck at home. The one dealing with the silence and the long distance. Everything about our life together was unfair for her. I chose this life. She did not."

"Yes she did!"

Elbows braced on the table, he braided his fingers together and stared at me with a blank expression I could only assume masked pain. His guilt about my childhood was nothing new. He berated himself my whole life, but now that I experienced Mama's life first-hand, Papa's emotions held an entirely different tenor.

He sprang back to his feet, shoving the chair away. I had never seen Papa this uncomfortable. Grandfather watched while he chewed. His expectant face would have been comical if I wasn't so upset by Papa's reluctance.

Papa paced. I gained my feet. "Out with it," I demanded. "Something is bothering you and it has been for weeks. It's only going to get worse. That's what you always tell me."

He growled.

I folded my arms.

He spun on his heel, jaw working. He propped an arm on his mantelpiece and ran a hand through already disheveled hair.

"It's not fair."

"What's not fair?"

A flash of his attention went over my shoulder, to where Regina had stood, and back to me. I felt a rush of gratitude she'd left, because I had a feeling that whatever came next, he wouldn't have said with her here.

"Regina gets the better part of me, which she absolutely deserves," he added more quietly, and with earnestness. "But the part of life that your mother earned, will never have, has arrived. These weeks without the Protectors is something Marie dreamed about, cultivated, and . . ." His voice trembled. ". . . lost. She worked hard for time with me, and she's gone. It's not *fair*, and neither was anything else about her life. That is what I have to say about the Protectors."

Spinning away to face the empty fireplace, he shoved a hand through his hair. The broad planes of his back moved up and down with fast breaths. Stunned, I sought for something to say. What could I possibly interject into a silence so loud?

"Gods, B," he whispered, shaking his head. "Every day I think about it. Every day I wake up with Regina at my side, and I can't stop hating how unfair it is to Marie. She waited. She endured. She longed for *these* days, when I would be free. When my time belonged to me and we could build a house and exist and . . ."

He choked.

My heart tied itself up. Cords wrapped around it, squeezing with vicious delight. If words had teeth, they'd be ravaging me now. I could barely breathe.

"And Marie can't," he whispered. "She endured all that loneliness and rigor and torment, for what?"

He straightened by shoving away from the mantle, his arms powerful and sure. His swift stride headed for the door, paused halfway there. He cast a haunted gaze to me, but it didn't quite meet mine.

"I'm sorry, B. I can't help you because I can't figure it out either. I don't know *how* Marie did it, and I don't know why. I only know that, in the end, it worked against her. I know that I have nightmares of the same happening to you. I know that I can't bear to see the same pain, to hear the same questions that

Marie must have asked. And I didn't . . . no, wouldn't . . . stop it."

My reaching hand lowered to my side. Protests died on my lips as I attempted to follow him into the twilight. My feet managed two steps before they faltered. Grandfather's quiet presence appeared at my elbow. He cupped a hand around my arm.

"Let him go," he said quietly, but with wisdom. "Believe it or not, Bianca, this is exactly what your father needs the most: space. But the curse of *space* is that we must fill it, and he, for the first time in his life, is finally filling it with the right questions."

Papa's anguish remained with me that evening, like black smoke curling around my heart. The dense clouds deepened as twilight approached, lowering over the forest with penumbra and the quiet cacophony of a settling forest.

I stood at the end of a well-known trail, the golden glow of my home far above. My breath strained as I calmed from the run. Somewhere overhead, candlelight bounced from the table. Leda's letters still waited for my perusal, but I ignored them again. I drew in slow, steady breaths, and waited for calm to find me before I returned.

A whisper of sapphire arose from the ground, slipped into my ankle. I felt the warm creep of Deasylva's presence like a balm.

"Papa's sad," I whispered.

Her reassurance, wordless but steady, was her only reply. But it was enough. Muted starlight echoed from behind the wild canopy, only visible in a brief, rare snatch. With a sigh, I turned to go. The stirring whisper of the forest elevated like swirling fall leaves.

She belongs to us.

We are yours.

The joy returns.

My heart skipped a beat. I paused, arrested. Had they said what I thought—

"Little troublemaker?"

I knew that voice. The rolling, nuanced timbre. The purring r's and deep intonation and hints of unrestricted adoration. I whirled around.

Merrick.

Chapter Six

He smelled like evergreen.

His hair was longer, pulled out of his face in a braid down his back. Loose tendrils cut across his temple, waving in a cross breeze over his shoulders. Tanned skin and a glittering, blonde beard, highlighted by his clean white shirt and brown breeches. No half-armor. No wounds. No obvious issues.

Those eyes.

Glimmering emeralds.

Forest canopy.

Brilliant summer.

My breath caught, stomach dropped. The entirety of my body might have collapsed and I wouldn't have noticed.

"Merrick?"

He grinned, white teeth sparkling. "Merry meet, B."

A spell brought me into his arms, slamming against him. He wrapped me so tight that distance ceased to exist. The dull thud of his heart was a reassuring song. A familiar rhythm whose memory used to lull me to sleep at night. I could barely catch my breath as I clawed him closer.

Six months!

Gone in a flash.

His fists tightened onto the back of my dress, pulling it taut around almost-paralyzed ribs. The muscles along his forearms flexed as he braced his legs.

"Hold on, little troublemaker," he whispered against the shell of my ear.

Hold on?

I had no plans to release him.

Ever.

Transportation blurred the world. As darkness engulfed us both, Merrick held true. Through the quick pressure bearing down on my hands, the contour of his body remained. He didn't leave me. We landed, together, at the door of my house.

He loosened his hold, but not by much. One arm anchored my waist, while the other touched my cheeks. He studied me so closely. As if memorizing again, or recalling what he'd always known.

"Why didn't you warn me you were coming back?" I breathed. "Your last letter was cut off. I've been worried."

He chuckled. "I didn't know they were recalling us. I reported to Rognvald, as usual, and then he cleared me. I came as soon as he released us."

Oh, his voice. The sweet burr. So rolling and steady, the cadence a thrill to my confined soul. I leaned back, studying him. The sculpted shoulders, brawny arms. He looked stronger than before, as if he'd been very active. Tan, too. Wherever he went, sunshine and food had been plentiful.

"Not hurt?"

He shook his head. "Wasn't that kind of mission." He pulled me in until my head tucked under his chin, as if he couldn't bear the distance. My eyelashes fluttered along the column of his throat.

"I'm . . . relieved."

"Me too. I've missed you, B."

The declaration led to a hot, thready, desperate kiss. I wrapped my legs around his waist and lost myself in his warmth for so long, yet never long enough. When he pulled away, laughing, I forced myself to take a breath.

"Now that," he drawled, "is a homecoming to dream about."

My feet touched the ground again, but not really. With Merrick this close, we might as well have been on the Volare. The tops of my fingers sprinted along his jaw. It glinted with hints of blonde, like his dirty-blonde hair, darker underneath.

"I have something to show you," I said with my own smile.

"Oh?" His gaze flickered behind us. "Does it have something to do with the lovely tree house at our backs?"

"It does. How did you find it?"

"The forest. It brought me here, then to you."

I threaded our fingers together. "Come inside my home."

Merrick stood at a window fifteen paces long, and eight paces tall, taking up an entire wall facing the forest. Thanks to a spell, the glass vanished in the summer and returned when winter encroached.

"I shouldn't be surprised that you live in a bloody tree," he mused, touching the wooden whirls with his fingertip. "I've known it since you wrote to me, but I am surprised to see it. How did you get over the height?"

"I don't look down much."

He snorted.

"The trees protect me," I added. "Goat fell the first week we moved in, but vines caught her."

"Well, sure."

Laughing, I lifted my hands.

"Letum Wood provided. Who am I to say no?"

He shook his head. "The Lady Witch of Letum Wood, indeed."

The honorific title warmed me through.

Merrick trailed his hand along the table top. He drank in the details. The grains of wood sliding through the ground, the shelves carved into the wall. On his way to my side, a smoky look bloomed through his verdantly bright eyes. When he stood in front of me, he grabbed my hands and kissed my fingers.

Pressing our foreheads together, we said nothing for a long, long time. I smacked another kiss to his lips, wound my arms around his neck, and squealed when he swept me into his arms. We tumbled to my bed together. I tucked myself into his side. He fluffed the pillow, pulled me close, and drew lazy circles along my back.

I held out an open palm, smiling slyly.

"Just one hint?"

A moment passed before he realized what I asked. "No!" he cried, laughing. "You know I can't tell you where I've been."

"Aw, come on! Just *one* hint. You're home now, so what does it matter? Besides, you don't have to tell me what you've been doing all this time. Just . . . you know. A hint of where you went."

Merrick's teeth dug into his bottom lip, pulling it through until it plumped out again. With a robust breath, he succumbed.

"Fine. Just one."

Something round, soft, and delicate landed in the center of my palm. An olive sat in the folds of my hand, slick and perfect and firm. A bright red pimento decorated the end, hiding a creamy center crusted with salt. He conjured another one and popped it into his mouth.

"Delicious."

The words *Eastern Network* lingered on the edge of my tongue, but I didn't release them. It was part of the code. Our agreement. Merrick would never break the trust of the Brotherhood. He maintained his secrecy, but every now and then, a hint or two arrived. It helped me feel somewhat involved despite the screen hiding that part of his life.

I rolled the olive between my thumb and index finger, enjoying the plump, but rigid, texture. While instinct said the Eastern Network, he might be tricking me. Before this long assignment, and with missions of less importance, he attempted to throw me off. Keep me guessing, for the sheer joy of the challenge.

Olives could be the Southern Network or the Eastern Network. Both enjoyed pickled, savory flavors, anything fermented. Smiling, I bit the end of the olive. His gaze dropped to my lips, so I puckered them extra tight, then laughed when he growled.

"Understood," I said in a poor imitation of his accent.

"Tell me about Rognvald. I saw your message in the notebooks right as our mission was ending. I've been stewing on it ever since."

Giggling, I relayed the tale in full. By the time I discussed my fading black eye—thanks to a spell from Leda—my stomach ached from laughing with him. He put a hand on my thigh, chuckling as mirth faded into shiny-eyed warmth.

"What now?" I asked.

"Rognvald gave me a few days to get things settled. See if I can get an apartment in Chatham City again."

With a roguish smile, I said, "You could always stay here."

"Can I?"

A hasty nod confirmed.

He grinned, pressed a kiss to my forehead. Deep thoughts swirled for several moments before he asked, "Do you think your father would filet me like a sea trout if I moved in with his daughter and hadn't put a cord of engagement on her wrist?"

His forefinger and thumb circled my right wrist, where it lay on his chest. "I'm not sure it's his business," I retorted.

Merrick chucked.

"Besides," I whispered, "That's easy enough to fix."

He smiled, but a distant note claimed him. The easy air slid into something with more ballast. How could I interpret his thoughtful stare or the sudden halt to the conversation? Before I could ask the question, he released my wrist.

"I'll take the offer, B. And gratefully. I'd do anything for more time together. Thank you." I beamed as he brushed a lock of hair out of my eyes. Greater curiosity ruffled the skin between his brow. "Any news on the Sisterhood?"

"Not yet. Leda is working on getting us a meeting with the Council."

"Still?"

"Perpetually."

He pressed a kiss to the back of my hand. "I'm sorry they're so slow to adopt what will be the best thing to ever happen to the Central Network."

"You think so?"

"Know so."

Until his confident tone bolstered my dream, I didn't realize how much I'd missed it. Relief was a rolling thing, gaining speed. Sheer shock had kept me paralyzed in his arms for probably too long. It bled to elation. Now, a thick web of solace and disbelief buffered me on all sides. I felt so much, I wasn't sure what to do about it.

So I sat there.

Drinking him in.

The way his sandy hair hung on his shoulders. The tired lines around his luminescent eyes. Nothing about him had changed dramatically, yet he dazzled me all the same. As if stars shimmered beneath his skin because he danced in the sky without me.

Merrick smirked.

"Stare your fill?"

"Never."

"Gods." He closed all distance until our ribs crashed together, foreheads touching, the slopes of our nose a gentle caress. "You unravel me."

I lost myself in his kiss. In the feel of his tight arms. The bands of security he brought. For the first time I could recall in months, the whispering trees slipped away, invisible, leaving me in a forest cocoon, suspended above all.

Chapter Seven

Despite the elation of Merrick's return, a restful night's sleep in his arms, and a delicious breakfast together under the canopy, life forced us to return to official business. Merrick returned to the Gatehouse and Chatham City. I turned my attention to the Sisterhood and Scarlett's weird letter.

Though I'd expected separation, even for a few hours, to be excruciating, it provided mental room. He threw me out of orbit, and I had to pull myself back within. To realign and think and breathe deep and find the new center of my world.

Ever changing.

Primed for distraction, I sat cross legged, in a short skirt and high sandals, on a tree branch above the house to read Scarlett's missive again. This time, I had the added bonus of insight from Leda.

My thoughts dwindled on several lines. *Silver-blonde hair, knobby knees, wrinkled socks, lusterless eyes, and a dim disposition.* Which, according to Leda, accurately described Scarlett's younger sister.

At five years old, she discovered her hovering talent. Which was the age Scarlett entered the orphanage. *By six years old she could soar safely down a set of stairs or the lower branches of a tree.* Which was the year she learned to read. *By seven she could cross four times that space.* The year she entered the official orphanage school. *And by eight she thoroughly exploited her abilities.*

Scarlett had been around eight when Ellie died. Which, in some way, I equated with the final line of the story.

Until they ripped off her wings.

A fourth read-through uncovered no other details. My main opinion stood. There was no way to know what motivation or intent inspired this unknown sender, but I presumed it wasn't innocent.

Why wouldn't someone claim it, otherwise?

If sinister undertones existed, we needed time to suss them out. I tucked it away to regard later, hiding it in my bookcase, between my two largest books. I finished a cup of tea, set it within the wash bucket, and glanced up in surprise. More than a glowing ice chip, but not attached to anything, was a single, bobbing blue flame suspended in the air.

Wryly, I said, "Merry meet, Gelas. I mean, Baxter."

Baxter often used Gelas' magic to navigate the witchy world. After the Battle for Letum Wood, Gelas destroyed all god magic amulets and the gods separated. Gelas alone cared for the mortals and demigods that the other gods left behind, abandoning them to the inevitability of fate and time.

In the intervening months since the battle, Gelas had come up with a loose tether to raw magic, allowing the demigods to still wield god magic in service of the former witches of the Southern Network. Invisible, without amulet, but something Baxter still managed to harness.

Which lent itself to the strangest kind of messages a witch might expect. The single sapphire flame sprouted into lines of ice that scrawled out a message.

Can you come? Southern Network.

"Yes."

The unexpected, flickering fire zipped away in a whoosh, leaving a trickle of black smoke behind.

Summertime in the Southern Network was a lush experience. The barren, bleak winters bottled up daylight, then unleashed it on the world, resulting in grassy tundras instead of snow fields, muddy mountains instead of glaciers, and trickling streams instead of ice pack.

Wildflowers littered a field far outside Zamok Castle, colloquially known as the Ice Castle, in colors of crimson and gold. They bobbed in a gentle breeze. The sun-kissed grass flowed between my toes.

In the exact middle of the field, sitting by himself, was Baxter.

I'd found him here several times since the weather turned warm. He enjoyed sitting in the wild tundras for short amounts of time, drawing in the fresh air and smell of sage. He leaned on his palms, head tilted to the sky, eyes shut. His tightly coiled hair tossed curls in the wind. He'd cut it shorter than usual, so the curls formed C's instead of rings. Their charming disorder lent a ruffled appearance to his usually pristine and tactful dress. His eyes, a unique blend of light green against his tawny skin, popped open as I approached.

"Merry meet, Baxter."

"Bianca."

We luxuriated in the field of wildflowers for minutes before he faced me. "So?"

"So?" I challenged.

"How are you?"

"Delightful."

A glint entered his eyes. "Has Merrick returned?"

"Just last night."

"Did I interrupt your happy bliss?"

"Not unwelcome, and not interrupted." I sprawled my legs, yanking my skirt to just above my knees so the sun brightened my shins. "Merrick has to catch up on Brotherhood gossip and meetings. How is Tipa?"

His affable amusement split in half as he cut me a suspicious gaze. "Why do you ask?"

As if speaking about our mutual demigod friend—if I could call her that, which I probably couldn't—was the most natural thing for us to discuss, I repeated my question. "How is Tipa? I haven't seen her in several months."

Baxter studied me for a long moment, eventually peeling his gaze away. There was definitely a reason for his nerves around the question. I'd long suspected that Tipa had some form of emotion around Baxter. He was handsome, a good-natured demigod, and genuinely cared about others. Neither of them were willing to acknowledge that something deeper than friendship might have grown between them.

"Fine." He waved an errant hand. "She's busy helping Gelas transition the mortals in Alaysia. Some of Tontes' many demigod children, and a few of my sisters, wanted to stay on the island that Prana pulled together."

"She did it?" I cried. "Prana let Gelas form all the small islands into one land mass?"

He nodded.

Incredulous, I whispered, "That's got to be a disaster."

The few weeks I'd spent in Alaysia, known as the land of the gods, hadn't been easy. Hundreds of islands of varying size littered the ocean, separated in shifting sections that belonged to each god. To have them conform to one great whole would be . . . dangerous. Demigods did not like mortals. Mortals did not like demigods.

Baxter snorted. "Not *my* mess, and thank the good gods for it.

Tipa's busy keeping the remaining demigods in line. Without amulets or god magic, the demigods are as good as mortals themselves." He winced. "Apparently, it's not going well. Ignis, Ventis, and Tontes have deserted them completely."

"I can't imagine," I muttered. "Gelas is still staying in the Southern Network?"

"In the winter, yes."

"The Southern Network is agreeable with him thus far?"

He nodded. "Alina and Gelas' wife, Syanna, get along well."

Alina, the Southern Network High Priestess and Highest Witch, had lost her magic along with the rest of the Southern Network years ago. Through his demigod daughter Tipa, Gelas gave Alina limited access to god magic. The power helped the Southern Network seal and improve their porous security. Vagabonds from the Eastern Network didn't take advantage of the South so much these days.

"Syanna likes the Southern Network better in the winter." He motioned around them. "This is pretty, she says, but it's not ideal. Syanna and Gelas will continue to live in his frozen northlands during the winter. Tipa prefers it there, too."

"A true daughter of the god of ice."

"Very much so."

A hint of something else propelled his agreement. Experience, perhaps? Tipa and I hadn't started off on the right foot. She thought I was a reckless, foolish witch who had problems, while I found her to be a potential future ally and friend . . . when she didn't roll her eyes at the sight of me.

"Demigods," Baxter said in a contemplative tone, "move very slow."

"False. You're quite fast."

"No, no. Not like *that*. In terms of . . . relationships."

Sensing he finally broached the boundary of a territory I'd long been wanting to hear more about, I fell silent.

"Tipa, in particular, is verrrrry slooooow about who she befriends, and who she trusts."

"I've noticed."

He muttered something that sounded a lot like, "You don't know the half of it," but I didn't dare interrupt him to clarify.

"There's a chance," he continued, as if something might explode should he say the wrong thing, "that I could eventually win Tipa over as not just a friend, but . . ."

"A lover?"

He shook his head. "No, that's not quite it."

"A partner?"

"Better." He hummed, then shook his head, "but still not quite it. In Alaysian, the word is *temeras*."

"What does that mean?"

"I don't think it translates directly." A quick shake of his head moved a curl out of his eyes. "It's something between a lover and a . . . boyfriend? Is that what witches say?"

"I guess?"

"You don't know?"

"No."

He chuckled. "I should have expected that. Regardless, I like Tipa. I think we have a friendship. I'm curious if there's more than friendship behind it."

"But you don't know how she feels?"

"Correct."

"I'd offer wisdom, but . . ."

"You're the last witch I'd ask." He sent me a winning smile. "Sorry."

His natural charm, and the draw of the demigod that witches had to constantly fight off, still didn't quite allay the inherent insult of his statement. I hexed him with a sneezing hex that ended as quickly as it began. He laughed through it.

"It's fair," I admitted. "Tipa and I are pretty different, and I'm really not the best witch to give relationship advice. Still, the fit between the two of you would be sound."

"Alaysia is keeping Tipa busy, anyway."

"Do *you* have news from home?" I asked, certain he'd understand my bold emphasis. Baxter had no home to speak of. With Prana combining the islands, and Baxter burning his father's *Rostina*, or gigantic, magical sand castle, the question went poignantly deep.

During the war between witches and gods, Baxter conspired against his father, Ventis, the god of wind, to help witches maintain Alkarra. As the gods descended with floods, tempest, and fire, Baxter worked behind the scenes in Alaysia to give us a chance to survive. Without him, we may not have won.

His jaw flexed. "No word from my father, if that's what you're asking."

"It was my next question."

"He hasn't spoken to me since his departure."

"Do you expect him to?"

A hollowness filled his tone. "No. Never again. And that's for the better, I think."

I set my hand on his arm. "I'm sorry, Baxter. It's good to hear that you can move on, but I'm sad that it's happening in such a way."

With a teasing smile, he said, "You know what isn't good?"

"What?"

"The Eastern Network. That's why I asked you to come here today."

I cocked my head, intentionally giving him the space to escape the painful thoughts. "Really?"

Frustration scrunched his brow. I no longer wondered why he wrote from the Southern Network instead of the East, where he tended to spend most of his days. With a concentration and annoyance that intense, he probably needed a break from the heavy-handed sea culture.

"Niko's brother, Cristian, is not an impressive High Priest. Or perhaps Derek jaded me, because at least he really cared. Niko had his faults, but Cristian?"

He whistled long and low.

"How so?"

"Cristian came to the throne amidst trauma and trouble, so he's clutching to power like a rich woman to her pearls." Baxter shook his head. "He doesn't trust witches, and his Council doesn't trust him. Rumors are swirling . . ."

"Of what?"

"Insurrection."

I sucked a breath through my nose. The Eastern Network had a habit of rotating through powerful families as often as every several centuries. Hundreds of years earlier, the Castaneda Dynasty had ended when the Aldanas burned them all alive in a cave and took the throne. They had been ruling ever since.

Lately?

They hadn't been ruling well.

Isobel Aldana, former High Priestess, had started the initial decline for trust in the Eastern Network. She had secretly hidden her life, betrayed her family, murdered her husband, and died in a battle against her daughter, Mabel, of the Central Network. Not everyone knew of her full betrayal as the Almorran Master until much later.

Niko also stepped into position amidst chaos, war, and turmoil. Though the Central Network ultimately won against Almorran magic and struck Mabel down, Niko's battle with his Council, with witches, and eventually with other Networks, had been constant and uphill.

"I can't say I'm all that surprised," I said. "The Eastern Network has been anything but stable for years."

Wryly, Baxter muttered, "Me, too."

"Do you think witches will actually rebel?"

"It's hard to say."

"It'll impact Tomasso," I said, speaking of Priscilla and Niko's son, direct heir to the Eastern Network throne. Cristian was acting on Tomasso's behalf until he came of age on his twenty-third birthday.

Since Niko died in the Battle for Letum Wood, Baxter had become a sort of step-in father figure for him, and acted as an intermediary for Priscilla, so she didn't have to engage with the Aldanas directly. Tomasso was a little over a year old, living with his mother who ran Miss Priscilla's School for Girls.

Baxter nodded. "It definitely will impact Tomasso, which is why I wanted to give you a warning."

"Does Priscilla know?"

"Of course."

"Is she . . ."

"Fine." He shrugged. "For now." His eyes narrowed ever-so-slightly. "The Network hired a groundskeeper for her, a witch named Jorge. He's quiet, but sturdy. While Priscilla can handle her own, I feel better that someone else is there with her . . . just in case."

My brow rose.

"In case *what*?"

He shook his head. "In case Cristian grows truly desperate and tries to harm Tomasso, giving him a more secure hold on the throne. I'll let you know if I think that's happening, but I didn't want it to be a surprise. Consider this your early alarm."

"Thanks."

With a friendly hand on my shoulder, he squeezed. "Speaking of the Eastern Network, I'm off to chat with Cristian again. I'll keep you updated if any changes happen, but be on your guard. And it wouldn't hurt to check on Priscilla, too. Just in case."

"Ava stirring up trouble?" I quipped, eager to shift the conversation to something a little less dark.

He rolled his eyes, said an exasperated, "Isn't she always?" and smacked the wildflower petals off his pants as he arose. "Being an uncle isn't as easy as I expected."

"You're more father than uncle."

"True."

I followed him back toward Zamock Castle. A few hundred paces away from the ice castle, I waved to a figure on the High Priestess's balcony. Alina. She waved back. Once Baxter left, I returned to the Central Network, stewing over mysteries and politics.

Merrick set a bowl of porridge in front of me the next morning, sprinkled with a golden crust of sugar granules. This particular sugar came from the Western Network. He grinned in a jaunty way, teasing me. The granules were meant to be another hint, but he'd countered it with a dash of dried cranberries, which definitely originated in the Eastern Network.

I quirked an eyebrow.

He grinned, and my heart melted. "Had some almonds, too," he purred. "Just a few flecks of them left."

Their tawny slivers decorated the top of my bowl, also a known import from the West. I picked up my spoon, giving him my best, most uncertain glare, and earned another laugh. A bowl twice as big as mine settled in front of him. He sat down, a hand on my thigh, our bodies close.

We ate in silence. I emerged from a deep sleep with the slow rising of the sun, washing the sky behind the branches with rosy hues. With porridge heavy in my stomach, my mind awoke. Goat stared through the window, slotted eyes trained on me and oddly fixated. Other Goat, hay dribbling out of his mouth, bleated.

Merrick drew my attention as he shoved his empty bowl away,

leaning back in satisfaction. "I need to report to Rognvald this morning. Finalize the whole mission. Should have done it yesterday, but he was busy. This should officially close it out."

"Will it open you for another mission?"

Lips rolled, he nodded. "Technically, yes. He's not likely to send me unless this one opens back up, for some reason, or things get weird and desperate."

I scraped the edge of my spoon along the bottom of the bowl, gathering little surplus. It had been a stupid question to ask. I already knew the answer. The Protectors defined their career by a mission-after mission emphasis. They could return from one and be called for another before finishing a bath, though it rarely happened that quickly.

In a snap of fingers, real life was restored. The haze of one day is all that separated us from routine.

So much build up . . . and back to work. How unerring some drudgery, despite the separation of months.

Merrick set down his mug of coffee. "It's unlikely," he added, "that I'd go anywhere soon. There's training I need to pass to prove I'm still competent with certain languages. And Scarlett wants to speak with me, too."

"All day today?"

He nodded. "Not all day with Scarlett, but part of the debriefing. This mission was instated by Rognvald, so he's having me report what we uncovered, with our conclusions."

No wonder Grandfather didn't know much about it, nor feel he should inquire.

"Which means we'll be able to meet up for dinner tonight?"

He smiled at my hopeful slant, kissing me softly. "Yes, little troublemaker. Dinner tonight. Do you mind if we go to The Pig's Snout? I've missed their biscuits."

"Not at all."

"Good. Tomorrow night, I want to see Mother and Drogo. I barely sent a word off to them when I returned from my previous mission, before I had to leave again on this one." He gathered our bowls and swung a leg off the bench. Before he disappeared to the wash bucket, he paused. "Later, can we talk?"

"Aren't we talking now?"

He smiled, but it was half-hearted. One hand nudged a spoon from side to side in a nervous gesture as he sat there, dirty bowls in his lap, uncertainty in his eyes.

"Yes, but I think we need to *talk*."

My insides locked up, as if he breathed ice on them, because I knew what he meant. He'd returned. That meant . . . things. It meant we should discuss our thoughts on this Protector life, how to survive it, if we wanted it. I'd blithely mentioned handfasting last night, and his expression had been odd.

He desired to discuss big things. Things I didn't have the answer for. Still, I replied meaningfully, despite my tight stomach.

"I think that's a good idea."

A wider smile resulted. He kissed my forehead and strode toward the wash bucket, chattering. In the midst of his ramblings, a voice floated from the stoop.

"Bianca?" Leda tepidly crossed the space, neck rigid. She looked straight ahead, clearly avoiding a downward gaze.

"In here!"

With a released breath, she stepped inside. Solemnity coated all her features, a shade deeper than what I usually observed. Merrick held up a hand in greeting, which she acknowledged with a nod and a half-hearted smile.

"Merry meet, Merrick. I'm glad you returned safely."

"Thank you. Good to see you, Leda."

To me, she said with a sharp irritation, "You were supposed to let me know when he returned."

"It's only been one full day! And good morning," I added with dramatic kindness. "To what do we owe the pleasure of your happy company this early?"

She strode past me, ignoring my question. A steely determination overcame her features. "We can discuss that later. There are suddenly other priorities. Merrick, a favor?"

He paused, hand submerged into the soapy wash bucket. "Me?"

"Do you have ten minutes?"

"Ah . . ."

She held out a hand. "May I transport you somewhere?"

He lifted his hands from the bucket, flinging the droplets off his fingertips, and reached for a towel. Briefly, his astonished gaze met mine in question. I shrugged.

"What do you need, Leda?" he asked.

"Access to the Protector's room in the Great Library of Burke."

"Oh?"

She said nothing else.

Pure surprise would be her only ally here. "Am I allowed to give you access?" he finally asked.

A dollop of rage altered her pretty expression for half a second. She composed it with an indrawn breath, her cheeks heating to a pink tinge.

"You're allowed to do what you want. I can promise it's not dangerous to open a door for me, and you can be back within the minute, if you desire. I can't go inside it without you, and it would take far more dire straits than this to tempt me to ask Caroline."

Another pause several beats long followed. His twisted expression seemed to ask *who is Caroline*? I couldn't help but echo the question. I had no idea.

Slowly, he said, "All right," and accepted her hand. The comical sight of them holding hands, Merrick shifting uncomfortably, nearly brought a rangy laugh out of me.

Leda turned to me. "Go to Scarlett. Immediately, please. She's received a second letter." Her expression turned grim. "You'll definitely want to see this one."

They vanished.

Chapter Eight

The first line of the second letter almost stopped my heart.
Marie Hazel was born with wings.
I lifted my head.

Scarlett regarded my reaction, dour-faced and pale. She stood behind her desk again, a strange surreality to how similar this felt to the first letter. Blinking, I looked at the message again. The tip of my finger traced the curves.

Marie.

Hazel.

Mama and Grandmother. The feeling of an arrow spearing through my chest took me by surprise. I had to swallow rising acid to focus again.

"Read on," Scarlett rasped.

Marie Hazel's parents didn't mind that she had wings.

In fact, they had wings of their own. Her mother didn't fly, of course. Some witches had limits for the amount of social disruption they would cause. Her father did fly, of course. Some witches loved any social disruption they could cause.

Marie Hazel grew up near the sea. Oh, how she loved the sea. The splashing tide. The crashing waves. She soared with aquilas over distant skies. She flowed in currents of air that became mighty storms. Marie Hazel comprehended hurricanes, rip currents, changing coral. She merged into and became part of the magic of that great clime.

Nothing stopped her.

Until the sea died.

The great tide disappeared all at once. Vanished. Salt-crusted stones emerged as the waters retreated. They hissed for the last time, departing to forgotten places, unseen. The animals, swept away. The sparkling blue expanse was there.

Gone.

This was tragedy enough, but the sea dared to take her mother.

There, it ended. I lowered the paper and gazed away. My heart had become a mass in my chest. A thumping knot that slammed with every dull reverberation. *Thud, thud, thud.*

"Agonizing," Scarlett whispered, "isn't it?"

"The details," I breathed. Parallels already filled my head, forming liked snapped ties. Mama at home, living so quietly. Papa wild in the world, so unapologetic. Mama dying.

But the sea . . .

As the daughter of Marie and the granddaughter of Hazel, I wanted nothing to do with this horrid piece of literature. With a sense of determination befitting the Head of the Sisterhood, however, I forced myself to read it again.

And again.

The letter rustled as I dropped it to my side, relieved to have finished it. For several moments, neither of us spoke. Words failed me. I didn't know what to say, where to start. The strangeness. The details . . .

Scarlett stood at her window, staring out. "Haunting, isn't it?"

"There is something about it that's . . ."

I shivered.

Scarlett crossed the space behind her desk, lowering with a relieved sigh. "What do you make of it, Bianca?"

"It's a far more clear threat."

"Threat?"

I hedged, unable to put my instinct into words. While there was nothing directly stated, the implicit details left it impossible to see this as benign. Particularly because this author included my family *and* Scarlett's family.

"It's been four days since the first letter, correct?"

She nodded.

"Do you remember when either letter arrived?"

"Noon for the first, about ten minutes before Leda left to summon you here for the second." Her attention darted to the clock over her door, and back to me. "About twenty minutes ago."

"Different times?"

Another nod.

"Was the message delivered by a witch or with magic?"

A deep voice answered from my back. "A witch," Hiddleston said. He stood near the closed doors, mirroring Scarlett's solemnity. By his dark expression, he understood that an implied threat lurked beneath the surface.

"Did you see the witch?"

"The Underassistant said that a man delivered it."

"Anything stick out?"

"Strange dress, she said. Top hat, purple cloak with a flower."

"Purple cloak?"

He nodded. I set that detail aside, as it sounded vaguely familiar, while Hiddleston continued.

"Well, she *thinks* that he delivered the letter. According to her, a man wearing a very garish cloak walked by, tipped his orange hat to her, and kept going. He appeared out of place, so she watched him leave. After he disappeared down the stairs, she noticed the envelope on the desk in front of her."

"It may not have been him?"

Hiddleston shrugged. Scarlett, perched on her chair, said nothing. A summoning spell brought the first letter to my hand from where I'd tucked it away at home. I compared the two letters. Same distinct handwriting. Parchment, spacing, evenness, all uniform.

I sent them to Scarlett, side by side, for her to observe. "Nothing changed, except for the length."

"I see."

"There's nothing overt yet. No direct threat, no . . . powder or infiltrates in the envelope."

The observations felt like desperate reaches. A scramble to create discussion or fulfill her expectation of me having the right answer. The Head of the Sisterhood should have an opinion on this situation. The problem was I didn't know if mine was the *right* opinion.

"Does any of it sound familiar to you, Bianca?" she asked.

Roughly, I whispered, "All of it. If you substitute Letum Wood for the sea, and take out the death of it . . ."

"It's symbolic," Hiddleston offered. "Both of them are. The wings are something shared between you."

Trouble grew on her brow as Scarlett thought that over, eventually shaking her head.

"Yes, but what?"

A dozen replies passed in and out of my mind. I had no idea how to line them up into something feasible, but Hiddleston must be right. Those were details we could suss out later. For now, I had to get my hands on who wrote these letters.

"Any parallels with you or your sister in this story?" I asked.

"No."

"Clearly, I am Marie Hazel, as you are Ellie Victoriann. What do we share?"

With a big breath and uplifted shoulders, she suggested, "A love of our Network?"

I scoffed.

"Mabel? Or," she clarified, "experience with her."

"Yes, but there's no real reference to her in here. It must be something else. Perhaps something also metaphorical."

Hiddleston advanced to study the letters side by side. "There's a lyrical quality to it," he said. "It's not quite poetry, but also not prose as most writers use it."

I reviewed it again. The slightly slanted words and letters had a song-like pattern, depending on how I read it. I could imagine someone carefully penning and sculpting each word.

"Almost like . . . maybe this story is from something else?"

Scarlett frowned. "What do you mean?"

I paced in front of her desk. My mind worked better when my body moved, though it drove her to distraction. "A poem, maybe, as Hiddleston suggested. A song. The sender may have copied a known piece of literature?"

She spread her hand.

"To what end?"

Exasperated, I said, "Who knows? If they've taken something that exists and twisted it to fit us, then . . . it might imply some sort of motivation to get our attention. There must be a reason they're sending these letters, and involving both of us in such strange ways."

"Not to mention remaining anonymous," Hiddleston added.

I agreed with a nod. "I'll keep both of them, if you're comfortable with that, High Priestess, and work more on finding a source, or the witch who is delivering them."

Scarlett appraised me with intent perusal as she nodded. I shuffled the letters into my dress pocket as Hiddleston bowed out, closing the door behind him.

"How are you?" she asked. Her tone reclaimed her usual crisp, businesslike state to which I was more accustomed.

"Fine."

"Merrick has returned."

Her lack of question made sense. She must know he was on her schedule for meetings today.

"Yes." I smiled. "Finally."

She echoed the sentiment, though it barely reached her eyes. "I'm happy to hear that, on your behalf."

"Thank you, High Priestess."

"Rognvald mentioned you helped him with a personal mission."

"Did he tell you what happened?"

"He did. He also mentioned that his cousin gave you currency in exchange for the assistance. Are you a mercenary for hire?"

I frowned.

"A what?"

"Are witches paying you to do whatever dirty work they don't want to deal with?"

Her surprisingly even tone reflected more searching than frustration, but I still couldn't tell what she thought.

"No," I said slowly. "Not that I'm aware of. I didn't ask for payment. She sent it, and I didn't know to whom I could return it."

"Do you need currency?"

"I'm . . . fine. For now."

Truth, mostly. Spring, summer, and fall made it easier to scrounge in the forest. Much of my sustenance came from the woods, or Grandfather, with whom I ate often. Come winter, I'd need new clothes and a fresh pair of boots. I traded for other necessities more often than I purchased them.

Scarlett's tone shifted slightly when she said, "Leda has secured a time slot to meet with the Council."

"Oh?"

I silently cursed Leda. She hadn't told *me*. Or, probably more correctly, I still hadn't answered her massive pile of letters. "That's wonderful news," I said.

"Yes, I'm very glad."

"When is it?"

"Six months from now."

My elation died a quick death. Six months?

"It buys us time, without being too far away," Scarlett said with an optimism that I struggled to share. "The Sisterhood could greatly benefit from you solving this riddle." She motioned to the letters in my pocket with a nod. "While Rognvald's task was kind of you to do, it's hardly the sort of thing we can use as proof of skill. We can't convince the Council to put you on any sort of payroll if you're a mercenary for hire."

I hid a sigh.

"I agree, Your Highness."

Scarlett hummed a prim, "Hmmm," and said nothing more. She spun on her heels, heading toward her bookshelf, where she pulled several scrolls and sent them to the hallway. Her bell-like skirt swayed as she slowed.

"I have every confidence that you can crack this before it becomes a problem, if it ever does. Thank you for your help. Let me know if you find anything. For now, I trust myself into your capable care."

"We'll figure it out, High Priestess."

Whether she responded to the confidence in my tone, or truly believed it herself, I couldn't tell. She nodded, gave me a smile, and dismissed me with a wave. Leda entered the room, face flushed with a triumphant smile as she announced Scarlett's next visitor.

Half an hour later, Leda daintily plucked a roll off the top of a towering pile and set it on her plate, out of reach of her other foods. At a configuration of jam dishes, she gazed disparagingly at several that had been disturbed by previous diners, and moved on down the row of food without scooping any for herself.

Our weekly tradition of meeting for lunch hadn't altered in years, except for location. Eating at the Chatham Castle Dining Hall was far preferable to the unnervingly quiet Great Library of Burke. The food was superior, too. I didn't have to provide my own, thanks to Grandfather's position as High Priest. I ate for free, and so did Leda.

"Scarlett has a point, you know," Leda said.

"About what?"

"You being a mercenary for hire."

My nose wrinkled. "What are you talking about?"

Leda cast me a long suffering glance over her shoulder, then continued past a bowl of pasta and toward spinach.

"I overheard Scarlett asking you about payment for helping Rognvald."

I rolled my eyes, grabbed three rolls, and set them on top of a steamy meat pie. "Right. That. His cousin sent me the coins, which hardly makes me a mercenary for hire. Also, it wasn't mercenary!"

"Definition of terms," she immediately countered. "Depends on what you consider a mercenary. You *did* conduct a service and then received payment for it, which is how she isn't wrong."

"Mercenary is a bit strong."

She shrugged, surveyed a ladleful of gravy, decided against it, and plucked a few carrots from a steaming pile next to the gravy boat.

"You know," she continued, "we could use your position as a mercenary for hire to our advantage. At least for the next six months, before we build up our case in front of the Council."

"Thanks for telling me about the meeting, by the way."

"If you would answer your messages," she said with glacial warmth, "then you would have known before you came."

"There are too many messages!"

With surprising aloofness, she said, "I know. That's why I had Merrick take me to the Protectors room." Her voice lowered. "Once we arrived, he was harder to convince than I thought, but I managed."

Oh, I couldn't wait to hear Merrick's view on their trip to the Great Library of Burke.

"Fine. Great. But I'm not a—"

"I know, I know. You're not a mercenary, per say. If you do offer services in exchange for currency, it would show the Council your value."

"I thought mercenary work was a bad thing?"

"Doesn't have to be."

Storm clouds shuttered her eyes, slowing the growth of motivation once there. Quick as the idea occurred to her, she dismissed it.

"No." She tutted. "That would only work if you had several very lucrative, big jobs that you executed flawlessly, with one particular skill, that would then open you up to others in the market. Then, creating scarcity, we could—"

"Leda . . ."

"Right! Sorry. All that I'm trying to say is that the Council doesn't yet understand your worth. It's our job to make it clear."

"To do that, I need assignments. But I can't get big assignments until the Council recognizes the Sisterhood as an entity."

"Hence," she trilled, "this letter situation with Scarlett. An ideal opportunity."

After plucking a shiny apple from a pile at the end of the line,

Leda swiveled toward the edge of the dining hall. I stuffed an apple in my pocket, one on my plate, and followed after her, ravenous. With a quick spell, I commanded a brownie to follow. Considering that Leda had only just gotten started with her updates, I summoned a second. They trailed after me.

Leda waited, napkin on her lap, fork tines probing her baked potato, at the farthest table in the room when I joined her. Without missing a beat, she asked, "How are things with Merrick?"

The rapid change in conversation made me halt.

"Uh . . . good?"

Her gaze flickered to mine. Eager to avoid discussing the *talk* he wanted to have tonight, I asked, "What about you and Hiddleston?"

She glared.

I waited.

The more surly Leda's response to banal questions, the deeper the emotions. Based on the fearful scowl directed my way, she cared about Hiddleston more than I expected.

"Fine."

Her hint of elongation was too blatantly obvious.

"Fine?"

"We are . . . spending more time together."

"Have you held hands?"

Heat rose on her cheeks. "Perhaps."

I hid a laugh. She'd absolutely destroy me if I showed any amusement to their relationship. With as much soberness as I could rally, I asked, "Are you still good friends?"

"We're not good friends." She countered with an air of riposte that pinked her cheeks further. "We're *very* good friends."

I tilted an eyebrow.

"Oh?"

"Not like that!" She scowled. "Just that we're . . . very good friends."

"Don't you mean very, very?"

If two Guardians hadn't sat down at the far end of the table, she might have stabbed my eye with her fork. "This isn't funny," she hissed, knuckles white around her utensil. Unable to hold it in any longer, I burst out laughing. Her murderous glare deepened.

"It's ridiculous, Leda! When are you going to admit that you like him?"

"Hiddleston is a good witch."

"So was Council Member Greyson at first, but look what happened to him."

If Leda was a cat, her ears would have flattened and her back arched.

"Don't compare the two! Hiddleston is not a traitor to his Network, and former Council Member Greyson, may he rot in Carcere prison, *is* a traitor. Hiddleston is a well-respected witch that accomplishes his tasks in a timely manner, isn't afraid to stay late to finish his work, and has . . . impressive insights into . . . projects."

"Why do you speak about him as if he's a job candidate?"

Pert nose in the air, she said, "I don't have to take this abuse. I'm done here." As she set her fork down and made to leave, I elevated both hands.

"Fine! Fine." Unable to help myself, I slid in my final jab. "We won't talk about Hiddleston, your very, very good friend. I swear it."

"Maybe we should talk about your handfasting plans instead?"

Her snippy comment shouldn't have surprised me, but it did. Merrick's response to my exploratory, casual mention of handfasting had cast a heavy shadow in light of his request to talk tonight.

"There aren't any plans."

"None?"

"Not yet, but I already know I want to handfast him."

As if she sensed something wobbly in my reply, she drawled,

"Go on," and watched me out of the corner of her eye. She moved her fluffy potato around with the fork ends.

"After three years apart, all we've been through, the whole Ignis debacle, and nearly dying, I figure there isn't much more required to convince me that I want to spend the rest of my life with him."

With a high-pitched voice, she asked, "Does Merrick know?"

"Yes."

She deflated. "Well, then. It's not like . . . that is . . ."

I rolled my eyes. "No, Leda. He's not going to be asking me to handfast him right away. At least, not that I'm aware of," I added, startled by the thought. "It's kind of hard to ask," I muttered, buttered roll halfway to my mouth. "You know, because he's never here."

"Do you really want to handfast a witch that will miss so much of your life?"

My immediate agreement hesitated just a beat.

"Yes."

Her lashes tapered. "Why do you want to handfast Merrick?"

Not for the first time today, I bit back the urge to ask her if she'd just joined my life. "Why wouldn't I? I love Merrick. Adore him. The time that I get with him makes up for all the days between."

Archly, she asked, "Do they?"

"Yes!" I cried. "I just . . . it's hard. I don't know how to communicate it. So . . . while I want to handfast him, I also want to figure out how to . . . talk about our lives without talking about them. You know?"

"No, I don't know. Nothing you said makes much sense, but I'm used to that. It's odd, isn't it?" she mused. "How some witches re-create the lives of their parents? You're in the same position as your mother. Do you think we reach for things that we understand without realizing it?"

"When will you start having babies?" I parried back.

Her high irritation turned to deepest loathing in the blink of an eye.

"There's a big difference between Mama and me," I said to dispel the building wrath. "For good or ill. Mama was at home with me and grandmother, running the Tea and Spice Pantry, the garden, taking care of us. I will have the Sisterhood. Besides, I know what I'm getting into handfasting a Protector. Mama had no idea."

"That won't make it any easier, especially if you're both on missions at different times. When will you even see him?"

Her query stirred up uglier, deeper questions. The insecurity should have been boldly obvious, but wasn't, because we hadn't yet been in that position. I had a feeling these were questions and realities we'd discuss when we *talked* tonight.

At this rate, we may never be in that position.

"I don't know," I concluded.

Leda savored a bite of potato, assessment still on her expression. "You and Merrick will make the right move, whatever it is. This will be fine. All of it—the Sisterhood included." She waved a hand, clearing the thoughts that trapped her. "Regardless, we're still close enough to what happened with the gods last year that no one has forgotten your work. We'll jump on the opportunity to show your power and ability to earn that official mark over the next six months."

The idea made me salivate. Having official recognition from the Council would be the realization of a dream. Like the Brotherhood, we could take assignments, potentially hire more witches. Nine other women making the Network a better place had never felt so close.

"Of course," Leda sang, spinning an idea like a spider along gossamer strands, "you have to convince a majority of the Council that the Sisterhood is a necessity that can draw from tax currency. The other very real problem is the awkward position Scarlett is in."

"Scarlett?"

"She wants the Sisterhood, but the Sisterhood lays on your shoulders. It's out of her hands and in yours. That's not an easy thing."

Had she just insulted me? Most of the time, that question wasn't worth answering.

"We have to establish a pattern," she continued, speaking more to herself. I couldn't fathom how Hiddleston tolerated this all day. "Not a series of one-offs. The Protectors go through a lot of rigorous training to prove themselves as consistent action-takers."

"One-offs?" I cried. I held up five splayed fingers, and touched the first one. "Defeating Mabel?" The second finger. "Going to Alaysia?" The third. "Figuring out the secrets behind god magic? Defeating *gods*."

Gently, Leda said, "For one, *you* brought god magic into the Central Network." I ground my teeth, a hot retort building in the back of my mouth. "And while it was notable that you helped get rid of the gods, so did everyone else. Bianca, you're a candidate. Yes, they're *interested*. But they're not convinced."

Knowing she was right only made it harder to swallow the jagged pill. With a deep inhale, I nodded.

"I hear you."

Despite the building angst that speaking with Leda inevitably culminated in, I couldn't help but feel gratitude. Her political savvy was far outside my interests, which would have sabotaged the Sisterhood into nothing.

She chatted about *building a profile* and *earning trust* and *individual approach before a collective* while I devoured my meat pie and tried to stay rooted into the conversation. The second letter tugged at my thoughts, narrowing the space in my chest with each reminder.

Someone knew a lot about me.

"In the end," Leda concluded with a breath. "The Sisterhood needs time. We can do it, but not all at once."

"It is a *we*, right?"

Firmly, she said, "I will help the Sisterhood however I can, as long as it doesn't interfere with my work for Scarlett."

"Can you?"

"Right now? Very easily." Her cutting retort brooked no compassion. "It's not like the Sisterhood is doing anything, and until we have a firm plan for approaching the Council, we may not for a while."

I winced.

Ouch.

"Thanks," I muttered.

"Just remember, there's no room for error. Not yet. Be confident, powerful, and imperfect. No one will believe a perfect track record, either. They want to see what happens when you fail."

Exasperated, I cried, "You just told me there's no room for error, and in the same breath, told me to be imperfect."

"Imperfect, yes. An idiot? No. Above all, you can't quit. You can't fail so disastrously that you give up. We need them to see you fail at something, pull it together, and then come out on top."

"Your expectations are impossible!"

"Stop being a martyr. It's all about timing. The success of the Sisterhood is tied directly into the Council's perception of Bianca Monroe. That's all I'm trying to say."

"No pressure."

Leda stopped, faint brows elevated. "There's a prodigious amount of pressure. We're facing a failure to get off the ground with the Sisterhood, which is the worst failure of all. If we don't get it just right, the Sisterhood will crash before it's gained altitude."

Chapter Nine

A manulele bird with a plum belly and orange plumage sat on my shoulder, head cocked, beak tilted to the sky. With a chirp from its throat, it zipped away, zooming into the bracken. Two other manulele, affecting the same pose, darted after it.

Ten more followed.

Then twenty.

All signs led to Ava approaching.

Less than a minute later, a rising vine brought Ava onto my stoop with a grin. She stepped off of the foot loop at the bottom of the vine, released her hold, and threw herself into my arms. The manulele birds swarmed us with fluttering, giddy chirrups and whistling wings.

Laughing, I caught her in my arms and squeezed tight. She pulled away as quickly, throwing herself onto a chair near the table.

"I'm so hungry!" she cried.

Food awaited, as it always did, when Ava made an appearance. "I figured. Eat away!"

She'd already made herself busy scooping preserves onto two slices of brown bread. I grabbed an apple from the top of the pile and crunched into it while Ava dished up a few spoonfuls of stewed greens, mixed with roasted leto nuts, and chunks of goat cheese.

"I only have a few minutes," she said through a hasty bite. Sweat glistened along her forehead and within her poofy black hair, which she hadn't braided in several weeks. As a mortal, she couldn't wield magic, but Letum Wood brought her to my house whenever she ran toward it. The forest had proven itself capable of transporting witches before, but was very selective. Sometimes I wasn't sure if it was the forest who transported her, or Deasylva.

Was there a difference?

Yes, but oh-so-subtle.

I had an inkling that Ava had Deasylva's interest, but it was only a hunch confirmed by the way the forest seemed to help Ava more than it helped most witches.

Lowering into the chair across from her, I asked, "How's it feel to be out of school?"

She rolled her umber eyes. "Fine. Miss Priscilla isn't as strict in the summer, but she still makes me practice reading everyday. It's good," she said smoothly, a carryover from Alaysia she used often. Her eyes flashed with wicked delight. "I found pirate books."

"Wonderful. Baxter is pleased with your progress."

This seemed to truly hearten her. Baxter, her uncle, was her only surviving relative. "I've worked hard."

"It shows."

Ava studied me, swallowed a large bite of greens, and said, "The Eastern Network lady visited again."

My interest piqued. "Niko's mother, Camila?"

"Yes."

"Why?"

Her young brow rose with a touch of too much innocence. Ava pressed a hand to her chest. "How would *I* know?"

"Because you eavesdropped."

She gasped.

This time, I rolled my eyes. "Give up the act. You'll never convince me you don't know something. You wouldn't have brought it up otherwise."

Conceding the point, she said, "I heard a little, but not much."

"What did you hear?"

A slow grin claimed her face. "Depends on what you offer."

My eyes widened. Ava returned to her food, but her sly smile remained. Oooh, cheeky mortal. I leaned closer.

"I won't tell Priscilla about the midnight runs you conduct at every full moon, or your request that I secretly take you to the ocean before you start your next term."

She couldn't talk fast enough.

"The lady was asking Priscilla about security and safety, and if Priscilla had seen any East Guards around the school lately."

My instincts tingled at the questions. The Eastern Network didn't have an official High Priestess. Cristian hadn't married, which put the unofficial title to his mother, a woman named Camila. Like most Eastern Network women, her role was mostly ornamental. She attended balls and cultural events at Cristian's side, provided support for the running of Magnolia Castle, and managed Cristian's life outside of politics, such as letters and schedules.

She was also known for a hint of subterfuge.

Camila frequently visited Priscilla and Tomasso. She sent toys, food, resources, with all the generosity of a truly doting grand-mere. Priscilla graciously accepted it all and used it to prepare Tomasso for his life ahead, but she did so with a hint of wariness. Everything Camila did might have roots in expectations later. Camila, if she was wise, expected Tomasso to be the savior of the Aldana Dynasty.

Tomasso, the true heir to the Eastern Network, would one day have to choose his ancestry in order to recover the Aldana name—unless Cristian destroyed all hope before then. If Camila had reservations about Tomasso's safety strong enough to discuss them with Priscilla, there must be reason for concern. Coupled with Baxter's *early warning*, I sensed something foul brewing.

With great energy, I reapplied my attention to Ava, who had already cleaned half of her plate. She watched me, waiting for me with a curiosity almost as powerful as her appetite. I cleared my throat.

"What did Priscilla say to Camila's questions?"

Ava shrugged. "I couldn't hear her. She was on the other side of the room, and Camila was closer to the door."

Sometimes, I felt deep gratitude that Ava couldn't wield magic. Who knew what would happen to the world in such an event? Other times, it seemed like the biggest wasted opportunity. Ava would be a ferocious wielder of goddess magic.

"But," Ava popped one finger in the air as she reached for a third slice of bread, "Camila had fewer questions after that, and she didn't sound stressed."

"Priscilla doesn't have Guards."

"She has Jorge."

I tilted an eyebrow.

Ava chortled. Her mention of Jorge didn't surprise me. Ava spent more time outside than in, which likely meant they saw each other often.

"A groundskeeper is hardly the same as a Guardian."

"He's strong."

Ava tore a piece of bread in half with one hand while she reached for a ball of butter with her other. She grabbed it with her fingers and used her thumb to smear it. Another carryover habit from her time in Alaysia, raised by mortals, who had different ideas around propriety than stuffy witches. Leda and Priscilla would have been outraged, but I didn't care.

"Strong," I countered, "is not the same as capable."

The rising of her ebony brows, and resulting wrinkles, told me she disagreed. She'd stuffed her mouth too full of food to state it, however. Taking advantage of her forced silence, I continued.

"Do you think Priscilla knows why Camila is concerned?"

She shrugged. "Priscilla hasn't seemed any different lately."

"That's . . . good."

Another shrug. Ava dragged her bread across the plate to sop up the juice from the salted greens.

"How is the school without other girls in it?" I asked.

"Boring."

"That's a sign that you made friends?"

"Yes. There are a few girls I like," she said after swallowing. "Baxter promised me a month in the Eastern Network if I have good behavior for three more weeks."

"Really?"

She nodded, all eagerness. "A month of sailing lessons too. Not that I need them." She scoffed, as if it would be an insult to suggest as much. "But it will reassure him if I have official learning."

With a smile, I said, "Congratulations."

A vine wound into the house, slipping across the room with lightning speed. It hooked the bottom of Ava's chair and wound around her ankle, tugging lightly. The jolt brought Ava's eyes to the clock. She cheeped a sound and jumped to her feet.

"Gotta go!"

The vine wrapped her calf.

"I'm going to be late for a book review."

Laughing, I stood and clamped her in a quick hug. "Good luck and thank you for telling me. Let Priscilla know I'll visit soon."

With a wave, Ava ran out of my house, jumped off my porch, and screamed through a free fall. Two seconds into it, the blood-curdling sound ended, and the vine disappeared with it. Transported again by the forest.

I stared at the spot where the magic whisked her away, then pressed my palm to the tree. Sapphire light swirled beneath my fingers as I asked, "What *is* your fascination with Ava?"

A gentle voice replied, startling me. *She has a mighty future.*

While Deasylva sometimes answered my often-metaphorical queries, it meant something that she chose to respond now.

"You certainly have a type of witch—or mortal, in this case—that you like, don't you?"

You are lucky I do.

Candles bobbed in between Merrick and I that evening, casting a strange glow on the silverware, the plates. The bustle of The Pig's Snout swirled in the background, distant, but not far. Despite my usual preference for a still forest, I was thrilled about the break in monotony that eating at a high-scale pub allowed.

Merrick sat across from me, washing in and out of attentiveness. Remnants of the biscuits he had greatly missed lay on his half-empty plate. His lashes drifted low, then bobbed high as he jerked awake. Smiling to myself, I wound my foot in between his ankles and rubbed my bare arch along his calf.

He woke up with another start, smiling groggily. I leaned over the table, a thin affair cluttered with a shared steak and still more of his favorite biscuits. Their golden, flaky crusts peeled apart. Sprinkles of cheese melted on top in sharp orange lines.

"Tired?" I asked with amusement.

Merrick chortled and rubbed a hand over his face. "I'm sorry, B. I'm exhausted. The meetings with Rognvald to close out the mission have been more draining than I expected. So much talking, answering, debating."

Disappointment was an icy flush through my veins, but I hid it behind a smile.

"You only just returned a few days ago, and you haven't really been home all that much. Late nights, and whatnot. I suppose being tired is normal."

He struggled to contain a yawn. "Rognvald and I have had to break things down, meet over the results." Unable to fight it any longer, he let the yawn split his lips wide. I struggled not to echo him. "We still have more meetings."

I grimaced.

"That sounds awful."

That side of Brotherhood work sounded utterly horrible. I had a hard time picturing myself in the same position, though Leda would happily force me to sit through meetings and analysis. Except, she wouldn't require this much of me. She'd be too tired of me by the end of a single day.

I hoped.

Merrick recovered from the yawn, straightened in his chair, and put forth another miserable smile. He picked up his fork to stab at the steak. My hand curled around the two letters in my lap. I'd hoped to ask him about them tonight. Merrick would have wonderful insight . . . if I could get him to wake up. A formal stiffness rang through his words when he asked, "How are you?"

"Good."

"Did you have a good day?"

"Fairly normal."

"Anything big happen?"

"After meeting with Scarlett this morning, I ate with Leda. Ava came over for her lunch. I had a swordwork session with Tysen. He's quite good. I like it. He challenges me."

Merrick nodded.

The plaintive notes of the conversation faded as I sawed off another bite of juicy red steak, and he chewed through a biscuit. Carrots dissolved to silk on my tongue. I couldn't help harkening back to the past six months, when I dreamed of Merrick returning from his prolonged absence. An awkward dinner, with little to say, had no place in my ruminations.

Of course, I welcomed any time with him, exhausted meals included. But it seemed easier in my daydreams to know what to say. More appropriately, where to start. We had a lot to catch up on, and six months was such a long time to bridge.

I swallowed the mouthful I managed to chew.

"Can you . . . that is . . ."

My tentative questions died before they gained true ground. I forced myself to loosen my hold on the scrolls. To his credit, Merrick stayed awake long enough to spare me a chance to finish the query. Maybe now wasn't the best time to get his opinions on the scrolls and who might have sent them.

"You mentioned being busy with Leda and Scarlett for Sisterhood plans in a recent notebook entry." His voice brightened momentarily. "Want to talk about that?"

"Sure."

I cast about to find an entry point, but struggled to know where to start. The letters aside, which would take too long to explain tonight, what else could I say? The Sisterhood had stalled.

"We have a date," I said brightly. "Six months from now."

"For?"

"Oh, to approach the Council and request funding."

"That seems important."

"Yes. Quite."

"Anything else?"

"Leda has this whole plan for it."

"Oh?"

"I can't quite remember the details."

He tried to hide a yawn, and failed. Chewing on my bottom lip, I speared a crumpled piece of biscuit. This topic seemed like a natural bridge to the letters, but when *had* the first letter arrived? Shortly before he came home, which made it . . . a week ago? I stalled, attempting to sort through where to begin telling him the whole tale when he cleared his throat.

Blinking, I looked up.

"You mentioned some tension with Derek?" he ventured.

"Oh, right. Sorry. I got lost in thought. Ah . . . it's not so much tension as . . . he doesn't seem well."

"Ill?"

"No. It's more . . . in his head."

He paused, waiting. In order to explain the tension with Papa and my request for advice on living with a Protector, I really needed to backtrack several weeks, but I wasn't sure where to start there, either.

I set my fork down, reached for a glass of water. Jikes, it shouldn't be *this* difficult. When Merrick was gone, I chattered endlessly with Goat and Other Goat, telling them all the things I couldn't say to Merrick because he wasn't here.

He'd arrived, and I couldn't conjure a word.

With a hesitant smile, I said, "I'm sorry. Really. I do want to tell you. It's just that I don't know where to start. It's easy to think about when it's all fresh in my mind, but it's harder to look back and categorize."

Seeming surprised, he said nothing, only brought another forkful to his mouth and waited. In the admittance, most of my motivation to talk about Scarlett and the Sisterhood waned. It wasn't really that exciting anymore.

Just perplexing.

"Anything new with Goat and Other Goat?" he ventured with a hint of desperation. Half of his dinner already sat in his stomach. Based on his twitchy hands, I could tell he held himself back from wolfing the whole thing down.

Didn't they eat while they had meetings?

Deciding to forego talk of Goat and Other Goat and ignore all the set up behind Scarlett's letters, I blurted out, "There's actually something else. Scarlett received a letter a week or so ago."

"I imagine she receives many letters."

"Yes, but this one was . . . odd."

"How so?"

"It told a story."

"Someone wrote her a story?"

"I guess? It's about her sister who died. It talks about her having wings and . . . it could be a vague, veiled threat. It's more symbolic than literal."

Fork poised halfway to his mouth, he paused. I hid a grimace. Surely *wings* flummoxed him, not to mention my horrendous accounting. There was so much more to it than what I said.

"And?"

"I have the original here." I lifted the scroll onto the table with a hopeful lift of my eyebrows. "If you want to see?"

He ate another forkful and eyed it, as if attempting to ascertain whether he had the energy. I swiped it back to my lap, immediately regretting it.

"How about later?"

With a relieved nod, he agreed.

A fretful silence stretched between us while I attempted to conjure a question that didn't involve his mission, which he couldn't talk about, and he seemed to do the same. My life must appear like a string of boring, routine work.

The fact that he had wanted to *talk* hung over us. Whatever subject he desired to broach hadn't yet arrived. I couldn't help wondering why he put it off. Sheer energy, probably. Though I couldn't imagine this horrid small talk was much less miserable than just getting it all over with.

"How's Marten?" he asked.

"Good."

"Regina?"

I nodded. "She seems fine."

His fork clinked against the plate. He ate faster. The fatigue in his eyes had grown. Deciding that withholding was the better part of pleasure, I reached across the table and put my hand on his wrist.

"Merrick?"

He slowed.

"Go to bed."

A questioning look crossed his face. I gestured to his plate with a tip of my head. "Eat the rest, then go home and go to sleep. I'll pay, finish up some more things with these letters, and then I'll see you in the morning. Sleep in?"

He hesitated. "I did want to talk. We haven't mentioned what I wanted to discuss."

"You're not going anywhere, right?"

"No. I have to close the mission out." He spoke firmly, as if he'd already discussed it with Rognvald. "We can't be tasked out again. Yet."

We.

A clue that another Protector, or several, had been with him.

"Then go. There's no reason to endure this when you're so tired. We can talk about what's on your mind and read Scarlett's letters together later. In the meantime I'll . . . make a list of topics to catch you up on. It's just . . . it's hard to think of them at the moment."

Relieved, he hurried through three more bites, pressed a kiss to my cheek, and transported away. Hand on my water glass, I stared at his disheveled plate, my half-full one, and slumped in my chair.

Romance was never what I expected.

Chapter Ten

The next morning, I studied a spell from Grandfather's book, *Invisibility Magic and Its Sources,* cast it, and waited to see how it felt.

It worked.

Featherlight and simple.

Magic purred in the background with little expenditure. When I shifted, the air rippled a little, but one had to be looking at the exact spot, near the edges, to notice. Similar to our usual invisibility magic, but different.

Only one more test to conduct.

Gathering my brain together, I kept the magic active and cast a transportation spell. A long enough distance to test whether it held up as part of a layered magic, but not far enough to be dangerous.

Plush carpet cradled my feet when I landed just outside Scarlett's office, behind Leda's desk. Which, thankfully, was uninhabited. The invisibility spell remained firmly in place.

Time for the second test to commence.

Would anyone notice me?

Unmoving, I eyed two Guardians that stood across the way, near the stairs. A full minute passed, and they did nothing more than yawn. Neither glanced toward me. Hiddleston didn't notice, either. He remained across from Leda's unoccupied chair, head on his desk. Envelopes fluttered around his locks. He ignored them with the same long-suffering that Leda managed.

Frowning, I kept the spell in place. Was it a good thing that no one noticed? Yes, but no. If this book had gone to anyone else, they could have done the same without detection, which might explain the delivery of the first letter.

"Hiddleston?"

His head lifted, eyes canvassing the area.

"It's Bianca. I'm over here, behind Leda's desk, and invisible. I'm testing a new spell. Is Leda with Scarlett?"

He returned to his work. "Yes."

"Any sign of another letter?"

He shook his head.

Time for test number three. Longevity. How long would the spell last without re-issuing? How much energy would it take? The book contained these details, but a wise witch always confirmed. Besides, I had a reason to stake out Scarlett's office. Another letter might arrive at any moment, and I'd be ready for it.

Might as well test out the new magic in the meantime. "Mind if I stay?" I asked.

Yawning, he waved a permissive hand.

I settled in.

No letter appeared that day.

Nor the next.

But I did manage to proof two different invisibility spells, as well as a listening incantation.

Morning dawned with a cooler edge on the fourth day after the second letter. I braced myself for another doldrums in the castle. Four days existed between the first and the second, and I anticipated four between the second and the third. There would be another, I felt certain.

Though Chatham Castle never truly slept, it dozed. At five in the morning, the entire castle had a lullaby purr, waiting for the day to start.

I hid behind Leda's desk, vetting a third invisibility spell from Grandfather's book, in which a cloak doused with magic made itself and anything beneath it invisible. It worked better than I expected, but I didn't enjoy the restrictive nature. The cloak made noise, swayed when I moved, and it trapped heat. Still, I'd test its edge of usefulness and make notes within the grimoire, despite Leda's insistence that writing in a book was akin to abuse and should be handled accordingly.

Fire boys and maids bustled down the hallways in sleepy waves. As the sun rose, they gave way to Assistants. Hiddleston first, then Leda. If they noticed me, they gave no sign.

Council Members flowed up the stairs and spread wide, followed by gaggles of other witches and many coffee mugs. Around the time Leda arrived, I slipped into the office. Scarlett entered through a hidden passageway hours after I stationed myself near Leda, and later than usual. Her voice filled the office with a low cadence.

Grandfather followed her through the same secret passageways. He strolled out of her office half an hour later and into his own. Not a single suspicious face walked by. No one in ostentatious purple, anyway.

My stomach growled as the clock ticked forward. My senses washed into a loose state as I opened my focus to sensation instead of sight. I stared at a fixed point dead ahead.

Magic filtered into my awareness in opaque layers. Powerful spells drenched Scarlett's office. One such spell prevented transportation inside. Such ancient magic, so old and mighty that it didn't even hum, had integrated into the stones themselves. They used magic differently back then. Higher cost, more intricate to weave and use, but it had a payout that lasted centuries. We rarely used such spells these days. Everything was quick, easy, short-lived.

Enchantments on Scarlett's desk, which teemed with magical life from the supplies, envelopes, and self-writing quills, immediately commanded my attention. I peeled my gaze away from the prodigious power source and placed it onto Leda's desk.

A hum drew my thoughts.

Not from Leda's desk, or the familiar envelope that appeared on top of it with a definitive handwriting, but on the magical thread that set the envelope there.

Faint.

Oh, so faint.

I slipped away from the wall, tugging on the magical pulse. Mentally grasping it, I followed my senses to the right, still hidden under the cloak. The fragile and tenuous thread of magic threatened to unravel, but I held it loose, coaxing it to life with silent murmurs. Gossamer in my fingers. The merest flinch, and I'd lose it.

A flash of brilliant purple splashed outside the office, drawing my eye.

The spell broke.

I lost the thread of magic, but not the witch that disappeared down a side stairwell. Without hesitation, I transported to a landing below.

Feet raced.

They raced *up*.

A flash of violet cloak appeared over the stairwells as I transported again, lost to the magic for less than a breath before arriving on a landing above. By the time I hit my feet, the distinctive purple cloak also vanished into a transportation spell.

I grabbed it, but with slippery magic. If the witch transported a long distance, I wouldn't make it. The spell came and went, depositing me in the heart of Chatham City.

Spinning in a circle, I stood half crouched and fully visible. The part of my mind that sought magic closed, returning my attention solely to visuals. At some point in transporting, I'd lost the cloak during the spell. Not unheard of.

Violet fluttered on the edge of my sight.

I whirled.

A male witch with broad shoulders dodged through the milling crowd, swift and sure footed. He wore a violet cloak that matched Hiddleston's descriptions. He didn't run, but his long stride didn't require it to pace away. He swung a cane at his side, whacking shins so witches moved out of his way. Commotion followed him with curses and raised fists. Not a subtle step in his escape.

I dodged toward him, then skidded to a stop.

A second male wearing the same cloak strode off a different way, at the same fast clip, down a less busy street. He looked exactly the same from behind, except *he* wore a garishly orange top hat. As I started for him, a third appeared, just to the side, with an obnoxiously large flower. Three options sprawled out.

Violently purple cloak.

Orange top hat.

Garish flower.

Which one was I supposed to follow?

Something obliquely familiar rang through this final one. He strolled down a quieter street. When I strained to hear, I swore I noted a casual whistle. Paralyzed, I hesitated as memory hit me.

I had seen this witch before.

At the Potionmaker's shop, while helping Rognvald. The outlandish witch stood in the crowd, regarding me with curiosity, as I attempted to calm the flailing child abductor. My legs began to shake as the realization slammed into me.

This witch, whoever they were, had been following me before Scarlett received any letters. This wasn't just a story.

This *was* a threat.

Shoved back into the moment by the sound of a braying donkey, I dragged my gaze around. The three males continued to stride away, in three opposite directions, with little impeding their path. When the third disappeared into a shop with an open door, I acted. Breathless, I raced into the little shop, slamming against the door.

"Stop!" I cried.

I needn't have bothered. No one stood in there. The shop-keeper, a wizened old woman with soft gray curls and wide eyes, asked, "What, dear?"

My hesitation cost the lead. Exasperated, I spun around and hurried back into the crowd. Minutes later, I'd all but confirmed that all three had disappeared from this area of Chatham City. The crowd surged relentlessly, as if the three apparitions of the same man had never been there. For good measure, I forced myself to walk the streets. After almost an hour, I found no sign.

A deception spell explained all of it, including the latter two males split into clean roads, and the first ventured through a crowd. The deception spells would have popped as soon as anything else touched them, revealing the truth, which is precisely why I saw no one in the shop.

Like a fool, I'd followed the wrong one.

Whoever we faced, they had definite skill at magic, and a penchant for playing games. Cursing, I transported back to Chatham Castle.

Something happens within the body when wings are lost. The clipping stretches into the tired soul, the wounded soul.

The deepest soul.

The orphans slept, blissfully unaware that after a grasp of strong fingers, a flick of wrist, Ellie Victoriann's life stood still. They took her wings.

She wept.

Oh, how she wept.

Loss changed everything about Ellie Victoriann. The way her skin reacted to the wind. The way her words sounded from her throat. The way her eyes comprehended all that lay before them.

She now understood the four elements of despair: unfettered restlessness, spiraling tragedy, insipid loneliness, and the pains of death.

Amidst these travails, Ellie Victoriann refused to relinquish hope. Hope, such an expensive commodity, yet never far from daydreams. It burns bright in the darkest of places. A seaside beacon. A thudding heart, never stopping.

She escaped and grew new wings and she flew. For months, years, forever. She broke the invisible shackles and soared on wind currents, only to crash right in front of Marie Hazel.

Fate, you see.

She's fickle. If one were to meet fate, you'd see her as a truth-

sayer, mindreader, futureseer, and pastkeeper. Fate holds a mirror, and the mirror sees all.

Marie Hazel vowed to protect Ellie Victoriann, her friend with wings. Her friend and destiny.

Her friend in fate.

They leaped into the sky, bound up clouds, cavorted through currents. Into thin air and stars the duo soared beyond cloud and wisp, to shimmering black sea and magenta night. They advanced so far, they could not turn back.

"Higher," Ellie Victoriann demanded. "We must press higher."

Selfishly, she gobbled the air. The stars became her pedestal.

Marie Hazel could not keep up. She was no true Protector.

Marie Hazel was going to die.

Scarlett's pale face stared at me as I set the third letter aside, lost in thought. A swirl of words played through my mind again and again.

No true Protector.

Going to die.

"This . . . witch," Scarlett whispered, shaking her head. "They know how Ellie died. How I didn't die, but I did . . ." A hand pressed to her heart. "In here."

"Well—"

"No." She cut me off with a slice of her hand. "They even know *how* she died. The line that says, *the orphans slept, blissfully unaware that after a grasp of strong fingers, a flick of wrist, Ellie Victoriann's life stood still.* When my sister died, the Apothecary had a medicine, administered by needle, that I thought at the time would save her. He grabbed me with one hand, pushed the needle in with the other."

Slowly, I whispered, "Grasp of strong fingers, a flick of wrist."

"Yes." She slapped a finger onto the letter, her voice hoarse. "Everything that follows still matches exactly what happened. *Loss changed everything about Ellie Victoriann. The way her skin reacted to the wind. The way her words sounded from her throat. The way her eyes comprehended all that lay before them.* All of that is true."

Silently, I related. When Mama died, the world completely shifted, like an earthquake shoving me to the side. "That's a natural response to grief."

Scarlett frowned, brow drawn together. "Yes, but I've used those words before."

"Who have you told about Ellie?"

Flustered, she said, "I . . . I don't know. Many witches, most likely. There have been speeches that I've given to help drum up currency for orphanage support, or discussions with friends. Anyone from the orphanage might know these details."

"Are you in contact with anyone from your orphanage?"

"No."

"The Apothecary who administered the medicine?"

"He must be dead by now."

Another perusal of the letter bound up my thoughts. So many parallels drawn, so many intimate details. Scarlett confirmed my hunch that this witch wasn't just playing a game. He had been watching for who-knew-how long.

"This witch is insinuating that I am going to cause your

death," she said, breaking the ice I had been ignoring. Her tone became suspiciously even.

I rolled my eyes, letting the scroll wind together in my palm. "I fail to be frightened."

"They might be setting up a situation to do just that."

"They might."

"Bianca, I will not . . ."

"Let's figure out their motivation and their name before we start assigning possibilities. Scarlett, for all we know, this will turn into something like advocacy for the orphanages."

She shared her own irritation through a glare. My stretch was a long one, but it conveyed my message more readily when drastic.

Scarlett's barren, bold whisper should have frightened me when she asked, "What do you suggest we do?"

I met her eyes. We'd slipped from *innocuous letter* to *suspicious story* and firmly into the lap of *obvious threat*.

Without fear, I stated, "We're going to find this witch. They've given us some clues, made it clear this is a personal and violent threat. Today, whoever it was wanted me to follow him. Trust me, Scarlett. The Sisterhood will track him down."

Chapter Eleven

I burst into the treehouse, words on the tip of my tongue, but stopped in the doorway. A glimmering rectangle, propped against Merrick's pillow, drew my eye.

The golden notebook.

"No," I whispered.

Frantic, I crossed the room and sped through the pages, all the way to the back. In it, Merrick had hastily scrawled a note.

B,

Rognvald assigned me to another mission. An extension of the mission from which I returned.

We thought it closed out, but it reopened. I'm sorry. I'm not sure the timeframe, but it's meant to be short.

I could almost hear the hesitation in his voice as I ran the pad of my thumb over the final words.

I'm sorry.

I tucked the notebook under my arm and stood on shaky legs. The rush of surprise gathered into a heavy, leaden ball. It sat on my chest, claiming me.

Jikes, but it happened so fast.

A snap.

Gone.

The idea that none of this should be surprising occurred to me. Papa did it all the time. Many were the times that Mama and I woke up to find his side of the bed empty. With most circumstances, he left an explanation or a farewell. Other times, he just left.

I stood at the window, peering out. Six days. He'd been home a mere six days before the Protectors reclaimed him. A silent question ballooned through my heart as I watched Goat try to play with Other Goat, who ignored her.

"Mama," I whispered, shoring up the anxiety and frustration that Merrick's unpredictable departure incurred. "How did you do it? It was supposed to be easier than this. I thought . . ."

The thought didn't finish, because I wasn't sure *what* I thought. That growing up with a father who left unexpectedly on dangerous missions would be similar to a lover who also left without warning?

Yes.

Like a fool, I fell into that trap. Papa's entrances and exits had been all I ever knew, and while there was a sense of normalcy in these strange movements, it didn't erase the misery. Merrick's departures dove deeper, and differently. They probed the edge of a wound that I hadn't known existed until this moment.

One that reeked of abandonment.

A quiet voice whispered amidst my thoughts, wondering if Leda was right. Was I re-creating my mother's legacy because it was familiar? I turned that thought away as quickly as it came and doubled down on my resolve to solve the Scarlett situation. I bit back tears and forced myself outside.

There were some things I controlled.

And some I didn't.

I knew which belonged where.

Leda eyed me as I settled at our mutual table the next day, at the far end of the Dining Hall, with a scowl. The last place I wanted to be was Chatham Castle, but we needed to discuss the third letter.

I couldn't bear to see it.

Leda's gaze drifted from my wild hair to my surly frown. "He left already?" she asked, but it was low.

"How'd you know?"

Her long suffering stare ended on my dress, which sported a tear along the sleeve, thanks to an early-morning sword work session with Tysen. He took one look at me, asked nothing, and we proceeded to attempt tearing each other apart with different sword routines. The release helped.

"Oh," she sang, "no reason. Certainly not because Rognvald apprised Scarlett of it this morning. I'm sorry."

"Thanks."

The slices of turkey and sweet potato were of little interest to me, but I picked up my fork anyway. Butter melted along the sides of the potato, oozing to the edges. I sliced it open, cutting it into even petals.

Thankfully shucking off the pitying voice, she asked with her business-like stoicism, "Do you know why he's gone?"

My fork hit the plate a bit more savagely than I expected. "Return to the previous mission. That's all I know."

"Good of him to write."

Her sincerity took me by surprise. I studied her. She rolled her eyes, spoon plunged into a bowl of butternut squash soup.

"It *was* good of him to write," she snapped. "I wasn't being sarcastic so don't look at me like you want to bite my head off. There might be times he can't write and you have to accept the silence. Any explanation, no matter how small, must be better than assumption."

Her astute observation into other shades of my future, however correct, wasn't welcome. Then again, I was the fool complaining to Leda. The concept of lending comfort in a situation driven by choice didn't exist in her brilliant mind.

"Right," I muttered. "Thanks."

"Are you going to come to terms with him being a Protector?"

"Eventually."

She scoffed daintily, sipping the soup off her spoon as if it were an art form. I pushed some of the gravy from the turkey into the potatoes, forming a river.

"You won't at this rate, but lie to yourself if you want. It doesn't seem to be going all that well."

An internal war raged through me. I could hash this out with Leda, and most likely walk away more frustrated, but with hard won clarity. Or I could put it off and torture myself in the treehouse. Stewing alone hadn't gone well in the past. If I was honest with myself, I'd admit that I wanted Leda's take on it.

So I grumbled, "It's hard."

"What?"

"Having Merrick gone all the time."

"Sounds like you didn't expect a relationship with a Protector to be difficult?"

"It's not *that*," I quickly countered. "I just thought that, with Papa being a Protector, I'd be more prepared. It seems like an easy thing to go through because I've endured it before."

"As a daughter."

"Yes, but—"

"There's a difference." She cut me off with the compression of eyebrows that spoke to mild and growing irritation. "Your relationship with Merrick is based on romantic love, not parental affection. Your mother was able to compensate for much of what Derek couldn't provide. You have no compensation with Merrick."

"True."

"In some ways, certainly not all. But there's no one here to show you the way for you and Merrick, either. It forces everything to the front in a particularly brutal way that most of us, in normal relationship situations, can reconcile."

Jikes.

She was right.

Unprepared for the insightful comment, I simply stared at the pile of potatoes that sat under my nervous fork.

I felt Leda roll her eyes. "Which means," she drawled, "you're going to continue to be angry and resentful until you realign the expectations for your relationship." She added a bit tetchily, "Not to mention the rise of the Sisterhood and all *that* will mean for you and Merrick. What happens when you're both on missions? Or if they overlap?"

A ball rose in my throat. Magma-hot. Roiling, singeing, like the god magic ripped from my body in Alaysia.

"The two of you will be a pair of fools in love," she concluded with a huff. The bite in her tone didn't suggest any sense of warmth or approval.

After a long pause, filled with the gentle sip of soup and the quiet chatter of conversation in the Dining Hall, I asked, "How?"

"How what?"

"Do I rearrange my expectations? For my relationship with Merrick, I mean. I don't think we can keep going on this way. Correction," I added gently. "I'm not sure *I* can keep going this way. We were supposed to talk but he was tired. Now, he's gone."

She stared at me with a blank expression, then cried, "How would I know? I've never been in love with a Protector," and returned to her soup.

I gripped my fork until the edges bit into the sides of my

fingers. With her astute powers of observation but inability to provide an answer, she'd make an excellent Council Member.

"Besides," she added, as if I'd asked another question, "you have to figure that out. You and Merrick decide what it would look like. Instead of having one Protector in the relationship, you will have two. That alters it entirely."

The weight pressed on my chest.

Yes, *entirely*.

No one else in Alkarra could model a relationship like ours. The closest approximation we might have was Regina, and she'd avoided relationships her whole life for this purpose. Mama, a close second, but she was gone. Papa knew Merrick's side. Grandfather had insight into sharing a partner with a too-big career, but he couldn't answer the question of how Merrick and I should navigate dual or overlapping missions.

We stepped into a tenuous, dark sky. Neither of us knew what we were doing, or how to talk about it, which left us floating around long absences, blissful reunions, or the awkwardness of the in-betweens.

"Now that's over with," Leda leaned closer, "we need to discuss the letter."

Grateful to set that aside, I set down my fork and nodded.

"Yes."

The third letter appeared between us. I glanced at it, but avoided comprehending the words.

"Set aside the obvious threat against you, and sort of against Scarlett, there's something familiar about the narrative. A rhythm and tone. Not quite rhyme, but close. It's not consistent or clear."

"Like a poem?" I suggested.

"Maybe? This feels like . . . something else."

Leda summoned copies of the other two letters, which she kept filed in the depths of her organized desk, and lay all three side by side. Her fingers tapped the first, the second, and the third.

"Same handwriting. Clearly, someone penned this themselves

or used the exact same quill and spell. Even the parchments match. But the letters themselves contain a different subject each time. Ellie, then Marie, then both. The cadence, feel, everything alters from letter to letter."

"All three arrived four days apart," I said.

"True."

"But at different times of day."

"Also true."

"So it's . . . chaotic."

"On the outside, it appears that way, but so does algebra if you don't know the rules."

Irritably, I asked, "What does it mean?"

She shrugged.

"No idea, except that we simply don't understand him, or his process, or his motivation yet."

I bit back my second wave of exasperation.

"Do you think we should involve Rognvald?" My fingers curled into a fist at my side, nursing the quiet fear that Scarlett might want to turn this over to the Brotherhood in protection of me.

Leda eyed me, brow raised high. "For your safety?"

"No! For Scarlett."

Her fixed stare rested firmly on me. "Bianca, forgive me, but I don't think Scarlett is the one in danger, and I think you'd have a hard time getting a Protector's assignment for the Head of the Sisterhood. Not unless there's a clear and obvious threat."

My mouth bobbed up and down as I attempted to reply, but no words issued. What to say? I could hardly go to Rognvald and ask for protective services, nor did I feel the need. But a target existed on my back, painted right where wings might sprout.

Of far greater concern was Scarlett's safety. The unknown sender might be intentionally drawing attention to me so that I grew slack in my care of Scarlett. I wouldn't run the risk.

"Does Scarlett have any travel plans over the next couple of weeks?" I asked.

"No."

"Meetings outside the castle?"

Leda's nose scrunched as she thought, then nodded. "Two. Both in Ashleigh."

"Rearrange them to occur here, please."

Without a moment's hesitation, she asked, "Anything else?"

"Have you made any progress on the Brotherhood communication magic?"

Her eyes widened with a moment's delight. Her lips curled in a coy, reserved smile as she pushed her half-empty bowl away.

"Not yet."

"Can you prioritize it higher? I'll need to know right away what's happening with Scarlett, and you're with her more than anyone."

A pinched nod.

"Thank you. I found records on the orphanage Scarlett grew up in, and I'm tracking any of those witches that are still alive for the next couple of days."

"Wise."

Sensing the end of the discussion, she cleared the copied letters. As I shoved away my lunch, hardly touched, she stopped me with a short gasp.

"Oh! I forgot to mention."

"What?"

"I've met with some of the Council Member Assistants to feel out what the Council Member schedules look like for the next several months."

"Why?"

Her eyes nearly rolled back in her head. "The Sisterhood! We need Council approval so we have access to funding currency."

"Right. And?"

Leda closed her eyes, jaw clenched so tight that she had to take a swelling breath in, hold it, exhale it, and then look at me.

"We need their approval before the vote."

"So?"

"So you'll need to visit with each Council Member individually and discuss the Sisterhood, the merits, and why the Central Network can't be without a Sisterhood in the future. A face-to-face basis will be the only way to convince them before the vote."

Her disdain made it clear that *this* should have been obvious.

"Georgette is our greatest concern, if you ask me," she added as a wry aside, standing. I followed her to the end of the table, where we peeled toward the hallway together. The thought of meeting each Council Member made my stomach hurt.

A scroll appeared in her hand, summoned from elsewhere. It contained a list with organized, tidy writing on the lines. She could write a book titled, *Perfect Penmanship, Speedy Quill*. Her gifts were lost in a place like Chatham Castle.

"These are some notes I've gleaned on the individual Council Members, though I haven't made any appointments yet. You can keep this scroll. I'll firm up plans next week, so we don't seem too eager."

She sent the list my way. To satisfy her, I skimmed the names, suggested meeting times, and tentative dates. My eyes nearly crossed. Eagerness. Motivations. Meetings. Leda lived and breathed these odd details, and thank the goddess for that.

Unfortunately, I was the one to see them through.

"Your heathen schedule is so unbound that I'm assuming we won't have any restrictions on your side," she said as we headed toward the main stairs. "However, I am going to wait until this whole letter debacle is figured out before we schedule the meetings."

"Why?"

"So we can add this to the list of Sisterhood accomplishments!

Can you imagine speaking with Georgette about the Sisterhood right now?"

Her pale, wide-eyed expression revealed intense dislike, as if I dared to suggest it. As we climbed the stairs, alone except for Guardians stationed at intermittent spots, I asked, "Can you tell me why you care this much about the Sisterhood, Leda? We both understand my reasons."

I thought she'd flutter those pale lashes and conjure a contrived response worthy of a future politician, but that faded as quickly as it arose. For all her indomitable spirit, Leda was underestimated as a chameleon. She knew herself well, but allowed different colors to display depending on who she spoke to and how they could serve her purposes.

She made no such mistake with me.

"The Sisterhood could be one of the greatest assets the Central Network might ever see. To be part of that would be noteworthy."

"Is that all?"

Leda's sidelong glance burned. "Someone," she said hotly, "has to keep *you* alive. I have my own plans for the Sisterhood, thank you very much, and I'd rather not dig another grave."

"Does your plans for the Sisterhood involve helping you attain a long, illustrious, and powerful political career?"

She hummed, saying nothing.

Chapter Twelve

Papa's cat, whom I dubbed Cat, twirled around my ankles with a quiet, rumbling purr. Discarded pieces of mouse, and a streak of blood on her paw, told me that she was self-sufficient as well as adorable. I patted her on the head as I advanced into his quiet home.

"Papa?"

Enchantments kept his house safe from prying eyes and strangers, but the magic allowed me inside whenever I wanted. An empty interior awaited, rife with the calmness of a house that hadn't stirred in a day or two. I searched for old bread crumbs or dried coffee stains, but couldn't even find a dirty plate.

"He's been gone for a few days."

I spun to find Regina standing in the doorway, silhouetted by daylight. Her unbound auburn curls lay wild on her shoulders in perfect coils. The casual house dress of before had been replaced by her usual pants, shirt, and vest.

"Oh?"

She trilled her lips in a gentle raspberry. "I have no idea where he went. He sent me a message, saying he'd be back eventually. I get the feeling he didn't know where he was going either. Just . . ."

"Had to leave?"

A nod. Trouble brewed in Regina's eyes, burdened as a cast off sigh.

"He's . . . restless," I said.

"Very." She straightened. "But if you leave a message, or send him one, I have no doubt he'll reply."

"Have you sent him any letters?"

"No." Her brow furrowed together. "I didn't want to bother him. He's obviously seeking something that he hasn't found here." Her voice trailed into a slant that I couldn't quite read.

"Is it frustrating to you that Papa still hasn't quite figured things out?"

A sincere smile spanned her lips. "That's the secret, B. None of us have things figured out. Certainly not adults. And no. Not frustrating yet. Understandable. I'm here for the good and the bad."

Her words, spoken so certainly, settled a ruffled terror in my chest that wondered if she would leave. This was a different Papa. Not the same man that I'd known even a year ago. Did that matter to her?

Regina's arms dropped to her sides. "I came to check on the cat, but she seems perfectly capable of handling herself."

I smiled. "It's good to see you."

"Did you need something? Are you alright?"

"I'm fine," I said quickly. Too quickly. A flash of curiosity illuminated her eyes before ebbing. Whatever she thought to ask, the words didn't cross her lips. She smiled and left with a hush of wind.

I stared at the empty house, and I wondered.

Grandfather studied Scarlett's three letters with pursed lips and an expression as still as pond water. My fingers dug into my palms as I waited for him to tell me what he thought, particularly as he skimmed the third letter twice. He finished, stacked them in a pile, and stared.

I asked, "Well?"

His querulous gaze met mine. "Well," he repeated with a languid elongation as he pulled his spectacles off. "I don't like it at all. Does your father know about these letters?"

"No, but I tried to ask his opinion. He's not home. I sent him a message after visiting his place last night."

"Did he reply?"

"Not yet."

"Hmm."

Grandfather leaned back in his chair. He sat behind a busy desk, clotted with papers and quills and memos that he'd arranged into neat stacks, organized by which task had to be completed first. In the chaos, he created certainty. If that didn't describe Grandfather, I didn't know what else would.

"It's a clear threat leveled at you, my dear. I'd wager there will be one for Scarlett, too, in the next missive."

"Me, too." I waved a hand over them. "I hid in Scarlett's office yesterday behind an invisibility spell, just to keep an eye on her. No one showed up, and no letter either. I was only there for a few hours. I've been tracking down former orphans that lived with her, speeches she's given about her life in the orphanage. Trying to find anything that matches."

"Any luck?"

"No."

"That's a good focus for now." *For now* echoed in the room. "What does Leda think?"

"Leda?"

He simply waited for me to reply. "Uh . . . she thinks a lot of things." I explained her thoughts at lunch the previous day, emphasizing Leda's desire to dive deeper into the poetic structure of the stories. "She thinks it might have been taken from something else and adapted."

"Wise. I see why."

Swallowing hard, I admitted, "I stayed up late last night, thinking up more unconventional ways to approach this problem and find the witch."

Interest piqued his tone. "What have you come up with?"

"First, finding tailors in Chatham City that might recognize the hat or cloak. It's a long shot," I reasoned, grateful to air my plan with someone before I set it in front of Leda, who would rip it to shreds. "The witch may have transformed the hat and cloak to its current appearance, or made it themselves. I don't have any other features that I recall which might make the outfit so unique."

"Worth a try. Also figuring out why he wore it at all? Think over the motivation a witch might hold to dress in such a way."

"It's very . . . loud. Garish."

"Exactly. He must have a reason."

Shoulders lifting with an indrawn breath, I continued. "And I thought that I'd ask Talmund to place invisible Guardians in the halls outside of Scarlett's office, to look out for this witch again."

"Another grand idea. This would require you to work with the Guardians. Does that bother you?"

"No. Should it?"

"Not in the slightest."

Understanding what he didn't say, I asked, "But you're wondering if *they* will want to work with *me*?"

He shrugged, and the uncertainty gave me a little shock. If Grandfather doubted Talmund's response, I might have reason to doubt as well.

"Talmund and I have a positive history. He helped me when the gods set Letum Wood on fire, and again at the Battle for Letum Wood."

"Your reputation was greatly helped by those events, but this is a different circumstance."

His eyes twinkled just enough that I sensed his question might be merely metaphorical. Given to make me think instead of act first. *The hardest part of leading the Sisterhood*, he once said, *will be making decisions. You can't care what witches say, or what they think. You have to consider all angles, and then bear the responsibility of choice. That is no small matter.*

"I'll keep that in mind," I said evenly.

He smiled, grabbed the scrolls, and handed them to me. I tucked them into my pocket.

"One avenue you haven't mentioned is the Great Library of Burke."

Frowning, I asked, "Why there?"

"There's a witch named Caroline. She's not the Head Librarian anymore. She surrendered her place to Abena years ago, but she's still in the library, haunting around. I can't fathom how old she must be . . ."

"You think she can help?"

"I think," he repeated slowly, still forming a thought, "that Leda might be onto something. If there is a poem or story that someone adapted to create this, Caroline would be the one to find the original. It might provide clues or context."

Grandfather tapped a finger to his lips, lost in thought. Removing himself from it, he said, "I've never worked with Caroline myself, but Mildred worked with her and Isadora a few times. Apparently, Isadora knew her well. From what I understood back then, Caroline could be a difficult witch to pin down. If I were you, I'd have Leda give you an introduction."

"Do I need an introduction?"

"A hunch tells me it might be wise. Leda worked at the Great Library of Burke and will surely know of Caroline. Until the Sisterhood creates its own reputation, Leda's position as Scarlett's Assistant and former worker in the library will give you sway, though there's no guarantee Caroline will care. Or listen," he tacked on.

"She sounds delightful."

"I'm rather interested to hear if it works." At that, his stare sharpened, closing in on me. "As the High Priest, I command you to keep me updated. When new letters arrive, I want to see them. Head of the Sisterhood or not, I won't have my beloved granddaughter in blatant danger without understanding what plan is in place to keep you safe. Do you agree?"

"I agree, Grandfather."

He softened, and sadness entered the wrinkles around his eyes. "Now," he murmured softly, "About Merrick's return to duty."

"I don't want to talk about it. Not yet."

With an understanding nod, he dismissed it. Waving his hand to beckon me, he stood, angled toward his bookcase.

"Come, my dear. Let's see what other grimoire acquisitions I have that might be of use to the Sisterhood. I can't tell you how pleased I am that the other book should have been so worthy."

The hallowed halls of the Great Library of Burke thrived because of witches like Hiddleston and Leda, who thrilled to the whispering book pages and murmuring Librarians. Ancient words suppressed, sleeping, enchanted. I had never been one of those witches, preferring the wildness of Letum Wood, and the freedom of open air, to the close hallways and sniveling strangers.

I slipped down a hall and spelled my shoes home to tread more quietly. The unnerving, magical combination of an ancient and aware library gave me goosebumps, and I wanted to feel as if I could hide within its dark halls. My fingers kept a loose hold on a small piece of parchment, the ends curled together. This letter might grant me greater admittance into the annals of the Library of Burke.

Leda's directions from earlier breezed through my mind, memorable only because of their strangeness.

"Just go to the library and wander," she said. "Find an Underlibrarian and give them this note. If Caroline balks, you tell her *I* sent you. She knows that I'm not afraid of her anymore."

The *anymore* had me very curious. Leda's testy tone meant she'd had run-ins with Caroline before.

I had only to wander and wonder . . .

A door creaked open just ahead, spilling a young man with copious freckles and wide, green eyes. He couldn't have been much older than fifteen. A line of books stacked high in his arms, wobbling precariously at the top. I reached up, tilting the three highest books closer to his center of gravity to prevent the whole thing from falling.

He smiled, as wobbly as his load. "Thanks. Do you need some help?"

"You work here?"

"Yes."

"Any idea where I can find an Underlibrarian?"

His chin notched a little higher. "I am one."

"Can you help me find Caroline?"

Did I imagine his cheeks losing pallor? He blinked heavy lashes, thick as midnight, twice.

"Uh . . . Caroline?"

"Yes."

"I can't . . . we're not allowed to . . . that is . . ."

"You're not allowed to find Caroline?"

His bald, flat statement of, "No," held a hint of terror.

I lifted the note from Leda. "I was sent here on a very specific errand from the Assistant to the Highest Witch. That errand is to find and speak with Caroline."

Yet another reason I found it odd that Leda hadn't come with me. She loved an opportunity to subtly throw around her power. After toiling away for years to earn a coveted Underlibrarian title and morsel of acclaim here at the library, she now held more ability as Scarlett's right-hand than she knew what to do with.

The young man swallowed hard. When the top of the pile threatened to plummet to the other side, I stopped the toppling dominos. With a spell, I helped him lower all thirteen tomes to the floor. Breath heavy from the exertion of balancing, he reached for the note, read it, and paled further.

His eyes met mine, studied the paper, captured mine again. His face wrenched down into an uncertain frown.

"Really?"

"Really what?"

"You *really* want to see Caroline?"

"Uh . . ."

"I mean . . . I can take you, but . . . " He leaned closer. "But most witches do everything they can to avoid Caroline."

"Does Caroline know the most about books, literature, and stories?"

"Well, yes."

I elevated both hands. "Then I want to see her."

His pile of books rose with a spell as he returned the note to me. "Then come with me, if you dare. She'll be in her first day of the week office, and the good gods help you in there."

Chapter Thirteen

The young man cringed and recited prayers under his breath. His shoulders hunched as he oh-so-carefully rapped on a nondescript door, hidden in a hallway of other nondescript doors, and slid to the side.

A woman's voice barked through the thick wood.

"What?"

The bite in her tone wasn't as frightening as expected. Upon hearing her voice, the Underlibrarian squeaked and darted away. Within seconds, he'd exited around the corner without another sound, abandoning the tower of books in his wake.

The door flew open.

A woman loured at me, her pure white hair pulled into a knot at the base of her neck. Random flyaways wheeled off her temple. Her bright eyes flashed, her disapproving lips pinched, and she glared through a hostile pair of glasses that topped the tip of her nose.

"What?" she demanded a second time.

Her screech had more robustness than expected. Beneath her snapping-turtle glare, she was a bitty, rotund woman, not yet given over to the ravages of old age and time, though it stamped across her face.

Mute, I held up the curled parchment.

She said nothing.

We locked into a silent battle of wills that, I realized two seconds into it, I could never win. Whether curiosity propelled her to accept the parchment, or sheer dumb luck, Caroline snatched it from my hand.

Her body continued to block the doorway as she peeled the scroll apart, devoured it. Color rose on her cheeks, blooming in a bright red fire as she crumbled it into a fist, stepped back, and held out one rigid arm.

"You have five minutes."

I scuttled to obey the silent entry command. The moment I hustled through the doorframe, she shoved the door closed. The office space had nothing except a desk and littered necessities on top. Stone walls. Wooden floor. Not a window to allow in fresh air or sunlight.

Wall sconces kept the room bright, as well as a chandelier with candles enchanted to prevent wax dripping. Another lantern flickered on a desk full of neat stacks of paper. Three quills lay near an open inkwell and an untouched blotting paper.

Not even a book.

"What's your name?"

"Bianca."

Caroline breezed past, almost knocking my shoulder. She didn't sit down because there was no chair. The desk came all the way to her sternum, allowing her to comfortably rest her forearms on it without bending.

"Well?" She twirled a hand. "What do you want?"

I pulled the three letters from my pocket and set them on her desk. "Can you take a look at this story and tell me if you've read it before? Or some version of it."

Caroline glanced at each of the three, allowing no more than a minute. She shoved them back.

"I have."

"Really? From where?"

Caroline tsked. "Where?" she snapped, head tilted to the side. Her eyes cast on the floor, brow ruffled. "Where is it? No, no, not *that* line, the other . . .yes, it's original, I'm sure of it."

The sense that she wasn't talking to me kept me stock still. The gods, but Leda had put me into an office with a madwoman. No wonder the young man had knocked and sprinted away. Caroline's head twitched to the side. Her brow lowered.

"Are you . . . yes." A hand lifted to her lips, tapping a staccato. She stared at the empty stones on the far wall, appearing for all the world like she studied something valuable and intricate.

With a jolt, she turned to face me again.

"I've read something similar to it before, but I'm not sure where. I have an idea of where the original text might be."

"Can you take me?"

"I don't know, can I?"

With further disbelief, I stared at her. Her eyes narrowed to slashes. "Isadora told me about you, you know. Bianca Monroe. Daughter of the High Priest. Aligned to the forest. Very strange."

Her unexpected reply caught me by surprise on several fronts, arresting my immediate response, which gave Caroline another moment to unabashedly study me. My knees felt like liquid and my courage trembled and I wasn't *quite* certain how to respond. I'd likely only been in Caroline's presence for two minutes and already my skin prickled with the urge to leave.

"Isadora?" I managed.

Caroline acted as if she hadn't heard. Her lips moved to one side of her face as she set a hand atop the second letter. Her fingers traced the bold lines and hidden promises of the third.

"Yes, yes, I remember. Not *that* room you ungodly . . . fine!" The authoritative loathing in her tone pinned my shoulders back, preparing my instincts to flee in a moment. "Take her, if you're going to be so self-righteously important about it. Yes, I *knew* you'd think it was there, but I don't agree. I don't think it's poetry. No! I don't know what it is, but . . . Fine! Do it!"

A light popped between us, drifting toward the door. Caroline, looking up, snarled. "Well?" she thundered, motioning to the fading light. "Aren't you going to follow it? Will-o-wisps don't just serve anybody, you know!"

Thankfully, Caroline did not follow.

The will-o-wisp led me to a circular room packed with books at the edges. It smelled like stale dirt and musty water, though no sign of wet stones lurked anywhere. A skylight three stories overhead spilled muted sunshine that didn't quite make it to the floor. Ladders side stepped their way up the room, ending on ledges with railings that allowed easy perusal.

"Here?" I whispered.

The will-o-wisp continued to ascend, floating higher and toward a specific section of the wall. I stepped on the closest ladder and chased after it, relieved when it landed on a single book. Once I carefully pulled the book free, the will-o-wisp swept to another one and waited.

And another.

With a spell, I lowered the books to a round table occupying the middle of the room. One panel lifted up, allowing someone to stand in the hollowed-out center, like a teacher instructing students. By the time the will-o-wisp finished its review of the room, I stood on the top ladder in the greenish glow of sunshine falling through Letum Wood's thick canopy.

Using a floating spell I had tested from Grandfather's book, which worked beautifully, I returned to the pile.

The will-o-wisp hovered nearby.

"This many possible books?" I asked. At least thirty scattered the desk. The will-o-wisp zipped around my head and disappeared into a puff. I reached for the first book. This could be a very long day.

The entire trove that the will-o-wisp located for me stretched thirty books long, packed with stories that didn't contain what I sought. While I didn't doubt the veracity of Caroline's claim to have read something similar before, this room yielded no results. No match.

Not even close.

Whomever—or whatever—she argued with before sending me away had it wrong.

With both palms pressed over my eyes, I tried to picture the next step. Tracking down witches in the orphanage yielded no leads. The sheer number of speeches Scarlett had made over the years, which hadn't been kept, narrowed to a few mentions in the *Chatterer*, but no clear records.

This had been a tepid hope, and I needed an idea.

Any idea.

Rognvald in the Gatehouse, striding around several Protectors, barking out ideas, receiving others in return, floated to the top of my mind. They had a sprawling table that Guardians and Protectors alike used, particularly when working on missions together. What would *they* do in a stalled situation?

My mind blanked. No inspiration flowed. Irritated, I shoved away from the shelf.

"I'm finished," I stated. "Thank you."

The books rose like a flock of ascending birds, flying toward the shelves. While I perused old titles, more will-o-wisps had gathered, as if curious. At my movements, the congregated little lights scattered. Soaring will-o-wisps rose from their perches along the shelves and raced to the door, forming an exit path.

The walls closed in, and I couldn't stand anymore of this stuffy room, locked into place. I followed the will-o-wisps, grateful to leave. They guided me through the hallways in a flock that gradually peeled away. I attempted fruitlessly to track the winding paths, the creaky stairs, the occasional flash of light from a window.

Ten minutes into the journey out of the Great Library of Burke, two witches stepped off a staircase and headed my way. The will-o-wisps dissipated into puffs of glitter. Before I could panic, a head of white-blonde hair cast instant reassurance. Leda looked petite and demure next to Hiddleston, who had his hand wrapped around hers.

All questions of the library and next steps concerning the violent but vague letters fled my mind in a moment. My lips parted, but I quickly slammed them shut. Were Leda and Hiddleston openly holding hands?

No.

It *couldn't* be.

They approached at a surprisingly rapid pace. If I didn't pull my shock together, I might scare Leda into whatever emotional hole from which she'd emerged. I barely managed to close my mouth and compose my face before they stepped into visible range. Hiddleston watched me with greatest intensity and wariness.

Leda acted as if nothing was amiss; her eyes lingered on my empty arms. I tried not to stare at hers, free of jerking or spastic movements that would indicate she attempted to break away. Not that Hiddleston would hold her captive, by any means.

But . . .

What other explanation was there?

"You didn't find anything?" she asked.

"Not so far."

She frowned. "That's frustrating."

"Tell me about it."

A focused expression crossed Hiddleston's face as he stared into the distance. I left him to it. Perhaps he'd see something in the paths of the past that might aid the search. Shaking back to life after only a few moments, he ran a hand over his face. Leda cast him a silent question, earned another shake of the head, and motioned back the way they came. I followed.

Slowly, they sauntered toward a stairwell. Leda, lost in thought, still hadn't removed her hand. I snuck a glance at Hiddleston, who cast me an equally sidelong look over the top of her head. His lip twitched ever-so-slightly as if to tell me he observed my disbelief, and yes, this was real.

"What will you do next?" Leda asked.

"Wait for the next letter. I'm following up with tailors in Chatham City tomorrow to inquire about the cloak, the hat, the flower. My expectations aren't high."

As we ascended another staircase, a beam of light cut through an overhead window. I stepped into its warmth with deep relief. The suffocating stuffiness of the buried library room dropped from my lungs. I yearned for the breezy forest to clear my mental cobwebs.

"Did Caroline say if she knew of other places to search?" Leda asked.

"Not that I recall."

"Hmm."

"Do you trust Caroline?"

"I do." The prim set of her lips belied her words, though her laid back tone seemed to agree. "It's just . . . it's odd."

"Why?"

Frowning, Leda said, "Caroline has a prodigious amount of power that she can access. It's not hers. It belongs to the magic of the library. I would have thought, between the two of them, they could find it."

"She speaks to the library, doesn't she?"

Leda rolled her eyes. "Constantly, yes. They have a rather . . . strange . . . relationship. Regardless, I'm most surprised that she didn't locate it right away."

"There are a lot of books."

"Yes, but the magic of this library shouldn't be ignored or underestimated. *It* should have found the book, then told her where it was located. There is only so much literature about the time of the kingdoms and the early days of Alkarra."

I paused. "Hold on. Why do you think the time of the kingdoms has anything to do with this?"

"The more I've thought about it, the more I've wondered if it has roots in the old Declan texts that I used to study. Though, now that I'm gone, things in that area of the library are probably falling apart."

Irritated, I snapped, "What are you talking about?"

Haughtily, Leda said, "Don't you remember the title I sought?"

"No."

She rolled her eyes. "Librarian over the Declan Language Division."

"Right."

With a little shake of her head, she said, "Just because I left the library to work for Scarlett doesn't mean that I've released my ties. I have friends."

Another shock. Leda didn't make friends, but she collected acquaintances and connections the same way dragons sought power. Hoarded them, really, but never dishonestly. Most witches that encountered Leda's good side seemed to intuit that it came at great cost, and didn't imply friendship.

She was supportive, but she didn't always care.

They weren't the same.

Which made her intimacy with Hiddleston all the more astonishing. We stepped into busier halls awash with light and the fragrance of lavender. Running feet hushed by a long hallway carpet raced past.

"Let me know if you discover anything you think is important," she concluded with a musing tone. "I don't imagine you'll receive formal help from Caroline again, but there's a chance you can make an ally out of the library. Be grateful for that," she added in a mutter.

"You don't strike me as a fan of Caroline's."

Her jaw tightened. "Let's just say it's better for everyone if Caroline and I don't interact face to face."

Hiddleston sent me a warning glance, but it was wasted effort. I ignored it. "How long has Caroline been around, anyway? She said that Isadora mentioned me."

Leda's brows dropped so low they turned to razors.

"Isadora?"

"Yes."

"She mentioned *you* to Caroline?"

I shrugged.

Leda's frown deepened. "That's rather strange. For Isadora to mention you to Caroline implies something, but I'm not sure what. Yet. No one knows how long Caroline has been around," she said absently, guiding us toward a room with a sprawling tiled floor, made of chips of marble and tile in a brilliant mosaic. A stained-glass dome soared overhead, spilling torrents of sunshine.

"No one?"

"It's fair to say she's probably ancient. The library must preserve her. The good gods know she's bathed in magic everyday, running this place. Like foresters that grow up and remain in the forest? They have slightly longer lifespans than most, if they're not dying from injury or sickness," she added wryly.

I tucked that aside to think about later.

"Do you think the magic of this library is Deasylva's?" I ran my fingertips along a wooden panel, considering the grains that burrowed under my touch. "It feels familiar, doesn't it?"

Hiddleston said, "I've never seen a grimoire for the library with any sort of claimant from a goddess on it." Hearing his deep, reverberative tone was a surprise after Leda's high-pitched soprano.

"That we know," I added.

He conceded with a tilt of his shoulder. A hint of light blue trailed my fingertips in quiet answer.

Deasylva's, for sure.

We passed under the dome, awash with sound and smells and life, so unlike the chilly catacombs of the library bowels. Leda had navigated with flawless ease and comfort. This is where she'd buried herself after Camille died, hoping to forget the horror of the War of the Networks.

My escape had been in the trees.

Running.

Just outside the dome, Leda paused. She whispered something to Hiddleston. He nodded once, so quickly it had to be an agreement to a request, because the shadow in her eyes lightened. He stepped aside, offered a quick departing wave to me, and wandered to the fountain. There he stood, hands in his pockets, and stared at the ever-changing water nymph.

Luxuriating in my forest again brought a sense of freedom flowing through my veins.

Leda turned to me. "Let me know what you find. Hiddleston and I have something to work on, now that we've assured your safe departure from Caroline's assistance. Scarlett is in her office for the next three hours. If you want to camp out there, I'm sure she'd appreciate the sense of safety she has when you are around."

Chapter Fourteen

The enchanted notebook didn't change from gold to rose gold that night.

Nor the next morning, when I stared at it after returning from a run, sweaty and disheveled. I regarded it while eating, washing dishes, feeding Goat and Other Goat, caring for the manulele birds, sending Ava a message, and preparing to visit Scarlett. To be certain, I checked the last pages.

No new messages.

A missive arrived from Leda as I prepared to transport to the castle.

Hiddleston is going to cover for me this afternoon so I can have a longer lunch period and try to crack the Brotherhood magic. It's complicated, but I think I can do it. Also, today is day four since the last letter. I'm sure you plan to be here with Scarlett.

My eye roll would have knocked a lesser witch over. Instead of replying, *Yes, Mother. On my way,* I pitched it into my cold hearth and leaned into the transportation spell.

Stay busy, I reminded myself, intentionally avoiding Merrick's notebook that stared at me from the middle of the table. *Stay busy, and get through his absence with a little more grace.*

Chatham Castle couldn't come soon enough.

Rognvald stared at me with a frown. "You want me to provide a list of witches that I think might harm Scarlett?"

"No." I jabbed a finger at the parchment. "I *have* a list of witches that may have a potential interest in harming Scarlett, and I want your thoughts on the list. Most of all, I wanted you aware of the escalating threat against the High Priestess."

Rognvald nodded at the door. Understanding the silent command, I closed it. Quick as I could manage while being concise, I produced the three letters and laid them on his desk, next to the original. He ignored the list of potential enemies to skim the letters while I sketched a concise review of what was happening. He stared at the wall until I finished.

"There's some risk to Scarlett's life, all things considered," he said, "but nothing that would justify a Protector. I agree with your list, too."

"Do you know of anyone else not on this list that might have a reason to threaten Scarlett?"

He scoffed, drawing a hand down his beard. "Loads of witches, but you've covered most of them. A few other outliers, maybe, from our latest missions."

I conjured my pencil. "Great. Who else that I haven't already included?"

He rattled off a list of names that I hadn't heard of before, most of them recent problem-makers that Protectors dealt with through their various missions.

"Thank you," I said. "It'll help me figure out this . . . threat."

"There's a threat here," he conceded, "but not to her." He tapped once on his desk. "The threat is for you."

Rognvald turned away, head tilted to the side, eyes distant. He appeared like that when using the Brotherhood communication magic. When his attention returned to the room, made obvious by a shake of his head, I asked, "Can you bring me back inside the Brotherhood magic?"

His gaze darkened slightly. "I wouldn't mind, myself, but it's against our protocols."

"Even while there's escalating threat against—"

"The exceptions I can make are for specific, extenuating missions. When we execute another mission together, yes."

"What if something were to happen?" I asked. "With Scarlett, I mean, and this weirdo sending her letters."

"Aren't you the Head of the Sisterhood?"

"Yes, which is all the more reason. Keep me away from the other Brothers in the magic, if you want."

"I can't."

"I can't access just you?"

His sharp stare unnerved me. "Not that I'm aware of."

"Lame magic," I muttered.

"*Do* you need help?"

Grudgingly, I admitted, "Not yet."

Rognvald rolled his eyes. "If Scarlett asks for our help, we would assign her a Protector, but as it stands, I don't feel one is required. Let's leave it at that. Ask Talmund. Maybe he'll assign more Guards."

Chapter Fifteen

An itch scoured the space underneath my skin, driving me toward the High Priestess' office with a relentless energy. The irritation of another letter possibly arriving today compounded the feeling that my skin couldn't quite contain me.

Chatham Castle purred like a contented cat. The reassuring and low soundtrack of life echoed off the stone walls, softened only by the hanging banners, floor rugs, and occasional divan or collection of chairs set near the wall. The smell of fresh hay washed up from the baileys behind me, welcoming a new market with vendors from the surrounding areas.

As I spun to climb the main staircase, a flash of color caught my eye. I paused, arrested more by instinct than sight.

My throat tightened.

A witch stood ten paces away, facing me. Royal purple cloak, gaudy flower, brilliant orange top hat. I knew the body structure, the spread of shoulders. He didn't smile, but regarded me with impassive, blank eyes that reminded me of a spring pond. Mossy, but oddly still. Unnaturally so. The basic structure of his face wasn't immediately familiar, but somehow, I thought I knew him . . .

His right hand held loosely to a bulging envelope.

He lifted it.

Shook it twice.

As he transported away, I sprang across the space and threw myself into the residual of his spell. The power clutched me immediately, as if he'd wanted me to follow. We plunged into the black.

The transportation spell left me two paces from a giant, stinking, steaming pile of cow dung.

Hay and mud and muck littered a pasture filled with black and white cows, lowing quietly in the early morning hours. No sign of Letum Wood lingered on any horizon, which meant we emerged deep inside the Western Covens.

The flash of a purple cloak transported twenty paces ahead. I didn't bother following his spell, but initiated my own. The spell swept me thirty paces out, so quick that I'd barely left the spot where I stood before I gained the next position. My feet hit seamlessly, without breaking stride.

As I transported, he did too, leading us on a merry chase out of the pasture, while only truly stepping three times. My gobs of practice darting over streams and giant root swells in Letum Wood paid off in the mad dash across dairy and field.

He climbed over a trough and disappeared, revealing himself fifty paces away, near a thatch-roofed building. Something in the confidence, the bold race, made me wonder if this switch *wanted* me to chase him.

Had he planned for this? Mapped out a route, or a vague idea? I could be playing right into his hands. Yet, what choice remained? Any Protector would do the same. Breathing hard, I followed. While leaping over a hay bale, a voice entered my head.

Bianca?

I shouted, tripping over the half-strewn hay, and barely recovered my feet. At the last second, I pirouetted away from an open well, managing not to fall in by sheer speed of my feet, and scrabbled against the ground with my fingers to stay upright.

My response was immediate.

Leda?

I'd felt this way before. Had allowed this magic entry into my thoughts in the past, which surely allowed its inception today.

The Brotherhood magic.

Don't panic! Leda said. *It's just me.*

Not now! I shot back. *I'm chasing the witch.*

The one who delivered the message? she said with a slight gasp.

Yes! Get Scarlett into her office and have Guardians inside and out.

I will!

The lapse in concentration almost made me lose track of my target. He continued to half-sprint, half-transport out of the pasture until he disappeared around a barn edge. I barely kept sight of his purple cloak as he headed toward a small town, transporting there like a rock skipping over a pond.

Foregoing the necessity, I spelled myself all the way to the small town where he headed. When I landed, he was only twenty paces away, facing me.

I crouched, snarling. A startled expression crossed his placid face before he grinned with the tucked corners of his lips and reappeared ten paces away. Off to the side, his cloak ballooned through the air. Abandoned, fluttering on a dying breeze.

A game.

He played a *game*.

Without a second of hesitation, I dodged through an alley, taking a calculated risk that it ended where I hoped it did, and sped onto a back dirt road. Ancient wheel marks and the discarded husks of vegetables littered the hard street. Familiar shoulders wove through a crowd of no more than ten witches. Though cloak-free, I still recognized him. As before, he didn't gaze over his shoulder, but strode purposefully.

Scarlett is safe, Leda said. *Where are you?*

Somewhere in the Western Covens.

I skidded to a stop at a crossroads outside of the farmer's market. No crush of witches packed this area, which lent an advantage of sight. No sign of the witch remained, nor hint of magic in the immediate vicinity. Working off sheer instinct, I darted across the road, to the most unlikely alley. Scuffling feet sounded at the end, close enough to make me press harder. A stitch burned against my side like a twisting, hot cork. My legs smoldered, but weren't yet tired.

Where in the Western Covens? Leda asked.

No idea!

The scuffling feet disappeared. I cast about, feeling for magic, and found empty air. No pulse of life. No reverberative sign. Nothing to indicate someone passed through here. I turned left, right. Panting, I spun in a circle, discovering nothing.

In a desperate move, I transported to the top of the closest building. Sunlight and wind flooded me as I raced across the top, running along the eastern sidewall to avoid falling through weak spots in the shingles. I spotted the witch along the road, loping as if out for a daily constitutional.

Hesitation stalled me for only a breath. I'd never successfully transported on top of someone. Certainly not someone rapidly moving in an unknown direction. That kind of specificity was extremely difficult, or very rare.

A Protector could do it.

One spell and two seconds later, I toppled him to the ground from behind. He collapsed beneath me, and I felt an absurd thrill that I managed it.

Leda's voice rang through my head.

Are you all right?

I ignored her, scrambling for traction against his sure and strong movements. He prevented my arm around his neck by flipping onto his back. I lurched onto my hands and knees. The witch planted a foot on my stomach and shoved. All the air raced out of my lungs as I soared into the sky. I flung a hand out at the last minute, grabbing his wrist to prevent his escape. I had no breath, but I wouldn't let him—

He transported, taking me with him.

With a mental screech to Leda that I wasn't entirely sure she would hear, I dropped into the encompassing, terrifying pressure of the transportation spell without enough air.

Compressing body and life into the folds of time and magic to leave one place and appear another was painful enough. Without sufficient breath, my body felt plunged into ice water. Kissed by a dark vacuum, all hope of life dissipating.

Seconds stretched into short eternities. Every heart thud, slow as they felt, came at great cost as my chest wrung itself out. Darkness swamped my sight, my mind, like a cloak drawing over me. Understanding narrowed, pulling me under, overwhelmed. I struggled.

Clawed for the surface.

Shouted for Leda.

A final pinprick of perception told me that this wasn't good, the pressure released. I thudded onto my spine and drew in a great, gasping breath.

The hiss of the ocean roused me.

Molten hot sand gritted against my cheek, belying the cool rush of waves ahead. Water splashed nearby, freckling my face with salty drops. My eyes popped open as a wave raced closer. I shoved upright just before the water slapped my cheeks. The soothing, cool sea banished the ebony depths. A weak shudder woke me further.

That had been . . . close. *Too* close.

Bianca?

Leda's voice edged me further away from the terrifying, deadly precipice where I dangled. Bleary, I rubbed sand granules away from my face. The ocean awaited. Crashing surf rolled in the distance, spraying white foam with each gentle crash and hiss.

Bianca!

The growing urgency in her tone clued me in.

Right.

A quick glance down confirmed my worst nightmares. Not only had I run through puddles of pig muck, cow dung, and who-knew-what-else, but I'd also managed to lose my only lead. The witch was nowhere.

I'm fine. I struggled to sit up. *I was occupied, sorry.*

What happened?

He transported me.

What?

Even across the distance, her screech made me grimace. I stood, brushing sand off my bare, sweaty arms. My lungs recovered, but my body still ached from slamming so hard into the sand. Not an accident, I'd wager. If I had been the witch, I would have ensured a hard landing to buy me lead time. It felt as if something had taken a hammer to my shoulders.

In the distance sat a little town, dotting the seaside. The Eastern Network had innumerable shores and beach access along the eastern edges, where the land snaked around the ocean. Salty marshes and wetlands eventually became the Southern Network along their distant border. The land mass of the Eastern Network was impressively large, though much of it was too wild for steady inhabitation. Based on the smell from behind, mixing with the fresh breeze welling off the sea, I'd landed somewhere near the southern area of the Eastern Network.

I'm in the East, I said quickly, gaining mental capacity as I studied the landscape. *I grabbed the witch to stop him from leaving, but he took me with him and brought me to a beach. There's a little village nearby. It's quite . . . idyllic.*

You know it's the East?

Fairly certain. I'll need a few minutes to track the sun to know for sure, but this doesn't clue me into the Western Network. There are buildings ahead, and they look more Eastern than tribal.

Though no one was nearby, I issued an invisibility spell and levitated above the sand. He must have done the same. No footprints led in any direction.

Did you lose him?

Yes. No sign of him.

He may have left you and transported again.

If true, the magical signature would be long gone. I rubbed a hand over my face, clearing the final bit of sand. At some point in the near future, I'd appreciate the story behind the magic Leda must have accomplished to establish the Brotherhood magic between us, but I set it aside for the more pertinent situation.

But why here? I asked.

Could it be his home?

Could be, I drawled, *but it's awfully small. And why would he draw me to his home?*

With her usual verve, Leda said, *The fact that he took you at all means* something. *If he wanted to get rid of you, there are better places than a beach in the Eastern Network. Or he didn't plan on you catching up to him. When you did, the transportation spell was underway and he couldn't help it. He dropped you and left again?*

How to convey the sense that he'd *wanted* me to follow? He'd kept himself visible throughout the chase, allowing enough space to keep me on his heels, but not so much I lost him entirely. Not to mention that when I faced him, he smiled.

It all felt like a game.

The letters.

The details of the stories.

The costume, appearances. Even his blithe smile.

I rubbed my forehead to stave off a headache, grateful that I didn't have to speak out loud to Leda and, thus, give my position away. Jikes, but navigating the communication magic was weird with Leda at the other end.

I'm going to check the village out.

Get a name as soon as you can. I'll look it up on the map. There's a legend of all places somewhere in the library . . .

She trailed away, and I was glad to lose her voice for a few minutes. Crossing the sand required little time with the levitation spell. Five houses congregated up the way, set back from surging tidal waters.

Whitewashed exteriors, storm shutters, and old crab husks littered their yards. Various footprints pressed into the wet sand, drying under a steady sun. I slipped beyond the footpath, overhearing chatter that confirmed our location. The words were *Ilese.* My knowledge of the Eastern Network language wasn't perfect, but passable. I conjugated the verbs in my head as I thought I heard them, parsing together the basic meanings of a low, daily conversation about fishing as I passed a house, still invisible.

The sandy road, lined with high grasses that waved in the sun, gave way to another rippling field that faded into the distance as I left the ocean. Near a divergence in the road, a sign stuck out of the sand.

Breton.

The little village is Breton.

I'll search for a map. In the meantime, I think you should return. Another letter just arrived.

I stopped home for a quick bath and change of clothes before I went to Scarlett. Leda remained silent in my head, allowing me space to stew. Fresh, hot summer air danced over my cheeks as I entered Scarlett's office. Open windows allowed a stiff breeze inside that didn't cool the space, but moved the heated stagnancy.

Scarlett stood on the other side of her desk, her cheeks reddened, but pale beneath. Her physical ailments hadn't improved recently. She held her body very still, wearing a loose dress with short sleeves and a wide neckline. The coveted *linea* fabric kept witches cool and hid sweat stains. The odd way she held herself, as if waiting for a physical blow, made me just as nervous. A bold anxiety lingered in the air.

Wordless, Scarlett extended a sealed envelope to me. The telltale scroll bulged inside.

"This arrived not long ago."

I accepted.

"Thank you, High Priestess."

With a quirk of her lips that faded as quickly as it arose, she said, "Don't thank me. Leda tells me you have an adventure to relay."

The envelope remained in my hand while I repeated the story. It seemed hard to grasp that it had been less than an hour ago when the chase began. Her engaged expression grew concerned when I admitted, "It was a set up, High Priestess. The witch wanted me to see him and chase him."

"Why?"

"I don't know."

"Did you recognize him?"

My lips parted in hesitation. "No," I said slowly, "but . . . maybe? There's something vaguely familiar, but I can't be sure it's not because I've chased him before, through Chatham City. Though I didn't see more than his facial profile that time. I can definitely sense transformative magic on him, but there's not enough to explain a total metamorphosis. Whatever he's transformed, it's not much."

Leda piped up from my side. "Hiddleston is looking into Breton right now, High Priestess. We're trying to see if there is any obvious connection or if Hiddleston can recognize the witch in the paths."

A stroke of inspiration pushed me to say through the magic, *Message Caroline. Tell her to look into a connection between Breton and the stories.*

Leda's head snapped to the side, meeting my eyes. A moment of cogitating thought passed before she blinked, said aloud, "I will," and retreated from the office. Scarlett watched her go, appearing startled.

"She will what?"

"Message Caroline."

Eyeing me sharply, Scarlett asked, "Is there something I don't know between the two of you?"

"Leda has created the Brotherhood communication magic between us. Or enabled it between us? I'm not sure, yet. I don't know the details. She popped into my head as I was chasing the witch. That's all I know. We're . . . getting used to it. Sorry."

"How advantageous," Scarlett murmured, staring at the door through which Leda left. Her musing expression grew slightly more concerned as she returned her gaze to the note. The office door opened again, admitting Hiddleston.

Scarlett asked, "Have you found anything, Hiddleston?"

"I was able to find it happening in Bianca's paths, Your Highness."

"Did you see the witch?"

"Yes."

Interest piqued her tone. "His face?"

"I didn't recognize him, Your Highness. Not with any certainty. The paths were . . . busy. Bianca had many opportunities. As I can see only for Bianca and not that witch right now, I cannot see his paths to know much more."

Thank the goddess I didn't have Hiddleston's vision. I'd never know all the ways that I had failed to choose the better path. If many alternatives existed, what kept me from chasing them? Was it possible I had chosen the best path amongst dozens of worse ones? Or did I have a habit of choosing the worst circumstance right away?

I didn't want that answered, so I made a plan to avoid Hiddleston the moment this meeting ended.

Scarlett drew me back into the present. "Is there anything in the paths to give us information or help?"

Hiddleston drew in a calm breath through his nose before reluctantly shaking his head. "Not yet, Your Highness. I'll continue to search."

"Thank you."

As he departed, Leda returned bearing Scarlett's tea tray.

Scarlett nodded to the letter. "I find I don't have a taste for whatever that letter might say. If you don't mind reading it elsewhere, Bianca, and informing me of your plan afterward, that would be most appreciated."

Leda kept a wary eye on Scarlett as Scarlett lowered to her chair, her chin high in defiance of exhaustion.

"Of course, High Priestess," I said. "Whatever you need."

"I must reach the top of the sky, Marie Hazel. I must! I battle wind and torrent and cloud and star. Help me reach the heavens."

"Why?" Marie Hazel demanded. "Why not stay here? We can return. The ride down will feel warm."

"For the betterment of the world! We must see the stars."

"We see them here."

"It is not enough."

The brittle words rang through the air.

It is not enough.

Marie Hazel reached for Ellie Victoriann. "I have no more to give."

Ellie Victoriann did not see Marie Hazel's stripped wings and gasping breaths. Only the plumbless stars and spawning heights. Only her own ambition. Only her own desire. They had advanced so far, they could not turn back. Marie Hazel's heart stopped.

Her slack wings stilled.

Chapter Sixteen

"I t's going to terrify Scarlett," Leda announced as she stared at the letter. Her pinched lips and pale expression drove the fear home. Hiddleston leaned against his desk, his powerful legs held him into position. His palms braced on a smattering of paperwork. He kept an intent stare on Leda.

She lifted her eyes to his.

"It's not good."

Frowning, I plucked it from her hand and skimmed it again. "It's odd." My thumb ran over a series of hand-drawn stars at the very bottom of the page. Four of them.

"It's allegory," Leda retorted, plucking it back. "It's all symbolic, Bianca. Obviously, you can't actually fly to the stars."

"I know that! But it's odd that it doesn't fit. Ellie Victoriann's selfishness to fly to the stars isn't at all like Scarlett. If Ellie Victoriann is supposed to be Scarlett and Marie Hazel is supposed to be me, it doesn't make sense. Scarlett's ambition isn't that singular."

"Disagree." Leda folded her arms over her chest. "Scarlett has great ambitions for you in the Sisterhood, she's simply approaching her plans in a slow-moving and insightful way."

"What ambitions?"

Leda shook her head. "They're not mine to share. If you want to know that, you can ask Scarlett."

I studied her high-handed, pursed lips for about five seconds before deciding against that. Despite some curiosity, I didn't need another mystery.

"Maybe another time," I murmured, and a fox-like triumph slipped through Leda's eyes. It scuttled away as quickly as it came, leaving concern fresh on her downturned lips. She brushed a stray lock of hair out of her eyes.

"This still leaves the problem of *why* this witch is sending them."

"A message," Hiddleston said. "Clearly."

"What message?"

"*That* is the better question."

"And what are these stars?" I waved the letter for them to see. "What do they mean?"

With a conceding shrug, Leda issued a spell, made three copies of the letter, and handed me the original. At home, I'd conduct the ritual tests and comparisons, but felt no magic, saw no variation in writing size, script, or parchment. Everything was the same.

While Hiddleston and Leda split apart for their separate desks, I asked Leda, "How did you do it?"

Her lips twitched. "You mean the Brotherhood magic?"

"Of course."

"It took awhile," she retorted with the energy and vigor of someone who had been waiting for me to ask. "It was harder than I expected, to be honest. The magic system has a name. Lokkan."

"Lokkan?"

She nodded. "The spells are few, but are as nuanced as I expected, if not more. It's a robust system. The Protectors don't use it to even a tenth of its ability, which *did* surprise me. There's a parent incantation, you see, and the holder—"

An exhausting day lay stacked behind us, rife with muddy pigs and Scarlett's worry and something else I couldn't quite grasp. The very last thing I had the capacity to track was Leda's assessment of a new magic system.

"The point?"

She released a sharp breath through her nose. "It was complicated," she finished in a snap, huffing at my audacity. "But I did it. I was able to bring you in right away, I think, because you had participated in this magic before, with the Brotherhood. Otherwise, I think it may not have been so simple."

"I'm glad."

She sounded genuinely eager when she asked, "Did it help?"

"It definitely will."

"It'll take time for us to figure it out," she concluded. "I'll need to discover what my boundaries are, and what constitutes an emergency. Ideally, you won't message me during the hours that I'm not working with Scarlett, unless it *is* an emergency, which will still need to be blatantly defined."

"When aren't you working with Scarlett?"

She didn't deign to respond to that, but answered instead, "I'll draw a schedule up and have it for you later. Naturally, I'll expect you to abide by it with respect, which means you'll forget about it and speak into my head whenever you want."

I resisted the urge to remind her that I wasn't one of her Underassistants. She'd only gloat about how many served her, or something equally irritating. No, I couldn't speak with Leda about anything else until I'd eaten, had a long, hot soak in a Northern Network spring, and braided my hair out of my eyes.

"Thank you, Leda." I managed to infuse sincere gratitude into the phrase. "It will be helpful and safer for Scarlett this way. I'll know that help can come much faster than before."

"Don't abuse it," Leda sniped, but there was a small smile on her face as she sat at her desk. "I'm only just beginning to delve into its intricacies. Give me a month, and I'll hold even the Brotherhood in the palm of my hands."

Hiddleston chortled, and they both settled down to work.

Tomasso shrieked, hurled a toy, and shrieked again.

At over a year old, he was a whirlstorm and a wonder. Watching Priscilla chase him around, praise him, scold him, keep him engaged, and not lose her mind, was another wonder. He reminded me of an octopus: all appendages moving at the same time. But an octopus with the potential to wreak extraordinary havoc on what could have otherwise been a quiet, peaceful life.

Leda, unbothered by the screeching and thudding, continued to drink her tea. A book poised in her lap, split halfway open. The title read, *Incendiary Politics,* and made me want to yawn. Enraptured, she pressed doggedly into the tome while Michelle and Priscilla chattered over delicate sandwiches and slices of fruit.

Michelle's two daughters, Sanna and Isadora, ran in circles around Tomasso on the floor. More correctly, Sanna ran while Isadora toddled. Tomasso and Isadora weren't all that far apart in age, though I wasn't sure how much.

I stood at the attic window of Miss Priscilla's School for Girls, staring onto familiar, yet different school grounds. A man with a wooden wheelbarrow pushed a load of weeds away from the manor and toward the forest. I tilted my head, considering.

"Cilla?" I asked.

Their conversation paused. "Yes?" she called. I tapped on the windowpane gently, so as not to draw his attention.

"Who is that?"

Priscilla stood to peer around my shoulder before saying, "Oh, that's Jorge."

Ah.

The mysterious groundskeeper that Ava mentioned. The strapping fellow was wide through the chest, with hefty arms and a serious expression. No smile lines graced a face like that. He meant business, whatever he did. Dirt speckled the front of his shirt, which was unbuttoned and sweaty around the neck.

"He's taken over as groundskeeper," she said.

"Did the Network provide him?" Leda asked with a slightly arch tone that suggested they had better, or they'd hear from her.

"Yes."

With a prim and approving nod, Leda returned to her reading. Isadora sounded an alarm that Michelle dealt with. Something in Priscilla's voice grabbed my attention.

"Jorge," I murmured again. "He looks . . . swarthy."

I wanted to say *intense* but couldn't summon the word. He would be in his mid-thirties, at least. A rugged life aged him. Priscilla shrugged, but I didn't miss a high color on her cheeks as I followed her away from the window.

"How old is he?" I asked.

"I don't know how old he is."

"Thirty?"

"I don't know."

"Handsome face." I tried for an idle tone as I lowered into a chair near the cold hearth. "Have you spoken much with him?"

The glare Priscilla shot me suggested I wasn't as subtle as I hoped. Leda peered over the top of her book, mimicking Priscilla's wry annoyance. She returned, like a lowering shark, behind *Incendiary Politics*.

I held up both hands. "I'm just making an observation!"

"Speaking of handsome men," Michelle said quietly, no doubt having promised Priscilla to save her from my inquiry should it arise, "has Merrick returned yet?"

Leda's eyes reappeared.

I sighed. "Yes, but he's gone."

Priscilla set her hands in her lap. "Really? Oh, Bianca, I'm sorry."

Michelle murmured something similar. I nodded, willing to

take the heat of the conversation for now. Later, I'd get the dish on Jorge and Priscilla and her uncanny nonchalance.

"How did the reunion go?" Michelle asked.

"Wonderful." I smiled, then added a wry, "And too brief."

Michelle and Priscilla nodded in unison. Thankfully, discussion pirouetted to the upcoming school class, and whether Michelle might be interested in helping Celia with some of the cooking, as Celia had finally mentioned retirement. A knock came on the door a moment before it snuck open. Baxter's light eyes peered through the crack in the doorway.

"Did I interrupt a ladies' lunch?" he inquired.

With a smile, Priscilla motioned to the tea tray. "Just a little catching up, but you're most welcome."

Tomasso let out a happy shriek as Baxter entered the room. He raced over. Baxter scooped him up, tossed him around, and laughed when Tomasso let out a peal of laughter. Baxter made weekly appearances into Tomasso's life. He and Priscilla had developed a friendship over the visits, but to my eye, nothing deeper. For her part, Priscilla seemed indifferent to changing her current status quo. Single parenting suited her.

"Well," Baxter declared, propping Tomasso on the ground to toddle to his playthings. "I have only a quick question." He glanced at the rest of us. "If you don't mind."

We shook our heads.

"Have you heard the news?" he asked, his gaze on me. Sensing an undercurrent of meaning, I tensed.

"What news?" Priscilla asked.

"There's a problem forming at Magnolia Castle right now. Just came from there. There are *Chatterer* journalists on the scene, even."

A grisly report, regardless of the cause. *Chatterer* journalists usually worked only within the Central Network, but these days, with borders between Networks open, they popped in and out wherever they wished. If they found a story, they chased it like relentless hounds. Most of the time, the information gathering worked in my favor, but Rognvald complained incessantly.

Mention of the words *Magnolia Castle* pressed Priscilla's lips together. With some faltering, she asked, "What news comes from Magnolia Castle?"

"Potential news," he amended, standing with his hands in his pockets and a slight frown. His shoulders hunched a little, and the slouching posture gave him an air of question. "East Guards surround it, while others are dispensed elsewhere. Cristian is . . . frightened."

"Of what?"

"Rumors." Baxter shrugged. "A rumor that Carcere's walls have been breached, along with another that said half the navy drowned. Another message said that Necce has been flooded with rebels, and yet another claimed that all the grains from a recent harvest were poisoned. There is no sign of a rebellion or any truth to support the rumors. Necce hasn't been flooded with obvious rebels, and all reports from Captains of the Ships indicate that the Navy is fine. But Cristian is . . ."

"Delusional?" Priscilla offered.

Baxter hesitated. "What do you think of Cristian?" The tense air in the room made it obvious that no one missed his clear avoidance of answering.

"I think he's Cristian," Priscilla replied. "It's hard to put a witch like him into words. I don't like him much," she said flatly, and without apology. "When Niko and I were engaged, he never wished us well or spoke to me. He's very tied into the Aldana family legacy. To him, it must look a certain way. I didn't fit into that vision. Much of Niko's hesitation around handfasting me stemmed from Cristian's opinions. We had as little to do with each other as possible."

Baxter nodded. "That's as good a summary as I assumed. Anyway, he's barricaded himself into the castle. By doing so, he's drawn negative attention to himself, and he can't afford that."

He rubbed a hand over his eyes and shook his head. "Oi," he whispered, a common exclamation in the Eastern Network, "there's no helping witches who don't want it."

Priscilla hid a smile. None of this seemed a surprise, but the rumors had me on edge.

"Is he researching the rumors?" I asked. "Please tell me he's trying to delineate fact from fiction?"

"Yes." Baxter frowned and added, "Sort of. Guardians have been dispatched, but he continues to change his mind. Asks one thing this minute, another the next. His advisors are making it difficult, too."

"They're a mess," Leda said.

Her voice, clear as a bell, seemed to break through the agitated waves of silence that held others back from saying the same thing.

Baxter sighed. "Since Niko's death, yes. Cristian was not ready to take over, and now he's not ready to remain. Yet, he won't give it up." With exasperation, Baxter asked, "Are all witches like this?"

Primly, Leda said, "Only in leadership," and set her book aside. *I need to tell Scarlett,* she told me through the magic, but avoided eye contact. *There's more to this than you think. I'll update you later.*

She drank the last of the tea, propped her book under her elbow, and said to Priscilla, "Thank you, Cilla. I'm sorry I must go. I'll return soon."

As Leda departed, I couldn't help wondering what possible connection any of it might have to the Central Network.

That evening, I sent Papa a message.

Where are you?

No immediate response drew me to the window, where I

stared out. Sunshine twined through the branches, bouncing off butterflies as they fluttered through the open space. Far from the forest floor, I enjoyed the benefits of fresh air. The thick darkness didn't reach this high. Sunshine still penetrated the storied heights.

A terrible, yawning emptiness unfurled. In the aftermath of all that happened, I wanted to tell Merrick. To speak about the day that tumbled through my mind. The four letters—the latest of which attempted to foretell my death. The witch I chased. The Eastern Network city. Priscilla's calm response to Baxter's update on the Eastern Network.

Grandfather would welcome me, should I seek refuge in his apartment. He'd distract me, certainly.

But I longed for Merrick.

Tonight, it felt as if the treehouse stared back at me. Last time he left, I hadn't moved in here yet. But now? I'd seen it with him inside, and I couldn't forget how different it felt. All wide windows, flowing space, lilting wood grains, and breath. In a turn of my neck, I could encompass most of it with my eyes. The gentle soundtrack of Letum Wood filled the background with contented and lovely murmurings.

Everything about this treehouse was linked to me, from the pots and pans I scrounged up to the rickety table that I repaired last year. Yet, without Merrick, it felt empty. I hated that I had to endure this again. His absence required me to work through the empty first days, so soon after he left. To reconcile the life I had to the one I didn't.

The hollow space would pass, eventually. But in the meantime, I had to battle the yawning pit, swelling with a wash of loneliness. As sweet as my reunion with Merrick had been, the equally low plummet to sadness took my breath away. The *speed* of the change.

As I stared into the quiet forest, a body appeared at my doorway. A pause, then a low and familiar voice.

"This is what I hated most about leaving Marie."

Papa leaned against the doorway, a distant expression on his face. He appeared tanner, a bit leaner. His clothes were dirty, but not torn. No dirt under his nails, no scratches on his face or hands. No clues to what he'd been doing since I last saw him.

The sunlight backlit his profile, casting his face into shadow. I didn't need sunlight to know what ghosts I'd see there. I could hear the turmoil in his voice. My shoulders slumped, as if the emotional load that he carried could be shared through a glance.

"What did you hate most?" I whispered.

"Besides leaving?"

"Yes."

"The silence. I knew that I left her to silence. That she waited. Powerful and strong as Marie had always been, she endured. I hated that she had to."

A lump rose in my throat, and the picture blurred. Quietly, I whispered the tolling truth that rang deep into the caverns of my chest. I couldn't help myself.

"This is harder than I thought."

I meant more than Merrick. I meant the Sisterhood. Scarlett's safety. My own safety. I'd bitten off more than I could chew . . . again.

Papa shoved away from the wall and crossed to my side. His arms swamped me, enveloping in a familiar warmth that I didn't always receive as a child. The heat broke through my crumbling strength with bolstering sinew. A sob peeped out of me.

"I thought there would be nothing harder than knowing, from afar, that your mother struggled through daily life without me. That our handfasting forced her to endure silence and loneliness that would make other women cringe. I was wrong."

His fingers clamped around my shoulders. The tips dug into my muscles in a reassuring way. Papa whispered, "It's worse to see you going through it, B. It's so much worse."

Another sob escaped me.

Papa, often denied the privilege of comforting me in the days gone by, held me tight as I cried.

Chapter Seventeen

The next morning, a letter tapped on my forehead with frustrating insistence. As I elevated from the layers of sleep, I tried to shove it away. It persisted.

Finally grasping it by the edge, I peeled my bleary eyes open and stared at it. I lay on my stomach, head canted to the side. Grandfather's latest book lay half-open in front of me, poised to a page discussing a tasteless, odorless, slow-moving poison known as *postamotent* that used to be wildly popular amongst the Factios in Chatham City. I must have fallen asleep reading the list of symptons.

The envelope wriggled out of my hands and unfurled itself.

I squinted through sleep.

Library.
Now.

No signature accompanied the bright green ink, so iridescent and obnoxious that I immediately understood who sent it. With a groan, I rolled off the bed. Though tempted to prolong the wait, I didn't dare.

Caroline's bold declaration swept us down yet another dark hallway. "I found the original book."

I yawned, rubbing my eyes with the heel of my hand, and gave up cataloging where we went. No will-o-wisps accompanied us, but I had a feeling they'd catch up as soon as Caroline cleared a way. Cobwebs and spiders would avoid someone like her.

"How?" I asked.

She half snarled. "Don't question the depths of my knowledge around the literature of this building if you want me to help."

"Sorry. Not quite awake."

"It's not my fault it took this long," she added with a bitter scoff, as if I dared to mention it. Her voice elevated, rising with her eyes, which glared overhead. "If *someone* had considered literature outside of short stories and poems a little faster, as I suggested!"

The jab, clearly not meant for me, remained unrequited.

We buzzed around a wide corner that split into three different hallways. Caroline chose the left hallway, which happened to be the narrowest. Torches didn't flare to life as we passed. She summoned one from its bracket along the wall and held it high, like a beacon.

"I take it the original isn't a short story or poem?"

"No."

"What is it?"

"I'll explain when we arrive."

"Where did you find it?" I asked.

"The Room of Ancient Eastern Network Texts."

"Oh?"

"Thanks to your message about the town of Breton, I thought to look there." Her glance held something like irritation, though not quite. "It's probably a good thing you sent it. Without the information, I wouldn't have thought of it."

The witch had led me directly to Breton, which meant he wanted us to make some sort of discovery. Was it *this* discovery?

If so, why?

With another gesture of her hand, we split down a different hallway, this heading at a diagonal.

"I've been studying the structure and cadence of the letters and believe Leda was correct. The story was taken and adapted from a very early version of the Declan language. They could be flowery with exposition, if they wanted. The familiarity told me I'd read something similar before, but nailing down the place and time was the hard part. Considering," her tone heightened again, "that *some* magicks are stubborn fools," she lowered it, "we're lucky to have found it. It's not truly literature in the sense one might think."

"Then what is it?"

"A game."

Blinking as we passed under a doorway that appeared to be on fire, though no heat accosted us, I scrambled to keep up with her steady stride. The word *game* shouldn't have surprised me. I'd considered it such for days now, but her confirmatory description hit me right in the chest.

"A game?"

She shushed me.

Her steps slowed from their high crescendo to pause near an ancient door. It looked like an original, with boards held together by wrought iron bands. Time had almost separated them, peeling apart to opposite sides. It groaned as Caroline pressed inside, shoving through despite the chance it could disintegrate by the sheer testament of time.

We stepped into a room where lanterns hung from pegs, illuminating lazily at a command from her lips. Scrolls shuffled and twirled softly in cubbies, as if waking from a long sleep. The animation lent a restless spirit to the room, stirring it to life with coaxing promises.

Caroline ventured a single step over the threshold. Her tapered, assessing gaze trawled over every space.

"This anteroom and the joined chamber of books was created by one of the original Burke family members," she said. "Thus, it is quietly powerful and very old. Vargas, I believe? Toward the end of his days, he desired a room to hold the traditions and cultures that he understood would be swept away by time. His traditions. His cultures. Brigands, original foresters, and the like. Of course, his wife, Nessa, spurred the idea. The library says she sponsored the room. She cared about notating history. Was an avid reader and historian, in fact."

Caroline's voice activated scrolls and parchment. Books shivered on their shelves, thick with dust. The brittle smell of ink and paper aggravated my nose, so overpowering my eyes watered. I sensed another magic stirring in the background. Something soft and tender and fierce at the same time.

"There." She pointed straight ahead.

In the middle of the room, atop of a small table laden with a glimmering crystal, stood a book. Beside the table, another door, ghastly black and overburdened with similar crystals and jewels. As if someone painted it with glue and flung glittering gems in a spray design.

"Of course, this is the anteroom to Vargas and Nessa's special chamber, which is on the other side of that black door," she said crisply, pausing next to the book. My attention roved over the walls, the shelves, the dark in the corners and the sides. The shelves lay empty, but surely they hadn't always been. Damp darkness pressed hard, as if it wanted to shove things out of corners. It smelled like loam.

"What's in the special chamber?"

"That," she said with lofty regard, "is none of your business."

As I reached to touch the book on top of the table, it moved an equal distance away.

"It won't let you."

"Why?"

Crossly, she said, "The *anteroom*," through gritted teeth, as if that explained everything.

Setting that aside, I asked, "Can I see inside?" The four letters appeared in my hand. I held them up. Caroline, seeing them, nodded once. I set the letters down on the table. As I set each scroll on top, the book slipped open, whirring through pages at the front and toward the middle.

I regarded it carefully, confused by the ink, which held flecks of embedded silver. The smell of hibiscus drifted free. This book, like this room, was old. Ancient. The parchment was brittle, yellow, and thin. Once the whirring pages settled, I noted a familiar arrangement of stars at the top of the page. The same that burdened the bottom of the fourth letter.

"This is it," I whispered.

"I know."

"You've read it?"

She nodded. "Studied it, yes."

The words on the page made no sense at first. While I knew most Declan verbs and basic conjugation, a language that I had to learn in force while working with Mabel, the blocky, squared letters made my eyes cross. It took several moments of perusal to understand that these words weren't written in Declan, only a strange handwriting. I could understand them with intentional concentration.

Caroline swung a hand in front of the book. Gently, it closed, revealing the front cover. The title, burned black into the leather, was one word.

Ludos.

"Translates to the word *game* from ancient Declan," Caroline murmured. "There was a type of logical puzzle very popular during that time period. It revolved around stories, clues, and an eventual ending that one sorted out by a series of other things: dice, a gameboard, cards, etc." She touched her earlobe. "One would hear the set up of the game, which followed a predictable pattern. They would establish characters, the quest of the game, and then decide the ending by whatever method chosen."

"The dice?"

"Or cards or gameboard."

My heart raced as I considered the first two letters.

"Set up," I whispered.

Unbothered by my wide-eyed breathlessness, she tapped the edge of the book, which spun backward until it opened to the first puzzle, delineated by a brilliant chapter heading swirled around the number one. She spoke delicately, as if she feared breathing too hard would disintegrate the paper.

"Here is an example of one of these logical puzzles. There's a set up of two opposing sides, or paths." The page flipped, revealing short-form story not unlike the first two letters, except the ink changed color and so did the names.

"The first character is set up in this mulberry ink," Caroline said, tapping her finger on the first page, then delicately turning to the second page, which scrawled in bright red. "The second character."

Just like the first and second letter. Beyond that, the pages shuffled to a navy blue writing. "The set up of the quest," she continued as my breath came faster, "and a blunt ending without resolution that leads into the rest of the game."

The third letter, and the fourth letter, respectively.

"There's a fifth set in some games," Caroline added, tapping along the paper edge. "In the fifth section—or letter, in your case —the Gamemaster invites the players to solve the problem at their discretion." Her nose wrinkled in deeper thought. "Some historical sources indicate that the position of Gamemaster was a privileged and hard-won title. There are paintings that reveal elaborate costumes, even. Tournaments, if you will. Players showed up in person to compete and solve the problems. The Gamemaster was indicated by a large hat, typically."

Weakly, I asked, "Costumes? Such as a bright purple cape, a gigantic flower, and an orange top hat?"

Surprised, she said, "Why, yes."

The gods.

It *was* a game. Every single aspect of it.

"I see," I whispered. My brain moved too quickly to conclude anything else. Blinking, I said, "Can we return to the story you think it resembles? Can we compare what is in the book with what's in the letters?"

With a breath of magic, the pages slid to the original opening spot. I recognized the familiar arrangement of stars on the page again, which confirmed that the letter sender *did* want us to discover this book.

Hungry, I devoured the first few lines.

There was a time when a young lad named Koda Bazool lived in a common home.

You'd observe nothing special about him. Penniless, black hair, pointed eyes, knobby knees, wrinkled socks. He held a dim disposition, except for one talent. He could read minds.

My heart hummed as I frantically re-read the initial paragraphs of the first letter, registering the oh-so-subtle nuances.

There was a time when a young girl named Ellie Victoriann lived in an orphanage.

You'd observe nothing special about Ellie Victoriann. Orphan, silver-blonde hair, knobby knees, wrinkled socks, lusterless eyes, and a dim disposition.

Changed gender, name, descriptions. Minute tweaks and details swapped around to more intentionally suit a story about Scarlett or her sister, Ellie. Whoever re-wrote the story, they had taken pains to understand and track Scarlett's life before her role as High Priestess, not to mention reiterate Ellie Victoriann's name.

Caroline asked, "Well?"

"Subtle," I immediately retorted. "The basic storyline is the same so far, except for nuances."

Speaking louder than before, she asked, "You can confirm that *I* have found the correct reference?"

"Yes."

With a satisfied smirk, Caroline pressed her fists onto her hips as I used a spell to make a copy of the letters, conjured a quill and bright blue ink, and made slashes above the words that were different. A book popped into the air next to me.

"Here," she said.

As a replica of the original, it lacked the same feeling of time and power. The ink was black, the papers cream, and the cover generic leather. Space between the lines and on the side of the pages left ample room for notes.

A beat of silence passed while I comprehended the inherent kindness of the gesture. I glanced at her, gave her a silent and rueful nod of thanks, and ignored her eye roll.

Returning to the letters, I said, "Can you stay and help me compare this? There could be important alterations or clues."

"For a few minutes."

"I'll take it. Please, continue."

The tedious process inched us through the first paragraphs and original storyline one sentence at a time. Thanks to the copy she provided, I could have taken the papers and retreated home, but the thought of being close to Merrick's memory, imprinted in the fabric of the air, kept me in the library.

Besides, it seemed more prudent to stay with Caroline and the troves of wisdom heaped inside of her. Her murmured additions, tapping nails as she pointed out one I missed, and more in-depth explanations, kept my quill writing so fast I almost summoned a second one.

The temptation to summon Leda flickered through me, but recalling that she was in meetings with Scarlett all day, withheld the temptation. Unlike the Brotherhood, the Sisterhood held boundaries within personal lives.

"Several phrases have no direct correlation with the original." Caroline sniffed, gaze focused downward. "That means whoever adapted this tale added several lines."

I shot her a questioning glance. "When was this written?"

Caroline tilted her head slowly from one side to the next, bones popping along her spine, as she studied the words. "A very long time ago. That's the end of the first letter, anyway, and plenty for you to study and figure out." She cracked her finger knuckles, as if preparing for a fight. "I'll be on my way."

"There's so much more."

Her steep irritation would have set me on fire under different circumstances. With deepest toleration, she said, "Yes, there's more. You're capable of dealing with all the rest on your own. Unless you want to run the library?" she added crisply.

"I thought Abena did that?"

Fury flashed in her eyes. "There are other ways to run a building, Miss Monroe."

Heat rose in my cheeks. "No, I just . . . nevermind. I'll figure it out. This room is private?"

"Very."

"Accessed by whom?"

"By myself, or the library."

"You can be certain?"

"Absolutely certain."

"Is this the only copy of the book?"

At that question, which she clearly hadn't anticipated, she hesitated. Her eyes cast low, to the side, in a stretch of silence that I allowed to ride, even though I didn't understand it. Her attention shifted back to me.

"No."

"Where are the others?"

"I'm not sure, and neither is the library."

"If a witch came here to read it, would you, or the library," I hastily added, "remember?"

Another pause.

"Yes, but only within a specific timeframe. It would have to be in the last year or so. Even then, details may be sparse. Names are only known by the library if given by the witch or someone with the witch, while in attendance of the building. The library doesn't just *know* who enters."

I tucked that information away for later.

"Could you ask?"

"I already have."

"Does it remember?"

"No."

My focus returned to the yellowing pages of the book, and then the copy. The handwritten lines looked like mirrors, near-replicas, of the original, except the paper was white as bone and swept clean. My heart trembled, as if staring at those words gave me a glimpse into the future.

By all accounts, I should be celebrating. Should feel wildly ecstatic that I'd managed to get ahead of the sender, and find another reputable witch who agreed with my assessment of this situation.

Yet, all I felt was dread.

A *game*.

I wasn't sure that I wanted to stand in this position, to be the one responsible for the lives of others. Not just *others*, but Scarlett. The High Priestess and a personal mother figure. A woman who had been present through the worst moments of my life.

But I swallowed that fear, shoving it down. These were the

moments Grandfather warned me about. When I realized that this life was a choice. At one point, both Papa and Merrick made similar choices, perhaps repeatedly. They decided to become the person that saved, not the person that stepped aside.

Filled with fresh resolve, I faced Caroline.

"Thank you."

She blinked, but lacked her fox-like suspicion. "Do you have everything you need?"

From what I could ascertain, Caroline had given me all the help she could. She acted as if it was grudging assistance, but she'd stayed without complaint. A highly valuable favor is what she offered. Somehow, along this path, I'd have to accrue many such favors. To remember that no one, not even the Brotherhood, acted alone. I'd be a fool to expect the Sisterhood to prove itself alone, too.

Perhaps the wisest thing that the leader of the Sisterhood could do was *this*.

Alliances.

Friendship.

"I have everything I need, yes. Thank you, Caroline. Is there any favor that I can offer you in return?"

Her lips parted, the only indication that I'd taken her by surprise. She shook her head. A quick back-and-forth, barely more than a nudge.

"Then keep the offer," I said. "I'll return anytime you need it, and help until what you've asked for is complete."

With that promise ringing in the air, Caroline strode out the door, sending me one last quizzical look before fading into darker hallways. In her absence, will-o-wisps winged into the room and cluttered in a teeming ball around the table.

I doubled down to work.

Chapter Eighteen

The next day, I woke up to the familiar hum of Letum Wood soughing through my mind. For several moments, I basked in the symphony, letting it pull me from dreams. As wakefulness arrived, reminders of the game that Caroline discovered soared into my mind, rousing the still tired corners. Late last night, I'd managed to finish reading the original game structure and the comparisons, which left me open to puzzle out the parallels.

Ellie Victoriann and Marie Hazel were the characters.

Obvious.

The quest? Ellie's search for the stars, perhaps. Or was it something else? I couldn't say it was entirely clear, but the other games in the book were sometimes equally opaque. The blunt ending which established the next steps of the game involved Marie Hazel's death, certainly.

Or did it?

Maybe I missed something. Caroline mentioned that dice, board games, and cards entered the storyboard next. At least, historically. How would *that* apply? Would we receive a deck of cards next, or a bag filled with die?

The gentle cadence of my thoughts untangled yet stranger dreams of sand and fire and library walls. Waving branches across the ceiling caught my attention as I opened my eyes. I blinked away the night, listening to the cadence of the trees as it slowed to a near-syrupy song.

She belongs to us.

We belong to her.

The joy returns.

My heart seized. "What did you say?" I whispered.

The joy returns.

I pushed upright to find a familiar, broad-shouldered figure striding through the open door. Merrick paused, emerald eyes locked on me. A steady assessment confirmed no obvious wounds. No bruises on his face. Normal Merrick, despite a thicker beard, tired eyes.

"B," he breathed.

I closed the distance between us with swift steps, slamming a hard kiss to his lips before he drew another breath. Relief made me weak-kneed, followed by a quick flow of disbelief. He gripped me close. Infusing all my internal tempest into each muscle, I locked my arms around his neck and held on.

Too long passed before he whispered, "Are you all right?"

"Yes. Fine. You?"

"The same."

He squeezed the dregs of breath from the bottom of my lungs. I pulled away. My hand pressed to his cheek in studious regard. No scars. My thumb ran along a wrinkle on his temple.

"How long are you here for?"

"Hopefully awhile. I have no information that should pull us back immediately, but I won't promise."

He nuzzled my neck. His breath was a warm caress. I had to swallow the pocket of tears forming in my throat. Had Mama experienced this each time? Papa rarely caught us by surprise, but not never. The ups and downs of quiet anticipation, of wondering, of never knowing, exacted a steep cost.

"B?"

"Hmm?"

He pulled away, peering into my eyes. "I'm sorry about all of this. Leaving so fast and returning unexpectedly and . . . it's not easy. I—"

Hushing him with a finger to his lips, I said, "Any minute with you is worth the hours without."

Recalled from deepest depths, the words had a haunting flavor. Mama always said it to Papa, when he returned full of apologies or they stayed up late, talking into the night, with me sleeping at the foot of their bed.

Merrick closed his eyes, pressed our foreheads together.

"I love you."

I answered him with my fingers in his hair and my lips on his. He lifted me and carried me to the table, where I perched on the edge and kissed him thoroughly. His stomach growled, and he laughed against my lips.

"Are you trying to tell me something?" I asked.

"I'm starving."

"You're always hungry."

"That's true. Let's get some food together, little troublemaker."

Finishing off a final kiss, I said, "Sounds delicious."

"I'll change first, if you don't mind. I came the moment Rognvald released me. I have to return to the Gatehouse tomorrow morning, but I have the rest of today."

After breakfast, we tangled on a branch, legs knotted, bodies close. His knees tilted up, and I sat in between, my back to his chest, and recounted all the letters Scarlett had received. Finally, I exhaled free all the words I had jammed up inside. Without the pressure, I found it easy to tell him about each letter, the uncertainty, the chat with Rognvald.

Everything.

How could it be so easy now, but not then?

His breath caressed the shell of my ear as he ran his fingers over my hair, tucking it behind my ear, then spiraling it around the lobe. The gentle, frequent touch sank deep into my skin. I relished it.

This.

This *was* worth it.

Enjoying the quiet afternoon as sunshine tracked through the day brought a special rush of relief and love. Without Merrick leaving, we never would have had these returns. *Mama,* I thought. *Is this what made it powerful?*

I turned, head tilted to better see him. "Can you tell me anything about the mission?"

He shook his head, a wariness in his eyes. I forced myself to smile.

"It's all right."

He splayed a hand over my cheek. "Thank you. I know it's not easy. It's . . ." He trailed away, as if he dropped the thought, and then picked it back up. "It's harder than I thought. The not telling."

I nodded, but fell into silence. Sometimes, I wondered if navigating this life was a simple matter of leaning into the moments we had, instead of thinking about the ones we didn't.

The trees stirred, their long boughs drifting back and forth with gentle sighs.

Not alone.

She comes.

Their voices stirred me from our deep musings. I shot to my feet, summoned Viveet to my hand, and crouched before a silhouette appeared at my door. Leda called out, "Bianca?" as I recognized her figure.

Her breathless question sent a bolt of panic through the air. Merrick stood up behind me as I sheathed Viveet.

"What's wrong?" I asked.

"Scarlett needs you! Another letter has arrived. I've been trying to get you through the magic, but you didn't respond."

"I didn't hear."

"You must have blocked me."

"Can I?"

"I guess?" she cried. "I don't know. I'm sorry to just show up. I didn't know—"

"It's fine. Don't worry about it. Are you sure? It's too soon for another letter. It would be out of pattern."

Helpless, she shrugged. I summoned the Volare, slung it over my shoulder, and pressed a kiss to Merrick's lips. "Sorry." I grimaced. "I guess it's my turn to leave unexpectedly this time."

His touch lingered on my chin as he gave me a wry smile. "Go, Sisterhood. You're needed. I'll see you sometime soon."

Chapter Nineteen

Instead of the office, Leda took me to Scarlett's personal apartment. The High Priestess wore a regular dress, arms folded tight over her chest. Her hair, instead of its usual bun, lay in a braid down her back. The effect softened her face, removing years. Her eyes and cheeks were too sunken for vitality, however. She appeared lackluster and bereft, despite the brilliant sunshine streaming through pristine window panes.

Her butler, a woman named Marjorie, puttered around straightening books, fixing wrinkled rugs, and checking a pot of tea at the fire, where Scarlett stood near the fireplace. She didn't speak as I entered at Leda's side, simply handed me a bulging envelope that contained a scroll. I accepted it.

"When?" I asked.

"Ten minutes ago."

"Here?"

She nodded. "I came to eat lunch in the quiet. Sometimes, it helps if I have a break from the office."

Too much time had passed for me to track any sort of spell, then. I regarded the envelope, which was no different than the others.

"How was it delivered?"

"A knock on the door. Marjorie answered it, said the envelope hovered in the air. I haven't read it yet," Scarlett added, a bit weakly.

I tore through the envelope and flipped open the scroll to find exactly what I expected. Two sentences that established the game play in perfect mimicry of the games I found the night before.

The purpose of this game is to establish whether Ellie Victoriann saves Marie Hazel's life, or lets her die. Game play will commence upon Gamemaster's indication.

At the bottom, no signature.

Leda frowned as she peered over my shoulder. "What is this?"

With a spell, I summoned the other letters. Leda passed the scroll to Scarlett, who skimmed, then re-read. Her white-knuckled fingers clutched more tightly with every passing second.

"That's it?" Scarlett whispered.

"It's a game."

With a spell, I flattened all five curled scrolls so they lay in order on the table, such a perfect recreation of the games in the book that it made my stomach hurt.

Scarlett, clutching the back of her divan, rasped a quiet, "Pardon?"

"I have some updates to give you. First, summon Rognvald. I'll explain it all together. Right now, I want to check outside. Of greater importance is *how* the witch managed to deliver the letter at your apartment."

Leda nodded, eyelashes fluttering as she attempted to rein in her surprise. "Y-yes. Fine. Of course."

Scarlett gave a weak nod. Following Marjorie's quiet insistence, she sat on the divan and reached for a ready tea cup. I issued an invisibility spell, slid onto Scarlett's balcony through an open window, and into the sweltering summer heat. From there, I transported to the only staircase that led to the High Priestess' residence from Chatham Castle proper, which the witch had to take if they personally delivered the message.

I landed on the desired staircase, still invisible. Daytime enlivened the ambience farther below. Maids, fireboys, tired Assistants keeping up with their workload to impress Council Members. Secretaries bustled around, attempting to finish their work before a long weekend.

The residence part of the castle was several stories higher, and far calmer. I scurried up the stairs, my heartbeat steady, the rhythm a flow that synced with all my muscles. When I focused on sensing magic, I realized that I had already opened my awareness to it. The skill became more second nature every day.

Leda, simmering with curiosity, asked, *Why did you go out the window?*

Because they might be expecting me in the hall.

Oh.

At the mid-level landing of a staircase not far from Scarlett's apartment, I paused. Two Guardians should stand on either side of the staircase. One watched the side ascending, the other watched the descending. No snores, sniggers, or sounds of distraction.

I crept across a worn carpet padding the stone landing. It ended as the stairs began. If the Guardians were worth their salt, they'd stop me any moment now. They should be sensing magical use near the Royal Residence hall.

I made it all the way up the staircase to find both Guardians on the floor, sprawled wide. My heart leaped into my throat as I crouched next to the closest one. Warm breaths caressed the back of my hand. I closely watched the other one, breathing light and steady. A bruise bubbled near his temple. The other wasn't visibly maimed. Hit from behind, perhaps? With a spell?

Send for Talmund, please, I told Leda. *Two Guardians have been knocked out at the main entrance to the Royal Residence hall.*

We need replacements, and for them to search the castle for a witch with a purple cloak, a flower, or a top hat with an orange ribbon. If none of those, a male witch, broad shoulders, dark hair, or anyone suspicious.

Leda didn't miss a beat.

I'm on it.

Certain they were fine, and that my time window winnowed with every passing heartbeat, I slipped invisibly away from the staircase. Shocking that no one else had found them yet, really.

No magic remained. No spells, certainly not well known ones. I passed several spots that reached out to me like a warm friend. Magical hotspots that revealed nothing. My invisible fingers slipped along the wall, discovering only chinks in the stone. Magical signatures were low, muted.

I prowled along the corridor, already certain of the truth. The sender was gone. Long gone. Having the Guardians study the castle was mere procedure at this point. When my personal assessment of each room finished, I returned to the growing commotion around the stairs.

Guardians swarmed the area, surrounding the two on the ground. One Captain, and one quietly livid Head of Guardians, Talmund. Last year, Talmund wasn't sure what he thought of me, the former High Priest's daughter. I'd brought an amulet into the Central Network, befriended a demigod, and then disappeared to the lands of the gods. Talmund had a lot of reasons not to trust me, yet, he rallied for the sake of the Central Network.

Talmund could handle a lot of uncertainty, but that didn't make him wholly eager to see me. Considering all the drama stirred up by myself and Papa, I couldn't say that I blamed him.

An Apothecary ran a burning stick around the nose of the closest fallen Guardian, whose fingers began to twitch. His right arm jerked as he roused from whatever blunt-force trauma the blow to the head had caused.

Talmund, hands on his hips, glanced around. His eyes skipped right over me as I approached. What a lovely incantation this invisibility spell turned out to be. Like Grandfather, I'd have to keep a tight hold on it. The more known a spell became, the less stealthy I could be with it. Usage bred familiarity, and a witch familiar with my arsenal of spells might detect me.

"Bianca," Talmund barked. "Where are you?"

I removed the magic.

"Here."

He stared at me, obviously surprised. With resignation, he motioned down the hall. "When I'm assured my Guardians are well, will you explain?"

"Gladly."

Talmund followed me into Scarlett's apartment. Rognvald awaited, close to where Leda and Scarlett stood near the hearth. A cluster of books and accumulating messages scattered the mantelpiece. Leda withdrew the recent arrivals free from the air and spelled them away, probably to Underassistants and Hiddleston. The lightest whiff of cumin and warm spices drifted around the room every time Scarlett shifted her weight.

"Your Highness." Talmund bowed. "My Captain is at the scene, handling the changing of the Guard, and gathering more information. Since we just arrived, and Miss Monroe has an idea of what's happening, I'll defer any further information from me and say only that the situation is being handled."

Scarlett nodded. "Thank you, Talmund. I apologize for what's happened, and appreciate your swift response."

They turned to me.

Explaining the letters, the discovery with Caroline, and today's latest arrival required fifteen minutes. Talmund didn't need specifics, only a general picture. The summation must have been sufficient, without being too barren, because he had only a few questions that I quickly cleared up.

"No sign of anyone in the halls," I said to Scarlett. Leda stood behind her left shoulder, hands folded demurely in front of her, a mask of concentration in place. A quill floating to her left jotted swiftly onto a parchment so long it reached the floor. Goddess bless Leda and her notes.

"You know they're male?" Rognvald asked.

"I've chased him twice now. I'm positive, based on general appearance. There's . . . something familiar about the witch, but I haven't been able to peg what. Light transformative magic has been present whenever I'm with him," I added, before he could ask, "but nothing extensive enough to hide a gender."

Rognvald absorbed that with a nod.

Talmund's gaze darted between Scarlett and myself. Since the Battle for Letum Wood, Scarlett and I had been a known unit amongst many witches. The Brotherhood and most Captains of the Guard understood that I worked for Scarlett's direct and general welfare. Until now, a situation this large and challenging hadn't arisen to affirm it.

The time had come to *own* this. Make it mine. Hold the Sisterhood high, and myself with it. I would expect them to take me as seriously as I took it myself.

That thought locked my gaze onto Talmund. Rognvald, I trusted. The Brotherhood had my back, but the Guardians were still a wildcard. That thought held my breath steady as I waited for Talmund to react, instead of reacting myself. I'd invited him to my party, and he had to act accordingly.

Talmund must have sensed something of the rising steel in my purpose, because he gave the barest nod.

"Well," he said, as if piecing together an idea of what to do next, "I suppose, having come into this at a later stage, the Guardians will ask for what you need?"

The words weren't strangled, but they clearly weren't certain. I couldn't decide whether the breach from procedure was the hardest for Talmund, or the potential for the Council being upset with him later. For all Scarlett's freedom to employ me, that didn't make the Sisterhood a bonafide entity.

Talmund's response was a statement, more to Scarlett than myself, of trust. I saw it in the glance that they exchanged, which would have been unreadable if I didn't know Scarlett so well. To Talmund, I nodded.

I took that win.

I brought it close.

I turned it into fire.

"Thanks to Caroline's help, I have a good idea what will come next," I said, grateful to speak directly to Scarlett. "That means my focus is free to figure out who this witch is, which is my next focus. I already have ideas on how to do that, but what I need most is reassurance that Guardians are patrolling the castle and aware of the active threat. I'd like a Guardian within your office door when you're there, and home when you're here."

"You have it," Talmund promised.

Leda's eyes flickered with a smile. The switch from *potential leader of this mission* to *leader of this mission* hadn't gone unnoticed. The quill wrote faster.

Scarlett's arms relaxed by her sides as she gazed on me with a sense of relief. Had Talmund not been present, I had a feeling she would have muttered, *Finally*, and asked me what took so long.

While Marjorie settled Scarlett and Talmund made himself scarce, I followed Leda to her personal room down the hall. Scarlett moved Leda's living quarters closer a few months back to spare her from walking all over Chatham Castle just to get to work.

Paperwork and books cluttered Leda's tidy space. She kept it clean, but not neat. She never took the time to straighten things, so the apartment was efficient instead of pristine.

Exhaustion tightened Leda's features as she firmly closed her door and sent a silencing incantation around it. Warmth stirred in the room, wallowing from a lack of movement. Leda waved to a window, opening it to allow fresh air skidding inside.

She stared at me, luminous in the ambient daylight.

"You were impressive just now."

As the first compliment she'd given in regards to my handling of the Sisterhood, I had to repress the urge to ask her to note it on her parchment.

"Thanks."

"When did you come into such ownership? You've always wanted the Sisterhood, but never stepped into it like this."

"It's recent."

Head tilted, she queried, "What motivated it?"

A dozen reasons, but I didn't know how to voice any of them. Like a rainbow, so many hues, variants, influences contributed. A little Merrick, a little desire, a little releasing a weight of fear.

"Growth," I said.

She hummed.

Her hair slipped free of its bun, spreading wide across her shoulders. For a flash, I saw hints of her younger sister, Bronwyn, in her pert nose and elegant profile. If her hair had been darker, she'd be a perfect match.

"Thank you," she said. "Having you respond so quickly, and with ideas of what to do . . . it was . . . comforting."

"I'm glad."

After a pause filled with a silence neither of us knew how to address, I asked the question that haunted me.

"Do you think we can do this? The Sisterhood, I mean."

She regarded me with a vague sense of surprise, as if I'd captured her thought. With growing confidence, she replied, "If you had asked me any other time but today, I would have said I wasn't sure. But after what you just did, and the way you commanded the situation? I can say yes. I think we, the Sisterhood, have a shot at finding this witch."

Chapter Twenty

That evening, Merrick cast me a sidelong glance.

"Hiddleston invited us to his apartment?" he asked, incredulous. The curl of his fingers around mine, the brush of his knuckles against my hip, sent quiet thrills all the way through me.

"Yes. Leda and I want your opinion on the latest development with these letters, and Hiddleston wanted to do a dinner together. Hence," I spread my hands, "Hiddleston's invitation."

"And Hiddleston is providing dinner?" Merrick clarified.

"Yes."

We turned a corner, encountering no one down a stone hall illuminated by the occasional beam of light falling through open doors. Windows suffused empty rooms, bringing life to the otherwise still corridor.

"Have you ever been in his apartment?" he asked.

"No, but you might want to get used to him. More friendly than passing acquaintances, anyway."

"Why?"

"Because," I sang, enjoying myself immensely. "I caught Leda and Hiddleston holding hands the other day."

His jaw dropped.

I pointed a finger into his chest. "Not. A. Word. She'd slice me open over a fire if she knew I told you."

Lips sealed, he agreed with a quick nod. Slowing our momentum, I stopped at a familiar door with a black H scrawled near the top left corner, and rapped. The door swung open.

"Welcome," Hiddleston rumbled, an arm spread open in invitation. His eyes slid to Merrick and he nodded with an extra-wide smile. "Glad to have you back safely, Protector. It's been a very long time."

Merrick accepted Hiddleston's arm clasp with a returning grin, a hand lingering on the small of my back as he ushered me inside. Having Merrick with me made everything a little brighter, every step a little less fraught with social expectation.

Hiddleston's personal quarters were less impressive than Leda's, but far cozier. Instead of books and clutter, he maintained order and a leisurely energy. There was a blanket tossed across a well-loved, but not shabby, divan. Rugs to soften the cold stone floors. His bed had been made up, thick with a plush cover and plump pillows. The armoire was closed. Everything was tidy, in its place, but lacked utilitarian machismo.

He gestured us to a table in the middle of his living space, where Leda already sat. Four chairs clustered around the waist-high rectangle. It provided enough area to lay out the letters and information, but not a lot. Merrick's eyes roved each wall with curiosity and bemusement.

"Thank you," I said to Hiddleston, my hands on the back of a chair. Merrick stood next to me. "I'm grateful for dinner and a chance to talk this out."

Hiddleston, normally a solemn witch, gave me a smile.

"It's my pleasure."

Leda appeared far more comfortable in his apartment than I expected. I still hadn't summoned the courage to ask her about their obvious hand holding the other day, and held a smidge of suspicion that she might hold the communication magic at large in retribution if I pressed her.

She passed her hand over her personal copies of the five letters on the table.

"Shall we proceed?"

"First, Merrick needs to read them. I've briefed him, but he hasn't had a chance to read them himself." I invited Merrick with a tilt of my head. "Leda and I have already scoured these until our eyes might bleed."

He complied with little more than a shuffling step forward and a curious gaze. A deep-seated relief swelled in my stomach knowing he'd clap his eyes on them. While Merrick read, Leda sent me a pointed glance and spoke into my mind.

Does Merrick know?

She didn't need to clarify her question for me to understand what she meant. *He doesn't know that you supplanted the Brotherhood magic,* I replied, *no. I'll let you tell him.*

Merrick stiffened, drawing my gaze. His spine had gone stick-straight, hand trembling slightly as he read the second letter. He glanced at me. A subtle shift of his brow motioned to the letter, then me, as if to ask, *Are you serious?*

I set my lips in grim reply.

A hint of a smile appeared at the corners of Leda's mouth, then vanished. *I admit,* she said, *that speaking without speaking is a wonderful thing. I've considered bringing Scarlett into this magic as well. What do you think?*

I blinked, startled by the idea. Why hadn't I thought of it before? *The Brotherhood doesn't do it,* I replied.

Her scathing response was all the reprimand required. *The Brotherhood doesn't live in a treehouse, either. Are you going to move?*

Nevermind, I hastily said. *Not a great reason, you're right. We should pull her in, as should they. I can't imagine why they haven't.*

Me either, she admitted. *The magic system is rather different than you might think.* A gleam of wickedness and delight appeared. *It's far more usable than the Brotherhood might know. If I understand their usage correctly, then what they do with the magic is a mere pebble against a rockslide.*

Could we pull Scarlett into it without her having to be present in the magic all the time? She doesn't need the distraction of chatter.

Absolutely. You blocked me out the other day, remember?

I'm still not sure how.

I am. I'll teach you later. Plus, it would be easy to make Scarlett part of it.

Then why haven't you?

Exasperation replaced her profound belief in her own brilliance. *Believe it or not,* she sniped, *we are in this together. Just because I was able to figure out the magic system, and wisely believe that I should be the originator of it, doesn't mean I think I run the Sisterhood. Both of us are aware, I hope, that you are the face and soul of this organization. If you agree, then we will proceed to bring Scarlett in, accessible only when she desires, and not to common chatter.*

We are agreed.

Hiddleston waited, hands behind his back, eyes downcast but not in the paths. Merrick straightened away from the table, chewing on the inside of his cheek. Our conversation ended as I turned to him with a quietly expectant question on my face.

He met my gaze, troubled. "Well, it's definitely a threat against both you and Scarlett, but it's fair to say you hold the majority of risk."

"I agree."

Merrick tapped the top of the fourth and fifth letters. "I don't like the game aspect."

"Why?"

"It's a risk."

"Everything is a risk!"

"No, the *game* aspect." The more he spoke, the harder an edge his voice adopted. "He's in control, and calling the shots. I don't like that."

"He can establish whatever game he wants," I said blithely. "It doesn't mean I'm going to play."

Merrick shrugged, and I saw a world of concern behind the gesture.

Copies of the book Caroline gifted me floated to Hiddleston, Leda, and Merrick as I sent them with a spell. In each, I'd notated disparities or differences from the original story structure, making it easier to study each side-by-side.

"Now that Merrick has finished reading, I'll bring us to my first point of discussion," I said. "A comparison of the original story against the letters. I'm wondering if we can find a pattern, or a clue, in the changes."

Leda sucked in a breath through her nose, hiding a morbid sense of excitement. Her fingers twiddled, eager to study as she leaned closer to the first page. Hiddleston read over her shoulder. Merrick studied with a deepening frown.

While they skimmed, I explained.

"The story and the letters remain largely the same line by line, except for minor details. A few of them are repetitive."

"Oh?"

With the tip of my finger, I tapped on the bright blue ink that highlighted changes.

"The main character in the original story is a man named *Koda Bazool*. He can read minds instead of fly. He doesn't want to ascend through the sky to find the stars, but wants to plunge the depths of the mind. There is another character, who is the same as Marie Hazel. His name is Berislav Kaverin, and he wants the opposite. He wants to find the source of dreams, not plunge the mind."

Merrick's finger trailed along a sentence as he read from the original story, set against a part of the fourth letter.

Koda did not see the depths of midnight thoughts that

Berislav sought. Only the swirling, midnight depths and yawning mind. Only his own revenge. Only his own desire.

Set against the fourth letter, the two were clear matches except the original said *revenge* instead of ambition, and an additional sentence at the end.

Ellie Victoriann did not see Marie Hazel's stripped wings and gasping breaths. Only the plumbless stars and spawning heights. Only her own ambition. Only her own desire. They had advanced so far, they could not turn back.

Marie Hazel's heart stopped.

I pressed a hand to the fifth letter. "The establishment of game play is word-for-word the same to the original, except for names."

"Rhythm and syntax remains largely the same, except for general changes," Leda murmured, eyes zipping over the words. "Even basic phonology. The original story is rather consistent."

"He copied it," Hiddleston said.

Leda agreed with a *hmmmm*.

"Not entirely." I held up two fingers. "There are two words he didn't use from the original text. *Gray* and *revenge*. He removed those." I shrugged. "They were adjectives, so probably not very important. Regardless, the sender clearly wants us to figure out who he is. He brought himself face-to-face with me. He transported me to a specific village in the Eastern Network, which led to the discovery of this original story. He's placed puzzle pieces. I don't think the end point involves Scarlett. I think it involves *me*. Which is good news."

After a moment of thought, Hiddleston asked, "What is your plan to figure out his identity, Bianca?"

With a silent spell, I summoned my list of Scarlett's purported enemies.

"We're going down my list. Thoroughly. To start with, Leda and Scarlett are going to clear a few witches as not guilty."

Leda picked up the explanation.

"I am coordinating individual meetings with Council Members and Scarlett over the next two days. She's meeting with each Council Member for an unexpected monthly-walk through of their Coven. During that time, Scarlett will broach specific questions, targeted to suss out if any of them know about, or are, sending these messages."

Hiddleston frowned. "How will you know?"

An array of beads, organized into a bracelet, appeared in the air. Gems graced the front of the jewelry in a gaudy display. The middle one illuminated with interior lights if a witch told a lie in its presence.

"A truth charm."

Merrick tilted his head, chuckling. "Smart."

"Tension is low with Scarlett and the Council," Hiddleston added, regarding the charm as it hovered. "She takes their advice into consideration more than former leaders, so it's unlikely to be a Council Member."

"I agree, but I want to *know*."

"It shows thoroughness," Leda added. "When we present this work to the Council to jockey for Sisterhood funding, it will show we can see through even mundane tasks and security requirements."

"They won't like that you did it with subterfuge." Hiddleston clapped his palms together and shook his head. "Council Member Georgette will protest."

"Add it to the list of things about me that Georgette doesn't like," I said wryly.

"Preparation," Merrick purred, "is Highest Witch. I have ideas on security at Scarlett's office to be ready. Hiddleston," he added, "you're part of that."

"I'm willing."

Merrick motioned to Leda with a nod. "I have advice on approaching the Council Member meetings. You could gain real information from their responses, you just make the questions as innocuous as possible."

Leda smiled.

"I'm ready."

Hours later, Merrick twirled me to a stop in the mermaid garden, near the edge of Chatham Castle grounds. A distant, faint song rippled from a moving stream. Fish glimmered in the clear, moonlit waters. Blooms as large as my head bobbed in a quiet summer breeze, stirring the smell of honeysuckle.

Merrick broke the hallowed summer song, our fingers tightly threaded.

"B . . . about your plan."

Deliciously full from a delectable meal, which Hiddleston himself cooked over the fire and with much chuckling while I attempted to help, I turned to face Merrick. It had been a relief to set aside the letters for a while.

"Yes?"

Merrick tugged me to a stop, pulling me close. Our chests pressed together. He pushed a piece of hair out of my eyes. Moonlight highlighted his features, limning them with a glow. His thumb stroked along my cheek bone.

"It's weird," he whispered. "You're the one engaging in dangerous missions. Taking this on. While I see the methodology behind your plan and agree with it, I'm . . . worried about you."

"I know the feeling."

"Is this what it's like for you while I'm gone?"

Lips twitching with a held smile, I asked, "What?"

"The worry?"

"Probably."

"I trust you." He palmed my cheek, stretching his fingers into my hair. "I know you're capable and wise and brave, but . . . I'm concerned. I want you safe, B. But I also want you to be happy. It's a war between two things, because you'll never be happy if you're playing it safe."

My arms wrapped his waist, intoxicated by the balmy evening, speckled stars, and the melody of his words.

"I'll do everything I can to keep myself safe, Merrick. You know that. And I trust that you do the same thing on your missions."

His forehead pressed to mine. "I know you will, but I've seen circumstances when everything *isn't* enough. I don't want to live without you, B."

"You won't."

"This is harder than I thought," he admitted, his voice stark. Hearing the same words I uttered to Papa drove me closer to Merrick, closing an open gap I didn't know existed.

He kissed me, slow and sweet, with a yearning I couldn't fix. We both sought the illusion of control. The idea that we could be exactly who we wanted *and* cheat death. After the many battles we'd already waged, such was a foolhardy hope. Clinging to dreams yielded few results, but neither would I let them go.

"I trust you," he whispered, "but please be careful."

"Same to you, Protector."

"You know I will."

With a sly grin, I said, "I need to speak to your sister about a different charm—one I want to put on Scarlett. Any chance you could jaunt north with me tomorrow afternoon? I'd love to see your mother, too."

"That sounds doable. I only have a few obligations in the morning, but the rest of the day is clear. Even if your jaunt involves my annoying little sister."

I kissed him as confirmation.

Life with a Protector meant I couldn't be dependent on Merrick in the traditional ways. The temptation to wind my day and my fate into Merrick's wouldn't be realistic at certain times. At others, we could intertwine our busy schedules with ritualistic ease. Certainty would be the novelty, not the rule.

Understanding that in a new light, I tightened my grip on him. How powerful that truth made this moment, and all the others, in which I had him. The pain of constant change might be the only steady thing we ever faced as a couple.

But oh, how worth it.

Merrick kept me tight to his chest while he stared up at the moon, soaking in the quiet majesty of the night. His arms draped around me, so I pressed my ear to his chest and relished the steady plod of his heart.

Chapter Twenty-One

Jacqueline sprawled her hands wide, gesturing to a brilliant, sparkling, chiffon-laden dress of cream and white. The dazzling array of fabric that I could barely comprehend had stunned me into silence.

"What do you think?" she cried.

"It's . . . lovely."

She squealed, fists clenched. "I know! I'm so proud of it."

"Who is it for?"

She trilled a raspberry. "It's my first handfasting gown as a hired designer outside of Balmberg Castle. A witch from the other side of the Network hired me. Stunning, isn't it?"

"It is stunning, Jacqueline."

The rich colors swirled in layers of silk as the dress elevated from Jacqueline's bed, swung to a mannequin off to the side, and slipped down the standing wooden structure like a hand into a glove. Still borne on a spell, it adjusted to the mannequin until it stood in a pool of sunlight.

Merrick's lower register drifted up from where he stood below, discussing something with his mother, Kalli, and her second husband, Drogo. Wildflowers bobbed in the field outside the window beyond. Hints of fall already graced these northern alpine slopes.

Jacqueline lowered to the edge of a quilt-covered bed. "It will be a lovely bridal gown," she said with a happy trill. "Thanks for looking. I've been stuck in this attic and wanted to share it with someone!"

Jacqueline had overtaken Kalli's attic with fabric, buttons, string, scissors, and more. Fluff burdened the air, swirling with sunshine and dust motes as Jaqueline leaned back on her palms and studied me.

"So," she said with a tone too level to be anything but problematic, "when will *you* need a handfasting gown?"

I paused, my hand lingering near the lowering sash of the gown.

"Sorry?"

Jacqueline smiled with all the power of a feral cat. "Are you going to let me sew your handfasting gown, too?"

My heart beat a thready staccato in my chest. Jikes, what a question! I bobbled for a reply, struck dumb, before Jacqueline bounced to her feet. She studied me sidelong while shuffling the fabric at the back of the dress. The mannequin spun to her silent will.

"You are going to handfast Merrick, aren't you?"

The coy smile was dramatically overdone. Jacqueline bore no ill will, but she was a little sister. Had Merrick put her up to this? It might be his attempt to explore how I felt about handfasting. I immediately banished the thought. Merrick would just ask.

"Yes, I'm going to handfast him," I said firmly, "but not yet."

Jacqueline twirled a finger around her ribbon. "When do you think this happy day will occur?"

My lips twitched.

I stared at her.

Hard.

She cleared her throat, coy smile dropping, and lowered her

gaze. "Sorry," she mumbled and flopped onto the bed with all the veracity of youth. We weren't that far apart in age, but somewhere in the battles, the grief, the fear, I'd aged beyond my peers.

Had I been like this, once?

"I just . . . I just want to see something happy!"

Tears collected on Jacqueline's lashes. Last year, Jacqueline had been a seamstress for the controlling Northern Network High Priestess Geralyn. Jacqueline had spied on Geralyn and passed information to the Patriot, a hidden witch that fought for the good of the Network against wicked Geralyn's orders.

The peppy, ecstatic, chattering Jacqueline once hid a far more calm, strategic young woman emerging into life. She confessed an adoration of potions, instead of fabric, and a deep, simmering love-hate relationship with a trollhunter named Finan. Finan had proven to be as slippery as water. He regaled his love for her, then disappeared. To see this unhappy side of her was . . . unsettling.

Her plea for a happy love story hid the truth. Quietly, I settled next to her, hands in my lap. We regarded the wall for a few heartbeats before I asked, "How is Finan?"

Welling tears splashed down her cheeks. She shook her head. I put an arm around her, pulled her close. She tilted her head to mine and cried. The quick transition from bright, gossip-seeking youth to the depths of heartbroken despair reminded me of snapping fingers. My compassion rose.

Oh, how well I knew these depths.

"Finan returned," she whispered.

Her admittance made my chest tight. Finan and I met once, and very briefly. He stopped by my cottage to check on Jacqueline. By his request, I hadn't told Jacquie he'd come by. A week later she'd destroyed an ankle bracelet he'd given her, complete with a charm that allowed him to find her whenever he wanted.

She hadn't spoken his name to me since.

"When did you see him?" I asked.

"A week ago."

"How did it happen?"

She shook her head, pale. When her false cheer wiped away, the vestiges of the real Jacqueline remained. The fact that she continued to work as a seamstress, though she'd once believed potions her true love, made sense. She was floundering.

"Pure accident," she rasped. "It didn't go well. He showed up at the castle to report to High Priestess Nadira about a troll problem in the northeast mountains, and I wasn't at all prepared. He walked in and I dropped a bowl of food and couldn't pull my brain together. He saw me as he passed through. He might have doubled back to find me, but I left as fast as I could."

My eyes closed. How awful. To be taken by surprise, without any indication, after so long apart.

Her fists clenched. "I hate him," she whispered with a passion that stemmed from simmering love. "I *hate* him."

"Have you seen him since the initial time?"

She fluttered a hand around us, sniffling. "I worried he'd find me at the castle, so I hid in Mother's attic."

Well, that explained the mess, the dress, and the giddy desire for something happy.

"He won't come here?"

She shook her head. "No. He won't face Mother after what he did. Telling me he loved me, then disappearing. He thinks too much of Mother to break her heart. Unlike mine," she added as a bitter aside.

"I'm so sorry, Jacquie."

Helpless, she looked at me through teary eyes. "I thought I was past it, you know? I really thought . . ."

"You're probably farther past it than you think, but right now it's fresh. He's forced you to reckon with something you tried to move past."

She conjured a handkerchief, daubing at her cheeks, as Merrick and Kalli's voices slid into earshot again. Heavy boots tread on the ladder as he called up, "B?"

"Yes?"

"Are you coming down, or plan to stay up there?"

Panicked, Jacqueline swiped at her face. As I issued a spell to clean up the blotchy cheeks and bloodshot eyes, I called down, "We're coming! Jacqueline is showing me a lovely dress. Unless you'd like to see this lace? The chiffon is exquisite!"

As expected, he hastily retreated. She smiled her gratitude, squeezing my hand.

"There's better out there, Jacquie. Let Finan go."

Jacqueline nodded.

"Do you mind if I ask you a different question about Finan?" I inquired.

"No."

"Remember that charm bracelet Finan gave you? The one you wore on your ankle, that he was able to track you with?"

"Yes?"

"Any chance you know where he got it?"

Her gaze tapered into slits. "No. Why do you ask?"

I clucked my tongue against the roof of my mouth. Jacqueline knowing where a witch like Finan obtained anything was a long shot. The man was part enigma, the way he handled trolls and other large problems in the mountains, yet moved like fog amongst his peers. How interesting that Finan should resurface right when I needed him.

"You say Finan has returned to Balmberg Castle?"

Far more warily, she nodded.

"Excellent, because it just so happens that he and I need to chat."

Finan was far easier to find than I expected.

When Merrick entered Balmberg to report to the Masters in person, I followed behind him under an invisibility spell. He wished me luck under his breath and turned for the Master's Tower. I peeled to the left, repeating his earlier directions under my breath.

Straight at the painting.

Down the stairs.

Through a long hallway with open windows reflecting the tumbling waterfall that splashed down the mountainside into which Balmberg was built.

His guidance led me to a dining hall every bit as busy as Chatham Castle, but without the smell of fresh, hot food. Balmberg's kitchens were buried far below. They cooked intermittently for Network dinners or luncheons. Witches brought their food to dine on at big, round tables, far less intimate than the varied options at Chatham Castle, but the cacophony was significantly less. I stood off to the side, watching.

For practice, I opened my senses. Detecting active magical systems in broad crowds was a hit-or-miss proposition. The attempts often overwhelmed me. To sense, think, deduce, and remain aware of myself and my environment required effort. Sometimes, chaos nullified my ability to listen or think hard enough. When I opened myself to sensing, other awareness broadened as well. Smell. Sound. Their intensity didn't change, but it felt steeper.

Today, the overwhelm was minimal, and so was the magic. Simple transformation spells mingled amongst an invisibility spell slinking along the far wall. Not to eavesdrop, if the constantly moving figure meant anything, but probably to escape. When a witch sitting at the table nearest that spell reached out, snatched the invisible signature, and yanked it down, my interest piqued.

The witch under the invisibility spell became visible. I closed my attention from sensing magic in order to direct it to the unfolding situation. A male, for sure. Nappy hair on top, cut close.

Blithe smile glazed with a little concern, and long, thick arms attached to broad shoulders.

Ah ha.

The witch in question.

Finan.

The woman glowered at him with intense, snapping eyes. He held up two hands, speaking fast, though I couldn't hear the words. I moseyed over, Finan's words becoming more audible. In the seconds it took me to carefully cross the space without bumping into a table or witch, he hadn't stopped speaking.

The female stood up, shoved him against the wall. She was a pretty witch, with stick straight hair, black eyes like umber pools, and an elegant dress. An Assistant, perhaps. Her clothes were too artistic to be a maid, and too businesslike for a seamstress.

"I'm sorry," Finan sputtered, what seemed like the tenth time based on her irritated eye roll. "It was never personal. I got busy!"

Thunderclouds built in her stare, and she closed the gap between them. He tried to shrink against the wall—comical, his sprawling shoulders pitted against her dainty features—but had nowhere to hide. As she readied to stand on her chair and shout at him face-to-face, I removed my magic.

Seeing me appear, Finan gasped. Slowly, the female turned to look at me over her shoulder. Her burning glare could have set me on fire.

"What," she ground out, "do you want?"

Though egotistical to hope that my name carried any power in a Network outside of my own, I invested in it. Papa's popularity, the Battle for Letum Wood, and Merrick's position at Balmberg Castle surely carried some weight.

"My name is Bianca Monroe."

A flicker passed through her. She didn't release her hold on Finan, but she did give me more attention. An appraising stare regarded me from head to toe. I had a feeling that if I hadn't given my name, she might have turned her wrath onto me.

"Go on."

Without looking at him, I tilted my head toward Finan. "I need to speak with him. Speak, only. I'd like to do that before you scratch his face into oblivion for whatever he's done. And probably deserves," I added, for Jacqueline's sake.

Finan growled.

I ignored him.

"After I finish," I continued, "you can have him. Or at least promise me that you won't harm him so much that he can't speak."

She glanced at him, then me. "Why would *you* want to speak to Finan?"

"Not for the same reason as you," I quipped, "I can promise that. He has information that I need."

The witch hesitated, clearly torn. Finally, after what felt like an impossible amount of time, she released him.

"Show your face again here," she growled to Finan, "and I will personally claw your eyes out. Do you hear me?"

Finan slipped away.

Before the slimy fish could go far, I shoved him through a doorway. We spilled into a hall. Grabbing the first door handle I could see, I flung it open to find a pantry. Without hesitating, he raced inside.

"If you leave," I growled, "I will find you. I invite you to transport away, try to disorient me, or try to hide. I. will. find. you."

The threat hit its intended mark. He held up one hand in surrender and shrank back, pressing his body against shelves lined with empty glass jars and dusty sacks of grain. A musty smell filled the air.

"You're welcome," I said next.

He scowled.

"What did you do to her?"

"The question is what she did to me," he retorted, straightening his shirt. Twist marks spiraled around where she'd gripped him. "Demmed trap she set up today. She knew I'd be here!"

"You weren't all that subtle."

"Trolls are easier than witches." His comment, probably meant to be lighthearted, came out far more grave than I felt he intended. His brow twisted together in question. "Why are *you* here?"

"Remember the charm you had on Jacqueline last year?"

The question changed his eyes, shifting them from curious to pained. He licked his lips, losing the impression within seconds.

"Why?"

"I need one."

He snorted. "Fat chance."

"I'll pay for it."

He hesitated. I gestured to his clothes. "You've lost weight. You're quite thin, a bit skeletal. You have three holes in the pants above your right knee," I pointed to each, then swung my hand to his other pant leg, "and one over your thigh. Both of your shoes are coming apart at the seams. It's warm out, but you're wearing a long sleeve shirt. I don't see any pack on you, though you might be staying in a room. I doubt it. You don't seem like the kind of witch that's comfortable in closed spaces."

His darting gaze, held breath, confirmed it. If possible, the panic in his glazed discomfort intensified.

"I daresay," I finished with a low drawl, "you could use some currency. Buy yourself some new clothes or a warm bath." I sniffed, grimaced. "You could use it."

"Look," he said. "I am not—"

"—my enemy. Correct, but you could be. I want that charm, and then I'll leave you alone. That's it."

He hesitated for far too long. With a growl, he held out a long palm. I noted scars, calluses, a few split nails. A bracelet appeared there. Braided leather, with several jewels inside. They had a muted sheen, like a cross between a gem and an opal, but no less lovely.

When I hovered a hand over it, a pulse, like a low-toned heartbeat, flowed against my palm.

"It's the last one. Assuming," he added with a touch of melodrama, "that Jacqueline destroyed the other?"

"Yes."

He affected a shrug that wasn't as careless as he probably wanted it to appear. "Then this is the final one."

"Who made it?"

"I won't say."

"Why not?"

"To protect them."

I frowned. "Are they dangerous?"

"No."

His lips closed around the word. He wouldn't say anymore, I could sense it. I hesitated, and asked, "How much?"

He flipped his hand over, dropped the bracelet into my hand.

"Free."

"But—"

"I can't charge you for it. It's part of the deal. But I can gift it to you. It's not much use to me, anyway. Hasn't been for awhile. I kept it because . . ." He swallowed. His eyes lowered so far the lashes almost touched. "Just take it."

Unable to help myself, I closed my fingers around the gift.

"Why can't you use it?"

"I don't have anyone I care about enough to track anymore."

I paused, letting that sink in.

"I owe you."

He shook his head. "No ties. If you want it to work, it has to be freely given, without debt. There's a vow that I took."

"Do I have to take the same vow?"

"No. Just tell me—"

He stopped again.

I could almost hear the words he didn't say.

Tell me about her.

He didn't ask. I could sense that he wouldn't. Nor would I tell him anything about Jacqueline. If he wasn't going to make it right, he deserved to live with questions.

Besides, Jacqueline had earned that moment to stand before him without agony or heartbreak. The woman in the dining hall might not know it, but there were worse places than rage. Finan had given me what I sought, and I had no reason to create an allegiance with him. Part of me wanted to.

"What incantation do I use?"

He repeated it for me. I said it three times, committing it to memory, and he nodded. "Put it on the witch you're tracking and say the incantation. If you're looking for that witch, open your hand and repeat the spell. A fog will appear above your palm, showing you where they are."

"Thank you." I transported the bracelet to the safety of my treehouse. "The offer of help stands with or without the bracelet, Finan."

A flicker of amusement rose and died as quickly. "Don't promise something you'll later regret."

I stepped back, and he seemed to breathe easier.

"I have a feeling I won't."

Chapter Twenty-Two

The next morning, Council Member Clare entered Scarlett's office with a steady gait, high chin, and sincere smile. Her auburn skirts flared with a lace trim that was as subdued as her close-cropped curls.

After Council Member Greyson left over a year ago in a flurry of drama and betrayal, Clare stepped into his place. She oversaw the Western Covens, a sprawling area noted for ranches and farmland. They grew the many crops that witches in Chatham and Ashleigh relied on.

As the final battle during the Battle for Letum Wood ramped up, the Council asked me to stand in as a distraction for the gods. A sacrifice, though they didn't word it that way, while Guardians moved into place. Clare had been one of the few against it.

Several Council Members retired after the gods invaded the forest. Halifax, Rafe, Rossana, and Massimo. The rest stayed on, creating a sense of balance between new and old. I would always remember Clare's frustration with the other Council Members who offered me up like a lamb to slaughter, but I did not know her well.

With obvious affection, tinged by professionalism, Scarlett

returned Clare's smile from behind her desk. The gentle glimmer of opalescent-like stones gleamed from her wrist.

"Welcome, Clare. It's always good to meet with you."

Leda grabbed the door handle.

All is well? I asked. Twenty minutes past, I'd made an ordeal out of walking into Scarlett's office, speaking with her and Leda about the meetings, and remaining within. Two minutes ago, I cast an unknown invisibility spell and strolled out. If anyone watched, they'd think I remained inside.

I'll be in touch, Leda replied. She stared right at my invisible form as she shut the door behind her, a truth charm glimmering from her wrist. She'd use it to perceive whether any of the current Council Members lied, thus indicating guilt around the letters.

In the meantime, I had somewhere else to be.

Animal life covered the Western Covens like a tapestry. Goats, sheep, barn cats, cattle, horses, and an innumerable plethora of other beasts populated the undulating fields that stretched across the horizon. The wide-open sky was liquid cerulean.

Hot straw and manure filled my nostrils as I strolled down a somewhat-familiar Main Street. A mercantile on the right hand side gave way to a livery, then an Apothecary, and finally a textiles store. Lush grass grew in between each building, where chickens and runner ducks scuttled.

To the east lurked the ranch where the sender first transported during the initial time I followed him. If this witch truly played a game, then *everything* must matter.

Even here.

No obvious clues presented themselves. I didn't see the witch meandering amongst the sparse inhabitants, nor anywhere near the village center, but I didn't expect him to pop up before my eyes either.

Like the creep of magic, my intuition rolled forward. If I accepted each letter, and the events around their receipt, as individual clues, I could paint a bigger picture. Or, at least, play the game. Here, with the Western Covens sun on my face and hints of fall rolling out of these wet hills, I imagined each clue coming together.

Western Covens.

Eastern Network.

A witch that knew Scarlett, and myself.

My breath arrested. Eyes widened. A flash of clarity sent a frozen chill into my blood like ice shards. There *was* a witch that fit all those instances. Every clue. But it would be impossible. He couldn't be here.

It couldn't be . . .

A prickling sensation along the back of my neck drew my attention. I spun on my heel. Before I saw the purple cloak and bright hat, I knew he'd be there. Felt the certainty of it all the way to my bones.

The sender awaited.

He stood in the middle of the deserted road, cloak flapping in a mild breeze. He held the obnoxious Gamemaster top hat off to the side. As I removed my invisibility spell, he spelled away the top hat and cloak.

We stared at each other.

The usual transformative magic was present, obscuring certainty around his features. I tried to peel back the facial structure, see if anything familiar lay there, but he called my attention with his voice.

"Follow me," he commanded.

"Why should I?"

He paused, not appearing altogether surprised by the question.

"It's the logical choice."

"It's really not."

"You're an intelligent witch, Bianca Monroe. That's why you arrived here protected by a rare magic system, hoping to find another clue. You always have been smart. I can see that you suspect who I am, which means that *logically* you have two options."

As he spoke, the transformation magic ebbed away. The facial structure widened. The hair lengthened. Eyes darkened. The sensation of magic withered away, leaving my senses wide open. My heart stuck in my throat. A familiar image formed.

But it couldn't be.

"Come with me and receive confirmation of your guess around my identity, which will enable you to play the game. Or you can stay and lose."

"What happens then?"

"By you," he continued, as if I hadn't asked, "I mean Scarlett. There are two witches I seek my revenge upon. Scarlett or you will come with me today. Let's make this far easier on Scarlett. Isn't that your job?"

My breath caught as the transformation spell finished ebbing. The cold draw of power in his eyes. The serious intent of his expression. The billowing suspicion, like a dark and thunderous plague.

Jikes.

I knew this witch.

Former Council Member Greyson.

He departed. Like a dancer drawn to a fiddle, his fingers played across these complex strings.

I followed.

The thread of his spell remained, allowing me to trail behind. I gripped the invisible strings with my mind, yanking them close so Greyson couldn't escape without me. In the midst of pressure and discomfort and pain, I comprehended only that this situation had to be impossible.

Utterly impossible.

This hellish grind lasted for what felt like minutes, pressing the bounds of my endurance. My heart threatened to burst out of my chest when I dropped onto hard sand.

My eyes flew open.

Greyson left no trace. No imprint of foot, nor magical signature. I glimpsed no hint of the white shirt and black pants he wore, nor his glacial gaze. Wherever he brought me, he promptly left.

I stood at the ocean's edge, alone.

A wide, churning sea, fluffed with rolling waves and giant sea eagles, lay ahead. The eagles soared, mammoth wings sprawled wide. Off to the side, close enough to cast the shadow in which I stood, was a structure I'd only heard about. Despite my lack of immediate experience, I knew it right away.

Carcere.

The magical prison occupied an isolated island off the Eastern Network's east shore. Built like a turret, the circular building spanned several stories. The prison occupied the top level, where Carcere's magic folded and hid space and time. Hundreds of cells and dozens of hallways and floors imprisoned an unknown number of criminal types. An entire world contained within a single floor.

Legends surrounded Carcere, which was little more than a magical mystery. Only the worst kind of witches came here. Witches like Council Member Greyson, traitor to the Central Network.

More than a year ago, Greyson attempted to join forces with a demigod, kill Scarlett, and take over leadership of the Central Network. At one point, I thought him an ally for the Sisterhood.

Then I returned from Alaysia to learn of his betrayal. Papa defeated the demigod that aligned with Greyson, and the Protectors caught Greyson in his own game. Papa, Highest Witch at the time, had Greyson shut away in Carcere.

A rush of cold trickled through my veins as I understood exactly why Greyson had led me here. A black hole gaped on the side of Carcere, blanketed over a spot on the enchanted top floor.

Right where the prisoners once lived.

Chapter Twenty-Three

The implications of what lay before me were too grisly to comprehend. Carcere breached?

When?

How?

Perhaps the most chilling question of all—by whom?

Standing before this destruction, the letters haunted me. In the second letter, Marie Hazel flew above the sea. Craved the sea. He mentioned even the *aquilas* that soared overhead at this very moment.

The game, indeed.

Where are you? Leda asked. *Georgette is wrapping up. We're four Council Members in and all of them have passed so far. Scarlett has an hour-long break after this and she wants to speak with you.*

Shaking my head forced me out of a wretched stupor. Questions abounded, locking my thoughts for another five seconds.

Bianca?

Sorry. I'm in the Eastern Network . . . I'll explain later.

When?

In ten minutes. Cancel all the other Council Member meetings and call for the Eastern Network High Priest immediately.

What?

Carcere has been breached.

A polite voice piped up from behind.

"Can I help you?"

I whipped around, hand on Viveet, with a hidden gasp. A squat man with a balding head, curious eyes, and a bland smile stood a few paces away, wrinkled hands folded behind his back. His manicured clothes were neat, pressed, clean. The sunspots and brown skin of a man that had been in the sun most of his life decorated his neck.

My fingers released Viveet, an action he noted with a quick glance. He smiled wider. "Is there something you require?" he asked.

"Yes. I mean, no. I just . . . I came to see—"

"Our tragedy?"

"Ah . . . yes. I'm sorry about . . ." I waved a hand at the entrance behind me.

His inquiry turned to despair.

"Me too."

A hint of the Eastern Network accent tilted his tone, but not deeply. It reminded me of something influenced by, but removed from, a mother tongue. The rush of panic that raced through me ebbed, leaving me embarrassed. Shock had stolen my better sense, not to mention the conversation with Leda.

"I know who you are," he said.

"You do?"

"Many do." With a tilt of his head, he motioned west. "We tracked what happened with the gods. Your face was in our newsbooks. Your pere, too."

"Can I ask your name?"

"Ricardo."

"It's good to meet you."

He closed his eyes, bowing his head slightly. His eyes fluttered open again. Before I could gesture to Carcere and ask when it happened, Ricardo spoke first. "You have unfinished business in Carcere?"

"Why do you ask that?"

"Why else would you come?"

A noise, much like a hum, reverberated through his throat. He tutted, peered past me into the fathoms of darkness. Carcere's shell pressed with a pulsing gravity, as if dark magic could breathe.

"A tragedy, that place," he continued.

"Oh?"

"So many witches, stuck in darkness. An army of misfits, criminals, innocents. Brilliant witches subdued unfairly, early in life. Their crime was intelligence. A brain that worked faster and harder than former High Priest's, which made them competition. Witches no one wanted. The screamers. The mad. The depressed. What a fix, eh? Crave an ending to pain, and end up in Carcere."

The sorrow in his voice spoke as much as his words.

"Do you work here?" I asked.

"I have served the Eastern Network all of my life."

His soulful gaze locked on the interior of Carcere with unnerving rigidity. There was a sincerity to his mourning that I wasn't sure how to address.

"Is anyone else here?"

He twisted at the hips, searching the empty island. "It has been just me for a long while."

"Where are the inmates?"

He fluttered a hand, doubling his sorrow. "Gone." The pronouncement came with no surprise, but I swallowed an uneasy rise from my stomach.

"When did this happen?"

"Many days ago." He set a more shrewd stare on me. "Are you planning on going inside? That would not be wise."

"Why not?"

"Layers and layers and layers."

"Of what?"

"Magic. Evil. Darkness." His nose wrinkled. "Filth. Sadness. Despair. Suppressed life. Enchanted items. Mirrors. Unknown."

My uneasiness doubled. "But the walls are broken. Doesn't that mean the magic inside is broken?"

He laughed, an old man giggling at the folly of youth.

"Can a behemoth like Carcere be destroyed in a single breach of its walls? No, my heart. No. That is not so." He shook a finger back and forth, lips wrinkling into a solemn smile. His eyes gleamed like quicksilver.

"Any idea who did it?"

Ricardo shrugged. "Does it matter?"

A great deal, I almost said, but returned his careless gesture.

"I suppose not. Unless you think Carcere could ever be repaired?"

He laughed outright, a deranged note in the hysteria. With each gusty breath, he shuffled a step to the side, edging out of reach. "The magic leaks into the sea, my heart! It returns to the goddess who originated it until all these stones hold nothing but pain and memory. Old bones. That's all Carcere will ever be."

A sense of horror overcame me as I stared at Carcere. The remnants of shattered minds and age-old prisoners existed somewhere up there. Moldering bodies. Forgotten souls. No, I did not want to enter, and I could see why he laughed at the mere suggestion. A seething sense of waiting breathed through the enchanted darkness.

I turned away.

It was just a building.

Nothing more.

Discomfort kept me company as Ricardo left, chuckling and wiping his eyes. It remained as I returned to Chatham Castle, accompanying me into Scarlett's office. Leda, without a word, stood and joined. Hiddleston remained in the hall, solemn as he closed the door behind us.

Scarlett waited, pale faced.

"Well?"

"It's Greyson."

Her eyelashes fluttered. For a full ten seconds, she didn't move. Thoughts swirled behind her eyes like smoke in a jar until she sank to the chair behind her desk, clutching the edge with one white-knuckled hand.

"The gods," she whispered.

Leda rushed forward, a second faster than me. Scarlett had already lowered to her chair by the time we made it to her side, but her color hadn't improved.

"Call for the Apothecary," I said.

Scarlett held up a hand, her tone firm, though weak. "No, please. I need only a moment to . . . think. Don't call anyone."

Leda sent a long suffering glance over the top of Scarlett's head. A silent riposte at me for saying it outloud. Of course Scarlett would protest, despite looking truly awful. After a few minutes of silence and Scarlett's deep, intentional breathing, she straightened. Her voice had more force.

"I'm fine."

To buy her time, I began my explanation. She nodded, scrambling notes, as I lay out each event. When I concluded, skimming through the details of my conversation with Ricardo, she'd fallen into a thousand-pace stare. Blinking free, she shook her head and leaned her forehead into her palm.

"The good gods, but I didn't see that coming."

Leda, irate, muttered, "The East isn't going to see us coming, either."

Scarlett sent her a quelling look. "After you have calmed yourself," she intoned with all the patience of a school mam, "you may write to Cristian and request his immediate attention. The meeting can be short if required, but must happen today."

Leda whispered, "Yes, Your Highness."

Scarlett's focus flickered to me. "You will also attend this meeting, Bianca."

"Of course."

"Thank you." She rubbed her hand over her eyes. "Leda?"

"Yes, Your Highness?"

"Please send for my afternoon tea tray. I'll need something to perk me up for this meeting."

"Right away."

Leda disappeared out the door. I rounded on Scarlett. "Scarlett, you don't look—"

"I'm fine."

"But—"

"I'm fine," she said more firmly. Her stony eyes bore into mine. "I would appreciate your trust, Bianca."

Protests surfaced, one after the other, driven by a swell of protectiveness. Questions littered my mental landscape. *Why are you so ill?* I longed to ask. *What aren't you telling me?*

Scarlett waited me out, the silence burdened, until I muttered, "I trust you, Your Highness." Unable to help myself, I added, "But you look sicker than ever."

Ignoring my addition, she tugged at her bodice, smoothed the hairs along her scalp, and lifted her chin.

"We will gather information from Cristian first, then . . ." She faltered, closed her eyes, and opened them again with exhausted resolution, ". . . we'll discuss what to do about Greyson."

Eastern Network High Priest Cristian Aldana was a bold man.

He stood a full pace shorter than most witches, had narrow shoulders, a sturdy jaw, a powerful face, and shadows across his thin cheeks. No one who met him would find his power lacking. Cristian had eyes like a sea eagle, and a passion that matched the roaring tide.

Except for today.

He stood before Scarlett's desk with a dimmed gaze and bowed shoulders, as if he tried, but couldn't quite, keep them upright. When Scarlett stood to meet him eye-to-eye, he appeared to hide a flinch.

To send a message, I remained behind Scarlett's left shoulder. *Right* behind her.

Cristian's studious eyes flickered briefly to mine, then back to Scarlett. Based on his tightening lips, he understood exactly what my presence implied.

Talmund and Rognvald stood off to the side, silent stalwarts with poorly hidden disgust etched in their expressions. East Guards waited outside Scarlett's doors, near Hiddleston's desk. One stood just behind Cristian, invisible, of course. His Assistant, a man named Aldo, perched at a desk that Leda provided. She hovered close to Scarlett, quills poised. Hiddleston waited outside, the door canted open to allow him to listen and access the paths.

I imagined a witch like Cristian must have very interesting paths, indeed.

"Cristian." Scarlett broke the tenuous silence, "I believe you have met Bianca Monroe?"

Curiosity sprang to his eyes, erasing as quickly as it came. He nodded once. "A pleasure, Miss Monroe."

I nodded in response.

Scarlett didn't bother introducing Leda, as Cristian met her mere hours after he assumed the Eastern Network throne.

I've warmed up a friendship with Aldo over the past year, Leda said. *He sent me a note before they arrived today and admitted that*

Carcere has been breached for weeks. They've been hiding it out of fear.

Slush trickled through my veins in response.

Weeks.

Enraging fool.

Scarlett continued with impressive political politeness. "I've just received a report that the magical prison, Carcere, has been breached. Care to fill me in?"

The offer was a merciful one. An attempt to keep friendship open. I imagined that Papa would have drawn a harder line, calling out immediate responsibility instead of discussion. He might have gone to the East, also, to make a point. Scarlett gave Cristian a chance to mollify her frustration before she acted.

Cristian paused for only a moment, jaw tense. With a sharp exhale, he said, "Yes, High Priestess. Carcere has been breached."

"Since when?"

"Six weeks ago."

If I hadn't mentally prepared for such a response, I might have lost my bearing. Six weeks. Our enemies—and theirs—had been loose from that infernal hellhole nearly two months. The reports from Baxter made far more sense. No wonder mayhem had loosed.

With a slight rasp, Scarlett said, "So long?"

He inclined his head.

More sharply, she asked, "Is there any particular reason that you didn't notify me that a witch known to be hostile with the Central Network had broken out?"

"The weeks following the degradation of that magical prison have been chaos," he said crisply, and with all the ugly sincerity a witch might muster. "We kept the breach quiet at first to keep panic at bay, and then because of widespread confusion. Some prisoners remained within the cells, others didn't. Some returned, most are lost forever. The originator has sown discord the likes of which we have never seen. This was not a singular event, Your Highness."

Cristian swallowed, his throat bobbing. His upper lip flexed, as if he hid his own revulsion at the admittance. "There have been many other disconcerting events that followed. Attacks on our Network from insurrectionists, if you will."

After a pause several heartbeats long, Scarlett said, "I see. Your lack of communication is most disappointing. It puts the Central Network in a situation with a severity you have not yet comprehended, but you are about to."

His shoulders shifted, as if he braced himself. I held myself still, one hand near Viveet, and waited for Scarlett to drop the news of Greyson and his threats. Instead, she drew herself together with a breath and calmed her voice.

"I imagine the time has been very difficult for you, Cristian. Based on what you say, I'm assuming that there is more going on beyond what the newsbooks report?"

Warily, he nodded again. Clearly, he didn't trust her calm, kind approach or he would have extrapolated.

"I'm sorry to hear it, Cristian. The same is true here. You remember our former Council Member, Greyson?"

Cristian went very still.

Without waiting for his verbal reply, she pressed on. "He has escaped Carcere and proceeded to, over the last three weeks, send threatening letters against myself and Miss Monroe." She met his gaze head on, her voice hardening. "Tonight, he revealed himself and the state of Carcere to Miss Monroe. This is why we have approached you."

To Cristian's credit, he had the presence of mind to appear pale. "I did not know," he managed to say.

"Of course you did," Scarlett replied with cool regard. "Though perhaps not particulars. Because Carcere has been breached, and my former Council Member at large, my life and Miss Monroe's are now in grave danger. I don't need to remind you of the force of power that stands behind me, ready to protect."

Cristian shook his head. The small back-and-forth hinted at humility, even if his livid stare didn't.

"But I shall remind you," Scarlett added quietly, "that Greyson has foisted himself against the Head of the Sisterhood, and Bianca Monroe is no ordinary witch."

I braced myself for the hidden threat Scarlett would lace through her words. Papa's name would forever inspire fear and respect in Alkarrans, and it had been used to cement my welfare more than once.

"She is known as the amulet-breaker, the lady witch of Letum Wood, and servant of the goddess Deasylva. If the might of the Central Network doesn't frighten you, any threat against my life should because she is personally responsible for my safety. If there is one witch in Alkarra I would not want standing against my Network," Scarlett said firmly, "it is Bianca Monroe, Head of the Sisterhood."

Her words dropped like echoing crashes.

It is Bianca Monroe, Head of the Sisterhood.

I kept my focus on Cristian, thrilled and humbled. Scarlett didn't use Papa's name to inspire fear and wrath. Not once. She used *mine*. My lips twitched, but I kept my composure.

"This is the witch upon whom you have thrown danger and drama, Cristian, and I am sorry for it."

Cristian closed his eyes. His lower lip blanched as he bit into it, nodding again. At this rate, his head bobbed more than a cork on water.

With great difficulty, he wrenched out, "I apologize, Your Highness. There is no excuse for my actions, except for fear. Please, accept my humble apologies and promises for clarity in the future."

Scarlett pressed her fingertips into the desk. "While kind, your offer comes six weeks too late. This is something I shall not forget soon. Regardless, I'm glad to hear you offer clarity, Cristian, because you are about to give it. Leda, please take notes. Cristian is going to tell us everything he knows about Carcere and what has happened thus far."

Cristian's summation of the Eastern Network's extensive issues lasted a full fifteen minutes. No one interrupted him with questions. An unsurprising story unfolded, but I still felt gutted by the timeline.

Six weeks.

Six weeks for Greyson to plan a revenge and murder plot that he enacted so carefully right now.

Preventable, all of it.

The most maddening aspect of the political realm was the degree to which mistakes relied on a witch's behavior. I couldn't reconcile myself to it. The smooth control in Scarlett's face said she already had.

By the time Cristian finished, he appeared exhausted and relieved, as if he'd unburdened. While the details built context, they didn't offer any further proof against Greyson or his plot. The Eastern Network High Priest spoke of an escalation of hostilities, tension, and affronted Council Members. He hinted at a potential attempted coup at the Network government level, but vaguely.

He departed not long after.

Scarlett stared at the door in a stewing silence long after Cristian exited, taking Aldo and his East Guards with him. The heady smell of magnolias drifted in his wake, staining the air with an intense perfume.

Scarlett turned to me, brows high.

"Well?"

The opportunity to share my thoughts first wasn't an accident.

I looked at her when I responded, but felt the weight of Rognvald and Talmund's eyes.

"The most surprising thing to me is simply the timeline. From what research I've done on Cristian, he's proud and has something to prove. How they've managed to keep it a secret for six weeks is my greatest shock."

Rognvald said, "We've had two Protectors in the Eastern Network for months, Your Highness. Cristian blames the rising tensions on Carcere, but he's wrong. The disrest and insurrection has been building long before Carcere."

"Thank you, Rognvald. I suspect Cristian is scared and needs an enemy to blame it on."

"He's blind," Rognvald spat.

"He's not," she countered calmly. "He's afraid. There's a difference."

Talmund gripped his sword with one hand, the other hung at his side, as he asked, "What are you going to do, Sisterhood?"

Meeting his curious stare, I said, "I'm going to find Greyson."

Chapter Twenty-Four

Merrick waited at my treehouse, concern etched in his face.

He must have just returned, because moisture glistened along the column of his neck, trailed into his shirt. He peeled his half-leather armor free. The scent of sunshine clung to clean sweat. A tantalizing, strange mix that wasn't entirely unpleasant.

He shucked the armor free, set it outside to dry. With a spell, I sent him a cold jug of water. He held it up in a salute, then drank with long, deep swallows, splashing the rest over his face. Rivulets ran over bronzed cheeks and a recently trimmed beard.

Tempting man.

Shaking droplets free, he ran a hand over his hair, then untucked his shirt from his pants. He reached for the back and pulled it off. I didn't avert my eyes, but appreciated the flow of muscles as they rippled across his chest when he tugged a fresh shirt on.

The man was *too* tempting.

Duly cleaned up for now, he grabbed my wrist and yanked me into him. His steady breaths rose and fell against my chest in reassurance. Everything about Merrick was steady. His confidence. His calm. The way he listened, observed. I traced the tips of my fingers along the coarse hair of his forearm.

He buried his face against my neck.

"Rognvald told me. He sent me to scout it out. I've seen it."

"It's ugly."

He squeezed tighter. The loose grip he held on my waist tightened, then faded. I placed a hand on his stubbled face. Anxiety lingered in his eyes. He, too, fought the turmoil of thinking. Someone cleared their throat. To my greatest surprise, Hiddleston stood in my doorway, brows elevated. I hid a smile at his expectant stare.

"How long have *you* been there?" I asked.

"Long enough. Scarlett asked me to look into the paths while you were at Carcere to see if we could glean any information."

Merrick grinned. "Close your eyes, Hiddleston. I'm going to kiss her."

As Merrick stepped forward, wrapped me in his arms, and inhaled so deep his shoulders expanded, Hiddleston mumbled something that sounded distinctly like, "Don't mind me."

While Hiddleston gave his back to us and stared into the canopy to mine the possibilities of my past, I held Merrick tight. After several heartbeats, he broke the delightful kiss and released me. His hand slipped down my arm, linked our fingers. He tugged me to the table.

"Mother sent dinner. I kept it warm for you."

"Thanks." I dropped into the chair in front of a plate. "I'm starving."

He sat across from me while I dove into fried potato chunks and a hunk of roast coated with warm gravy. The plunge through different places, the workload of magic, and the gradual settling of events in Scarlett's office knackered me. The hot food provided a boon. I ate. Merrick stewed. Hiddleston sought.

A note transported onto my table with Baxter's handwriting.

Cristian just returned to the Eastern Network and summoned me to his side. He authorized the announcement below after speaking with Scarlett. I didn't know or I would have told you.

I'm ready to help at a moment's notice.

A newsbook appeared next to the parchment, splayed to the first page. The Eastern Network didn't have a scrolled news system, like the *Chatham Chatterer*. They used a novelette. The articles winked in and out just like our newsscroll, only in book form.

A bolded headline drew my attention.

Carcere Breach

The well-known island prison, Carcere, off of the eastern shore, has been breached.

Details from Magnolia Castle remain scarce. The High Priest's Assistant has written a formal statement, as follows:

"Please take care during the next several days as we work to clean up a developing situation that occurred off the coast. We will provide updates. Local towns should consider evacuation."

Updates pending.

"Evacuation? Developing? That's a bold call. Particularly considering this happened weeks ago and there's nothing *developing* about it."

"Damage control," Merrick muttered with a scowl. "They're going to act like it just happened so they appear on top of it. You forced their hand."

I scoffed. Too little, too late. I didn't envy Baxter the headache of dealing with dramatic High Priests.

"You've been in the East for a while, haven't you?" I asked.

Merrick nodded.

"But not at Carcere?"

He shook his head.

"If I received Rognvald's permission to hear about your mission, could you tell me?" I asked.

"Yes."

I filed that away for later. Rognvald and I had several things to discuss. A plan to deal with Greyson already bubbled at the back of my mind. I allowed it to simmer. Hiddleston stirred, drawing our attention. He rubbed a hand over his eyes.

"After looking into your paths, the only conclusion I have is that Greyson might have a clear plan. There weren't many branching paths for you, which means he likely had a singular focus. Sometimes, there are paths that the magic doesn't reveal, but that's because they weren't obvious to you at the time. According to what I see from your side of events, Bianca, Greyson didn't have other motives. He wanted to reveal this detail, and leave. I could be wrong. It's difficult to interpret his motive through your possibilities, but that's my instinct. Otherwise, I saw one possibility where you entered Carcere. All went to black."

Went to black meant *death* in the Defender magic.

"Jikes."

Hiddleston's hands came together, pointer fingers pressed to white as he tapped the edge of the table. Darkness clouded his features. "The lesson there is to not go into Carcere."

A windy sigh from the trees announced Leda. Eyes drawn and face pale, she slipped into the treehouse after completing a trans-portation spell. Hiddleston, attention fixated on her, beckoned her to stand by him.

To my surprise, she did so.

Leda met my questioning gaze. "Scarlett is fine. She dealt with a problem in the Eastern Covens and retired to her apartment for dinner. Marjorie and two Guardians are with her. One inside, one outside. They're doing full interior checks every half hour, and have an extra pair on either end of the Royal Residence hall."

Talmund had promised as much before he left, but Hiddleston and Merrick relaxed at the report. It was a robust comfort that the Guardians existed to keep protections around Scarlett. Would the Sisterhood integrate so fully into the culture of the Network that we could surround Scarlett with the support she required?

Current plans indicated the goal.

"Thank you for the update, Leda."

"Revealing himself and Carcere was bold, Bianca." Her steely tone failed to hide concern. "It was not a threat, but a promise."

"I agree."

"Then how will you find him?

"Three witches: Baxter, Papa, and Rognvald."

Merrick's brows lifted ever-so-slightly. A sign of startled uncertainty. He didn't see my angle, which confirmed my plan.

Wryly, I asked, "Are you opposed?"

"Only surprised."

With as much innocence as I could muster, I said, "About what?"

Her martyric sigh would have terrified a lesser witch.

"With you, Bianca, everything is a surprise. Keep me updated via the communication magic. We'll take this one step at a time."

Leda and Hiddleston left a vacuum of life in their wake. Merrick stood at the table, hands braced on the back of a chair, his jaw working. He met my gaze, which ballooned the rippling silence and ominous foreboding of his quizzical expression.

"Merrick?"

Shaking his head, he said. "Just thinking."

"This whole thing is . . . kind of a mess."

Closing the distance between us, Merrick pressed a kiss to my hand. "You'll figure it out. The midst of a high-stakes mission is disorienting, uncertain. This is normal."

The reassurance helped.

"Thanks."

"What did Leda mean when she spoke about the communication magic?"

"Oh. Ah . . . Leda pulled the Brotherhood's communication magic grimoire out of the Great Library of Burke. She's figured out how to use it."

He straightened. His cheeks became taut. "With me?"

I nodded.

"That's what she went into the Protector room for?"

"Yes?"

"She didn't tell me that!" he snapped.

With an agitated scowl, he paced behind the table. His long strides ate up the room before he turned.

"I could get sacked!"

"We have no plans to detail how she accessed the room."

He scoffed. "You think they can't trace it? You think they won't eventually figure it out?"

Could the Protectors track it? Would they? I had my doubts Rognvald would waste the energy. Merrick stopped at a floor-length window, hands stacked on his hips, and stared out. My heart sank.

"I'm sorry, Merrick. There was no plan to get you into trouble. We just . . . we need to be able to communicate."

His soft reply of, "I know," sent greater fear through me. Almost as softly, he continued. "I didn't understand it before, but now I do."

"Understand what?"

"Derek's . . . insecurity . . . about his relationship with Marie."

My hands trembled as I paused to soak that in. The *talk* we hadn't managed to schedule into our day had arrived.

"What do you mean?"

Merrick spun to face me. His face cleared of emotion. "Derek has always been hard on himself about Marie, hasn't he?"

"Yes, always."

Merrick fell into thought. "I imagined it was a weak spot, insecurity, or maybe a control problem. I don't know. But . . . now? I see it. I feel the same way, I think."

"About me?"

"Yes."

Bristling, I asked, "You don't think I can handle it?"

"I know you can," he immediately said, and with such force I believed him. "That's not what Derek thought about Marie, either. Obviously, she handled it with confidence and grace, or you wouldn't be who you are today. But . . . the unfairness."

I sank into a chair.

"Oh."

He squinted a little as he studied me. "I'll be gone, B. Maybe all the time. When I return, you could leave. I left for six months, and little happened with the Sisterhood. Now that I'm here, your mission has ramped up."

"It's bizarre."

"With Carcere broken into and insurrection rising in the East, there's a chance I might have to return. Rognvald tries to switch us through longer rotations, so no one has to take the majority of the weight, but he can't promise anything. The needs of the mission come first. If the East doesn't get this under control, I could be assigned there for a very long time."

Drawing in a long breath, I said a shaky, "I know. I can handle that. Can you?"

"But should we *have* to?"

"What's the alternative?"

"I leave the Protectors."

I hid my gasp. That he'd even *say* it shocked me. Calmly, I managed to reply with a careful, "You'd still be in the Masters."

"Yes."

"With the same problem."

Too gravely, he said, "Not the same. Not exactly. The Masters aren't as busy as the Protectors, and they work mostly out of the North. The Protectors tend to go everywhere. I'd have to live in the North, though."

None of this conversation shocked me. I'd hashed this and similar problems out before. They rolled through my mind at night, or during my weekly Leda meal, or with Grandfather, clarifying the truth: I wasn't a little girl pretending anymore.

This was the stark reality of living.

Merrick added, "We might *both* be on missions at the same time," before he drove a hand through his hair. "Perhaps the only reason Marie and Derek worked is because your mother was always available. Which," he added gently, "wasn't fair to Marie." A sad chuckle accompanied his final pronouncement. "I never understood it until right now. Gods, I feel I owe Derek an apology. I thought him mad."

The swelling heart that I'd carried around since Merrick returned—again—shriveled. Nothing could lessen my love for Merrick, but the stacking problems were a cold reminder that love wasn't easy.

Entirely too much vulnerability entered my voice when I asked, "Do you want this to work?"

Astonishment flared his eyes. He reached for me, taking my cold fingers in his.

"B, of course. I want it more than anything. I just . . . I don't want to go into it with expectations we can't maintain. Whatever we have to figure out, we will. I've already lived without you for three years," he added fiercely. "I won't do it again."

Mollified, I squeezed his fingers. He pulled me into his arms.

"And finally," he added with a bit of a grimace, "there's my dual loyalty to consider. It isn't an issue for Rognvald or Regina, but in the future I might be forced to choose. You have the Sisterhood, I have the Brotherhood and the Masters."

He trailed away.

The needed transparency aired big problems, even if the weight of it dimmed the giddiness of his return. Did this whiplash range of emotions happen to Mama? Sheer delight when she experienced Papa again, then the cutting kiss of reality as he left?

If so, she hid it well.

Mama and Papa carefully kept disputes between themselves, separating me from that part of their marriage. They argued in front of me, but not often. Was that an advantage, or a disadvantage?

Merrick's hand reached up, tilted my chin higher. I met his gaze, though it required effort.

"B? What are you thinking? I feel like I've done too much of the talking, and now you're upset."

Hesitation lasted only a moment.

"I don't want you to be assigned again while I'm working for the Sisterhood," I admitted. "But I also don't want to say an elaborate *merry part* every single time we have to be away from each other, and I won't give up the Sisterhood."

"I know." His flat tone, void of the despair in his gaze, didn't convince me.

"I'm worried, Merrick."

"About what?"

"That our relationship can't survive what our chosen paths will ask of us."

The words, though true, felt like poison. Terrifying to release, but more dangerous to hold close. I monitored his reaction while holding tight to swirling doubts. Giving him those words made me want to vomit, but damming them inside would break us in a different way.

Merrick leaned back.

"What?"

"I know what it's like to be a Protector's daughter," I rushed to say, because it seemed we were rushing to say everything these days, "but not what it feels like to be his partner. This is new for me, just like it is for you. It's different. I thought it would feel the same, but this is infinitely more scary."

Tension zipped through him like a rod. "You think we can't do it?"

"That's not what I said."

"If you're having doubts," he snapped, "better air them out now. Before—"

He broke off.

"Merrick, I don't doubt the way I feel about you. I don't doubt *us*. We just . . . we don't know what we're doing and there's no one else who's doing it. We have to forge our own path, and that's hard."

"I love you, B. Nothing changes that."

"I love you too, but how do we not talk about your missions? How do we process the things you need to think about? We haven't even figured out how to catch up on everything you missed after you've been gone for six months."

He opened his mouth to reply, then stopped.

I swallowed hard before continuing on, fraught as this *talk* felt. "We don't know how to be in a relationship that, by necessity, has secrets."

"Your mother—"

"Is gone."

"But Derek—"

"Won't talk about it. Besides, we're not them, are we?"

He hesitated, mouth bobbing open and closed. He whirled around and began to pace again. I had an idea that it had less to do with movement as it was gaining space.

The air had swollen between us, crackling like a thunderstorm.

I couldn't withdraw the words, and wouldn't. They needed to be said, but that didn't make it easy. After an eternity of quiet, he stopped. I lifted my head to find that none of the turmoil had left his eyes.

"You're right. We don't know how to . . . be *in* a relationship. We've always been under duress, or gone, or separated, or fighting. Something. We haven't had to live, day to day, with the threat of another departure."

Grateful he understood, I nodded. His review of our history had lingered in the back of my mind for days, but I hadn't the courage to call it forward. Perhaps *this* is what relationships were. One doing what the other couldn't, wouldn't, or didn't know how to do. A sort of imperfect balance.

What happened when neither of us knew what to do?

If possible, his agitation increased. "We need time, B. Time, I think, to get used to something normal. To talk it out and figure out how to do it."

I countered with, "You can't talk about your missions."

"No, but . . . "

He turned again, heading the other way, hands clasped behind his back. I almost shared memories of Mama and Papa with him. Mama's unequivocal acceptance of Papa's silence, and her lack of questioning, but quelled the urge. Why share it with him if I couldn't promise the same? Could I give the same space without angst or bitterness?

I didn't know.

Merrick's brilliant green eyes churned under the weight of a powerful storm when he asked, "Do you want this, B?"

"Yes," I breathed.

"Because I want to ask—"

He cut off.

When he hissed, and his brow crashed, and he turned his head to the side, as if listening, I knew exactly what had happened. My heart almost stopped when he lifted his gaze to mine. His scowl could have ignited water.

Heart slamming in my throat, I asked, "Rognvald just spoke to you?"

He nodded.

"A mission?"

Another tight nod, then a gesture to ask me to pause. He sat on the edge of a chair, knees bent, forearms propped on his thighs, and steepled his hands. They propped up his chin. With every exhale, he issued a feral little growl. Still listening, no doubt, to whatever Rognvald had to say. Every so often, his eyebrows twitched, as though he spoke with some invisible opponent.

I focused on tightening and relaxing my fists. The cycle of building and breaking tension was a welcome release.

Merrick stood, muttering a curse word. He pulled in a sharp breath through his nostrils, released it. His nose twitched as he strode to my side. Gently, he took my hand in his. I splayed my fingers, opening them for his touch.

He spoke without meeting my eyes.

"Rognvald is calling me back to the previous mission."

"In the East?"

He nodded. Though back to the East, that didn't mean he'd be near Carcere. I still didn't know what he had been doing there in the first place. He regarded me with an apology that went deeper than words.

"B, I'm sorry."

"I know."

"This is hard."

Reluctantly, I nodded. Did Mama admit weakness before Papa left? Did she allow him to see the difficult waves of his departures?

Did it matter?

I wasn't Mama, and Merrick wasn't Papa.

Merrick's jaw flexed, highlighting the golden sheen and

glimmer of his beard along his jaw, like sunlight captured in a stream. When he inhaled a deep breath, his shoulders widened.

"Rognvald expects me in ten minutes."

"For how long?"

"He didn't say."

"Any chance we could see each other?"

The desperation in the question was thready. I shouldn't have asked. He licked his lips.

"No."

The rock in my stomach turned to grinding mortar and pestle. It broke, broke, broke, anguish in a bottle. Difficult to tolerate, but impossible to ignore. Jikes, what if another six months lay ahead?

"Take the notebook?"

Merrick's barren gaze became dull. "Not yet. Leave it on the shelf, by yours. If I have a moment when I can summon it, then I will."

Another smolder of my grinding stomach.

It must be *very* dangerous.

My heart gave a wild beat against my chest as I threw myself into his arms. He grasped me close, hands locked around me, breath fast. He pressed a rough kiss on top of my head.

"I'm sorry, B. I'm sorry."

His words rang in my ears long after the hasty farewell. He vanished with pain in his eyes, whisking my heart with him.

Reeves opened Grandfather's door. The aged butler took me in with a glance, stepped aside. With brimming gratitude, I slipped by him.

Grandfather stood near the hearth. Dozens of memories from my time in this room bubbled to life as I swept past comfortable divans, a painting of Mildred, and walked straight into his waiting arms. The sounds of Reeves' departure were a closing door and resulting silence.

Tears bubbled free.

Grandfather's soothing hand smoothed the hair away from my ears and over my back. I felt like a lost child in his arms as I cried. The stiffness with Merrick, the uncertainty of the future, and his latest departure, swept my metaphorical legs out from under me. I longed for Papa, but couldn't share this with him.

Not now.

Grandfather rubbed my shoulder. Somehow, he already knew.

"I'm sorry, my dear. So very sorry."

There, I cried.

Chapter Twenty-Five

As always, I found refuge in Grandfather.

That night, I slept at his apartment. By the time I'd washed my face, summoned new clothes, and laced my sandals, tendrils of the sad funk had fled. Seeing Merrick's mission through the lens of sleep and time and Grandfather's promises that *all would be well*, gave me greater perspective.

Not peace, but distance.

With distance came clarity.

Clarity brought her own relief and misery. With sunshine streaming through the windows, I leaned toward relief. The knowledge that I had a High Priestess to keep safe propelled me out of the bedroom and into the apartment.

Seeking Grandfather and breakfast, I wandered down the hall. A breakfast of warm toast and sweet jelly, as well as a calm conversation about my plans for the day, would escort me out of the sad funk of Merrick's latest departure.

I found Grandfather amidst piles of books. He peered at me through glasses perched on the tip of his nose, his bald pate shining merrily against streaming sunlight.

"There you are, my dear. Would you like to help an old man?"

"What are you doing?"

"Still sorting! Reeves announced that you'd awoken, so I thought I'd better be useful while waiting for you to emerge for a shared breakfast."

He sorted through some of Mildred's old books. I held up a tome, read the cover aloud.

"*High Priestesses and Their Oddities. A step-by-step guide to getting the most out of your relationship as Ambassador.*"

Grandfather chuckled.

"A classic. Donate it."

Snorting, I set it on a pile of books he gestured toward, likely destined for the Great Library of Burke. I reached for the next thing. A wooden box, filled with a plethora of moldering quills, dried ink bottles, and a sundry of Ambassadorship. I handed it to him. He set it in a pile that looked like rubbish.

"Are you ready to talk about Merrick leaving?" he asked.

With a sigh, I said, "I suppose so."

"What happened?"

Grateful, I aired it all. Emotions surfaced with the retelling, but not with the same power. I swallowed them back more easily, allowing nothing more than smarting tears as I concluded with, "I'm just not sure *how* to run the Sisterhood and love a Protector without losing my mind and my heart."

"You have precious few witches to call on for advice, too. Few Protectors take a wife. Some do. Most don't."

Grandfather set aside another book, leaving it in the pile to go to the Great Library of Burke. All of them disappeared as he leveled his thoughtful stare on me, no doubt transported directly to the library.

"Well," he said lightly, "you almost had it right with the idea to ask your father for help."

"That's wrong?"

"It's not *you* who should be asking Derek for advice."

The gentle implication wasn't lost.

"Merrick?"

"Mmm, yes. Derek cannot truly fathom the underside of the life your mother endured. But he could help Merrick."

Well, in hindsight, that seemed perfectly obvious. Grandfather's eyes twinkled when he smiled at me. "Like Derek, I don't enjoy seeing you go through this. Unlike Derek, however, I have answers and advice rooted with experience."

Hope buoyed me.

"Really?"

"Mildred and I were in a similar position not long after she defeated Evie. We had *something*, but no one to model it after. We had pressures that we couldn't control. No one could know of our feelings, I was the Ambassador, active traditions worked against us, etc. No one existed that we could ask questions of."

My breath caught at the pristine clarity of it. Of *course*. What little I knew of Grandfather and Mildred's relationship was clouded by history. I had no access to who they had been together. Mildred and I had so little time before Mabel killed her.

With a warm smile, and a chuckle, Grandfather set a hand on my shoulder. "Time, dear girl. Give yourself time. While I can't speak to what it feels like to be six months away from someone, and then return, I can tell you that with time, you find answers. Try different things. Be patient. You and Merrick will come through this, because you have what matters the most."

"What's that?"

He tapped a finger over his breastbone.

"Love."

Tears filled my eyes. I didn't need someone to tell me what to do. Not really. Merrick and I were different, but the same. I needed something different than what Mildred required, and Grandfather knew it.

Grandfather squeezed my hand.

"Just like with the Sisterhood, you'll discover the right path for you. This will pass, and you'll be stronger. I promise that a lifetime of toil, dedication, loyalty, and love is worth it. Even if, in the end, it looks different than you dreamed."

He swept two books closer to my side. One of them, a tattered black cover with elegant crimson scroll work I recognized right away. The other, a leather-bound tome as thick as my fist and either brand new, or protected by incantations.

Picking up the tattered black book, I exclaimed, *"Mildred's Resistance?"* with shocked reverence.

He smiled faintly. "There's only one copy."

"Stella lent it to me years ago."

Another wry chuckle. "Yes, she told me. I was glad. It's the best way to tell the story of the Resistance, really. Lavinia did an admirable job of it. Anyway, with them gone, Lavinia gifted it to me. I felt that you should have it."

I cradled the book close to my chest, grateful to feel my heart thump against the hard cover. It healed some of the smarting wounds and wrenched heartstrings that ached.

"Thank you."

He tapped a finger on the other, thicker one. "That is mine. It's precious to me."

"What do you mean?"

"My journal. I've been writing in it for most of my life. Shorter expositions in the beginning. Mostly flow of life. The rest? Well, I found a bit more of a writer in me as I aged. Particularly after I found out about you."

My mouth split. "You're jesting."

He shook his head with a simple, "No."

Gingerly, I cracked the cover to better explore the pages. Handwriting whirred by as I fanned through each spread, studying every line. Ink color, letter size, slanting detail, changed as the years passed. Emotion welled up in my throat, inspiring another threat of tears. He gave me more than part of himself.

He gave me *me.*

The history that I had been denied. The parts of Mildred that I would never know. The weaving of my own tapestry that he played into, however subtle or uncertain at the time. My breath arrested with the gift.

"Grandfather, thank you."

With a mysterious air, he said, "I have a feeling it will come in handy one day, though I can't predict when or how. Perhaps it never will, and I simply express the hopes and desires of an old man that loves you and wants his life to have come to something. Either way, it's yours. I am deeply grateful for you to take it."

From without, Reeves intoned down the hall.

"Breakfast is served."

Clutching both books to my chest, I clasped Grandfather in my arms, again whispered, "Thank you," and felt love pour from him. Before I pulled away, he patted my back.

"I adore you, my dear. That's all you ever need to know."

Sneaking around Magnolia Castle was too easy. Far too easy for a Network experiencing major upheaval. A little transformation magic, a bright smile, an occasional stint with invisibility, and there I stood at Baxter's personal apartment.

The door shook on its hinges when I rapped with my knuckles. He called out, quelling my fear that I wouldn't find him here, because who knew where else in Alkarra he might be?

The door breezed open.

He startled, then smiled.

"Bianca!"

I shoved inside. His expression fell as he took one look at my face.

"Please, come in."

The door closed behind me with a firm *snick*, and I sent a spell around it. The wide open patio, admitting a fresh sea breeze and scudding white clouds, would pose a different problem for privacy, though I couldn't imagine who might listen in.

"Something I can do to help?"

I nodded to the windows in silent question.

He waved it off. "Not a problem. Different spells protect it from listening ears. No one can hear anything. What do you need?"

"When did you learn about Carcere?"

"When you summoned Cristian." He set his hands on his hips. His dull eyes and furrowed brow indicated deepest irritation. "I'm not happy about it."

"Why would they keep it hidden?"

"Instability. Didn't want me to tell you, because he knows I would have, and right away. A lot of reasons." Baxter's lips compressed. "Rising insurrection chief amongst them. I believe Merrick might know more about that?"

The words weren't idly spoken. I lifted an eyebrow.

"Pardon?"

Baxter waved a hand. "A few East Guards said they suspected the Central Network sent Protectors out but had no proof. With all the rampant violence on the streets of various large cities, I have little doubt Rognvald is watching."

"Reportedly. Has anyone from the Brotherhood approached you to ask about Carcere or recent developments?"

"No. Why would they?"

I rolled my eyes.

Naturally. Rognvald didn't think of asking Baxter, the demigod liaison, if he had any insight. Why Baxter wasn't the *first* place the Brotherhood went, I couldn't fathom.

"Two reasons for me to involve you." I upheld two fingers. "One, I want to clear any demigod involvement, just to be thorough. Two, you work and live in the Eastern Network as much as anyone else to whom we have official political ties. You might have more access to other sources or witches that have information about the breaking of Carcere."

He granted me a quick smile. "Your focus on me is unconventional, obviously, and very flattering."

"Any chance it might have been a demigod that broke through Carcere's walls? Could god magic break a goddess system? Carcere held such powerful magic. I'm not sure how a witch accomplished it."

"I hadn't thought of it, to be honest."

"Well, think of it now!"

He stared into the distance. I thought I saw falling puzzle pieces in his eyes, so I remained quiet until he broke it.

"There's *some* chance," he said diplomatically, "though I can't imagine which demigod. Gelas keeps a relatively firm handhold on the demigods. The other gods destroyed the amulet system entirely and retreated, probably for hundreds of years."

"So . . ."

"I can check with Gelas." He hefted his hands into the air. "It won't hurt to clear it. He'll know if someone used his magic in that way, because he would have to give permission. Based on what you've described, and what I saw myself a few hours ago, I doubt even the strongest demigod could have created this destruction without using an amulet."

He meant the raw strength demigods possessed, far above the most physically capable witch. "This wasn't a physical ransacking and robbery accomplished by sheer force, no. Demigods might be physically powerful, but this was . . . an obliteration."

With a resolute nod, he promised, "I'll check."

"Will you send Leda a message if the Brotherhood asks you about demigod involvement?"

"Sure. But why?"

"Oh, no reason," I said lightly. "Just checking whether or not they're as thorough as we are. When can you talk to Gelas?"

"Immediately."

"Notify me as soon as you can?"

"I'll have a reply soon."

Papa stood outside of his house, staring into the forest, with his legs locked in a powerful stance and his arms across his chest. Based on the tension in his jaw, I approached a witch very deep in thought. A hint of caution almost stopped me from speaking with him, but I shoved it away and stood at his side.

He didn't relax as he came back into himself, receding from whatever distant place he cavorted. He cleared his throat.

"B."

"Papa."

Another stretch of silence, in which I soaked up a measure of the forest. The hallowed whispers rose. Saplings, fresh after all the battles, had adorably infantile songs. They repeated, *her her her her*, over and over again in my presence.

Papa cast me a sidelong glance. "How are you?"

"Busy."

"Oh?"

"Being busy isn't your problem at the moment, I'd wager?" I asked, gazing round.

The grass around his house appeared immaculate. Signs of construction had utterly dispelled. Shavings swept free. Mortar chinked the seams of his house; the windows sparkled. He hadn't manicured a garden, but a sense of intentional wildness returned to the vegetation around the living space. The same unfettered cleanliness and control continued inside the walls, as well.

"No. Busyness is definitely not my problem this week."

"When did you finish the house?"

"Last week, when I returned."

"From where?"

"Everywhere." He shrugged. "I just . . . needed to go."

The pain in his eyes made me ache. When Papa left the position of High Priest behind, it had been naive to think that he slipped into an easier life. In some regards, it *was* better. In many others, it remained far more difficult.

He was beginning to learn what Mama and I had always known: the quiet sometimes stared back.

For his sake, I'd rather stay and while away the hours with him, but that wasn't meant to be. We climbed different mountains now, and it had to stay that way. I couldn't save Papa from himself.

"I can't stay long," I admitted, and hated that it was true.

"Any time with you, B, is well worth it. Even if it's only for a few minutes."

"I need you to answer some questions about former Council Member Greyson."

His head snapped to the side.

"Sorry?"

Unbothered by his shock, I firmly repeated myself.

"Greyson."

He frowned, then said in an elongation that told me he'd already suspected what I was about to say, "Don't tell me . . ."

"He's out of prison. I take it you haven't heard about Carcere yet?"

The question was easy to answer. Fury tightened the lines around his eyes. He squeezed his arms, gripping them so tight the knuckles blanched white.

A stiff, "No," responded.

"It's been breached, the magic broken. I think from the inside, but it's not terribly clear. I'd have to go within to know for certain." Recalling the malodorous magic and fetid air, I shuddered. "Baxter's going to clarify whether or not a demigod was involved," I added as he opened his mouth.

His lips sealed again.

"Seems odd," I mused. "There's hardly any information for the origin of such a magic, according to Leda, and I haven't heard mention of a grimoire. It might have been a simple matter for a demigod to break it open and destroy the powerful place."

"Might have."

"The Brotherhood hasn't come to you?" I asked.

"No. Why would they?"

With exasperation, I said, "You were the last witch known to speak to Greyson before he was shoved into the belly of Carcere last year."

"And?"

"I figured you were the obvious choice for more information."

"It is a Sisterhood mission, no?"

"Yes, but I've intertwined with a Brotherhood mission too. Rognvald hasn't yet confirmed."

He grunted. "The Brotherhood haven't asked because all ties have been cut. I'm not part of their ranks anymore. Obviously," he added caustically, as if some hope had remained that Rognvald might need him.

I said nothing.

He eyed me askance. "What exactly do you want to know?"

"I wondered if you had any ideas about Greyson? You stopped Greyson's attempts to work with the demigod Dayla and usurp Scarlett. What did you think of him at the time? Of his crimes, of . . . who he was? What did he say the last time you spoke to him? How did he appear? Did you deduce his motivation? All of this happened while I was in Alaysia," I tacked on.

"True," he murmured. Papa thought for a moment. His tough stance melted, distracted by this new conundrum. "When I met with Greyson in Carcere, he surprised me. So calm and measured. We didn't say much. His affect was mostly neutral, flat. Impressively so, now that I think about it."

"Did he betray his motive for attempting to dethrone Scarlett?"

"The challenge."

"*That's* what he said?"

"Yes."

Combined with his insistence that I play his game, I shook my head. "It doesn't make sense."

"He was a witch in a position of power during a tenuous time. He saw an opportunity, snatched it, and failed. Doesn't have to be much more complicated than that, B."

But it does, I wanted to say.

Papa didn't have a truly accurate picture. If he didn't know about Carcere, he wouldn't know about the letters. I didn't want him to. Different paths, and all that, but also an overprotective father with only time and boredom on his hands. The Sisterhood had to rise on her own.

"Carcere's breach had to involve someone from the outside," he mused, a fist over his lips. Deepening thought nearly claimed him again. "But *how*? The suppressive magic should have prevented it."

"I have no idea. The East hasn't released much information, and Cristian didn't offer explanations."

He ran a thumbnail along his lip with a distant gaze. After a stalled pause, I asked, "Anything else I should know about Greyson?"

Papa rubbed a hand over his face. "Be careful. That's the most that I can say. I walked away with an impression of latent evil in his eyes. How he hid it all those years, I'll never understand. Things like this don't just happen, B. There's something else moving in the background, and don't think Greyson is the beginning or end of this problem."

Chapter Twenty-Six

Rognvald eyed me the way one might a troll: with a great deal of skepticism.

Did he fear I would berate him for taking Merrick again? Tempting, but not worth the repercussions.

I sat on the proffered chair opposite his desk, setting aside my typical preference for standing. Rognvald hadn't changed the office decor after Matthais died. The barren walls, solitary desk, and functional cupboard space remained utterly unmoved, and a bit lonely. Not a thing lay in sight. Not a parchment, envelope, or quill.

"Well," Rognvald said with a head tipped toward me. "How are you?"

"Fine. You?"

He gave me a pointed look. "Tired of trivialities," he growled.

I flashed a grin. "Me too, but I'm waiting."

His eyebrows elevated halfway to his hairline.

"Are you?"

A knock came on the door. It *snicked* open, and Leda peered inside. She might be petite, but nothing hinted at frailness as she stepped inside without invitation.

"This is Leda."

"I know Leda," Rognvald muttered, with a look that suggested I'd lost my mind.

"The *other* member of the Sisterhood."

His mild annoyance bled to surprise. He leaned forward. "Say what?"

"Leda is part of the Sisterhood. Have I not mentioned that before? Few witches, aside from Scarlett and I, know about her role. She's integral to the Sisterhood. Her behind-the-scenes research and spell work is unparalleled."

Leda's neutral expression didn't falter as she lowered to the chair next to mine. She reserved all judgment from her face, though she'd expressed disinterest in Rognvald as his tenure as Head of Protectors progressed. She didn't hate him, but wasn't excited about his leadership.

"We'll need her here today because the Sisterhood has a favor to ask of you."

"Go on."

"We came for two things." I held up both pointer fingers, then dropped the left. "First, we are going to extend an invitation for you to join the Sisterhood communication magic. It's the same magic as the Brotherhood, but Leda is the originator of it. That's why she's here."

Rognvald's eyes bulged. "Sisterhood communication magic?" he repeated, as if the words were as fragile as glass. "Same as the . . ."

"Brotherhood." Leda beamed with an acute enjoyment of his discomfort. "If you're willing, I'll explain."

He hesitated, running his tongue along his teeth. Questions burdened his eyes, but he didn't release them right away. The time he took sifting through each word told me a great deal more than I expected.

"No one else has this magic," he said in astonishment. I

couldn't decide whether I saw respect or utter terror. "The grimoire is locked up."

"Correct," I said.

Rognvald turned to Leda, finger pointing. "The only way you could originate the same magic as the Brotherhood is if you snuck into the Protector's room at the Great Library of Burke," he barked. "Who let you in?"

Leda regaled him with a glacial haughtiness worthy of Mabel herself. "You presume that I don't have my own connections to the Great Library of Burke after working there as an Underlibrarian for two years, and as Assistant to the Highest Witch?"

He faltered.

"The grimoire is safe," she said with only slightly less venom. "No one else has access to it. You can see the grimoire whenever you want in the library. Not that you would," she tacked on, as if she couldn't help herself. "Considering that no Head of Protectors has accessed the grimoire in decades. If you'd bothered more than a cursory glance, you'd realize how little you use, against how much power is available."

My tense muscles uncoiled when I realized she'd very thoroughly cleared Merrick's name with her annoyed regard. To my utmost delight, Rognvald didn't question her. While he didn't appear cowed, he was wary.

"You're the primary?" he grunted, and the question was a concession.

Leda shook her head. "Not just a primary." He scoffed, but she continued. "I'm the Priestess."

Rognvald stared. "Priestess?"

Magical lines formed a structure in the air between the three of us. She conjured a visual of the magic for Rognvald's sake, proving her assumption around the depth of communication magic.

"The magic is split into levels," she said primly, gesturing with two fingers. The entire bottom row, which displayed nine circles below a horizontal line, illuminated to a bright azure. "Most of your Protectors are on the lowest level. You, as the primary, are the level above." A light green circle pulsed above the others. Lines, like an umbrella, kept the nine circles locked beneath Rognvald.

He sucked on his front teeth, nodding a little. "That is how it was explained to me. And?"

"The magic has room for three more primary spots, each higher than the last. A witch cannot ascend to a different primary unless invited by the Priestess."

She paused, eyebrow tilted in a silent query. Rognvald waved her off, refusing a chance to ask questions.

"Let's say we had a Sisterhood with five female witches in it," she continued. "The magic would select another primary magic holder for the Sisterhood. They will be here."

A row of four red roses lined above Rognvald's circular symbol. On top of the Sisterhood symbols, another circle appeared, this one red to match the others. I hid a smile as Rognvald motioned for her to continue again. Tension lined his eyes, his silence.

Leda motioned higher as two additional levels appeared. A row of orange rectangles topped by a matching circle, and a final set of primaries and subordinates with white stars. Leda's teeth flashed with a smile.

"Then, there's the Priestess."

Spiraling over all the others, at the apex, stood a golden crown that rotated in position.

"All primary witches, and all their subordinates, are under the power of the Priestess, who can hear and access all of them. The magic functions without the Priestess when there is one primary."

Rognvald's arms stiffened so tightly he might have cracked from the inside out. Knowing that someone else had usurped authority and could potentially control the Brotherhood communication magic hit him as hard as I expected.

He leaned forward.

"How did you do it?" he snapped.

"Everything is in the grimoire," Leda said. "I understand that you might feel threatened by the move, but the Brotherhood has had access to it whenever you wanted. You're not the only witch with subversive methods, Protector." She arched a brow. "In all due respect, a Sister never reveals her secrets."

Well done, I crooned.

Leda's lip twitched, but she brooked no revelation on how she felt.

Quietly, I said, "We felt that you should know the Protectors could have been subverted in their own communication magic and never known it. We also want to offer you a connection with the Sisterhood, so we can all communicate."

"The Brotherhood has fallen into a routine with their communication magic," Leda said crisply. "You've used a hidden magical system for centuries without revisiting it to learn what's possible. As such, there's a great deal more to it than you thought."

Rognvald widened his eyes, as if to say, *no kidding.* In the intervening minutes, he had relaxed ever-so-slightly, but studied the magical map with continuing intensity. He ran a hand over his face and muttered, "The gods, but what if someone else managed the same?"

"I've already set up a primary for the Sisterhood," Leda said, and the crimson roses glowed like brilliant, shining foil. "I am the primary *and* the Priestess, because the goddess bless the Central Network if Bianca was in charge of something so logical, structured, and mundane. We have been using the magic for days, and it's very helpful."

Rognvald's teeth clacked as he considered, his gaze cast surreptitiously to the top, where the Priestess lingered, her icon greater than the rest. He tipped his head toward the Priestess.

"And her?"

"Hears it all, should she desire it." Leda drew a line from the red roses to the circles, indicating immediate communication between the two groups. "Communication works through the primaries," she added, considering her own visual aid. She drew a line from one rose, to the second primary, down to the first primary, and to another circle. "If Bianca wanted to speak with Chi, for example, you and I would hear it. But no one else."

"So you—"

"I can hear everything you say to the Brothers," Leda calmly added, "but I have not. The ability to quiet your line is there. Out of respect for you and your witches, I have done so. I stayed only long enough to confirm that I could hear your voices, then backed out."

A sweltering round of thought gave his reply. Rognvald braced his forearms on his bent knees. He sucked on his teeth for a moment before saying, "First of all, I owe you gratitude for exposing a weakness we didn't realize existed. This could have been . . . far worse. Thank you."

Leda accepted his gruff appreciation with a nod.

"Second, it seems fairly obvious what you're going to ask next. You want access to the Brotherhood through the communication magic."

"And the Brotherhood will have access to the Sisterhood," I said.

He paused to study me. After ten seconds, during which I held his gaze and understood that a storm of protectiveness belied it, he nodded.

"Agreed."

Leda said with a gleeful smile, "Consider it done! It'll only take me two minutes to finalize the connection between myself and Rognvald, which will open up the Brotherhood and Sisterhood for communicating. It shouldn't be much different than you experience now, Rognvald."

Chapter Twenty-Seven

A letter from Baxter greeted me as I left Rognvald's office.

No demigod involvement.

I crumpled it and turned it to ash. Leda, already striding toward a meeting with Underassistants, messages whirling around her head, didn't even say *merry part*. I watched her go, undecided. Despite the exhaustion of Baxter, Papa, and Rognvald's visit's wrapped into one big day, the last place I wanted to go was home.

Alone.

With Merrick gone, I avoided the prospect of a lonely tree-house by stopping at Scarlett's office. No Assistants protected her doorway from the hall. When I eased around Leda's prodigious desk and peered through the partially opened door, Scarlett sat in her chair, staring out her window. Her jaw created a sharper, more obvious line than before. Had she lost weight?

The reverberative *tap-tap-tap* of my knuckle swelled into the room.

"You may enter, Bianca."

A few steps into the office, the dampening sunlight confirmed my growing suspicion: Scarlett had worsened. Her sickly visage had a limp tenor, a quiet pallor that spoke to exhaustion and deepening despair.

I lowered into the chair across from her desk, using a spell to close the door. Scarlett's quiet declaration, spoken to the window with a neutral tone, stirred greater fears.

"I'm having nightmares."

"Of?"

"Ellie."

Unsure of what to say, I remained silent. Scarlett proceeded, her voice distant, each word a sigh.

"Every day, I go to bed and fall right to sleep, my exhaustion is so great. Inevitably, nightmares plague me. Terrors, wracking my mind, of the night Ellie died. I toss, turn. Sometimes, these awful dreams are so stark and gaunt I cannot possibly return to sleep, so I lay awake. If I manage any rest, it's fitful."

A pause, then she weakly continued. "Tea cannot boost my energy much longer, Bianca. I cannot . . . I cannot account for this change in my health. Ellie has been gone for years. Years and *years*," she whispered, as if puzzling over a broad challenge. "Yet, I worsen. The lack of sleep makes it all worse."

Shaking her head, she breathed a quiet, "I am at my wits end over it. If I wasn't so tired, I might summon greater outrage. I am too young for this."

An untouched tea tray lay on her desk, a sundry of teas littering the top. Herbal ones, mostly.

"Have you—"

"The Apothecaries don't know what it is. They've tried sending me sleeping potions and draughts and tinctures and teas and—" She fluttered a hand in the air. "They don't help."

Panic erupted in my chest, like a cloud of butterflies turned loose. I sat there, letting them flutter and wreak havoc, until I thought my voice might have some control.

"Has stress over Greyson caused this?"

She whispered a plaintive, "I don't know," that cut right to my heart. Her eyes fluttered closed. She leaned her head into her hand. "Forgive my outburst of emotion and feeling, Bianca. It doesn't seem right to burden you with the problems of a High Priestess."

Swallowing, I said, "If the Sisterhood can't be here for you whenever you need it, whatever that looks like, then what good is the Sisterhood?"

Her eyes fluttered open, meeting mine. Bemused, exhausted, she gave a wan smile before her eyes drifted closed again.

"Indeed," she murmured sleepily. Her lips opened, as if to speak another word, but she dropped into repose.

At my treehouse, tension intensified.

No matter how hard I tried to shuck the building dread in my chest after speaking to Scarlett, I couldn't help but feel as if something was wrong. Wind stirred through the trees as I paced back and forth across my home. Marjorie had joined Scarlett as I left, promising to care for her with a concerned look at the High Priestess.

An hour passed.

My discomfort increased.

Something wasn't right. Scarlett's ill health might be attributable to stress, but she'd experienced far worse than this. The night terrors, the weakness, the general lethargy and yawning.

To Leda, I asked, *Is it possible that Scarlett has been poisoned?*

Leda responded several moments later.

What?

Quickly, I recounted our visit, finishing with, *Marjorie was going to take her upstairs once Scarlett awoke.*

Eventually, Leda said, *I suppose I can look into it, but she hasn't been eating much. Her appetite is down. Mostly, she's drinking broth and tea . . .*

She trailed away.

My terrible supposition elevated like acid in my throat. How many times had I heard Scarlett requesting Leda bring her tea lately?

What tea? I demanded.

Hold, please, Leda said with a note of flurried panic. *I'll go check.*

While waiting, I tilted my head to the side, lifted my chin to the sky, and forced myself to relax. Slowly, my head dipped to the other side in an exaggerated stretch, tilting Goat and Other Goat. They peered at me, lower jaws working, as they chewed grasses brought up from the forest floor by Letum Wood. My deepening dread grew.

The hairs on the back of my neck lifted as the trees called out a warning.

Peril returns—

A stiff breeze slammed into me from behind. The forest washed into stark silence as another voice spoke over the trees.

"Evening, Miss Monroe. My, my. How busy you have been today. Such effort, flittering around your Network, solving problems that aren't yours."

Viveet, laying across the room on my table, shot into the air on my command. The moment her handle touched my palm, I spun. Her azure flames bloomed as I dropped into a crouch and faced the main door.

Acid rose into my throat as Greyson appeared in my doorway. His usual impassioned face regarded me with haughty disregard. Gone was the playful delight of last time, when I chased him all over the Western Covens and landed at Carcere. Something far more sinister changed his expression.

"How did you find me?" I snarled.

The trees keened. Sapphire light pooled at my feet, but Deasylva didn't speak. The forest hardly breathed.

"You may be a beloved witch, Bianca, and hailed as the Lady Witch of Letum Wood, but that doesn't make you indomitable."

My jaw clenched as I muttered, "Demmed close, though. You have two seconds to leave before—"

He snorted. "Before your tree dispatches me?"

"Before *I* dispatch you."

"Then Scarlett will die. Surely, you've seen how awful she looks these days. Do you really want that?"

The gleam that entered his bland expression was a frightening sign. Hardly a heartbeat later, Leda's panicked voice spun through my head.

Bianca! It's Scarlett. She's collapsed. I just came to check on the tea she's drinking and found her on the floor with Marjorie. I've called for Apothecaries. We can't rouse her.

Stark, I whispered to Greyson, "What have you done?"

His features rearranged into a cold, cruel smile. "Initiated the game, my dear Miss Monroe. All your hard work to discover the truth and answer the building questions has finally come to its inevitable end. The Gamemaster has arrived."

The violet cloak, garish top hat, and flower appeared all at once, belying the sinister edge of his voice.

He reached into a pocket. I elevated Viveet halfway up my chest and into mid guard, bracing my feet. A smile flickered across the corner of Greyson's mouth as he comprehended the movement. Unbothered, he withdrew a thin glass vial. It sparkled in his hand, the width of my pinky finger, and as long.

"Inside is the antidote to the poisoned tea Scarlett has been steadily consuming for the last six weeks. The general accumulation of it in her blood will lead to seizures within . . ." He paused, glanced toward my twig-like clock on the far wall, and back to me, ". . . three hours. But not if you administer the antidote."

Fury ballooned like a cloud.

"This is your game?" I asked through clenched teeth. "You want to quietly poison our High Priestess?"

"Dear Bianca," he said patiently, "life is but a game, and Scarlett is not my only prey. To Carcere with you!" he cried, his dark eyes brightening with a maniacal fervor. "The game shall commence as soon as you step inside those hallowed halls, although Scarlett's own life ticks away. There is no time to rally the Brotherhood, even if the Sisterhood wanted their support. Certainly, you don't need it, do you?"

His drawling scorn rankled almost as much as his words. My breaths were long, hissing things as they expelled. Greyson ticked an eyebrow higher as he replaced the antidote in his pocket.

"Tick tock, Miss Monroe. You shall need every single second of those three hours to save your darling High Priestess' life."

Bianca! Leda insisted. *Can you hear me?*

Swallowing hard, I said, *I hear you.*

I need you.

Greyson smirked, as if he knew what Leda said. Impossible, but it wouldn't take much to guess. He would know that I wouldn't look so panicked on only his information. He drew himself taller, shoulders expanding. His smile flashed with wicked, white teeth.

"Enter Carcere and find your way to me. If you make it, you will have an opportunity to fight for Scarlett's life."

My heart nearly stopped as he vanished into a transportation spell. The moment he disappeared, the trees activated, as if his presence bound them. Their shrieks and terrified cries created a discordant chaos not unlike that which came alive in my mind.

A trap.

Greyson laid a trap. I could go to the Brotherhood, take the time to explain, form a plan, and then approach, but what if Scarlett died? The maniacal pleasure in his eyes told me that he meant every word.

Heart pounding in my chest, I made the decision. Foolhardy

or desperate, it didn't matter. I had to follow. To Leda, I calmly said, *It's poison. Greyson just found me—he has the antidote. He's started the game.*

What?

I'm going after it.

Bianca, no!

We don't have an alternative. In three hours, she's going to start having seizures. He said it came through the tea. Do everything you can to counteract it or find its source. Grandfather might have a book —ask him.

I ... I will.

Stay close to Scarlett, and—

I'll be available to you, too. Whatever you need, let me know.

I will.

Bianca? she said hastily.

Yes?

Be safe.

Her plea echoed in my head as I closed my eyes and drew in a deep breath, activating the transportation spell to Carcere.

The gaping hole in the side of the circular turret whistled in the wind, drawing my attention. I stood before Carcere, on the quietest island I had ever set foot on, without invisibility. Waves crashed, muted. Sunlight scattered brilliant white diamonds over the sea top and into the wave troughs, yet all I comprehended was that black hole.

Carcere.

A wicked, broken place.

On my first visit, Ricardo's presence and sheer haste prevented me from noticing the little details, and each told a story. Based on the rubble scattering the sand, the explosion likely came from within, though I'd need to go inside to confirm. Char marks meant there had been some kind of fire.

It would be foolish not to assume that Greyson tracked my every move, so I kept my contemplative stare on the slowly breaking turret, my thoughts deliberate and slow. Knowing Leda had my back bolstered my courage for whatever lay ahead.

I'm outside Carcere, I said.

Talk to me as often as you can. With any luck, the suppressive magic is gone. Talmund and Marten are here. Rognvald is on the way. Apothecaries are congregating now. No change in her status.

Don't tell them—

I haven't, but I won't be able to avoid your grandfather much longer. He keeps looking at me.

What can you tell me about Carcere? I asked.

With increasing confidence, she said, *Off the cuff, I can tell you that the magic for the prison isn't well understood. It was erected hundreds of years ago, and the original witch to put it together very intentionally kept themselves apart from it. There's no attribution to their name because they didn't want to be remembered for it.*

Staring into that deep, dank hole, I felt a shudder that had nothing to do with the air temperature.

Can't say that I blame them.

Give me a few minutes and I can find more facts.

Send me whatever you can about the interior, the layout, whatever is known.

Whatever I find might be from legend. There's notoriously little information regarding Carcere. Some reportedly escaped prisoners have spoken about enchanted objects, but, also reportedly, no one has ever escaped alive. At best, there might be accounts from East Guards.

Send whatever you can.

Not a soul stirred on the island as I padded through the sand, cognizant of each passing minute. If I didn't think of Greyson, the game, the antidote, then the panic and fear simmered below the surface.

Underneath Carcere, glittering window panes and flower boxes and views into a well-maintained interior occupied the other floors. The disparity between the ghoulish top and the luxury apartments apparent below was haunting.

What the Aldana's used those floors for, I couldn't say. In fact, I didn't know what they'd *ever* been used for. The polished, refined feel of the place lent to some sort of retreat, perched below the most infamous case of restrictive magic Alkarra had ever known. The idea was mildly horrifying.

Who could spend their time here with any comfort knowing what sat above them?

An open door swung on squeaky hinges on the first floor, so I stepped inside and paced through the circular interior. A hall ringed all the way around, leading to interior rooms. A staircase led me higher.

On the second floor, nothing revealed itself. Another set of stairs led me higher until I paused at a door with charred black edges and half-obliterated. It opened onto a branching staircase, thin and carved into stone. Wood chips littered the stairs and ground beneath it. No one had cleaned it up, because they probably left as fast as they could. I crunched over rubble to peer up the abandoned enclosure, a draft of shivery air washed by.

I think I found the entrance.

Great timing. Leda sounded breathless. *I conjured a book I remembered from before. It has accounts from witches who worked there. Guardians, mostly. The problem is that none of them corroborate.*

What do you mean?

They're all different. Some talk about circular cells, others square. Some report windows, others report utter blackness. One of them talks about mirrors that reflect anomalies that aren't real.

Anomalies?

I don't know.

The prison could change in different places, I suppose, I mused as its foul exhalations washed over my cheeks.

Assume great instability, Leda said.

Staring into the awaiting abyss, I paused. The dank smell was overwhelming with rot and time. Though I saw only a single set of stairs that evaporated into darkness, a sense of overwhelming size loomed.

Carcere prison had the feel of an ancient, breathing, livid monster. Something that wanted revenge.

Something that seethed.

In general, Leda continued, *I've found only information about irregularity and circles and vanishing staircases. Mostly from East Guards interviewed in secret. I think most of them were under an oath not to speak about the prison, but they must have broken it.*

A magical oath?

Must be.

That would be painful.

I would assume so.

The only window in the stairwell displayed the final hints of the moon hiding behind the thrashing clouds outside. The sea raged and waves frothed, a tempest-laden background to this terrible day. I didn't know what I'd find once I crossed this threshold. With Greyson waiting and Scarlett's life on the line, lingering wasn't an option.

With a spell, I conjured a torch. The smell of torch oil emanated with crisp notes reminiscent of moldy cheese. A spell lit the end with a flare of light and blazed with a friendly burn, sending light onto the dank walls.

I'm going in.

Chapter Twenty-Eight

Ghostly tempest and silence welcomed me as I shuffled into the shadows, leaving behind Alkarra to discover a more tenebrous, livid world. The sense of shifting from one realm to another accompanied me, as if I truly left them behind.

Can you still hear me?

Yes.

Relief was a warm rush through my veins.

I forced my feet to continue. Within a few steps, Carcere's main Guardian post came into view. A desk, a canted chair, and whispering pages lay on the floor. Speedily abandoned, it appeared.

No friendly, kind chatter from an old keeper. No vague smile or blithe questions or uncertain glances, attempting to understand my reason for coming. Only the ringing, empty quiet of long-dead days. Carcere poured out of its dark, swilling hellhole and spilled onto the island in dull, reverberative notes. My stomach churned.

Hesitation accompanied me as I worked past the moldering main desk and moved steadily upward. As if my heart didn't pound, or mind didn't race, or questions plague me as to whether I made a big mistake.

Leda's steady voice had a slight edge, as if she swallowed her fear. *What can I do to help? Do you need any further information? No changes on Scarlett, though Marten has retrieved several books. They're speaking about different poisons now.*

I'll let you know, I promised, grateful that her chatter broke up the terrifying, bleak canopy ahead. *I don't know if magic will work while I'm deeper inside. If you don't hear from me in two hours, send Rognvald. But not before then, just in case.*

Malodorous air drew me up another set of steps. Rustling parchments shivered on the cold stone floor, littered near an abandoned shoe, candle stubs, and an overturned lunch pail. The contents had long been swept away by wind or rodents.

Cooler air poured over my flushed cheeks. The tenor of it had changed, but I couldn't put a finger on how. A weird echo warbled forward. The repeat of each shuffling step. Everything felt different.

I think I'm approaching the threshold into Carcere, beyond the Guardian's desk. I'd wager it was an intake spot. I think . . . I think this *is where Carcere truly begins.*

I'm noting these directions for Rognvald, just in case. Tell me any change in your plans or directions. After a pause, she added, *Be safe, Bianca.*

Two hours.

Two hours.

Rubble populated Carcere's floors as readily as sand. As I advanced into a hallway as wide as a carriage, my boot soles grazed along broken stones. Hollow, heavy pieces that might have been bones. Less than a minute had passed when I glanced back and saw nothing. When I elevated the torch, no ceiling became apparent. The feeling of expansive air loomed overhead.

The mystery of Carcere defied understanding.

While I wasn't sure where I stood in relation to the broken exterior wall, it must be close. A burned smell soured the space, mixing with centuries old air. Whistling, distant wind picked up and then died at regular intervals.

I kept moving.

"Greyson?"

Of course, he gave no reply. I brought Viveet out of her sheath and used a spell to levitate the torch. Thank the goddess, the magic still worked.

Darker recesses contained chains hanging from the wall, near stains so dark they could only be old blood. Rust dusted the manacles along the ground, which lay in wet pools that stank. Char marks spiraled on the floor where a fallen torch had burned for a number of minutes after falling. I nudged it with a toe and listened.

Stillness.

The torch revealed more details of the area, enough to assume we stood in a main passageway that cut narrow and straight, with other halls petaling to the side. Cursory exploration revealed cells in clusters of four, all closed with wooden bars. No sign of life existed except discarded items that, at one point, were likely weapons of torture. Mallets. Sledgehammers. Giant nails.

I shuddered and moved on.

"Merry meet?"

My own voice called in return.

Meet . . . meet . . . meet . . .

On second thought, I paused, conjured an invisible, protective shield. It flared in a shimmer of light that radiated ahead of the torch, then settled with a sigh. Feeling marginally better, I pressed on.

I winged my left elbow out to follow the stone wall, rubbed

smooth after years of use. On my command, the torch swung to the right. The passage had an upwards tilt, moving higher. My eyes adjusted to the dark, noting the slanting floor, rounded ceiling, and the increasing number of cell clusters. Twenty four, and no other hallways. Each scuffle of footstep rang through the cavernous space with surprising force.

How *big* was Carcere?

Can you still hear me, Leda?

Yes, but you're distant.

Will you remind me to ask Grandfather about spells to see in the dark?

Sure. A few heartbeats, and then, *You're deeper inside, then?*

Yes.

What's it like? Where are you going? Narrate what you can, just in case.

The brilliance of her idea would keep me from thinking too hard about this horrifying situation. My throat tightened when I admitted, *It's suffocating. Very dark.*

Literally suffocating?

No.

With Carcere, one never knows.

She fell silent. I listened, waiting for a shuffle of movement, a squeak. Something. Nothing stirred. What a strange place. Full of so much, but so little. Unable to bear it another moment, I called, "I'm here!"

A voice hissed ahead, serpentine and hideous. "You are here," it slithered, "but you are not yet proven. No witch enters Carcere without first answering to me."

Hold on, I said to Leda. *Something just spoke to me.*

Like what?

No idea.

Light flared ahead. Subdued, despite the suffocating darkness. Muted ruby flowers appeared, one at a time, two paces above my eye line. They flourished along trailing vines, swooping horizontal to the right and left. At exactly the same distance, they dropped down. Ten. Twelve. Fourteen. Twenty. They paused, then swirled inward along a viridian vine to form a rectangle. As they glowed, a light appeared.

No, a witch.

I sucked in a breath through my nostrils. My heart galloped until I recognized my own pale, shocked face.

A mirror.

As quickly as I realized it, I angled my focus off the silvery surface and onto the rosebuds gracing the edges. Any fool knew never to look directly into an enchanted mirror when one didn't know what magic hummed behind it.

Madness, mayhem, or a deadly mixture of both awaited those who dared.

Just beyond my right shoulder, a ghostly visage appeared in the mirror. More lines than substance. I whirled around, found nothing. In the mirror, the vapid skeleton remained. A glacial rush trickled down my head like an egg broken on top, lifting goosebumps on my arms.

"Who are you?" I asked, gaze averted to the bottom edge. The flowers glowed, carmine and bloody. The mirror wraith grinned, eye sockets and teeth brilliant in the reflection. The voice hissed at my right ear, distinctly feminine in her pitched strands.

"I am Spira."

I whispered, "Spira?"

The word loosely translated to *death* in the language of the Ancients, but not a physical death. *Letum* meant the expiration of the body. *Spira* represented the expiration of the soul.

Leda?

Yes?

Her immediate response brought instant comfort. If nothing else, a tether to the outside world remained.

Ever heard of an enchanted mirror named Spira?

Spira?

Conjures a ghost visible only within the mirror.

Spira swiveled around, twirling in a circle until she hovered near my sternum.

I'll research now.

"Look into my eyes, witch, and I shall allow you passage into the lands of Carcere," Spira called. The odd sibilance of her voice wavered a little.

Lands.

I swallowed rising hysteria. Of course, strolling inside had been too easy. I whipped to the right, seeing nothing as the chill swept nearby. She cackled as a cold breeze crawled across my collarbone and to my other shoulder. Risking a quick glance at the mirror, Spira hovered near my other ear. Her breath was a shivery hiss.

She smiled at me with all her teeth, her lips appearing and disappearing every other moment. I kept the mirror visible out of the corner of my eye.

"What happens if I don't look into your eyes?"

She wheezed a breathy, "Look into my eyes to proceed, or turn your back, and I shall eat your bones."

Spira's demand drove a maddening chill through the air. I attempted to breathe normally, buying time, but had no idea what to say. Proceed or turn back? Either way I met my probable death. A metaphorical rock and hard place. Look at her, go mad. Leave, she'll attack.

Carcere.

What a delightful place.

"See me," Spira growled. "See me, witch who dares. Witch who comes on her own feet without the Guards to accompany her."

Leda? I sang.

I'm looking! she cried.

Time is of the essence.

Her snappy, *I get it!* silenced me.

Right. On my own for the moment. My mind raced. Spira, clearly a dark magic imbued into a mirror, hadn't been affected by

Carcere's explosion. That made sense, since the communication magic also worked.

There would be no way around her. Dark, crimson ribbons spiraled near the mirror, reaching for the sidewalls. She was a net, of sorts. An intentional net. Spira must be separate from Carcere, though I didn't doubt they forced prisoners to face her. She mentioned it herself.

Why?

Did she assign cells? Predict the future? Read minds? Such a nefarious mirror must have a purpose. I'd known of a few mirrors that acted as truthsayers. They peeled back all layers of a witch that peered into them, revealing foundational facets. Some witches sought truthsayers, seeking their heritage or their past. Others avoided them.

"You stall!" she squealed.

To buy another moment or two, I admitted, "Yes, I do," because lying to a truthsayer was a poor strategy.

A sense of hesitation stole over her. "You do not lie," she hissed. "Why?"

Ah. If not a truthsayer, then something close to it. Her question meant she didn't guess. How interesting to experience in a prison.

"Why would I lie?" I asked.

"All who enter lie."

I found a grimoire, Leda's hasty voice came. *Give me two minutes.*

"All who enter lie?" I countered. "That sounds a little dramatic. I would wager most prisoners were too frightened of you to lie."

The frigid kiss of air swirled in a circle ahead of me again, like ice in a whirlwind. Agitation? Curiosity? Whatever Spira thought of my comments, she probably didn't like being challenged.

"All witches lie to themselves."

"That," I murmured, "sounds right."

"You are attempting to learn something," she drawled. "You are stalling."

"Correct. Like you, I'm curious. There are a lot of reasons for a truthsayer to inhabit a prison. Are you a truthsayer, Spira?"

"I am not only a truthsayer."

"Oh really?"

Spira circled near me again. The white, trailing wisps were visible only in the mirror as she floated around. Different parts of her body came into sight, in various stages of reality. A shoulder, then bones for ribs. A full, lithe neck, but sockets for eyes. Her nose flashed, a gaping hole, then smooth ridge.

As a truthsayer, Spira would be bound to a certain physical proximity from her mirror. Anyone who peered into it would face exactly what Spira gave—the truth. Themselves, as they were. Past decisions, lives, mistakes. I had little interest in the distraction.

"You insult me with your question," Spira said. "You don't believe I am more than a truthsayer?"

"Forgive me, I never intended to offend you. I was called to Carcere. I don't enter these halls with guilt."

"I see that you speak the truth."

Spira, Leda said, *is an ancient enchantment. She was a witch that lived before recorded time. Something about a broken heart . . . cheating lover . . . lost child . . . tragedy undercut her life. She eventually retreated into an enchanted mirror and survived for millennia. From what I can see, she was known for being a truthsayer. Rumors abound that she had the quadrille—was truthsayer, mindreader, futureseer, and pastkeeper, but it's largely understood as false.*

Counterspells! I cried. *Any sort of counter spell?*

I'm searching.

Spira's cold breath raced across my cheeks. "Your reply requires too long, and I sense your stirring words. To whom do you speak?" Her tone had a dragging, saccharine curiosity. "To whom are you discussing Spira?"

"You're also a mindreader?"

"I am more!" Spira thundered. "I am truthsayer and mindreader. I am futureseer and pastkeeper. I am Spira!"

A glacial wall of wind whipped over my face, cutting into my cheeks like sharp slivers of ice. Her words turned my attention on its head.

Futureseer.

Pastkeeper.

I knew those phrases. Not from Alkarran folklore, but from the third letter, when Ellie Victoriann and Marie Hazel met fate. My heart raced with new understanding.

"Yes," Spira crooned. "I hear your beating heart, singing to me. Oh, how it pounds. Oh, how it thuds. Chirp, little heart bird. Chirp for me."

The cold collected over my heart. I forced myself to hold still, not flinch. Thus far, she hadn't moved any closer to me. She swirled overhead, or close to, but not behind. By some luck, I must have stopped at or just before her boundary. Unless she wanted me to think that, and would strike at any moment.

I found a spell! Leda said. *Are you in front of Spira now?*

Yes.

Oh, Bianca, this is too complicated!

Spira hovered close. Had she a body, she might have been smelling me. "What do you desire to know, Lady Witch of Letum Wood?"

Ah. Mindreader, for certain. "Why are you here?" I asked.

"See me!"

"Not yet," I immediately countered. Beyond the mirror, I thought I saw movement. Spira hovered in the air, clearly borne on a spell. No legs, no cords held her from above or below. With a silent command, I conjured a flame in my fingers. Light flared, dissipating as quickly.

Magic was still possible.

A good sign.

"You are Bianca Monroe." Spira twisted again. I had a feeling she hovered right in front of my eyes, but I saw nothing except the gilded, flowered edge of the mirror. "You came to save your High Priestess and prove yourself worthy of leadership."

Affecting as mild a tone as possible, I said, "Correct, pastkeeper."

Spira slipped closer. Her fetid, cool breath rattled across my cheek, as if she leaned in for a kiss. I imagined her empty eye socket hovering just in front of mine, peering inside. Could she reap all the truth and motivations for coming here?

"Did you come alone?" Her breath rasped over my neck. "Yes, yes you did. You came alone, as bidden. Except you didn't. I sense the other witch in your mind. Her voice stirs. Your thoughts agitate. How very strange."

Ah.

That is why Greyson placed her here. A checkpoint. He wanted to make sure I brought no one with me, that I had no escape plans.

"I see," Spira murmured, her voice garbled. "I see your mind, Bianca Monroe. The dark pits. The chasms. The places saturated with fear, and others with love. What a wild mind you have created . . ."

I'll try to repeat it to you, but it's long, Leda said.

No. Wait.

Leda fell silent.

"My turn to ask a question," I said crisply. "Why did Greyson put you here?"

The vapor retreated, and stale air replaced it. I doubted these stones had ever been warm.

"He did not put me here."

"The Guardians did."

"Yes," she hissed.

"Greyson took ownership of you. You're bound to him."

Mildly, Spira said, "You already knew, so why did you ask?"

"I suspected," I said with brutal honesty. "Greyson's making sure that no one follows me."

"You speak his name twice."

Her surprise confused me. Why wouldn't I speak Greyson's name? "I imagine you and I are not so different. Are you lonely, Spira? Do you miss the sunlight?"

"I am bones."

"Me too."

"I am death!" she shrieked.

Spira was bound to her mirror and to a witch, Leda continued. I could imagine her whipping through pages, scouring each sentence. *In order to defeat her, you would have to break her bond to one, or both. The incantation will do both, but it's too complicated to do without the book.*

Turning away from Leda's whispers, and with real sincerity, I said, "Forgive me, Spira. I figured you were truth, not death."

For a hallowed silence, Spira said nothing.

Silver, Leda said. *You can drive something made of pure silver into the mirror to break her bond with it.*

What about her bound witch?

The spell.

There's no other option?

Well . . . I'm not sure. I just found an article . . . Bianca, I think that she can't be Spira. She was destroyed ages ago, and that is confirmed by many sources. If you're looking in an enchanted mirror that calls itself Spira, it's probably something else.

"You speak to the other one," Spira, or not Spira, purred. She'd stopped moving, hovered in place. The writhing fog became less frantic. It hung, limp and dank, like a lost cloud. Half of Spira's face flashed into sight in the mirror. "You are trying to kill me."

"I'm definitely not."

"What else would you say to the other witch in your head?"

"Not that."

"What *do* you say?"

"You can't tell?"

"Your mind is a slippery lake, Bianca Monroe, daughter of Deasylva, runner of trails, the Lady Witch of Letum Wood."

Which part of her saw those truths? Futureseer, or pastkeeper?

Spira must not know what Leda and I said. Perhaps she detected flows of magic. The systems, not the nuances. Yet that didn't make sense. She knew what to call me, my connection to Deasylva.

I noted those disparities for later.

The unnerving truth that Spira sorted through my mind without me sensing it made me want to vomit. It had been bad enough when Isadora searched my future paths, or Hiddleston my past. There was a particular intimacy to them knowing everything that did, or could, happen.

I returned my focus to the task at hand: getting out of here. *The letters,* I said to Leda. *The answer is in one of the letters. It has to be.*

Ask her about herself while I search, Leda suggested. *They love to be heard. Say her name, too. It's flattering for them, apparently.*

"Even wraiths have preferences, no? Do you prefer sunshine or darkness, Spira?"

After a moment of pause, she purred, "Neither."

"I'm curious how a truthsayer of obvious power, and such beauty, found her way into a place like this."

At the edge of my vision, Spira paused. She lingered near the mirror, a set of bones in swirling mist. I edged a step to the left.

"I was the first, and the last."

Her mournful tone set the hair on the back of my neck on end. *The first.*

Just like Ellie Victoriann, the first orphan—prisoner?—who could fly. My breath hitched.

"The first prisoner?" I ventured tentatively.

"Yes."

"In Carcere, you mean?"

Lashing, she shouted, "Yes!"

The ghostly sound wailed down the corridor.

Not Spira, I said frantically to Leda. *She's the first prisoner, somehow bound to the mirror.*

I'm on it, she said calmly. *I'm looking at the letters now.*

"You're not the real Spira, are you?"

In a weepy voice, she exclaimed, "No."

I gentled my tone. "How old are you, Spira?"

"Hundreds of years."

"Why were you bound to this mirror?"

"Punishment."

Her voice crinkled like fallen leaves, touched with mourning and a hint of disbelief. As if, after all this time, she couldn't believe it either. Instinct cautioned me to go slowly. Everything Greyson did thus far had been purposeful.

"Tell me, Spira. What did you expect to find when you read my mind, spoke my truth, sought my future, and viewed my past?"

"Hatred. Murder. Determination."

"Did you find them?"

"Only two."

"Which ones?"

"The latter."

"Murder and determination," I mused. "Whose murder?"

"His."

The lone syllable rippled almost out of sight. A rigid slant filled her voice. *His.* She didn't say his name. Could bound witches speak the name of the witch to whom they were enslaved? A distant stirring in my mind thought not, which explained her surprise over why *I* said Greyson's name.

She thought I was bound.

In a way, she had it right.

I can't find anything specific in the letters to what you've told me, Leda said. *At best, in the third letter, is the line: Fate holds a mirror, and the mirror sees all. But that's rubbish. Nor is there a definite path for overpowering such a thing. At best, some witches have had luck with a shield or mirroring spell. One attempted to do both, but the results aren't written. Nothing in the letters either, but I need more time.*

Frowning, I recalled a powerful mirror spell in the books Grandfather had given me a few weeks ago. The incantation I remembered roughly. Enough I could eke the magic free, but perhaps not harness it with great skill.

I paused, drew a deep breath. Spira stopped her gnashing. My gaze, locked on the bottom line of the mirror, caught sight of her agitated movement decreasing. I couldn't think of the spells too soon or Spira might mindread them. Couldn't consider a plan, either. My thoughts skipped around.

As I did so, Spira went utterly still, flashing in and out of sight. An arm. Her hair. I thought of Papa, and my pulse calmed, breath steadied. Spira's half-bald head tilted to the side, as if further confused.

"I cannot read you, Lady Witch. I do not understand your calm state."

I pulled in a deep breath.

Time to go.

Mirror and shield spells at the ready, I whipped around to face Spira head on. The reflective surface, tarnished with black spots in the middle, had degraded in the intervening minutes. When I first glanced at it, it was silvery, whole, and beautiful. Accelerating time wore on it. The hideous flowers faded to gray. The once-green streaks had long tarnished with the blotted black spots in the middle.

I cast the magic.

First, I strengthened my existing shield spell, then commanded the mirror spell second.

When I met Spira's face, I attempted to look into her eyes. Distractions built behind her, making it almost impossible. Fire. Flames. Tree branches. A familiar visage—Mama falling to the floor. Papa, on the ground, a sword skewered through his chest, blood bubbling from his lips. Merrick keeled over a wall, then disappeared as he fell off.

I sucked in a sharp breath.

The gods, she accessed and displayed my nightmares.

The unexpected assault of every fear I'd ever harbored caused me to waver in my spellcasting. The mirror spell disintegrated before it fully formed. Spira screamed, drawing me further from my intent as she whirled across the shield spell, mouth gaping open several paces wide, and attempted to devour me. The shield saved me.

At the last second, I abandoned the mirror spell. No, that wouldn't work. Too expected, too obvious. A ghoul like Spira, who worked in a well-trafficked prison with all types of unsavory witches, would have warded herself better.

The line from the third letter resurrected in my mind.

Fate holds a mirror, and the mirror sees all.

My shield spell disintegrated into granules of sand as Spira swooped a second time, overpowering it with magic and a shriek that made my ears ache. I re-cast, strengthening the shield with a repetition that cost me time.

Spira's attacks chipped away at the spell. I reforged it, wasting more precious time, until she caught me in a desperate spell loop. I couldn't win, because I couldn't stop defending. Spira would only gain power. Once she fed on me, her mirror would be larger and more dense. Her powers would be greater.

Bianca?

Not now!

The terrifying, bass roar that emitted from Spira's throat drowned Leda's voice. Spira doubled in size, even as the mirror shrank. It waved like a shriveled fruit, lowering and shrinking with every minute that passed.

Spira stood ten paces away. Her form gained greater solidity. She had a torso, a long skirt. Her arms were still bones, but all her hair had returned. Behind her, horrors continued. I didn't dare look at them. I'd see Mama, Papa, Merrick.

Instead of recasting the shield spell, I threw my life-force into a chance. I silently cast a deception spell of the mirror, commanding it to hover in the air above me. It would appear immediately across from the mirror, and near Spira herself.

The roars fell to silence.

Spira floated above me, the ends of her lush skirt trailing into nothing a pace above my body, which now lay on the floor. I didn't remember ducking. Didn't notice the cool press of stones against my spine until this moment. I'd stared so hard into her eyes, I hadn't paid attention to whatever else happened. Spira regarded herself through my deception spell mirror, and at the perfect replica of her mirror prison.

Her hand elevated, touched the surface of my deception-spell mirror. It didn't break, because Spira had no real substance. The horrors she revealed bled away behind her, scattering to smoke.

"All these years," she whispered, "and I have not seen myself. Have only seen others. You, young warrior. You set me free."

With an explosive *bang*, Spira, her mirror, and all the light in the dim corridor, went absolutely dark.

<h1 style="text-align:center">Chapter Twenty-Nine</h1>

The sound of a breath, as if someone experienced deep relief, followed Spira's final exclamation. Through the darkness, Greyson's voice curled toward me before I had the presence of mind to stand up and grope around for my forgotten torch.

"I see you, Bianca Monroe."

I whipped around, shoulders pressed to the damp wall. Nothing revealed, but I hadn't expected it.

Spira's gone.

Leda didn't reply.

Greyson wouldn't forfeit his element of surprise. Thankfully, he kept speaking. I couldn't fathom anything more horrifying than that silence.

"Welcome to Carcere, Bianca. Care to share your thoughts on the experience so far?"

"Your guard dog was lovely."

His chuckle amplified, as if I had moved into an underground grotto. Belatedly, I realized that Spira hid the entrance to some grander place. I saw nothing, but a sense of massive size sprawled overhead. Cool air trickled past. A distant drip of water made me wonder exactly *where* I ventured.

Attempts to conjure a candle failed.

Leda?

You're faint, she replied, and so was she. Until her voice answered just above a whisper, I didn't realize how much I clung to it. Something about the cavern must suppress the magic, or was it Greyson?

I'm fine, I said. *You may not hear me anymore, but I'm fine. I'll contact you as soon as I can. Don't leave her side.*

A very distant, *Be safe.*

"Are you afraid of the dark, Miss Monroe?"

I put a hand on Viveet and yanked her from her sheath. Brilliant blue flames, sparking with power, crackled from the blade. Not only did she cast light on a stony wall, narrowing slightly ahead, and wet with moss and general dampness, but her comfort blanketed me.

A flash of eyes awaited. Greyson, dim in Viveet's flickering flames.

"No."

Despite the strange magical suppression, Viveet worked. Did that have something to do with Deasylva's power? Perhaps the goddess gave me a boon in the most unexpected of ways. Or maybe Carcere had a strange way of devolving some magic, but not others. Did rules exist in a building like this?

They must, but one had to discover them.

"Follow me, Miss Monroe. We shall end this game."

"Sounds fraught with opportunity to go wrong."

"I wagered that you'd defeat Spira, you know," Greyson said, his voice as resonant as if he shouted into a barrel. He disappeared into shadows, his consonants fading in power with each syllable. "I gave you all the answers."

I shuffled forward, Viveet ahead of me. Unable to see anything but a step or two ahead, I wondered if I could track his position by his voice. Retreating footsteps sounded directly before me, so I followed. Wherever we walked, I sensed no walls, no ceiling.

"Spira claimed to be the first prisoner," he continued conversationally, "like Ellie Victoriann was the first orphan to gain flight. Is that why you decided to free Spira instead of fighting her?"

"You freed Ellie Victoriann. I figured I might as well try the same."

"Very good." His clinical voice had little inflection. "Had you fought Spira, you would have died. How did you know about the deception spell instead of a mirror spell?"

"I didn't."

"Really?"

"Instinct."

He cleared his throat, much farther ahead already. Irritated, I swung Viveet around to orient, but the effort led to nothing.

"Some things in this life seem to defy logic. You, Bianca Monroe, are often one of them. I anticipated as much, although it was a very Derek-Black thing to do."

"Thanks. I think. Would the mirror spell have worked?"

"No."

Viveet blazed as I passed a cell. Crossing iron bars blocked us from entering a rectangular space with nothing inside except old hay and a warped wooden board. Few indications that it ever held a prisoner.

Greyson asked, "Carcere is an interesting place, isn't it?"

"A regular paradise."

Light flared at least fifty paces away, revealing a dark hole in a wall, shrouded with chains. The light came from within what appeared to be a cramped, empty space. Black rock, drilled with holes, showed many of them side by side.

"I stayed in that cell on your right for a month," he said.

I still couldn't find him. His voice seemed to come from everywhere and nowhere. I advanced, wondering if this wasn't a little like Marie Hazel in the second letter, seeking answers in the retreating ocean.

"Was the service in your cell as exemplary as you expected?" I asked.

"You can't imagine."

The rolling evenness of his tone, devoid of malice or amusement or *anything*, sent a shiver through me. How could any witch contain such large amounts of nothing?

"I hope imagining is all I'll ever have to do about this place," I said in an attempt to match his sardonic tone. "You must be devastated that it's broken."

As I inched forward, the acoustics changed. I cast Viveet around, finding a juncture of branching halls that bisected a few paces ahead. Attempts to map the location in my mind failed utterly.

If I could keep Greyson talking, I might *find* him.

"Continue, Miss Monroe. The Gamemaster beckons, and greatness and antidotes await."

"Lovely."

With Viveet ahead, I feared no creatures or monsters, as I might in Letum Wood. Though I couldn't help the irrational fear that Spira's unbound skeleton might leap from the cracks and crevices.

Nothing attacked.

Nothing alive, anyway.

The creeping, awful darkness that poured onto Carcere island had intensified, so thick in these buried walls that it choked every breath. A mossy scent stung my sinuses as I stepped over another puddle. Where did all the water come from? Footsteps issued ahead. I swung Viveet that direction and found Greyson striding into an alcove.

Leda?

No response.

"I am a witch of sound understanding, Miss Monroe." His

voice carried from within as he vanished around a corner. "Logic and facts ring true for me in more ways than you might think possible. As a witch, I seek the challenges and mysteries of the world. As a Gamemaster, I seek the ability to solve difficult circumstances and prove myself."

Following, Viveet held in both hands, I called after him, "Including how to steal power and rule the Central Network?"

"All challenges," he blandly replied.

I barked a laugh.

"I am not interested in a match of physical prowess, Miss Monroe, though I would undoubtedly be able to overpower you."

"Undoubtedly?"

As I neared the juncture that he'd taken, I almost opted to stay in the safety of the main passageway, but curiosity drew me forward. I listened, venturing slowly. A light glowed at the far end, more suggestion than shine. Hesitating, I glanced behind my shoulder to see the same velvety wall of darkness. It seemed foolish to leave the known, steady path, but this was Carcere.

Dark magic.

Evil witch.

I wandered into the junction, noting the turn, keeping the mental map high in my mind, as Greyson explained his factually-stated arrogance.

"As a young man, I kept my body in prime physical shape, thanks to life in the Western Covens. I am physically strong. My prowess is capable. As a male, I have more upper body strength and brawn than you. Logic follows."

Before I could swing Viveet's blade into his condescending spine, he continued with, "But I find it barbaric and inefficient to prove ability on sheer might alone. No matter what you think of your skillset, Miss Monroe, I *am* bigger and older than you."

My teeth gritted.

Jikes, but I couldn't wait to take him down.

Goading me into a frothing rage might be part of his plan, and that was the only thing that calmed my ire. Inciting emotion in order to make me do something stupid would be a capable and wise strategy. If that was his aim, he certainly emphasized the correct sensitivities. I wouldn't let him goad me this soon.

"If there is nothing physical to prove your obvious superiority, what did you have in mind?"

Something rattled in the cavern I exited. The wet sound echoed through the hallway half the size of the previous one. The ceiling was so low that the top of my head nearly brushed the apex. My left hand trailed along the rough stones. Viveet led the way, undimmed.

"A challenge of logic and magic that shall satisfy my desire for revenge."

My gut twisted.

He had the wrong Sisterhood member for a game of logic.

"Go on," I sang.

My voice tripled, repeating in a strange singsong that sounded as if someone else distorted it.

On, on, on.

The muted glow became a shine from behind a wall. Greyson had already disappeared inside. I closed in with deepening uncertainty.

"You win the game by having higher intellect and mightier magic, Miss Monroe. You are a young opponent, but perhaps the most worthy opponent in the Central Network."

"You're pandering."

"I'm not."

He spoke with such seriousness in his tone that I no longer doubted him, despite the plethora of witches he glossed over. Leda. Hiddleston. Grandfather. Papa. Scarlett. Of these, I might have been the most accessible.

"Then I should be honored," I replied, closing three more steps. "I'm not."

"You should," he replied immediately. My sarcasm wasn't lost on him. "I wasn't lying when, years ago, I sought to support you in the Sisterhood. I believe you are capable of great things. You are clever. You have strength. But you also have weaknesses. Laying out logic, removing emotion, making decisions based on presented data, isn't something you do well."

"Hence, Spira."

"Indeed."

"You're exploiting my slant toward emotions instead of logic?"

"Why, yes. It's only methodical. Creates a greater challenge."

"You knew all of the details about Scarlett and her sister because of your time working with her, didn't you?"

"She revealed much in our chats. We were . . . friends . . . of a sort."

"What about me?"

"Oh, Miss Monroe. Your popularity is far greater than you've accepted. It wasn't hard to go into the annals of the *Chatham Chatterer* and gather information. Much of it I heard while working as a Council Member."

His smooth response, so unbothered by my irritation, made my molars grind. He was too smooth and calm. Something about this situation stank, and it had nothing to do with Carcere.

Perhaps I should be more afraid. I should be more wary walking *toward* this strange witch, but I reserved that feeling for the moment I found him.

"You failed last time," I said carefully. "You didn't overtake the Central Network. That's what you're doing now, isn't it? Proving you can pull something over on Scarlett because she pulled something on you."

"Assuming she is my target?"

His annoying question gave me pause. If not Scarlett, then who? His bland tone set me on edge. I had a feeling that nothing had ever mattered as much as that response.

"How did you choose the story to copy?" I inquired, changing the subject.

"That game has always been a favorite of mine. Seemed appropriate to use it."

The shine became a flicker of candlelight. Every painstaking step brought me closer to a bend in the wall ahead, on the left. Cells passed on my right, vacant. No sign of prisoners or a breakout. Had these cells been empty when it fell apart? Surely, this close to Carcere's entrance . . .

Or was I near the entrance at all?

It was impossible to know how long I'd been walking through this vapid darkness. Magic pressed like a dark fog, obscuring everything. The lack of environmental cues made it impossible to tell basic time passage or orientation. Opening my thoughts to sense existing magical systems in a place bathed with magic might overrun me entirely, and wouldn't help much.

Leda? I don't know if you can hear me, because I can't hear you. If you can hear me, mark that I was in a grotto-like area and came to a junction of halls through a doorway, set into a wall on the right. There were three branches. We turned right into the first junction, and right again. There's a slight glow. Cells on my right, light to the left ahead.

Talking to her kept my thoughts from jumbling and helped me solidify my escape path. Instability followed each step down this side passage. The floor sloped down gradually, with loose steps and stones. I hesitated outside of an illuminated doorway. Dozens of candles must be lit within.

"Tell me the rules," I said.

His curling voice lost its ringing wild. It came from ahead, around the other side of the wall. "Join me, take a vow, and then we play."

My nose wrinkled. A vow meant I'd have to touch him, which also meant that whatever waited ahead ended with Greyson. If he truly wanted a game of magic, then how would that work? Carcere suppressed magic for me.

Unless . . .

I paused a breath away from turning within. As expected, when I attempted to sense magic, a glut of sensation overwhelmed me. One that punched with sheer might. As quickly as I opened my mind, I closed it. Was that system Carcere? Or something Greyson put into place?

On the other side of the stone wall, the smell of torch oil almost overpowered the general stink of stagnant time.

"What's my guarantee that you want an actual game? This might be a trap."

"But how can I prove myself your intellectual superior without it being fair?"

"Why do you care?"

Greyson spoke in a lover's murmur. "Because, Miss Monroe, there is nothing more I desire than revenge on those who put me into this hellhole, and to share the agony of such a punishment with them. You have no other option. You will not be able to leave Carcere under your own power unless you win. I have put steps into place to ensure it, and Spira pales in comparison to them. Not to mention the antidote." A pause, and then, "Scarlett has two hours before her imminent death is irreversible."

With an irritated grimace, I rallied my courage and stepped around the wall. Greyson stood behind a broad table in his game regalia and smiled with feverish eyes.

"Miss Monroe. Welcome to the game."

Chapter Thirty

The seriousness that I'd always noted in Greyson hadn't changed much after his time in Carcere, except to deepen. If anything, he'd sunken more wholly into an emotionless state.

I paused within the light. Viveet's bouncing flames combined into strange shadows on the walls, casting him in alternating light and dark.

Greyson had always been a handsome man, with a broad face and a serious expression, as if conducting steep deliberation. Carcere had leached some of his vitality. Pale skin, hollow cheeks, dark smudges under the eyes. His hair, trimmed short, appeared clean and fresh.

All too quickly, I remembered the anxiety of the Council Meeting in which I first approached him with the idea of the Sisterhood. Half of the Council stood against me, while others were undecided. Greyson, alone, listened to what I had to say. He weighed my answers carefully. His questions had been poignant and significant, not the annoying fluff of those who hated me because I was Derek Black's daughter. At the time, Greyson had an obvious alliance with Scarlett. I had leaned on him with hope. Eventually, he evened out the vote against me.

The irony of this moment wasn't lost.

The varnished wood of his broad, elegant table gleamed. Candelabras dripped wax down black candles. As expected, signs of game play scattered the area. A deck of cards, a parchment, an elaborate golden hourglass, and a sundry of candles littered the table. The fingertips of his right hand pressed into the polished tabletop. He peered at me quizzically, as though he worked out a puzzle. The entire set up reeked of planning and malevolence.

But *why?*

The undying question rippled with such strength that I couldn't ignore it.

"You haven't changed much," he observed.

"You have."

He lifted his chin, but didn't reply. His perusal ended upon my eyes. We locked our gaze for a silent ten seconds. "Are you ready to represent yourself as the Head of the Sisterhood and save your High Priestess, Bianca?"

Without the rippling expanse of his voice in fathomless caverns, I felt an odd intimacy that was hard to understand.

"I already am the Head of the Sisterhood."

He smiled with small, white teeth. *I'm standing in front of Greyson,* I said to Leda, comprehending a magical barrier stronger than before. *I'm with Greyson.*

No use.

Leda didn't respond.

Greyson gestured to the table. "Let us begin, Miss Monroe." His focus turned to the objects, skittering over them one at a time with the tops of his fingertips. He kept them all within hand's grasp.

"You see the deck of cards, the book of spells, and the game of *Networks.* You choose."

"Choose what?"

"Which we will use for our game. You see? I'm allowing you to participate in proving yourself the most worthy witch. You can speak to your natural strengths, thus giving you a slight advantage."

Studying each, I said, "Oh, yes. This has *advantage* written all over it. You'll bring me into a magically suppressed room, in a forgotten hellhole of a dungeon, with the lurking threat of murdering myself or my High Priestess."

He didn't bother to smile.

I frowned, gazing at the book, the deck, the game. "What will I do with them after I choose?"

That feral smile. "Choose wisely. Once the decision is made, you cannot go back. You say the words, the choice is locked."

"Just like the fourth letter? *They had advanced so far, they could not turn back.*"

He lifted an eyebrow.

Uneasy, I skipped over the game of *Networks*. Definitely not that. Game strategy on a board with pawns was my ultimate weakness. Leda would excel, for predictions of strategy and defined rules were her particular strength. I had a feeling Greyson had suspected as much, thus putting it on the table.

Next to it, a book of spells. Tempting. Magic was an easy path to rely on. Spellwork and incantations were instinctive, but I wagered he'd expect me to choose magic. It would probably be something diabolical and impossible.

That left the deck of cards. Of the three, it was the least potentially dangerous. Unless, of course, something special existed in these cards . . .

"Tick, tock," he said. "Your time expires in ten sec—"

"The cards."

The others vanished.

I fought to keep my irritation under control. He'd confirmed that the magical suppression was *his* spell. He somehow blocked spells outside of his own. Somewhere in the twisting hallway, I must have passed an invisible barrier.

Brilliant. Magical suppression spells were complicated, requiring little repetition for time. One could set them and have them stay for a year, so circumventing the magical block that stopped me, but allowed him, would be a wasted effort.

"Prove myself?" I asked silkily. "Yet you suppress my magic?"

His lips twitched. "One can never be too careful, Miss Monroe. Don't worry. There are opportunities for your own safety. I guarantee that all will lay within your power once we begin."

He waved a hand to the deck of cards, but didn't look at them.

"You have chosen. Now, I set out the terms. Through the letters, I told you a story, but I didn't give you an ending. I have written the entire story down, so it cannot be altered."

A curl of parchment appeared on the table next to him. A seal marked it, branded with black wax and a design I'd never seen. Slashing lines crossed it in a zigzag pattern. The scroll's thickness indicated the story had more heft than expected. I had an idea, should I peek inside, the handwriting would mimic the letters.

Greyson set a hand on top of the parchment. His eyes flickered to mine. "This is the story in its *finished* entirety. You are going to use the cards to tell me the story. The whole story. Flawlessly." He stated every vowel with grating purpose. "Without a missed detail, and using every single card." A smile curled his lips. "I hope you paid attention. And I *hope* you understand how this ends."

Greyson extended an arm.

"Shall we vow on it?"

I stared at his open palm, the waiting agreement, and quietly asked, "What is it you want from all this, Greyson? Revenge, sure. But revenge comes from a desire for something else."

He grinned. "That's the right question, Bianca Monroe, and what I always loved the most about you. You asked the questions no one else bothered with. *What do I want?* That is what you must answer through our game."

In theory, Greyson asked for a recitation of the story, told out in exquisite detail, through a deck of cards he surely rigged to be wrong. There might be cards that didn't fit the story. Not to mention the unknown ending. I couldn't help but wonder what the game of *Networks* would have required.

I made him stand there, arm extended, while I considered.

"If I don't recite the story through the cards, and predict the ending with exactness?" I asked.

"You won't receive the antidote."

"If I win?"

"As part of this vow," he intoned with exquisite sobriety, "I promise to submit while you return me to the Central Network and the care of the Brotherhood that you so deeply rely on."

The words stung.

So deeply rely on. Did he say it to bait me, or did he understand that the Sisterhood, so fledgling, couldn't survive on our own? Didn't matter.

"Should you win, then I will not fight nor will I try to escape. You can transport me to Chatham Castle and put me in the dungeons."

"Is there a time limit for the challenge?"

"One hour."

Jikes.

He smiled wide when I said, "Tell me your exact wording for the vow."

Magic brightened his hand, swirling through his palm. He'd initiated the magic, but that didn't mean I had to accept yet. It wouldn't apply to me until I grasped his forearm.

"If Bianca Monroe can prove her prowess of cleverness and magic by using this deck of cards to verbally retell the actual story that I have written in this parchment, which actual story perfectly replicates the theme of the letters sent, and tells the same ending as what I have written in the final parchment, all within sixty minutes, then I vow to submit to her. With her spell, I will be transported back to the Central Network, without me attempting to break free, and put into a prison cell in Chatham Castle. If she does not succeed in any regard, or she recounts one single detail or event out of order, I shall not surrender the antidote."

Buried in that lengthy, wordy vow, the words, *I shall not surrender the antidote,* meant I signed Scarlett's life over to a madman. While I'd expected something like this, hearing it hit hard in my chest. Just like everything Greyson did. Strange, but logical. Grim when you stared it in the face.

His fleeting amusement ebbed into somberness. For a long time he stood there, the vow magic spiraling through his palm. I repeated every word aloud, sifting through each nuance, and earning a nod of agreement when I'd gotten it right.

A true test of cleverness, of prediction. Not magic, but sheer, dumb luck. Or was it? Had he planted clues in the letters?

Heart thrashing in my throat, I clasped Greyson's arm.

"I accept."

As the magic dissolved from my arm and swirled into a pinprick over my breastbone, the deck advanced into the middle of the table. The hourglass flipped, and granules scattered along the bottom in maniacal bounces. Twelve shimmering, golden rectangles formed between the candelabras. They glowed, edges simmering like live coals.

I hadn't forgotten that he'd claimed this would be a test of magic *and* cleverness.

"There are twelve cards in this deck. You will assign the final flow of the story into these spaces." With two fingers, he motioned to each. "You may arrange and rearrange outside of these place-holders, but when you are certain you have the right order of events," he added softly, "and *ending*, then you may place them here. This will be your final answer. Once placed, the cards cannot be retracted."

A space existed between me and the rectangles, allowing ample room to reposition them. I ignored the stolidness of the glimmering gold, opting not to deal with the pressure it imparted. Viveet's blue light extinguished as I put her in her sheath, but kept one hand on her hilt.

I hesitated, one hand hovering above the cards.

He chuckled, a dark, rolling sound that moved like shadows. "They won't bite you."

Irritated that he'd read my concern, I lifted the top card free. A scrolled design decorated the edges. The word **Wings** filled the bottom in a heavily scripted font almost impossible to read. Time aged the cards. They were a thick paper, unglossed, like many other cards. Cuts and curls marred the ends. The intricate details in the filigree caught me by surprise.

I set it aside.

The second card, **Orphan**. Designs scattered the interior, so tiny I could barely make them out. Broken toys, perhaps. I set that aside, already streaming the story of Ellie Victoriann through my mind. The details weren't that hard to remember, and the general storyline was simple enough.

The next, **Sky.** Clouds inched along the sides, both bright and tempestuous in ribbons along the edge.

Death.

Sea.

Blood, complete with shredded feathers.

One at a time, I lay out each card. There were only twelve, though the deck appeared much thicker when I chose it. Across the table, Greyson hadn't moved. His fingertips pressed into the top, knuckles slightly blanched. He stared hard. The candelabras inched closer to me, allowing light to flood the space where I laid each one out.

Friend.

Hope.

Despair.

Return.

Greyson's terrible stillness might be the most frightening thing about him. Carcere itself, a broken, historical, ancient structure that leaked old magic like a severed artery, wasn't the monster. It was stone and memory, but no longer magic.

Greyson was the true terror.

He fancied himself fair and superior, but stacked the literal and metaphorical deck against his opponent. This wasn't a challenge, nor was it logical. This was unbridled revenge, and I'd be a fool to consider it anything else.

I turned over the final two cards at the same time, confounded by what I saw.

Gambler.

Vagabond.

What were those? Nothing related to the cards, certainly.

At my frown, Greyson chuckled, then laughed. His strange mirth stretched across the darkness, as if he'd captured midnight and held it in his cupped palms. I swam in the ebony waters, seeking the top.

Attempting to control my expression as much as I could, which apparently I hadn't managed well, I turned my focus to studying the scrolled edges of the **Gambler**. Scattered coins, wrinkled fabric, and spilled purses. Not helpful.

The **Vagabond** contained trees, a hammer, and a pack. Nothing to do with Marie Hazel or Ellie Victoriann. These must apply to Greyson's motive, to the thing he desired. The ending, perhaps.

I resisted the urge to look at Greyson and interpret his expression. He'd only distract me, perhaps attempt to throw me off if I let him follow the path of my thoughts. So I did the only thing that made sense.

I spoke to Leda.

Leda, who wasn't there, but to whom I spoke out my ideas all the time.

Ellie Victoriann began the story with her wings, I said, tugging on the **Wings** card first. I pulled it into position at the beginning of the line of twelve, gently scattering the others to the side.

I hesitated. Did she receive her wings first, or was she an orphan?

Orphan first.

I pulled that card into position. Greyson didn't so much as shift. His glittering eyes regarded me through the shadows, as if nudging me further and further along this path. I didn't bother with second guessing myself. Instinct first. I trusted it.

Imagining Leda listening along the other end of the magic helped me picture the letters as if they sprawled in front of her. The flow of events came more readily.

Which came first? **Sea** *or* **Sky?**

Carefully, I nudged **Sky** ahead of **Sea**. Ellie Victoriann had been flying in the sky before she almost crashed into the ocean. I nudged **Friendship** into the next position. With a cock of my head, certain that must be right, I moved on.

Memory flowed through me, making it easy to tell Leda the story and shuffle each card into position.

Marie Hazel becomes Eliie Victoriann's protector, and they form a relationship as Ellie Victoriann attempts to find the top of the sky. This gives them . . . hope?

Tentatively, I set a finger on **Hope** and pulled it to position six. That left six cards, which put me halfway through the story. Things turned violent while they flew amongst the stars, which made sense, because **Blood** and **Death** and **Despair** waited in the pile of cards not yet assigned, including the confusing **Gambler** and **Vagabond**.

For several moments, I allowed my thoughts to swirl, braiding in and out, thinking, pulling, attempting to uncover connections. The utter silence of broken Carcere forced me to avoid the fact that I had no timeline.

I blinked.

Hold on . . .

Scrolled along the edges were intricate designs. Little will-o-wisps, almost.

Leda, I whispered to the blank expanse that would never reply, *what did that third letter say about hope?*

The details of the story replayed through my head, almost as if Leda spoke the words to me from afar.

Hope, such an expensive commodity, yet never far from daydreams. It burns bright in the darkest of places. A seaside beacon. A thudding heart, never stopping.

The designs told the details.

Carefully, I lifted the **Gambler** card, inspecting the edges with renewed fascination. The coins, overturned purse, warbling footpaths, elaborate question marks. What did the ending have to do with gambling?

"Ah," Greyson crooned, "you see the designs, don't you? An excellent display of attention to detail, Head of the Sisterhood."

I gifted him with a glare. He didn't appear flustered or concerned, he simply stared at me with a placidness I couldn't fathom. This truly was a test of cleverness and logic. *My* cleverness and logic. The weight of Scarlett's life rested in the balance, and I felt the damming pressure.

I set the **Gambler** card down again. The designs would provide hints. I could easily retell the story at the end, including every possible detail just to make sure I completed the picture. With time ticking, I couldn't think of that now. Every second that passed lowered more sand from the hourglass and inched Scarlett closer to death.

As if he read my thoughts, Greyson stated, "A reminder that

any wrong detail will count against you as a failure. One failure leads to the loss of the antidote."

I swallowed the rising lump.

I could do this. I knew the details. I knew *those* details, because I was a thorough Sisterhood leader. I'd poured over those letters until I had almost memorized them.

The rest of the cards slid into place quite easily. **Blood,** then **Despair.** Finally, the obvious ninth card, **Death,** slid into the space, leaving three remaining.

Return could apply to the descent both Ellie Victoriann and Marie Hazel experienced as they plummeted from the stars. I put it in a tentative tenth place, but slightly down. It *might* apply to the ending and the remaining cards. **Gambler** and **Vagabond.**

Here lay the gap. The unknown. How did the story end? Studying the edges revealed factors that I couldn't quite piece together. Answers I wasn't sure I could draw from my head. Not with—my eyes flickered to the hourglass—half my time left. Greyson's thirst for revenge lay thick in the air.

A diabolical smile curled his lips as he watched me internally debate. I could feel his attention, as much as see it out of the corner of my eye.

There are three uncertain cards, Leda, I thought with a hint of growing desperation. Up until this point, there had been only forward movement, a finite understanding of the next step, what it meant, how to deal with it. The crux had arrived.

I had to make decisions.

Greyson wants revenge, but revenge isn't broad enough to explain the gambler and the vagabond cards.

My eyes darted over the images, reviewing again and again the pictures on the edges.

Greyson said, "Thirty minutes."

My heart thumped. I opened and closed my fists. The demand of thinking faster made me think less, like stalling out in the middle of a run. I forced my thoughts to calm. The flickering candles along the prison walls drew my eyes to the cards and to Carcere, this miserable swamp where souls went to die.

Based on his word alone, I continued, *there are two people he wants revenge through. Ellie Victoriann, who represents Scarlett, and Marie Hazel, who represents me.*

That felt right. A toe ledge of certainty woke my quicker thoughts, and I plunged down the first of two alleyways this provided.

Ellie Victoriann as Scarlett: he would want revenge from her because she was instrumental in putting him into Carcere. She allowed the Protectors to fake her death so that he would move, and he did.

Made sense.

Despite the fact that Scarlett continued to occupy the throne he once wanted and could never have. Logic, and all that. Scarlett reigned supreme. I moved on, caching that information in a corner of my mind.

Marie Hazel . . . why?

Confidence stalled here. I had no idea why Greyson would want revenge against me. Me, whom he twice had stated intention to support before his attempted uprising. The sincerity in his words had been real enough. He didn't strike me as the type of witch to speak without meaning what he said, or without having thought deeply about what he agreed to.

I stared at the two remaining cards. *They* held the answers. Somehow, I must know it, even subconsciously, or else there would be no victory for him. No proof of his superior intellect if I guessed my way through it. I understood enough of his arrogance and purpose to understand *that*.

Which meant the answer was present, yet hidden. That provided a necessary surge of hope.

My eyes lifted to the row of ten cards, lingering on the vague details each provided. Each card provided a trait about the two other characters. **Orphan** for Ellie Victoriann, as well as **Wings.**

For Marie Hazel, **Sea** and **Friendship.** The words **Gambler** and **Vagabond** fit with neither.

But perhaps an unknown witch.

My breath hitched. Of course. There was someone else, in addition to Scarlett, that he wanted revenge against.

The **Gambler** and **Vagabond** fit that witch.

"Ah." Greyson tsked. "Do you see?"

"Not yet," I breathed.

My mind raced with the hunch that the **Gambler** and **Vagabond** applied to the other witch on whom Greyson desired revenge. I tapped along the edge of the final two cards, sliding **Return** firmly into place as the tenth card. The designs along the edge showed not clouds or falling stars, but a tower, fire, sandy beach.

Carcere.

Return applied not to Marie Hazel and Ellie Victoriann, but to the unknown ending. But then . . .

I paused, staring at **Death.** No, there hadn't been death. There had only been an allusion to death. Ellie Victoriann and Marie Hazel had fallen, but not passed. With a breath, I pulled the card out of the line up.

"Twelve minutes," he said.

Crowding my thoughts back to the **Gambler** and **Vagabond,** I turned the focus to Greyson. If he desired revenge through Scarlett's death and something else . . . that meant . . . what? It didn't make sense! I didn't contribute to his downfall. At the time Papa caught Greyson, I had been in Alaysia. They put Greyson in Carcere.

My heart skipped a beat.

Papa.

I lifted my eyes to meet Greyson's gaze. Burning intensity met mine, like smoldering stars. No longer did he appear the stern, logical witch that simply wanted to spar minds, but a man hungry for that which he sought. I knew then, staring into his eyes, what Greyson wanted the most.

It wasn't me.

Not Scarlett.

Nor power.

There was a witch more powerful than Greyson. More powerful than logic and plans and subterfuge. A witch who played the odds constantly, and sometimes didn't win. A witch wandering through his days, trying to figure out the next step. A gambler. A vagabond.

He wanted Papa.

Greyson sought to enact that revenge through me. Set up a near-impossible situation so that he killed Papa's beloved daughter and the leader of the Central Network. This was the ultimate revenge.

Greyson's malevolent smile spread, as if he noted the moment understanding clicked in my eyes.

"Don't forget to save minutes to recite the story, Miss Monroe. It will take . . . time."

A sense of cool washed over me now that I understood the angle. Knew where Greyson approached this from. So much fell into the light that previously seethed in the unknown shadows.

Lines clicked.

Pieces connected.

Except for one.

How did the story end?

The whirls and designs along the edges of the final two cards gave hints at how things might flow. When I studied the cards, it became clear that Greyson designed them to reflect the story in the interior and real life along the exterior.

"Eight minutes."

But still . . . something niggled in the back of my mind. I almost dismissed it, but paused long enough to listen. A stirring remembrance from the vow, taken less than an hour ago, and the subtle wording he carefully employed.

He wanted *the actual story* as presented in the scroll that *perfectly replicates the theme of the letters sent.*

Cheeky witch.

I knew just what he desired. I understood, with bold clarity, what sort of logic and magic this test provided.

With certainty, I shoved the three remaining cards at the end. **Gambler** as number ten, **Vagabond** as number eleven, and **Death** as number twelve. His eyes gleamed as they lifted, meeting mine.

"Let me tell you a story."

Tension strapped my chest into a narrow cavity as I pressed the tip of my finger on top of the first card. **Orphan.** With a little nudge, I slid it into the golden rectangle. It flared to light, then settled.

The card issued a little *click.*

Greyson nodded once, affirming its rightful place. I pointed to the designs on the top left corner of the card and worked clockwise. As I spoke, my finger trailed along the card, past the image of a house, clasped hands indicating two sisters, and along the right hand edge where the image of two headstones appeared.

I recited the actual story.

"Scarlett was an orphan, along with her sister, Ellie. They were very close. Their mother, Victoriann, died in childbirth and their father from an accident."

With each image along the edge of that card accounted for, I lifted my finger off it and slid to the right. The air around me lessened with intensity, flowing slightly. Some of the oppression had ceased.

Only *some.*

Enough that if I hadn't been paying attention, I wouldn't have noted it. The light around the card altered to a brilliant green, reflecting the emerald of Letum Wood.

Quietly, and without emotion, he said, "Correct. Proceed."

A wave of relief swept through me. Greyson's story involved Scarlett, myself, and Papa, not the characters he had created. Had I retold Ellie Victoriann's story, as well as Marie Hazel's, I would have lost.

The thought shaved a little fear free.

I could do this.

Beginning with the top left corner of the second card, I started with an image revealing books, wings, and broken shackles. "Scarlett, a wise child, had her intelligence to elevate her above all the other orphans. Her knowledge gave her wings, I suppose you could say, and they were the eventual key to her freedom."

The barest nod.

Another affirming viridian glow around the second card as it clicked into place, becoming part of the table.

My fingernail slid to the next card. Two links in a chain, one of them broken, leading to what appeared to be a coffin. The tale flowed more easily now, or perhaps that was the lessening aura of Carcere.

"Ellie, whom Scarlett deeply loved, died. This almost broke Scarlett. One might say it took her intelligence, her love of learning and books, away from her." My finger swirled to the right edge of the card, hesitating over scattered, haggard feathers. "Breaking her wings."

We watched each other with all the wariness of predator and prey. His nose twitched, jaw tensed.

Greyson nodded again.

Relieved I had worded it correctly, I lifted my finger, breath held. The lines around the card swirled to green.

"Three minutes," he growled, lips lifting in a half smile, half grimace.

Quickly, I moved to the third card, but spoke in the same cadence. Haste would cost Scarlett's life. I discovered the story with each image on the card sides. I didn't know every single step or nuance, but the details held my fate.

The third card, **Sky**, and the fourth card, **Sea**, passed muster in less than twenty seconds. Each affirming *click* and sprint of emerald light around brought a deeper ridge to his brow. Greyson inclined his head as I proceeded, speaking with greater strength. I knew this story. Most importantly, I knew *Scarlett,* because I was the Sisterhood.

I knew my work.

On cards five, six, seven, eight, which were **Friendship**, **Hope**, **Blood**, and **Despair**, I switched tactics and repeated the details from the top right corner. The story moved counterclockwise. Another clever trick on his part.

As I anticipated the switch, he betrayed a ripple of annoyance. Those cards sped past. I hurried through, gratefully seeing the green lights illuminate, indicating I had guessed correctly.

"One minute," he said, so softly it might have been a snarl. The darkness of the room thickened around him, as if his growing resentment built ballast. I breathed steady, completely in the moment, vaguely aware of the powerful release of pressure in the air.

My finger settled on the **Gambler** card's middle top edge. "On the night you gambled for the Central Network throne," my finger hovering over a symbol of a crown, looking oddly like a throne, "Papa also gambled on whether or not you'd believe that Scarlett had died."

Greyson's arms shook as I pressed my nail to a cluster of grapes. "Papa knew you were hungry for the position of Highest Witch." I tapped on the cluster of trees next to it. "Not just for power, but for the Central Network."

A flash of fire in his eyes.

Hungry, indeed.

I leaned into the sense of growing space around us. The lifting of a power, ever-so-subtly. Quietly, I asked, *Leda?* while I drew in a too-long breath.

A wafting voice replied.

Bianca?

Greyson's sharp eyes shot to mine. He'd noticed, which meant he not only lessened the magical hold on the room, but he kept his senses open to detect my magical use. The blip of magic that speaking to Leda required drew his attention. He could rationalize it away. I acted as if I hadn't noticed his suspicion by continuing to speak.

The final edge of the **Gambler** card awaited with one symbol. A cluster of stacked coins.

"Papa thought you would act in the face of your first chance. And you did. Which leads to the eleventh card."

As I removed my hand from the **Gambler**, I held my breath. Slowly, the gold shimmered to emerald. Each card had grown a darker shade of green, winnowing almost to black.

"Thirty seconds," he whispered.

While turning my focus to the next card, I threw up an invisible shield spell, one from Grandfather's book. Like the communication magic, Greyson might sense a vague magic system, but he wouldn't know it.

My eyes devoured the edges of the **Vagabond.** This was the true crux. I had to know the end state that Greyson desired. Had to know exactly what end he wanted for Papa, which could be any number of diabolical, terrible endings. Torture. Death. Retribution. Time in Carcere himself.

I braced myself.

There were only four symbols, one on each edge. I'd glossed over them before, not understanding what they meant. Why would a vagabond have four symbols, anyway? And then I realized what they were. The four elements of despair mentioned in the third letter.

Of course. Greyson didn't care about me. His whole plan revolved around creating the worst kind of despair for Papa. He planned to destroy me and Scarlett so Papa would destroy himself.

"Twenty seconds," he called, voice rising. A maniacal gleam brightened his eyes. Sucking in a breath, I scrambled to know which to say first. Greyson might have listed the symbols by least to most painful, to ensure that Papa would suffer.

Truly suffer.

Throwing trust into instinct, I said, "Because of his gamble to oust you, Papa became a vagabond. He lost his title, freeing him to suffer the four elements of despair."

"Fifteen."

My heart thudded as I tapped the first symbol, a cape unbound, appearing to tumble in the wind. "Unfettered restlessness," I repeated from the story and moved to the second. A circle, swirling into itself, collapsing in the center and pulling through like a dying thread.

"Spiraling tragedy."

The third. A flat, straight line. "Relentless loneliness."

"Ten seconds!" he shrieked.

"And the pains of death!" I cried. The edges of the card emblazoned with a brilliant, nearly black green.

My hand slapped the final card.

"As a result, Papa will die. *This* is your revenge: Papa's death. It's the final card. You brought me here to gain your revenge against Papa by taking that which he loves the most. He'll die literally," I gestured to the headstone, then a heart, cleaved in half, "as well as emotionally."

As I ripped my hand away, the last grains of sand dribbled to the bottom of the hourglass. Greyson's hands fisted at his side. All twelve cards illuminated. Magic sprayed in screens of white fire on top of the cards. I dropped, arms thrown over my head, as a shout bellowed from his throat.

An explosion burst from the middle of the table, borne out of the cards. As I shoved power into my shield, cinders rained on top. The shield rippled with their impacts. Despite their small size, the cinders slammed like giant boulders.

Not cinders.

Blighters.

Green blighters, whose hues matched the tone of the successful cards. Hundreds of green blighters. The magical balls of energy spanned as wide as the length of my thumb, and would paralyze me on contact. If the shield gave way, the deluge would kill me in seconds.

My shield bowed under the pressure, the offshoots of brilliant sage pounding like hail. The raw defiance, the barreling nature of this assault stole my breath. Greyson played this game so I would figure out his end game, but he never expected me to see Papa in it.

What had his opening vow statement said? *Can prove her prowess of cleverness and magic.* I might have won with cleverness, but I hadn't won with magic. After all that effort with Spira, the cards, the details were only part of the game.

The true end had just arrived.

I slashed open my magical ability and poured it into my wavering shield. Hidden behind the cards, Greyson did the same. He devoted an equal amount of magic into the blighters, which appeared like a constant stream, forcing us into a brawl for prowess.

I leaned into it.

Opened myself again.

Dug deep.

My magic sprouted like a tempest. I thought I heard Greyson screaming. Blighters collected on the floor in a green sea, like fallen leaves at summer's end. They thickened the air, focusing on my shield.

As I pressed harder, he met me.

My reserves began to falter, and so did the shield. The winnowing ability weakened me like a tired sigh. Consciousness hovered on the edge, threatening to give way. A dark chasm awaited.

The *pains of death*, to borrow a phrase from the letters.

Over the thudding blighters, Greyson's guttural shout wrenched the air. I silently pressed hard to empty myself out. It would be a battle of who lost consciousness first. My feet turned numb, my hands ached. The emerald thrum of blighters wanted my shield. They wanted *me*. I wouldn't give in, but I needed more.

I found more.

A powerful center buried deep, deep within, accessible only as all these layers poured free. When all was given, I found the end. The bottom. The very edge of *life*. It teemed a brilliant, brilliant cobalt.

Familiar.

Too powerful, I shrank away from that center. So much was loaded in there. So much I couldn't bring myself to touch it. I didn't know this power resided in me. I regarded it, half alive, torn in a place between here and there.

Hadn't I been there before?

I sent one last pulse, the dying edge of my ability, into this vague ether. *Deasylva*, I whispered, but the voice was in my head. *Is that you?*

Yes.

You're here?

Always.

I need more.

You have enough.

With a cry, I touched the burning bead.

Something shattered in a gossamer spray. Greyson vanished. The onslaught of blighters cooled like calming waves. Irreverent thuds altered to sloshing. Time passed. Minutes. Desperate minutes that I couldn't afford to lose if I wanted to save Scarlett from the poison.

Slowly, vision returned.

Consciousness, too.

The barrier that spewed blighters retreated into the table again. Blighters disintegrated with sprays of powder, raining over twelve black rectangles burned into the tabletop. I slumped over the smoking holes, fighting for breath. Powder spiraled like spindrift in whirls. Staggering, I peered over the far edge of the table.

Greyson lay on the floor, pale and unconscious, with manacles around his wrists.

Lowering to the ground, I pressed my back to the table and slowed my breathing. One torch, then another, flickered to life. Candles resurrected from where they stood on the ground, amidst the shattered remains of thousands of blighters. The magic that blew them apart pieced them back together.

I closed my eyes, tilted my head back, and muttered, "Physical brawn, eh? Bastard."

Chapter Thirty-One

BIANCA MONROE, I'M NOT HAVING THIS ANY LONGER!* Leda screeched in my head. *You reply or I'm sending every last Protector into that building to find you!*

I'm fine, I managed to gasp. *I'm fine.*

Where are you?

Carcere.

Yes, Leda snapped, *but where? You disappeared, came back, then said nothing! Rognvald said that Merrick is reporting flashes of lights and yells from outside. They've had to restrain him from going after you.*

Her words cluttered my mind. I couldn't comprehend them all at once, so I shook them out.

Merrick?

No idea where I am, I barely managed to say. *Grotto* and *turn right* and *boom* mumbled through my thoughts. Her frantic prattling faded to the background. My arms trembled as I crawled under the table, closer to Greyson. The vow remained intact. I felt it humming in my chest. Vibrant. Until I delivered him to the prison cell, it would remain intact.

For a moment, I stared at him. Comprehension dawned slowly. I had won. Greyson clasped Scarlett's life in those foul, loathsome hands, and I snatched her back from the very brink of death.

No.

"Not me," I whispered. "It wasn't me."

A familiar voice said, *Yes, you. You who are willing to travel to the depths. You who are willing to give all to find me in the moments of greatest requirement.* Then, with undeniable affection, Deasylva murmured, *Clever witch.*

I laughed, feeling deranged.

Clever.

Yes.

I *was* clever. But more than that, I knew the story, my mission, and asked the most important questions about the right people. No one in the Brotherhood would have managed the same. Wasn't that the point?

The Brotherhood and the Sisterhood conjured and created different outcomes by sheer force of personality. It's why the Sisterhood *and* the Brotherhood had a place. I saw it, which meant I could help the Council see it.

I shook my head, forcing my attention back to Leda's rambling. After pouring all my ability into Greyson's defeat, the energy that sitting required felt too monumental. I was an empty husk. A shell without a core. Only the vibrancy of the vow kept me anchored to the moment so that I might fulfill it.

Merrick is leading the search for you, Leda said. *Rognvald says they're going in.*

Tell them to stop.

A pause. *What?*

It'll take too long to find me, and I'm fine. I have Greyson. If they want to be useful, have them meet me in the dungeons, with a cell ready.

Chatham Castle's dungeons?

Yes. I would highly *recommend they use Mabel's old cell. Suppressive, and all that.*

You . . . you have Greyson?

Yes.

And the antidote?

Shuffling through his pockets, I eventually wrapped my fingers around the vial. The liquid gleamed.

Yes.

Her voice steady and strong, without a hint of celebration or judgment, she simply said, *I will relay the message now. Do you need any help?*

No, but thank you.

With great regret, I put a hand on Greyson's sleeve. The vow provided some magical energy of its own—enough to transport both of us to the castle and fulfill it. Thank the goddess for that.

I had nothing more to give.

The empty dungeons of Chatham Castle awaited. The moment the transportation spell finished, the vow was complete. The last breath of magic faded.

It would take me weeks to recover.

Greyson didn't stir as I stood on wobbly knees outside of a particular cell, clutching the opposite wall to steady myself. I shouted a hoarse, "Guards!" The distant scrambling of feet followed.

Before the Guardians arrived, Rognvald appeared a few paces away. Leda followed, breathed a sigh when she saw me. Rognvald's eyes widened, then dropped to Greyson. He swore under his breath and stepped into immediate action. I slumped against the wall. Upright, but barely.

"You're all right?" Leda whispered, holding me upright.

"Barely. He shouldn't fight," I said weakly, "but I'd get him inside the cell. There's a decent chance he's faking his unconsciousness. Don't put anything past him."

Rognvald issued no questions as he hovered Greyson inside with a spell and secured the heavy door. The Guardians stumbled to a stop, gawping. I produced the antidote, which I kept in my palm on the trip over.

"Here."

Leda accepted it, but didn't release my shoulder. "I'll take this to the Apothecaries. Can you hold your weight?"

"Yes." I transitioned my weight off of her. "Thanks."

While Rognvald issued spells that rippled, blanketed, and zipped around the outside of the cell, Tysen and Merrick appeared. Merrick swept to my side in three strides, hauled me into his embrace. Unable to speak past the lump in my throat, I let him hold me up, my arms tucked against his chest.

Only when his warm arms comforted me did I appreciate that the nightmare had truly ended. Death had hovered with close and dangerous wings.

Jikes.

That had been a mess ready to explode at the first catastrophic failure.

Merrick pulled away, studying me. He swiped a piece of hair out of my eyes. After the filth of Carcere, the blast of magic, and a torrent of blighters, I probably looked and smelled a mess.

"You're all right?" he asked, low.

I nodded.

With great reluctance, and a bit of a grimace, he released me, but didn't go far. I loved him endlessly for not coddling me in this moment of accounting and victory. His presence bolstered me for what must follow: my review.

Rognvald, appeased that Greyson was secured, commanded Tysen, "You stay. I'll have Talmund send his two best Guardians to watch him until the High Priest has established a plan." He waved to the two Guardians hovering in the hall. "Go back to your post. Talmund will arrive to explain things shortly. Until then, my Protector will remain."

They saluted as Tysen took up a position in front of the cell. Rognvald surveyed me with an upturned eyebrow. He had the audacity to laugh as he clapped me on the shoulder.

"You look like death."

The moment I walked into Scarlett's apartment, Grandfather imparted a teary-eyed smile. It was a beautiful sight worth fighting for.

While Apothecaries rushed in and out of the hallway that led to Scarlett's personal bedroom, Marjorie sent me a cup of tea infused with cream and sugar. Sipping it bolstered me with new energy and a grounding warmth in my belly. Good reports poured out of the room, including *she's stirring* and *she's obeying commands.*

An hour later, Talmund, Leda, Hiddleston, Rognvald, and Merrick attended my debriefing with Grandfather.

I set aside the harrowing fear of dying to focus on the facts, and kept the explanation succinct. The angles in which these military figures wanted information were different than the emotional angles Leda, Grandfather, and Scarlett would later desire.

The telling passed more quickly than I expected. As it always did, the verbal review helped settle the events in my mind. Grandfather's twinkling eyes misted, but cleared, often. He kept smiling, nodding, frowning, sighing.

Rognvald and Talmund launched into a back and forth discussion on what to do next, which gave me a moment to breathe.

Merrick stood at my side. While they honed into a plan, he reached for my hand. My fingers twined through his. I wasn't too proud to lean on him.

Leda watched me from the other side of the room, concern in her pale features.

That was really scary, but you did it.

Thanks. We make a good team.

With a shake of her head, she said, *I suppose I'll have to get used to this.*

You and me, both.

My attention drifted to Grandfather's frequent and worried looks, thoughts of what my vagabond father was up to this moment, and concerns over how to tell said vagabond what transpired. He wouldn't be pleased. But . . . maybe he didn't *have* to know.

Papa walked wild paths these days. I wasn't entirely certain *he* understood who he was anymore. Telling him may not be the kindest path.

Yet.

One day, when he was ready, I'd reveal it. For now, Papa had more important things to figure out.

"Bianca?"

I startled out of my thoughts to find Grandfather peering at me. Clearing my throat, I shook my head and said, "Yes, Grandfather?"

"Thank you to *both* members of the Sisterhood. You have saved many lives this evening, including Scarlett's, for which the entire Central Network owes you its gratitude. Tomorrow, the Council will receive a full briefing, if you're up to it."

Before I could think about it, I asked, "Can we wait?"

His brow rose.

"To tell the Council," I clarified.

Rognvald turned to face me. Merrick sent me a sidelong

glance. Leda blinked, as if I'd slapped her. Only Grandfather didn't appear surprised.

"You want to wait?" Leda hissed. "Bianca! This is your chance to show them what you're capable of in Scarlett's defense."

"I know. I want to wait."

"For what?"

With great hesitation, I admitted, "I don't know, but I think it's in the best interest of the Sisterhood if we just . . . wait."

Leda's silent floundering, visible across her contorting facial expressions, became comical. Seeing me roll my lips to hold in my amusement didn't help her foul mood. She visibly surrendered by lowering her shoulders from their earlobe-high perch.

"But—"

"I know what opportunities might be sacrificed if we hesitate to display our success. I can't explain my feelings on this, but . . . I'm going to ask you to trust me. At the very least, give me a week to let my feelings on this settle."

Grandfather said, "I have to explain Greyson's imprisonment."

"Sure."

"I can't do that without giving you credit."

With a weary shrug, I said, "That's fine. But can the accounting and details come later? Tell them only that the Sisterhood defeated him, and promise a later explanation."

"Very well." He swept both hands toward me in a dismissive gesture. "We will strive to keep the details between all of us. We will allow the Sisterhood to reveal what they want in the time the Sisterhood is ready."

All agreed with low murmurs.

Relaxing, I said, "Thank you."

Chapter Thirty-Two

Grandfather transported me to my treehouse, allowing Merrick the chance to wrap up his report with Rognvald and return later that night. Completing my mission against Greyson had somehow freed Merrick from his elusive mission for the next week.

Or perhaps the Brotherhood had a heart after all.

As Grandfather pressed a kiss to my forehead and then departed, I heard a soft song soughed from the trees.

She has come.

We welcome her.

She is ours.

You belong to us.

Tears sprang to my eyes as I leaned against the smooth bark. The ageless branches didn't waver. They remained stolid, unending, crisscrossing.

"Long day," I murmured.

Their chorus rose in a swelling crescendo that might have been amusement. A heartbeat at a time, they calmed. Their whispered chant skirted the edges of hearing, like a flash of light out of the corner of the eye.

Finally, another voice arose. Ancient and vibrant with wisdom. *You have returned, daughter of the forest.*

I smiled. The rich, billowing timbre of the voice had a dramatic resonance, with a reverb that slid all the way into my soul.

"Have you been waiting, Amanthis?"

The tree in which I lived said, *The daughter of the forest is one with all. We did not fear for you.*

A wispy smile overtook me.

"Thanks. Next time, I'll try to share the confidence."

You are seeking her. We sense your heart's desire.

Amanthis spoke of Deasylva.

"I want to thank her. She provided help over there. *In* there. Viveet, and power at the end, and . . ." I trailed away, not entirely sure I could put into words my experience. The bright blaze of magic within, buried at the bottom of what I thought had been my limit.

She does not require it.

The words swirled in my head. At the blithe mention of the forest goddess, saplings sang. A wind stirred their voices to my ears. They rose with affection, and then dissipated.

"I want to," I whispered.

A tremor of something stirred my heart.

Then allow us to sing your gratitude on your behalf.

The old tree settled into a hum, as much a chant, but without words. The soothing cadence threaded through my thoughts, winding like silk into the warm chambers of my heart. Here, I could finally release my emotions.

I sank to the branch, knees to my chest. An outpouring of thought and emotion accompanied the next hour of stunned silence. I may have dozed in and out of sleep. Or perhaps my review of the events was so thorough that I became lost in the analysis. Replaying each harrowing moment, I let it slide through me like water.

No judgment, Papa had always taught me. *You replay it after it happens, but you don't cast judgment. Whatever you did was what you could do. Afterwards is the real magic, B. Afterwards is when you learn from it.*

Those nuggets of wisdom, spoken under a forest canopy like this, remained as vibrant and true today as before. The forest song calmed to the distant edge of a whisper until it tapered off. Amanthis' rumbly voice returned, but this time I had no more space to hear the nuance of great love and affection.

You belong to us, Amanthis said.

"I belong to you," I whispered.

A scuff sounded behind me, too loud to be an animal.

The joy has returned.

She belongs to us.

My heart hopped into my throat. Merrick stood a few steps away, agony and relief etched in his expression. He didn't advance.

"B, I'm so sorry—"

I sprinted across the branch and threw myself into his arms with a cry. Relief. That's all I could feel. Not exhaustion over our disagreement before he left again, the unpredictability of our life together, the ache of missing him, nor the frustration of frequent missions. All former agony dissipated as I held him close.

"I love you."

He buried his face in my neck and drew in swelling breaths. I tangled a hand in his hair in my attempt to draw him ever closer.

"Thank you for coming back," he whispered.

Laughing, teary-eyed, I said, "You, too."

"I love you, B. Whatever it takes, we'll figure it out."

The vines and moss and quiet forest life teemed in the background as I held him close, glorying in the moment, the breaths of Letum Wood synched with the tandem thud of our hearts.

A week later, Scarlett's warm smile and bright eyes greeted me into her apartment.

She sat on her divan, surrounded by a bevy of paperwork, a glass of water, and her feet propped on a settee. Marjorie bustled from one side of the room to another, sashaying around Leda, who scrawled furiously on letters and notebooks from a table not far away.

"The Sisterhood returns," Scarlett cried. "I owe you a debt of thanks."

She cleared a spot on the divan with a spell and a flurry of fingers. Parchment scattered, scrolls flew into the air, and quills zipped away. In the empty place, I sat down. To my surprise, she wrapped her arms around me. Her embrace felt like steel.

After she pulled away, I studied her. The pale features had disappeared. Her skin had flushed with color and vigor, her features reanimated. Ferocity replaced exhaustion in her eyes. This was the Highest Witch I would gratefully serve for the rest of my life.

Every moment in Carcere came full circle.

Scarlett was worth it.

"You appear much improved, High Priestess."

"Very much improved, thanks to you." With a shake of her head and an exhaled breath, she silently summarized my feelings on the matter.

Utter bewilderment.

Squeezing her hand, I said, "I'm glad the ordeal is over."

"We share that sentiment. I interrogate Greyson next week."

"So long from now?"

With a scowl, she muttered, "Let him stew in his worries for a bit. Besides, I wanted to be strong and healthy when he saw me again." Scoffing, she added, "Him and his tainted tea."

"But how—"

"Leda has tracked down the tea," she said, correctly anticipating my question. "Greyson posed as a well-known tea merchant and offered up a new blend that was certain to promote health and decrease stress. He offered it to the kitchens and my Apothecary, to be thorough. At least, that's what we have been able to ascertain. It worked. I discovered the tea on their suggestion and enjoyed it."

"Promote health." I snorted. "Right."

She sighed. "Unfortunately, it *was* a delicious tea, and it did provide a boost of energy in the midst of a day packed with meetings. Laced with poison," she tacked on, and I had the maniacal urge to giggle at her casual tone.

Her nose wrinkled. "I think I'm quite done with hot drinks for the time being. I seem to have lost my taste for them."

"Can't say that I blame you."

"We'll see what winter brings." She held a finger in the air. "Lavender seems a safe bet. I might start there, once this blasted heat subsides."

Ah, Scarlett. She had returned, indeed. The vim and vigor of her expressions were a welcome sight.

"We'll be certain of it," I promised.

Sobering, Scarlett lay her hand on top of mine and squeezed my fingers. Tears sprang to her eyes. "Bianca, truly—"

I returned her familiar squeeze. "I know, Scarlett. It was worth it."

Clearing her throat, and blinking rapidly, she turned to a safer topic. "Leda reports that you have asked to stall an audience with the Council. Any particular reason?"

Hesitating, I said, "Ah . . . a hunch, I guess. The mission with Greyson gave me things to think about for the future of the Sisterhood. I can't put into words yet what I feel. Grandfather has some responsibility here. It's his fault I'm questioning everything."

Her brow arched.

"Oh?"

Slowly, I explained. "He challenged me a few weeks ago. Told me that, as High Priest, he wasn't looking for the Sisterhood to be like the Brotherhood. He didn't seek merit. He wanted it to be . . . different."

A hum indicated deeper interest, but I didn't have much more to recount. I ran my bottom lip through my teeth.

"The Sisterhood *will* be different," I concluded, in the most holistic summary I could manage. "I can see now why that's necessary. I just . . . I don't know *how* yet. If I stand before the Council and explain how we acted, but I can't form a sentence regarding our goals, our purpose, our plan, then it means I've failed. We aren't ready for that."

After several minutes of thought, Scarlett quietly concluded, "Bianca Monroe, I have never been more proud of you than this moment. Your self-awareness is impressive." With a less maternal tone, and infusions of the High Priestess I knew well, she said, "But the fact remains that we have a Sisterhood to form so that you could change Alkarra for the better. I suggest you figure. it. out."

Her finger jabbed once into my thigh with each word, drawing another laugh. With a bow, I promised, "Yes, Your Highness, I shall. Give me a little time, and I will tell you exactly what the Sisterhood is about. I vow it."

Grandfather's apartment smelled like lemon and a hint of orange. I pulled in a deep breath, savoring the swirl of the flavors at the bottom of my lungs.

"Much better," he crooned, "isn't it?"

He stood a couple of steps away, rocking back on his heels, as he surveyed the organized shelves. Books remained, but only a fraction of what he began with. The dusty pages that stuck out of them had been swept free. Reeves, with his light but efficient touch, had cleaned each book with a damp rag and his usual tender care.

"I don't know." I cocked my head to the side. "I sort of liked the mess."

He winked at me.

A tray bearing hot scones and a fresh pot of tea whisked closer, settling on the empty coffee table across from Grandfather's favorite divan. It was an old, slightly shabby thing that I had a feeling Reeves waged war against. No surprise that it remained here, out of sight, in Grandfather's reading room, which used to be mine. There was comfort in the repurposing. When we moved away, others moved in. A constant wheel of time.

While Grandfather poured the tea, I ran my palm over a stack of books that swung over on a spell. At the top, a book titled, *Quiet Incantations,* drew my eye.

"They're quiet," Grandfather said, "not because they're intended to be used with silent magic, though you can. They're quiet because the intent of them was never great popularity."

"Oh."

"The author of that book, a witch that I met years and years ago, wanted only to impart some of his favorite spells. Spells that he used daily, but never heard of anyone else using."

"What an interesting book."

I cracked it open to riffle through while tea steamed in front of me. For minutes, we sat in companionable silence, sipping tea, perusing books, listening to the silence of the High Priest's apartments. I broke the quiet span of air.

"Where is Papa?"

Grandfather set down his tea. "I don't know. He's responding to my messages but I haven't seen him."

"Is he all right?"

"Physically fine, I would imagine."

I studied him, but saw no worry. "Have you spoken with Regina?"

"Briefly."

"Does she know where he is?"

With his hands folded in his lap, Grandfather said only, "No. She knows that he's coming and going at his leisure, which is fine with her. She's a surprisingly patient witch. In her words, *I know where he went, but not where he is,* and I think that summarizes it well enough."

Worry held my heart in an icy grip that faded when Grandfather smiled. He held such warmth and confidence that I couldn't maintain the fear for long.

"He'll be fine, my dear," he murmured. "Just fine. Your father is . . . figuring himself out. He's doing what most of us do in our late teen years. He never got the opportunity, you see. He locked himself into the Guardians so young, and all has been decided for him."

With a sip of tea, I said, "I know, but . . ."

"It has nothing to do with you."

I wasn't entirely certain I agreed with the sentiment, but I didn't know where the rebuttal would come from.

"I hadn't planned on telling him what happened with Greyson," I admitted. "At least . . . not yet."

"Wise."

"Really?"

Another soft chuckle at my enthusiastic response. "Really," he repeated in his usual, calm way. "An appropriate plan, I think. You're an adult now, Bianca. As you continue to be so, and your life changes, your relationship with your father will also change."

"I know, but . . . I miss him."

"Me, too."

I swallowed, unable to fathom what Papa might be doing. Wandering Alkarra? Experiencing the world? I had a hard time imagining that anyone knew more about Alkarra than him. As Protector, and Head of Protectors, he hadn't adhered to the same restraint around crossing the borders and going into other Networks when the Mansfeld Pact had been in place.

He'd only been High Priest for three years, and even that had taken him *out there* instead of keeping him firmly here.

And yet . . .

I let the thought draw out, eager to understand Grandfather's view of Papa. If there was any witch I could trust to understand Papa and what he might need, Grandfather was that witch. He'd known Papa . . . always.

"How are you?" Grandfather asked, and his poignant expression spoke worlds to his question.

"I'm fine. Truly."

"Close scrape."

I nodded. "Yes, it was. I've . . . never faced a situation like that before."

"Impeccable life experience," he said with a weak smile that spoke to a little nausea, perhaps from how close it had come. Mere seconds too late in the story and Scarlett may not have survived.

"Sure," I said with a laugh. "That's why I did it. Life experience."

"In a way, yes."

"Have you spoken with Greyson?"

Grandfather shook his head. "No. Scarlett has, though."

"How did it go?"

"Leda hasn't told you?"

My lips trilled in a raspberry. "Not yet. She's been rather busy. For her, it's a hard balance between the two. Sisterhood, Scarlett."

He scoffed. "I can't fathom it, myself, but if anyone could, it's Leda. Talmund attended Scarlett's interview with Greyson. Rognvald as well, except he was invisible. Whether or not Greyson knew of his presence, I very much doubt it."

"What did Greyson say?"

"Full confession." Grandfather leaned back, a hand to his

mouth, as he stared at the tea spread across the tray. "According to Scarlett, not a sense of hesitation or repentance within him."

"What is she going to do?"

Here, Grandfather hesitated. "She will not execute him."

Shock stilled my voice. "I'm sorry," I whispered, "What? We didn't execute him last time and look at what—"

"There are greater concerns."

"Like what?" I exploded.

Grandfather met my outrage with utter calm, and I wondered if he hadn't planned to be the one to break this news to me after all. *This* might be why Leda didn't tell me, because she knew I'd inquire and . . .

"Forgive me," I whispered, blowing out a long breath. "I'm surprised, that's all."

Grandfather smiled again, forgiveness in the way he tossed it to me, as if it hadn't been necessary.

"There are greater things at work in the Eastern Network, and it turns out that Greyson may be involved in it."

I groaned.

"You *have* to be kidding."

Concern darkened his eyes. "I wish I was. The Protectors have been noting signs of stirring insurrection amongst the Guardians in the Eastern Network, but also the populace. Enough that Scarlett and I have spurred a new resolution behind finding our next Ambassador. They haven't been strictly needed yet, but I feel that is about to change."

He had another sip of tea. The way he watched my reaction out of the corner of his eye told me all that I needed to know. I set aside talk of the new Ambassador. Surely, they wouldn't change my life at all.

"Just how strong are these signs that the Brotherhood has observed?" I asked. "Strong enough that a certain High Priest named Cristian reached out to Scarlett to ask for help?"

Grandfather tapped his nose. "Right on. If I had my say, my dear, I'd say the Sisterhood may get a chance to irrefutably prove herself after all."

About the Author

Katie Cross is ALL ABOUT writing epic magic and wild places. Creating new fantasy worlds is her jam.

When she's not hiking or chasing her two littles through the Montana mountains, you can find her curled up reading a book or arguing with her husband over the best kind of sushi.

Visit her at www.katiecrossbooks.com for free short stories, extra savings on all her books (and some you can't buy on the retailers), and so much more.